John Sheehan

The Bentley Ballads

Comprising the Tipperary Hall Ballads

John Sheehan

The Bentley Ballads
Comprising the Tipperary Hall Ballads

ISBN/EAN: 9783744777568

Printed in Europe, USA, Canada, Australia, Japan

Cover: Foto ©Andreas Hilbeck / pixelio.de

More available books at **www.hansebooks.com**

THE

BENTLEY BALLADS,

COMPRISING

THE TIPPERARY HALL BALLADS,

NOW FIRST REPUBLISHED FROM

"𝕭𝖊𝖓𝖙𝖑𝖊𝖞'𝖘 𝕸𝖎𝖘𝖈𝖊𝖑𝖑𝖆𝖓𝖞,"

(·1846).

WITH PREFACE AND NOTES BIOGRAPHICAL AND CRITICAL

BY

JOHN SHEEHAN,

BARRISTER-AT-LAW OF THE INNER TEMPLE;
AUTHOR OF "THE IRISH WHISKEY DRINKER PAPERS," "THE KNIGHT
OF INNISHOWEN."

An entirely New Edition,

LONDON:

RICHARD BENTLEY AND SON.

1876.

PREFACE TO THE THIRD EDITION.

"He beginneth not with obscure definitions, but he cometh to you with words set in delightful proportion, either accompanied with, or prepared for, the well enchanting skill of music;—and with a tale;—he cometh to you with a tale, which holdeth children from play, and old men from the chimney-corner."—SIR PHILIP SYDNEY.

THE ENGLISH BALLAD, which in old times was a tale or story in verse of love, chivalry, or marvel, or even of mirth and humour, has gradually assumed a less exclusive application, until within about a century back it at length attained a generic character, and was understood to comprise several species of lyrical composition. The title of THE BENTLEY BALLADS consequently has been adopted as the most suitable to the collection of poems, the choicest of their respective kinds, which appeared in 'Bentley's Miscellany' over a space of about fifteen years, during which it was under the auspices of the New Burlington House.

In this new and much enlarged edition of those Ballads the reader will be glad to recognize a selection from the Golden Legends, it having been fairly considered at length that any array of the lyrists of the Miscellany in its palmy days which excluded one of its most brilliant contributors—*inter primos*, if not the very first—were partial and incomplete. Unfortunately, the length to which, almost in every instance, the Ingoldsby Poems extend, rendered a larger selection impossible; but those chosen for the present volume have always been considered the best. The circumstance is moreover the less to be regretted, as the whole of the witty and humourous Canon's metrical contributions to the Bentley periodical have been republished by the old House in New Burlington Street, and form, with the ample and most agreeable biography appended by his son, one of the most popular and pleasant works in our language.

Another specimen of the rare humour and versatile genius of the author, the Rev. Richard Harris Barham, not one of the Golden Legends, but an emerald set in native gold of the old Lagenian mine, is also added in *Mr. Barney Maguire's Account of the Coronation*, which appeared first in the 'Miscellany,' and was afterwards transferred to the columns of every newspaper in the United Kingdom. It was the opinion of the best native judges that a more perfect piece of genuine Irish fun was never before thrown off, and very seldom equalled. That an Englishman should have been the author was deemed the more wonderful, when the thousands of miserable attempts at Irish song-writing made by the herd of public-house poetasters throughout England for generations past was taken into consideration, and it was acknowledged that only one good Irish song had ever before been written by a Saxon, namely, Hudson's *Barney Brallaghan*, which also appeared in the 'Miscellany,' with a Latin metrical translation by Prout, and which holds an honoured place in all the editions of the 'Bentley Ballads.'

The next in merit, of the school of 'The Golden Legends,' is one whose *incognito* has been preserved to this day. He displayed much of the great master's savour, as well as his quaint expression and metrical facility. His 'Temptations of Saint Anthony' enjoyed a high reputation; and it was thought by many excellent judges that it only wanted

the appendage of the Ingoldsby name to have entitled it to
rank amongst the happiest of the Golden Legends themselves.

Amongst the various tales or stories of the passions
given in ballad style and metre in the present volume are
excellent specimens from that master of humour and pathos,
the author of *Maid Marian* and *Headlong Hall ;* from
Thomas Haynes Bayley, one of the most popular in his day
of the song writers of England ; from Professor Longfellow,
whom we may call, with his truly English heart and expression, the Poet Laureate of Transatlantic England ; and
from other writers of high reputation in their day, some of
whom are still living, and others have passed away. They
form a separate class, coming between the ' Ingoldsby Legends' and the ' Inman Ballads,' totally distinct from the
former as regards the human sympathies to which they
appeal, and differing from the latter in their gentle thoughts
and easy-flowing numbers.

The bold and exulting ballads of *The Buccaneers*, and
Haroun Alraschid, which display unquestionably great power
and originality, are the productions of a self-educated mind
and solitary spirit, which owed more to its own fine faculties of observation and induction, than to book-learning or
literary refinement.

The lays and songs of the Tipperary Hall series, a selection from which is given in the present volume, might have
been republished in a collected form, but that they lacked
in quantity what they maintained in quality from the public
award of their day. The *cadre*, or framework of the prose
dialogue in which they were set, had scarcely more than a
current interest with the generation and times in which it
was written, being conversations from which, according to
a strict rule of the ' Miscellany,' everything like political
acerbity was excluded. The party politics of 1846, when
the alarm on the question of the people's food took posses-

sion of the public mind, and was the turning point of Sir Robert Peel's commercial policy, are almost the only feature of their home history during that ever-memorable year of which Englishmen care to be reminded. If the piquancy of the political allusions of the hour, and those of a most uncompromising Conservatism, were eliminated from the re-publication of the *Noctes Ambrosianæ*, and the trenchant personalities on various public characters from *Father Prout's Reliques*, republished also a few years before Mahony's death, their success in a literary or commercial point of view would have been very doubtful; and the truth as to the evanescent value of the conversations of the Tipperary Hall symposia, however popular they may have been in their treatment of the lighter subjects of their day, would be the more apparent. Had that festive atmosphere been charged with party electricity, what bolts of indignation in prose and verse would have been hurled against the heads of our late Premier and the then noble leader of the Protectionist party, Lord George Bentinck, in the Commons for their bitter personal attacks on Sir Robert Peel! What lurid flashes would have darted in all directions, lighting up the darkness of the bucolic mind! What a theme for a poet of the people, the great Free Trade Minister falling at the very moment, and in the very arms of victory! For this was the eventful moment, when just as the Corn Importation and Customs Duties Bills had received the Royal Assent, that Sir Robert, deserted by the bulk of the Conservative party in Parliament on the Protection to Life in Ireland Bill, placed his resignation in the hands of Her Majesty. When the 'Morning Chronicle' was a pure Whig paper under the proprietorship of Sir John Easthope, and the editorship of his son-in-law, Mr. Andrew Doyle, and supported Lord Melbourne's administration, the Everard Clive of Tipperary Hall had contributed to it a series of political pasquinades in verse of such exquisite flavour and fancy, that even in the highest literary circles they were attributed to the gifted author of the old *Rhymes on the Road* and the *Fables for the Holy Alliance.* It will be remembered that the ' Morning Chronicle ' in Mr. Perry's time had been the vehicle of Moore's happiest efforts in this line ; and that it was not until a few years after the retreat of the Melbourne Whigs from office his brilliant intellect fell into that moral torpor from which death at length released him in 1852. What a noble pæan on the great triumph of freedom, humanity, and common sense, should we not have had in the July (1846) number of the *Tipperary Hall* from the author of the *Lay of the Derby,* who celebrated in June the triumph of Mr. Gully's horse Pyrrhus, and in May the victory gained by Cambridge (his own university) over Oxford in the great annual boat race on the Thames, if the injunction respecting political parties and men set forth at the opening of the convivialities had not been rigidly observed :

> Si quis Plebi faveat, faveat decenter ;
> Si quis Optimatibus, faveat silenter :
> Omnibus Politicis nisi temperentur
> Cor cructat nimium, esuritque venter !

The opinion broached in the last line, it may be said, by the way, had less reference to Tipperary Hall than to the hungry, and too often, as in those very days, virulent side of the House of Commons which goes by the name of Her Majesty's Opposition.

There was one great national contest, however, which occupied the minds of all parties in the country earlier in the year, before the great and final parliamentary fight on the Corn Laws had come on, and the glorious issue of which was hailed with equal joy by all, namely, the Sikh war in India. A triple victory conducted the British forces to the banks of the Sutlej. The battle of Sobraon seat-tered to the wind an immense barbaric host, furnished with all the material of European warfare, and guided by the skill of European discipline. Within three months from the encampment of our troops on the north bank of the Indus the British flag floated on the ramparts of Lahore; and our eastern dominion was advanced to the confines of Thibet. English, Irish, and Scottish soldiers fought with equal bravery and the most generous rivalry in the truly heroic campaign. They exhibited the same qualities which shone in other days of our history, and proved that the spirit which breathed in Clive's soldiers at Arcot and Plassy had not vanished nor grown weak—that the same pluck which prevailed over fearful odds at Assaye and Delhi still remained in unimpaired vigour, to confront the murderous onslaught of a formidable artillery and the fierce violence of savage horsemen; and that to such men as Hardinge, Gilbert, Gough, and the Hero of Aliwal might well have been delegated the consummation of a work begun by Clive, Coote, Lake and Wellesley. As the glad tidings of each successive victory over the Sikh forces arrived in England, a Tipperary Hall ballad celebrated it in strains which the victors themselves soon learned and rejoiced to sing; and it was of no ordinary significance at the moment that the Whiskey Drinker's portion of those strains, so peculiarly adapted to the sympathies of the Irish soldiers, were most popular amongst them, whilst the Young Ireland ballads were just at the highest point of their native popularity, scattering the wildfire of an unavailing disaffection amongst the Irish middle classes and peasantry at home.

Tipperary Hall, a series of conversational papers on literature, art, and social questions, extending over a period of six months in 'Bentley's Miscellany,' 1846, was the joint production of a couple of young barristers of the English Home Circuit, and a physician, also young at the time, who has since become one of our most distinguished philological and ethnological writers. One of the barristers who wrote for a long time in the 'Miscellany' under the signature of the 'Irish Whiskey Drinker,' having a few years after the appearance of the Tipperary Hall papers married a lady of sufficiently good fortune to enable him to indulge in the more congenial pleasures of literary ease and foreign travel, lost sight for a long time of Messieurs the attornies, who, if the truth must be known, never had their eyes much upon him ; for in those days they fought very shy of undisguised literary members of the bar, and managed to do the best part of their legal business without them. Talfourd was the first to break the ice of this very vulgar prejudice ; and the other young barrister of the Tipperary Hall party having won his way not by political or family influence, but by downright professional industry and ability, to high judicial rank, sent it floating down the stream of time, never again to chill with its hardened selfishness the genial aspirations of a noble profession. And it is worthy of remark that, so far from abandoning literature as he felt himself rising to the highest position in the legal world, he devoted his leisure hours to the composition of one of the most popular works on military history in our language—a work which the New Burlington House had the honour of publishing and which has gone through several editions. His Tipperary Hall *nom de plume* in the morning of his professional career was *Everard Clive.* The young physician contributed under the guise of the *Travelling Bachelor,* a sort of peripatetic philosopher to whom (once every three years) the University of Cambridge gives or used to give a handsome pecuniary *viaticum,* requiring in return a *bonâ fide* tour of observation in foreign countries, and a report thereof within a reasonable time.

The late gifted and lamented Edward Forbes, when at

the head of the Government Geological Museum in Jermyn Street, wrote the song of *The Potato Commission*, an exceeding clever *jeu d'esprit*, full of wit and humour, although on a grave subject apparently. The ridicule, however, was purely from a scientific point of view, showing how little the commissioners were able to do, and the utter hopelessness of ascertaining the prime causes of the terrible rot itself, which is still reckoned amongst the mysterious visitations of Providence. Sir Robert Peel, it will be remembered, appointed in 1846 a commission of scientific men, who laboured with great zeal and industry on the spot on the question of the failure of the Irish root. The result of their labours was that they told us, as regards the effects of the disease, what we knew before ; whilst, as to its real origin, they came back as wise as they went. Forbes was one of the brilliant company which Everard and the Dew-drinker, who rented the place together, used to assemble now and then to spend a pleasant evening at Tipperary Hall ; and sang his song of *The Potato Commission* on one of those occasions for the first time with great applause. It appeared shortly afterwards in the 'Miscellany.' The author of the song frequently afterwards favoured the 'Red Lion Literary and Scientific Society' after dinner with it, in presence of Professor Playfair, the chief Potato Commissioner, who enjoyed it as much as any one present. He died a few years back Royal Professor of Botany, at the University of Edinburgh, in the prime of his years, much lamented by a numerous circle of friends, who all esteemed him for his manly principles and great abilities, and loved him with a warm love for his gentle manners and most amiable disposition. Tipperary Hall was not a poet's myth, but a comfortable and somewhat prosaic looking reality. It stood on no mountain's brow with magnificent sea and land views to elevate the imagination. It did not command the entrance of rocky dell or flowery vale, with foaming cascade or sweet streamlet in front of its Gothic porch. It was not—

> " a lodge in some vast wilderness,
> Some boundless contiguity of shade."

Nothing so romantic, but a long, low, primitive-looking cottage dwelling of several gables, with one portion of the roof thatched, another tiled, and another again slated, showing, as the different geological strata show the world to be a good deal older than our grandfathers and grandmothers took it to be, that the building had been put together in detachments, as civilization crept on, and the funds or families of former proprietors kept increasing. It stood a short distance northward of the village of Highgate, on the Finchley road, flanked on one side by a large dairy farm, from which the celibates drew their supplies of milk for their celebrated Tipperary Hall punch, and on the other by a garden which had less fruits than flowers in it, the boys of the neighbourhood being accustomed to look after the former long before they were ripe, and the latter being of the wildest description, in all respects like Goldsmith's " blossomed furze, unprofitably gay." The excellent tap of *The Wellington* seemed opportunely placed for an opposite neighbour. Within a half mile or so farther north, was *The Bald-faced Stag*, whose hanging sign had no reference to a leading zoological feature of the famous railway year, 1846, but had hung there from the old coaching times, and long before them, when Hogarth painted his March to Finchley.

The contributions to the 'Miscellany' by Maginn and Prout were of a prior date by some years to the Tipperary Hall papers. Both of those celebrated littérateurs had in fact contributed to its first number (January, 1837), the Doctor giving the *Opening Chaunt*, and the Padre a goodly number of his classical comicalities. The latter was going off as the Tipperaries were coming on, and the former had gone off four years before, leaving a blank in 'Frazer's Magazine' and 'Bentley's Miscellany,' which it was most difficult to fill up. In 1842, that splendid Irish genius, at once vigorous and fine, and so eccentric and unfortunate throughout a comparatively short career, passed away from amongst us for ever. One of his best lyrical efforts in a serious vein was his *Soldier Boy*. It appeared first in the 'Miscellany,' and is given in the present edition of the Ballads.

Prout contributed in verse much more largely than his friend, the Doctor, to the 'Miscellany;' and although he first rose to literary fame with the Prout papers in 'Frazer's,' where his polyglot facetiæ took the world of scholarship by surprise, so signally and so agreeably, it may be fairly said that the gems of a similar description with which he enriched the 'Miscellany,' were equally brilliant and of the first water. He also gave several original lays and songs to the New Burlington Street periodical, such as the *Song of Saint Januarius*, and the *Redbreast of Aquilania*, which may be considered amongst his best. Prout's pure and idiomatic Latinity and mediæval quaintness of thought, displayed through the medium of his exquisite monkish rhymes, were something extraordinary. It is accounted for in this way, that having received the rudiments of his classical education in his native city of Cork, he pursued and completed it in more than one of the Colleges of the Jesuits abroad. During his boyhood, Cork, whatever it may be now, was famous for its accurate training in what may be called the junior classics, and especially as regards a philological, if not an otherwise deeply critical knowledge of them. Indeed, throughout the province of Munster you could scarcely find a village which had not at the head of its school one of that class of teachers called *red-wigs*,—laborious and conscientious men in their line, and terrible disciplinarians, who taught Latin and Greek, and the elements of mathematics, up to the University entrance requirements, and taught these branches of primary education well, for they spared no *pains* or *penalties*— in the strictest sense of the terms—and would have the business done. Those were the days, and Munster was the country of the "poor scholars," who wandered about from tutor to tutor, the charitable farmers of the neighbourhood affording them in turn a week's board and lodging for God's sake, just as the students of the Middle Ages, thirsting equally after knowledge, and equally poor, were received throughout the schools, not only of Ireland, but the Continent.

Prout's career *in literis humanioribus* on the Continent, was a distinguished one. It was under foreign Jesuits that he learned to write Latin elegiacs, hexameters, alcaics, and sapphics, with ease and elegance, and it can be easily understood that the curious felicity of expression to which he afterwards attained in his published productions, was greatly assisted by the copious Latinity he acquired in the upper schools of philosophy and theology, in which it was the language of thesis and disputation. He spoke it with facility when a young man, on leaving the Jesuits, and when he made his first appearance as a periodical writer. French and Italian, he spoke nearly as well as his mother tongue.

These few observations on the most famous Latin verse writer of his day, and the means by which he acquired his truly classic elegance and facility, may not be uninteresting to academic readers, especially at a time when change after change is taking place in the educational course, not only of our great public schools, but of our old Universities; when we already begin to contemplate the ignoble picture of the future in which our grandsons shall be seen turning away from the ancient fountains from which even the humblest drank the mystic waters, and felt a generous glow ; and when old and young worshippers alike are beginning to ask, are the voices and echoes of the haunted groves and streams of old to be lost before long, as we go down "the ringing grooves of change," amidst the roar of the steam-engine and the iron way?

Of myself and the space which I fill in the 'Bentley Ballads,' I may not speak, more than to say that when far away from England, after having lost sight of the New Burlington House for years, it did me the honour of selecting for the first and second editions of the 'Ballads,' some of my contributions to the old 'Miscellany,' amongst these my Latin rhymes (*et ego in Arcadiâ*), for I too before going up to the Dublin University, and afterwards to Cambridge, received my primary education at the Eton of Ireland, Clongowes Wood, from the men who taught Prout how to write Latin verses. For these or any other selections in this volume I am not answerable. I cannot say with Montaigne :—"I have here only made a bouquet of culled flowers, and have brought nothing of my own but the thread that tied them."

The flowers have been culled, the bouquet has been made by other hands; nor is the thread which binds them together mine, unless the thread of my discourse, the *quodam commune vinculum*, be deemed such, which binds me to the spirits who are gone—the leading spirits of the 'Miscellany.' This publication was purchased by Mr. William Harrison Ainsworth from the New Burlington Street House in December, 1854. Mr. Bentley has recently re-purchased it, with a view of consigning it to "the Tomb of all the Capulets."

With this plain avowal, I will now say to the reader, *Ave et vale!*—HAIL AND FAREWELL!

J. S.

CONTENTS.

THE TIPPERARY HALL BALLADS.

GENERAL BALLADS.

THE

TIPPERARY HALL BALLADS.

THE LENGTHENED CHAIN.

I COULD have gone away, afar,
　　Nor cared where winds or waves might speed me;
And looking on some distant star,
　　Let it mislead me.
I little recked for fatherland,
　　As little cared for home;
And had been free for land and sea,
　　At choice to roam.
　　　　But when I roved the furthest,
　　　　　I lengthened most the chain,
　　　　For one soft feeling ever
　　　　　Could draw me back again.

A dimple on a fair, pale face,
　　With a sweet smile around it,
Had won my heart, both child and man,
　　And firmly bound it.
Else had I climbed the Andes,
　　Where ice gleams high and bold,
And found a home as distant there,
　　And not more cold.
　　　　So when I found that roving
　　　　　But lengthened out the chain,
　　　　I turned my steps, but not my heart,
　　　　　And hied me home again.

TRAVELLING BACHELOR.

THE RICHMOND TIDE.

Air, " The Lincolnshire Poacher."

'Tis very well
   For a yachting swell
  To talk about the sea,
His flowing sheet,
His bark so fleet,
  And the breeze so fair and free.
You may call it dull
On the Thames to scull,
  But 'twill do very well for me.
Oh, I like to glide
On the Richmond tide,
  And my lady love with me.

Oh, come, my dear,
To the Temple pier ;
  We'll steam to Battersea ;
'Tis there my boat
Doth lie afloat
  Expecting you and me.
We'll go at our ease
As high as we please,
  From the swell of the steamers free.
Oh, I like to glide,
On the Richmond tide,
  And my lady love with me.

My skiff she's neat,
And quite complete,
  To carry a fair ladyè.
And I'm the man,
That manage her can,
  As you, my dear, manage me.
By gentle skill
We work our will,
  And taking it easily.
Oh, I like to glide
On the Richmond tide,
  And my lady love with me.

With my skulls so trim
I'll lightly skim
  By lawn, and flower, and tree ;
And look up, and view
Your eyes so blue,
  Still looking down on me ;
And the music hear
Of your voice so clear,
  In its soft and silver key.
Oh, I like to glide
On the Richmond tide,
  And my lady love with me.

Everard Clive.

TIPPERARY!

Don't talk of Horatius Flaccus,
  And the suppers he gave at his farm ;
Neither whiskey's delight nor tobacco's
  Had he got his old Romans to warm.
And Augustus, how he must have paltered
  Amongst the few spirited chicks ;
Why, he owned he left Rome mighty altered,
  Having found it a city of bricks.
      Away with such fine botheration,
        And each classical son of a gun:
      Tipperary's the gem of the nation,
        And we are the boys for the fun.

Sure they showed their ineligant manners,
  When they carved with their fingers their prog,
And they'd neither cheroots nor havannahs,
  Nor sugar to sweeten their grog.
Then a bumper in gratitude filling
  For the time of our birth, bless the stars,
'Twas delayed till the days of distilling,
  And till Raleigh invented cigars.
      Away with such fine botheration,
        And each classical son of a gun ;
      Tipperary's the gem of the nation,
        And we are the boys for the fun.

Irish Whiskey Drinker.

1—2

THE POTATO COMMISSION.

HAVE you heard the report—the last Edition—
　　Sent out by the great potato commission,
Who crossed the water to find some new
Materials for an Irish stew?
For since 'twas vain to put the pot on,
When every blessed root was rotten,
Sir Robert thought to improve the mess, sirs,
By a brace and a half of roast Professors!
　　　　(Sich a row there's been of late, O!
　　　　All about a rotten potato!)

King Dan had said, "the horrid cracks on
The skin were the work of the hoof of the Saxon:"
Back'd by Prince John and Smith O'Brien,
His word Repealers all rely on;
For when the Liberator takes a fancy,
Through the thickest mill-stone he will and can see.
"The rot," says he, "those fellows came fishin' here
Was fostered by the Times' Commissioner!"
　　　　(Who say in return that the great O'
　　　　Connell's a rotten-hearted potato!)

The report is both a short and sweet one,
And if not profound, is at least a neat one;
It states—"All ways that we could guess
We tried of praties to make a mess,—
We tried them boiled—we tried them roasted,
We tried them fried, we tried them toasted,
All sorts and sizes, till, *heu vanum,*
Nothing came out but smashed *Solanum.*
　　　　(And wasn't that a dreadful fate, O!
　　　　To come of taking a rotten potato!)

"Some say that grub is the cause of the rot;
But we, my Lords, affirm it is not;
For, isn't it plain, and there's the rub,
For such potatoes won't do for grub.
We've taken the matter feculaceous,
And tried to make it farinaceous.

'Twon't do for dinner, tea, nor tiffin,
For if fed on starch, you'll certainly stiffen,
 (And that would be a precious state, O!
 Resulting from a rotten potato!)

Some cock their glasses up to their eye,
And mushrooms in the cells descry,
But we, my Lords, have looked as well,
And think such notions all a sell;
Decaine in France, in Germany Kutzing,
Have sought the rot all manner of roots in,
And proved that those have looked with a loose eye
Who said 'twas caused by fungi and fuci.
 (Sure never since the days of Plato
 Was there sich a row 'bout a rotten potato!)

Now these, my Lords, are our opinions—
It's a bad look out for the British dominions.
We know as much as we did before,
And we don't think we shall know any more!
As for *Solanum Tuberosum*,
It's a very bad job for them as grows 'em.
We think the weather has made them scurfy,
And we've proved the same by consulting Murphy!
 (And if our report don't please debaters,
 They must get some other common-taters!)
       Professor Edward Forbes.

THE FLIRT.

Tell her that her eye is blue,
 And she'll tell you that she knows it
Ev'ry bit as well as you:
 Ev'ry morn her mirror shows it.

Tell her that her voice is sweet,
 That 'tis heaven to behold her:
And she'll ask you, "Why repeat
 What a thousand more have told her?"

Either coin some awful lie,
　　That with novelty may strike her;
Or in silence watching by,
　　Let *her* try to make you like her.

Let her speak her mind the first:
　　Then the game is most diverting.
Women's vanity will burst
　　Ere it lose a chance of flirting.

　　　　　　　　　　EVERARD CLIVE.

THE SUNBEAM'S COMPLAINT.

You've heard how Alexis electrified London,
　　And Elliotson doctor'd the Misses O'Key;
How Wheatstone's expresses have time and space undone;
　　Finally, Faraday's magnetized me.

Mercury, iodine, acids had all but
　　Made me as lank and as latent as Heat:
And I fondly imagined that Moser and Talbot
　　Had fix'd my conditions, and made me complete.

So I sped from the skies, in my radiance brightening,
　　As free as I moved on the morn of my birth;
When, just as old Franklin maltreated the lightning,
　　Did Faraday lower and link me to earth.

Attracting, repelling, he went on and on, 'stead
　　Of passing me free to my regular goal,
Till at last I inclined, like the heiress of Wanstead,
　　With a quivering tremor, and turn'd to the *Pole.*

And now I'm converted—the Whitechapel Sheenies
　　Who stick to their faith are far better than I:
I'm a sort of Sir Lopez Manasseh Ximenes,
　　A physical fiction whose day is gone by.

Dishonour'd in England, where never a ray shone
　　Except to be analyzed fifty times o'er;
I'll fly to the clime of the right generation,
　　Where Magi revered me, and Guebres adore.

I'll go to the East, where I'll build a Kiosque, of which
  All the high priests shall have nothing to do ;
So I'll be safe from Mosotti and Boscowitch,
  Possibly safe against Faraday too.

Or else to old Ireland—for Eastern bloods run there—
  And undulate free as the quavers of Hullah :
Since Science is more at a discount than fun there ;
  And trust to the mercies of Lloyd and Maccullagh.

So you my susceptible sisters in—*icity,*
  And you my dear brothers galvanic in—*ism,*
Would you retain independent felicity,
  Steer clear of the Doctor, and fly from his prism.

Else, sure as gun, he'll go off to assail ye, as
  Convertible forces to change at his call ;
And Matter himself must look out for an *alias,*
  Or he'll end in becoming no matter at all.

TRAVELLING BACHELOR.

SIR RODERICK MURCHISON.

Who first survey'd the Russian states ?
  And made the great Azoic dates ?
And work'd the Scandinavian slates ?
Sir Roderick.

Who calculated Nature's shocks ?
And proved the low Silurian rocks
Detritus of more ancient blocks ?
Sir Roderick.

Who knows of what all rocks consist ?
And sees his way where all is mist,
About the Metamorphic schist ?
Sir Roderick.

Who draws distinctions clear and nice
Between the old and the new Gneiss ?
And talks no nonsense about ice ?
Sir Roderick.

Let others, then, their stand maintain,
Work all for glory, nought for gain,
And each find faults, but none complain,
                    Sir Roderick :

Let Sedgwick say how things began,
Defend the old Creation plan,
And smash the new one,—if he can,—
                    Sir Roderick :

Let Buckland set the land to rights,
Find meat in peas, and starch in blights,
And future food in coprolites,
                    Sir Roderick :

Let Agassiz appreciate tails,
And like the Virgin hold the scales,
And Owen draw the teeth of whales,
                    Sir Roderick :

Take thou thy orders hard to spell,
And titles more than man can tell,—
I wish all such were earn'd as well,—
                    Sir Roderick.
          TRAVELLING BACHELOR.

THE COLD WATER CURE.

Air—" Drops of Brandy."

Oh, 'tis just since the days of Deucalion,
    And my countryman, Misther O'Gyges,
When Pyrrha came out as Pygmalion,
    And the pebbles became Callipyges ;*
Since the days of Narcissus, who hung
    O'er the flattering fount a divine eye,
And those of Arion, who sung
    His sonnets *in usum delphini.*

To this the good year forty-six,
    When the world's all mad with Hydropathy;
And Priesnitz takes off with his tricks
    The poor souls that escape Homœopathy :

* The false quantity is only the Whiskey Drinker's fun.

I ne'er knew a lass or a lad,
 Son, father, or mother, or daughter,
That didn't go moping or mad,
 As soon as they took to cowld water.

The element's precious indeed,
 As Pindar assures us—to lave in ;
And the ocean may serve us at need,
 As it served Polyphemus—to shave in.
But if you've regard for your life,
 Oh keep it away from your pharynx :
'Tis as bad for the throat as a knife,
 And worse than a rope for the larynx.
     IRISH WHISKEY DRINKER.

JESSIE.

Air—" One bumper at parting."

'TWAS when you were ailing, dear Jessie,
 Our hearts were as heavy as lead,
As for laughing or loving, why, bless ye,
 They never came into one's head.

Now your roses return, you sweet crayture,
 And the physic is laid on the shelf,
There's a general rejoicing in Nature,
 That Jessie again is herself.

   EVERARD CLIVE.

᾽ΙΕΣΣΙΙ.

"Οτ' ἀσθενεῖς, 'Ιέσση,
Συνασθένουσ' "Ερωτες.
Φρούδη μεν 'Αφροδιτὴ,
Φρούδοι γέλως, χάρις τε.
Σοί δ' αὖθις εὐπαθούσῃ,
"Οτ' ἐν καλῇ παρείᾳ
Θάλλει τὸ πρόσθεν ἄνθος,
'Εφήδεται τὰ πάντα.

   EVERARD CLIVE.

SOFT BE THY SLEEP.

SOFT be thy sleep, my lady love !
 And sweet thy dreams to-night.
No mortal watch is kept above
 O'er one so pure and bright.
Fond angels flock to guard thy bed,
 Throughout the night they stay ;
And, as they hover o'er thy head,
 Deem thee not formed of human clay,
 For heavenly thou art as they.

Soft be thy sleep, my lady love !
  My lay shall wake thee not;
No look entreat I now to prove
  That I am not forgot ;
But here, till morning's early smile
  Shall gild the eastern sea,
I linger on, and hope the while
  One brighter still to have from thee,
  In guerdon of my minstrelsy.

Wake, softly wake, my lady love !
  The night is well nigh o'er ;
May I not have one smile, dear love ?
  I ask but one—no more ;
For that will be so sweet a one,
  That I shall still delay,
Till morn shall own her smiles outdone,
  And, all o'erclouded, pass away,
  Or, blushing, redden into day.
              TRAVELLING BACHELOR.

THE JAUNTING CAR.

You may pull away, scull away,
  Boat away, float away,
Moisten your throat away, smoke your cigar,
  'Tis all botheration,
  Such slow navigation,
Compared with the rowl of the Jaunting Car.
  'Tis sporting and spacious,
  'Tis genteel and gracious,
Likewise efficacious 'gainst hail, rain and snow ;
  To go any way hence,
  From Dublin to Mayence,
Take the Irish conveyance wherever you go !

  Pelides, Tydides,
  The great Alcibi'des,
Car-borne, each tried his proud foemen in war,
  Likewise noble Hector,
  Troy's valiant protector,
Of fleet steeds the rector, rode out on a car.

Cytherea and Rhea,
Queen Boadicea,
And that charmer Medea, when wandering afar,—
Old Ossian's great heroes,
Singing lillybulleros,
They all of them rattled away on a car.

Long life to car-driving,
And long be it thriving,
For courting or wiving, in peace, or in war.
If at elbows you're out, sir,
And in love are devout, sir,
Put your coat up the spout, sir, and hire a car,
To show the girls' faces,
And set off their graces,
At reviews and at races, wherever they are ;
And for soft conversation,
There's no situation
Comes up to the side of the Jaunting Car.

IRISH WHISKEY DRINKER.

OUR NEXT MERRY MEETING.

THE winds were made for blowing, boys,
The clouds were made for raining ;
The streams were made for flowing, boys,
And bowls were made for draining.
'Tis bad to try a speech or song,
And fail to give the whole out ;
But 'tis a greater social wrong
To fail to drink your bowl out.
Fill, fill, my boys, once more,
Fill up before retreating,
One long last libation pour
To our next merry meeting.

There's not a gleam of life's delight,
But's purchased by a sorrow ;
The eye so bright that beams to-night
In grief may lour to-morrow.

Wealth, knowledge, power, are little worth
  Their price of toil and quarrel,
And oh, the deadliest leaf on earth
  Is aye the leaf of laurel.
      Fill, fill, my boys, once more,
        Fill up before retreating ;
      One long last libation pour
        To our next merry meeting.

Oh, where is he that does not know
  The pang of loving blindly ;
The self-contempt, the jealous woe,
  E'en when she meets you kindly.
And where is he that has not proved
  The pang that still is stronger,
Of being by another loved,
  Whom you can love no longer.
      Fill, fill, my boys, once more,
        Fill up before retreating ;
      One long last libation pour
        To our next merry meeting.

Since pleasure then by pain is bought,
  At least life's lightest part take :
The head-ache from the bowl that's caught
  Is better than the heart-ache.
He lives the best with open breast,
  Who welcomes joy the longest,
And 'gainst each ill with iron will
  Collects himself the strongest.
      Fill, fill, my boys, once more,
        Fill up before retreating ;
      One long last libation pour
        To our next merry meeting.

EVERARD CLIVE.

PHASCOLOTHERION BRODERIPI.

Hail to the patriarch Phascolotherion!
  Owen has had him to build a new era on:
Grant did the same to found many a query on.

Found about Stonesfield, where limestone so shelly is;
There he's embedded, and keeping right well he is:
Look at his jaw, and you'll guess what his belly is.

With him there dwelt by the primitive river a
Similar genus of small insectivora;
Free from the then uninvented carnivora.

Nothing appeared in the scale of creation
Higher than he through the Wealden formation—
Even the chalk could not show a cetacean.

Hail to the first of the British Mammalia;
One of the order of Marsupialia;
Nearly at present confined to Australia.
Travelling Bachelor.

THE CAMPAIGN OF THE SUTLEJ.

Air—"Paddy O'Rafferty."

Have you not heard of the fighting in India, boys?
  Sure 'twas at Moodkee a beautiful shindy, boys.
Better than hunting the fox from his cozy shaw
The hunt of the Sikhs from their camp at Ferozeshah.
At Alival, too, we complately astonish'd 'em,
Over the water we coax'd and admonish'd 'em,
Though bullets fly fast as bad eggs in the pillory,—
O we are the boys that can spike their artillery!

CHORUS.

Come to the Sutlej, where loud the guns roar, my boys!
Come ere the fun and the fighting's all o'er, my boys!
Come where there's honour and plunder, galore, my boys!
O! who's for a shy at the siege of Lahore, my boys?

II.

Hardinge's a hero; bowld Gough is another, boys,
Don't they call Napier " the divil's own brother," boys?
Ne'er in the East such a gallant commander was
Since on the Indus the great Alexander was.
Under Sir Harry Smith foes we could thump any:
Who'll serve the Queen and the East India Company?
Shew them our soldiers, the right sort of men are all;
Fight for the Crown and the Governor-General.

CHORUS.

Come to the Sutlej, &c.

III.

Rid the Rance of her Punts and her Punches, boys
Serve them a mouthful of lead for their lunches, boys!
Down at their river we will not stay long, my boys!
Smash into smith'reens their fine *tête-du-pong*, my boys.
If the powther is scarce, and the guns they won't play on it,
Try the cowld steel, and push on with the bayonet!
Once we're safe over, we'll then have a slap at all
Comes in our way, their cash, camels, and capital.

CHORUS.

Then come to the Sutlej, where loud the guns roar, my boys!
Come ere the fun and the fighting's all o'er, my boys!
Come where there's honour and plunder, galore, my boys!
O! who's for a shy at the siege of Lahore, my boys?

IRISH WHISKEY DRINKER.

DRINK, BOYS, DRINK!

Air, " *Take me when I'm in the humour.*"

(JULIEN'S SETTING.)

OH, what care I for wet or dry,
    For the sun that shines, or the storm that lours;
While thus we troll the flowing bowl,
    And the smiles of those we love are ours?
Your fancied wise may search the skies
    For fav'ring hours, with toil incessant;
Read ladies' eyes, and *they*'ll advise
    No time with them is like the present.

Drink, boys, drink !
Fill to the brink ;
Drink to those we love the fondest
Drink, boys, drink!

The stars may gleam o'er the crystal stream ;
Give me blue eyes o'er the red wine's glow ;
There's nought above like what we love,
And what's within our reach below.
Aurora's light is a lovely sight,
When she rises high the east adorning ;
But you, my dear, have a glance more clear,
And a rosier smile when you rise of a morning.
Drink, boys, drink!
Fill to the brink ;
Drink to those we love the fondest!
Drink, boys, drink !

We're weary soon of the sunny noon,
But beauty's sunshine never tires ;
Though her eyes may gleam like the noontide beam,
And her soft lips thrill with all its fires.
And, oh! 'tis sweet the fair to meet
At eve around the bowl we drink of,
When our spirits rise as the daylight dies,
And the less we see the more we think of.
Drink, boys, drink!
Fill to the brink ;
Drink to those we love the fondest !
Drink, boys, drink !

EVERARD CLIVE.

THE TOP OF THE GLASS.

WHAT is the top of the glass for, man ?
I wish you would tell me why
The bottom must stand like a mill-pool, man,
And th' upper half be dry.
'Tis the best part, and the broadest part,
And the part we first come to ;
And what do you think, if it isn't to drink,
The top of the glass has to do ?

There's nothing in Nature useless, man,
  And not very much in art.
So crown your glass with the liquor, man,
  For the top is the noblest part.
    'Tis the best part, and the broadest part,
      And the part we first come to ;
    And I'm wondering still, if it's not to fill,
      What the top of a glass has to do.

Now, if you're thinking of spilling, man,
  And the tale of the cup and the lip ;
Steady your hand with a bumper, man,
  And the deuce a bit will it slip.
    Oh, the top's the best and the broadest part,
      And the part we first come to ;
    And I'd rather in all take no measure at all,
      Than take a half measure with you.
                  TRAVELLING BACHELOR.

THE BATTLE OF SOBRAON.

BRAVE boys, now the war is all ended,
  The peace is come back from Lahore ;
But if e'er I saw fighting so splendid,
  I wish I mayn't fight any more.
We've heard both by land and by water,
  Of mighty great battles, I own ;
Sure they're all in regard to manslaughter
  But cock-fights compared with Sobraon !
A fig for their musketry flashes,
  Their cannons and mortars and stuff,
'Tis the bay'net that settles their hashes,
  And lets the smoke out of their buff!

At the brink of the Sutlej the Sirdar,
  The Sikhs, and the Sings were drawn up ;
Sir Henry cries, "Boys, shove 'em in further,
  Sure I'd like in their camp for to sup."

"It was rousing strong tay," says Sir Hugh, "boys,
   That we got, when we blew up Hongkong ;
But this morning for breakfast with you, boys,
   I prefer the Rance's Tay-du-pong."
A fig for their musketry flashes, &c.

The trumpets play'd up a bravura,
   The great guns they open'd the ball,
And the Sikhs who were train'd by Ventura,
   They didn't object to the small.
They'd been drill'd too by ould Avitabile,
   And, if the plain truth I must tell,
Faith he hadn't instructed them shabbily,
   For they fired most remarkably well.
A fig for their musketry flashes, &c.

Now what you call brisk cannonading
   Our infantry thought mighty slow,
So 'twas after some little parading,
   Faugh a ballagh, and at 'em we go !
To the Tenth our brave General beckon'd,
   "Twenty-Ninth," says he, " charge 'em in line !"
Lead the way there, my brave Sixty-Second,
   And the Fifties won't loiter behind.
A fig for their infantry flashes, &c.

Not a shot we fired off in advancing,
   Each man to his orders was true ;
But such howling, and growling, and dancing
   Was inside, when the breach we dash'd through.
There was Lal Sing, and Fal Sing, and Ral Sing,
   And ev'ry damn'd Sing of them all,
Crying out, " Oh, we never more shall *sing*,
   Or we'll *sing* most confoundedly small."
A fig for their musketry flashes, &c.

Bould Thackwell the batteries surmounted,
   With the ould Third Dragoons, one by one,
Which for cavalry horsemen was counted
   A feat mighty handily done.

Their fortifications we shiver'd,
   Their pontoons we broke up and down,
And those who escaped being skiver'd,
   Jump'd into the water to drown.
A fig for their musketry flashes, &c.

So, Sergeant, my boy, drop your halbert,
   The powder we'll rinse from our throats;
Let us drink to the Queen and Prince Albert,
   And the Houses of Parliament's votes.
Here's the Generals who took the surrender,
   And the heroes of ev'ry brave corps,
Who march'd in the utmost of splendour,
   All round the proud walls of Lahore.
A fig for their musketry flashes,
   Their cannons and mortars and stuff!
'Tis the bay'net that settles their hashes,
   And lets the smoke out of their buff!

THE LAY OF THE DERBY.

THE cloudless sun of May shone forth o'er the array,
   Where joyous thousands cluster'd along the course's line,
And the fairest of the fair with sunny smile beamed there;
   Oh! brighter than the skies above, those eyes appear'd to shine.

The fated hour is near, the gallant steeds appear
   In the lustre of their beauty, in their pride of strength and speed;
Oh! many a heart beat high, gaz'd many an anxious eye,
   And many a fortune lay upon each bonny, bonny steed.

They part with gentle bound, they have gained the destined ground,
   They are forming into line for the desperate career,
And hark! a gathering shout from the watching crowd breaks out,
   "They are off! they're at the turn! they are coming, they are here!"

As the sea bursts o'er the dykes, rushes first Sir Tatton Sykes,
   Close, close, the bold Epirote is thundering on his flank.
They are here—they rush past—swift, swiftest at the last
   Springs Pyrrhus by the orange to the victor's vanward rank.

" Twenty-two, twenty-two," the conqueror's symbol view,
The talisman of triumph, or beacon of despair.
The race is lost and won ; the banqueting's begun,
Fill high the sparkling crystal, and the blithe repast prepare.

Aloft on circling wing the feathered heralds spring,
O'er many a town and hamlet to waft the winner's fame,
How Mr. Gully takes as his own the Derby stakes,
And Pyrrhus is the First in fact as well as name.

EVERARD CLIVE.

REGULÆ AULÆ TIPPERARY.

DULCE est desipere ; tædet sine jocis :
   Sed desipiendum est legibus et locis.
Sanciatur igitur Momus his in focis,
Si accedant suaviter seria jocosis.

Nimia dicacitas torrens est veneni.
Pinge duos angues : exulent obscœni.
Migrat in insulsum si quid eget frœni :
Bacchus est quem sequimur, non asinus Sileni.

Si quis plebi faveat, faveat decenter ;
Si quis Optimatibus faveat silenter :
Omnibus Politicis, nisi temperentur,
Cor eructat nimium, esuritque venter.

Pauca pocla suppetunt ; modo bibas horum
Singulis nominibus singula nostrorum ;
Et amicis omnibus omnium amicorum,
Et amatis omnibus omnium amatorum.

Satis sunt facilibus, satis sunt formosis
Duo pleni canthari, si e generosis,
Dona sua Gratiæ negant ebriosis ;
Et in bilem vertitur vappa crapulosis.

Μέτρον ἐστ ἄριστον—si sat metiare—
Et Ἄριστον ὕδωρ est cum vini parte pare :
Sic, si nostrum compares alio cum Lare,
Inter aulas emicat Aula Tipperary.

TRAVELLING BACHELOR.

2—2

THE OREGON SQUATTERS.
1846.

'Tis we that have left Alabama,
    Each arrayed like a primitive palmer,
  With hand on the rifle,
  That is not a trifle,
And the bowie-knife—ain't it a charmer?

We're gents as is come from Arkansas,
Pikers, and gunners, and lancers.
  Each a democrat dog,
  That will go the whole hog,
And stand for his own like a man, sirs.

We come from the old Indiana,
As hot as a lighted havannah.
  The Britisher rout
  Shall soon be kicked out,
As by Jackson from Louisiana.

And we're from the woods of Kentucky,
So gallant, and spicy, and plucky.
  Let the Company's spies
  Look out for their eyes,
For there's gougers agog from Kentucky.

We're pilgrims from fair Massachusetts.
You should worship the print that our shoe sets.
  We'll take a firm stand
  On our own promised land,
And wander no more like those Jew sets.

We're a mission sent here from Missouri,
To teach gospel and trial by jury.
  We're come to patch holes
  In the Indian souls,
And to send them upstairs, we assure ye.

And we've come a long way from Ohio,
Where our chalks have run up to the sky, oh!
  We'll wash out our smalls
  In the Willamette falls,
And the Britisher's claim is my eye, oh!

                TRAVELLING BACHELOR.

WHAT MAKES THE WORLD GO ROUND?

UPON my soul, it's the alcohol
   That makes the world go round;
And gravitation is botheration,—
   Just when the liquors abound
On earth down here, each higher sphere
   Sets to all spinning away;
And toe and heel, keeps up the reel,
   And rests nor night nor day.

If it were not so, 'tis the heads below
   That would take up the fumes instead;
And it's we that would spin, when the liquors were in,
   Whilst they would be quiet in bed.
But now it's the sky, 'stead of you and I,
   That reels when the wine mounts up,
When, instead of our ears, it sings in the spheres,
   To the tune of the bowl and cup.

             IRISH WHISKEY DRINKER.

CAROLINE.

CAROLINE, tell me truly,
   What mean those smiles on me?
Come to the Spa at Beulah,
   I'll treat you all to tea.
Send your little sisters
   Out of sight to play,
Say your feet have blisters,
   And sit by me all day.

Omnibuses are leaving
   The Elephant every hour,
Railroads are receiving
   All who come in their power.
I've a gingham umbrella,
   So never mind the rain;
Call me your dearest fellow,
   And come by an early train.

Caroline, you're so handsome,
　You've made me sigh all night;
My chest requires expansion,
　My waistcoat's grown too tight.
Surrey groves are shady,
　And Norwood lawns are fair,
So, my adored young lady,
　Let's go and take the air.

Then at eve returning,
　As along the road we creep;
Gaslights round us burning,
　Half the party asleep;
We'll sit next to each other,
　And talk the long day o'er,
And hope your father and mother
　Will ask me in at the door.

　　　　　　　EVERARD CLIVE.

HOLD YOUR OWN!
1846.

A FEARLESS stand on ill-got land
　Is what a rogue may make;
And hands unjust may stoutly trust
　The sword for glory's sake.
By brow of brass and heart of steel
　Are grasping scoundrels known;
The man that plays the noblest part
　Will simply hold his own.

To let your sway take headlong way,
　Unchecked by shame or sin;
To deem nought done till all is won
　That force or fraud can win,
Are "shadows, not substantial things."
　A better pride is shown
In being merely firm and fair;
　And holding just your own.

That often Might has vanquished Right,
　Is now a thrice-told tale.
But there's a word above the sword
　Shall make the Right prevail.

'Tis they who think before they strike,
  And strike for Right alone,
Make good their claim to deathless fame,
  And always hold their own.

Then let them think that we shall shrink,
  Because we calmly stand.
If war must be, right soon will we
  Unteach them sword in hand.
Let Yankees boast their force for fight—
  That fight they can they've shown,—
But so *can* we, and so *will* we,
  Before we yield our own.
                          TRAVELLING BACHELOR.

THE QUEEN'S VISIT TO IRELAND.

1846.

AH, who is on the *say?*
  Says the Shan Van Vaugh;
Ah, who is on the *say?*
  Says the Shan Van Vaugh.
In the merry month of May,
She'll be here without delay,
And 'twill be in Dublin Bay,
  Says the Shan Van Vaugh.

Who is on Dunleary's Sand?
  Says the Shan Van Vaugh;
Who is on Dunleary's Sand?
  Says the Shan Van Vaugh.
The Queen is on the strand,
With Prince Albert in her hand,
And she'll bless our own green land,
  Says the Shan Van Vaugh.

Ah! who will meet her there?
  Says the Shan Van Vaugh:
Ah! who will meet her there?
  Says the Shan Van Vaugh.

On the Curragh of Kildare,
'Tis the boys will meet her there,
And the girls in fine repair,
  Says the Shan Van Vaugh.

And who will lead the van?
  Says the Shan Van Vaugh:
And who will lead the van?
  Says the Shan Van Vaugh.
If there's one before ould Dan,
Let him step out says the Shan,
Faith, I'd like to see the man,
  Says the Shan Van Vaugh.

Won't she go to Tara's Hall?
  Says the Shan Van Vaugh:
Yes, she'll go to Tara's Hall,
  Says the Shan Van Vaugh.
We'll build up the ould wall;
She and Dan will lead the ball,
And the Harp it won't sing small,
  Says the Shan Van Vaugh.

Will she wear the Irish Crown?
  Says the Shan Van Vaugh:
Will she wear the Irish Crown?
  Says the Shan Van Vaugh.
Yes, 'twill be in Limerick town,
Where Sarsfield gained renown,
And the Trayty was put down,
  Says the Shan Van Vaugh.

Will she call at Darrynane?
  Says the Shan Van Vaugh:
Will she call at Darrynane?
  Says the Shan Van Vaugh.
Yes; and to her health we'll drain,
The whiskey and champagne,
Sure she won't go home again,
  Says the Shan Van Vaugh.

                    IRISH WHISKEY DRINKER.

ALE!

Air,—" Home, Sweet Home!"

O'ER ent-grass and chalices the eye may like to roam,
And our pewter may be humble, but 'tis ale that makes it foam,
The taste that you prize surely waits for you there,
Oh, the flavour of such malt and hops was never found elsewhere,
Ale, ale, double X ale,
There is no drink like ale!—there is no drink like ale!

Some tell me their small is good, but for me I do not heed it;
And I don't like your fourpenny, nor yet your intermediate.
The gin it don't agree with me, the brandy makes me pale;
But the reason I'm so jolly is, I stick to drinking ale.
Ale, ale, double X ale!
There is no drink like ale!—there is no drink like ale!

An exile from Knight's, liquors dazzle me in vain,
Oh give me my seat at the Christopher again;
The jolly little pot-boy that came at my call;
And give me my glass of ale, dearer than all.
Ale, ale, double X ale!
There is no drink like ale!—there is no drink like ale!

EVERARD CLIVE.

ANNEXATION.

1846.

YANKEE DOODLE wants a state,
Oregon or Texas,
Sends some squatters in it straight,
And quietly annexes,
Yankee Doodle, Doodle Do,
Yankee Doodle Dandy,
He can do the Britishers
And Mexicans so handy.

Canada's a pleasant place,
So is California;
Yankee Doodle wants them all,
But first he cribs a corner.

Yankee Doodle, Doodle Do,
   Yankee Doodle Dandy,
He can do the Britishers
   And Mexicans so handy.

Yankee Doodle went to sleep,
   Among his bills of parcels,
President Polk he stirred him up,
   And cocked his tail so martial.
   Yankee Doodle, Doodle Do,
      Yankee Doodle Dandy,
   He can do the Britishers
      And Mexicans so handy.

General Cass he made a speech,
   Archer called it splutter,
He swore he'd tear the British Jack
   And wipe it in the gutter.
   Yankee Doodle, Doodle Do,
      Yankee Doodle Dandy,
   He can do the Britishers
      And Mexicans so handy.

Jabez Honan took an oath,
   By the living Jingo!
Cuba soon shall be our own
   And so shall Saint Domingo.
   Yankee Doodle, Doodle Do,
      Yankee Doodle Dandy,
   He can do the Britishers
      And Mexicans so handy.

Yankee has some public works,
   Well he may parade them,
English money paid for all,
   And Irish labour made them.
   Yankee Doodle, Doodle Do,
      Yankee Doodle Dandy,
   He can do the Britishers
      And Mexicans so handy.

Then hey for Yankee Doodle's luck,
  And for Annexation;
Hey for Yankee Doodle's pluck,
  And for Repudiation.
    Yankee Doodle, Doodle Do,
    Yankee Doodle Dandy,
  And hey for Sherry Cobbler too,
    Mint julep and peach brandy.
TRAVELLING BACHELOR.

THE DESCENT OF ORPHEUS.

WHEN Orpheus descended a long time ago,
  To bring back his wife from the regions below,
The row he kicked up with his wild harp down there,
Turned the whole of the Shades into Donnybrook Fair:
Such jigs and such reels, and such going down the middle,
Queen Proserpine joined in the high-diddle-diddle;
Like a May boy the King twirled round on his stumps,
And leathered the boards till he wore out his pumps.

Ixion came down from his old spinning wheel,
And with Tityus and Theseus took share in a reel.
Poor Sisyphus jigged down the hill from his rock,
And set to with Charon—that hearty old cock.
The unfortunate colander-filling Danaides
Found partners again, and with waltzing made gay Hades;
And even old Tantalus growing quite frisky,
Groaned for water no more, and kept shouting for whiskey,

At last Pluto cried—"A blue blazing bowl mix,
The hottest, the strongest, e'er brewed by the Styx;
If it won't suit this harper so newly to hell come,
Whate'er he likes best he may call for and welcome."
"Then give me," said Orpheus, "a draft of new life;
I'll call, with your Majesty's leave, for my wife."
"Take her off," cried the king, "but remember my order,
You must not look back till she's over the border."

The lovers took leave of the king of the dead,
Nor once did Eurydice turn round her head ;
But when within touch of earth's boundary stone,
Orpheus peep'd o'er his left,—and his charmer was flown.
Stern Pluto's decree !—and no power could shake it ;
"'Twas a bargain," said he, "and I knew you would break it ;
I've done the most merciful deed of my life,
For you're too good a fellow to plague with a wife."

Irish Whiskey Drinker.

BOAT SONG.

Pull away, pull away—pull, boys, pull,
  The tide's on the fall, and the moon's at the full.
Oarsmen, row with a steady stroke,
Steersman, steer with a ready yoke.
Pull away, pull away,—row, boys, row,
Swiftly and steadily on we go,
Under the shade of tower and tree,
Out where the stream shines broad and free.
    Our oars flash white,
    In the pale moon's light,
And her rays they dance in our wake so bright,
As on we row through the silent night
        Swiftly and steadily,
        Swiftly and steadily,
        Swiftly and steadily, oh !
Pull away, pull away,—row, boys, row,
While the moon shines bright, and the night-winds blow,
Rippling the streams as fast they flow,
      Row, boys, row !

Everard Clive.

CHILLIANWALLAH.

Air—"Nora Creina."

'Twas near the famed Hydaspes' banks,
  Where Alexander thrashed King Porus,
Lord Gough incensed the British ranks,
  And the Sikh artillery spoke in chorus.
Our troops were tired;—the Khalsas fired;
  And they're the lads that seldom bungle:
Quoth Gough at the noise, "Screw bayonets, boys,
  And drive those blackguards out of the jungle."
    Sabres drawn, and bayonets fixt,
      Fight where fought great Alexander,—
    Paddy Gough's a cross betwixt
      A bull-dog and a salamander.

On every side our luck we tried,
  And found the showers of shot and shell come,
Where'er we went to our sweet content,
  The Sikhs they gave us blazing welcome.
The woods went crack, the rocks went smack,
  The clouds were black o'er Chillianwallah;
But our General's Irish blood was up,
  And our battle-cry was "Faugh-a-ballagh."
    Sabres drawn, and bayonets fixt,
      Fight where fought great Alexander,—
    Paddy Gough's a cross betwixt
      A bull-dog and a salamander.

The Third Dragoons, they cut right through,
  And back again—'twas mighty plucky—
But the Fifth Bengals disliked the balls,
  And every one of them cut his lucky.
But 'twould have done ould Homer good
  To see that charge of General Gilbert's;
Right and left his path he cleft,
  And smashed their skulls like mouldy filberts.
    Sabres drawn, and bayonets fixt,
      Fight where fought great Alexander, —
    Paddy Gough's a cross betwixt
      A bull-dog and a salamander.

Brigadier Dawes gained great applause—
  His fighting lads were all in clover,
'Twas as good to be there, as at Donnybrook fair,
  And no police till the fun was over.
At length the Sikhs they cut like bricks,
  Shere Singh sheered off nor looked behind him
And the old chief Chutter did swear and splutter;—
  But nobody cared at all to mind him.
      Sabres drawn, and bayonets fixt,
        Fight where fought great Alexander,—
      Paddy Gough's a cross betwixt
        A bull-dog and a salamander.

And none shall scoff at brave ould Gough—
  Oh! he's the chief for a soldier's choosing:
We lads abroad will always applaud,
  Though "The Times" at home is always abusing.
By the Jhelum's side their might he tried,
  And tamed the pride of the Khalsa gunners:
And he laid them flat at Goo-ze-rat,
  With his English-Irish dose of stunners.
      Sabres drawn, and bayonets fixt,
        Fight where fought great Alexander,—
      Paddy Gough's a cross betwixt
        A bull-dog and a salamander.

Horatius Flaccus sang, they say,
  About "*Quæ loca fabulosus
Lambit Hydaspes;*" and his lay
  Our General's high renown discloses.
Sure with the utmost classic grace
  He goes against these Punjaub caitiffs;
Horace's river licks the place,
  But Paddy Gough, he licks the natives.
      Sabres drawn, and bayonets fixt,
        Fight where fought great Alexander,—
      Paddy Gough's a cross betwixt
        A bull-dog and a salamander.

                    IRISH WHISKEY DRINKER.

GOOZERAT.

Air—" The Pretty Girl of Derby, oh !"

COME all you Anglo-Indians, in her Majesty's dominions,
    Hear a fighting bard's opinions of the glorious day,
February twenty-first, when we saw the sunbeams burst
    O'er the banners of the Affghan and the Sikhs' array.

From the Jhelum's rocky shore they had doubled on Lahore,
    But the British bayonet gleamed across the Chenab's ford.
Oh ! 'twas Whish that turned them back on their bold and bloody
    track ;
And Gough was soon upon them with his vengeful sword.

All fearlessly the foe turned to bay to bide the blow ;
    Their thousands were three-score 'neath their famed Shere Singh,
Of his battle-ground the chooser, at the ancient town of Goozerat,
    He stood resolved for life or death the dice to fling.

From false Affghanistan they had summoned Akrham Khan
    To join their class of Singhs all so blithe and gay.
Like a singing class of Hullah's, they rehearsed between two nullahs,
    And prepared a hailstone chorus with their guns to play.

Awhile in grim repose our General watched the foes,
    Scarce four miles from their camp was his final halt ;
Till he called in from afar the scattered streams of war,
    To swell one mighty torrent for the stern assault.

'Twould take of odes some volumes to describe Lord Gough's own
    columns,
On the Jhelum that sought glory in the cannon's mouth.
And Whish's gallant warriors, that had stormed Moulradj's barriers,
    Came hurrying in by thousands from the East and South.

Oh, those lads who captured Mooltan, fear nor Sirdar, Khan, nor
    Sultan,
Through all the sunny orient they shall have the sway ;
And to make our party snugger there came closing from Ramnugger
    Dundas, and other heroes of the proud Bombay.

With our guns in front arrayed we marched, as on parade,
  To break the foeman's centre and bear down his right;
We were scarce in range to kill, ere he unmasked his whole artillery;
  And his cannon flashed all eager to announce the fight.

Then our guns moved forth and spoke, and the ranks were wreathed
    with smoke;
  Oh, Alexander! mighty son of Ammon, oh!
In the East you did some wonders, but your fabled father's thunders,
  Compared with eighteen pounders, were all gammon, oh!

Three hours with deadly roar the iron storm did pour,
  Till their batteries were all dumb and their hearts all low.
Then our level bayonets glance and our scarlet lines advance
  To plunge among the masses of the reeling foe.

As the cold steel glitters nigh, the braggarts turn and fly :—
  Spur forward, gallant cavalry, and hew them down —
Till night closed deep and black, red havoc marked our track,
  Where we smote the routed rebels 'gainst the might of England's
    crown.

Oh joyously that night did we celebrate the fight,
  In the foeman's captured camp when the sparkling wine was
    poured;
While around us lay the spoil of the day's victorious toil,
  The cannon, and the banner, the buckler, and the sword.

For ever has the sway of the Khalsa passed away:
  We'll crush the fierce fanatics, whom no mercy could subdue;
And they, our rule who hate, shall tremble at the fate
  Of Asia's best, with England who the struggle dared renew.

Bold Gilbert and his power have marched upon Peshawur;
  And soon its shattered tower shall confess our wrath;
Without troubling spade or mattock, we'll assault and carry Attock;
  And woe to the false Affghan that shall cross our path.

The annexing of the Punjaub you may reckon that a done job,
  And Dost Mahommed in the dust we soon will lay;
Then, just for a diversion, we'll polish off the Persian,
  And conquer back to Europe our triumphant way.

Our renown shall live for ages, and 'twill shine in history's pages,
 (When Radetski is forgotten, and pugnacious Bem),
How Shere Singh was the loser at the bloody game at Goozerat,
 And Gough won for his coronet its brightest gem.
 EVERARD CLIVE.

"THE CLARET CUP."

Drink of this cup.—Old Lovegrove sips
 The same at Blackwall below;
And this he gives to cool the lips
 Of the guests who for white-bait go.

Drink of this cup. The ice within
 Is fresh from Wenham's stream.
'Twill make the summer's dust and din,
Its tongue so parched, and fevered skin,
All melt away, as your draught you win,
 Like a long-forgotten dream.

Then off! off! says the Drinker,
 Off! off! and away;
If we swallow more we shall sink her;
 So, Bachelor, boy, give way.
 EVERARD CLIVE.

ADELAIDE.

He, who loves thee, wanders lonely in the gardens of the spring,
 'Mid the soft enchanted lustre that glimmers through the shade
Of the tremulous tree-branches, and the buds that on them swing—
 Adelaide!

In the snow-sheen of the Alps, in the sparkling of the streams,
 In the golden hues of heaven when daylight has decayed,
In the starry fields of midnight thine image on me beams—
 Adelaide!

Small silver Maybells lisp along the grass,
 Evening breezes whisper in the green leaves of the glade,
Nightingales sing, and waves murmur as they pass—
 " Adelaide!"

From this fond and faithful heart, when death hath stilled its grief,.
  Will spring a blooming flower, o'er the lover's grave displayed,.
And distinctly will there glimmer on each little purple leaf—
  " Adelaide !"

TRAVELLING BACHELOR.

IBRAHIM PACHA'S IRISH TRIP.
1846.

OH, who has not heard of great Ibr'im Pacha,
  How he came to old Erin across the blue wave,
With his beard of the longest the world ever saw,
  That 'twould take twenty barbers at least for to shave ?

To see him at morn, when just entering the bay
  Of old Carrickfergus we spied him afar ;
O'er the black funnel smoke he blew up far away
  The clouds of his royal Havanna cigar.
As nearer he came in the gallant Athlone,
At the old fighting-cock such bright glances were thrown,
And many a soft bosom wished him her own.

Here the band of the 93rd Highlanders swells ;
  Here Pat round his head his shilelah is swinging,
And here some wild bard, 'mid a chorus of yells,
  The great Pharaoh Necho's high welcome is singing.

Or, to see him at eve, when he sat down to dine,
And gulp'd a whole flood of the infidel wine,
How his jokes flew about like a quick fall of stars,
And o'er coffee and Cubas he talked of his wars ;
Till at last such slow work he no longer could brook,
And he call'd for Bush-Mills, and the Prophet's chibouke.

" Oh, Allah is great, but," said he, " I am thinking
This juice of the barley is wonderful drinking.
In Egypt there's corn, and in France there is wine ;
But Erin has both in her whiskey divine !"

His Highness and suite drank till midnight away ;
Till they set to at last, like young tigers at play ;
And he order'd ten puncheons for Cairo next day.

Next he walks round and talks round the town at his ease ;
And th' authorities show him whatever they please,—
Foundries, factories, warehouses, tall merchantmen ;
Such things he's oft seen, and he'll see them again,
So no longer his Highness's patience to tax,
They took him to see Mr. Richardson's flax.

On board, then, once more, he bade Erin to hope
    That he'd see her again with his smoke-jack unfurl'd ;
The 93rd Highlanders played Johnny Cope,
    And he sailed from the pleasantest isle in the world.
IRISH WHISKEY DRINKER.

MAY MORNING.

OH, the May-morn of yore was a blithe one, I ween,
    When they danced round the pole on the old village green ;
When the maids gathered dew at the break of the day,
And they wove a bright wreath for the Queen of the May.
Though the good times be past, and the world has grown cold,
Still the dew and the flowers are as sweet as of old ;
Still the sky laughs with love, and the earth with good cheer,
And the birds sing their merriest song of the year.
      Wake up, lady fair, come away, come away !
      'Tis Love's merry morn, 'tis the morn of the May !

Our steeds but thy coming, fair lady, await ;
Hark ! the neigh of Black Gipsey below at the gate !
Her bridle I've wreathed with the freshest of green,
And I've cull'd thee a rose that is fit for a queen.
The hedge-rows are sweet, and the meadows are fair,
But the breeze of the Downs is more racy and rare :
O'er their soft turf careering together we'll go,
As the sea-birds skim light o'er the waters below.
      Wake up, lady fair, come away, come away !
      'Tis Love's merry morn, 'tis the morn of the May !
IRISH WHISKEY DRINKER.

THE CAMBRIDGE AND OXFORD BOAT RACE

FOR 1846.

THE morning breeze of early spring
Ripples the river with its wing ;
And men who roost in London, wake
A somewhat hurried meal to take :
Then up the Thames they speed.
For this is the appointed day
When Oxford oars-men must essay
The laurel wreath to wrest away,
That now is Granta's meed.
Awake, arise—we must be bonne
To see the gallant strife e'er noon ;
They start where Mortlake's waters flow,
And down to Putney piers they row.

Oh well I call to mind the time
When I was in my boating prime,
When such a match as this to view
I used to join some eight-oars' crew ;
Or, doomed in solitude to float,
Could sport at least a wager-boat.
Now, as the Queen in Hamlet saith,
I'm getting fat and scant of breath.
So at mine ease to watch the race,
I in a steamer take my place :
'Tis nine o'clock : we're all on board,
The bottled porter safe is stored,
Cigars are lit of various sizes
And cheerily their odour rises,
As high the thin smoke curls ;
The engines champ, the wheels begin
Their spattering, fizzing, seething din,
Merrily up the Thames we spin.
(" Childe Harold " is the boat we're in,
She's chartered by the Searles).

Flat Chelsea, on thy Reach's tide
  The racing shouts are heard no more,
No more contending cutters glide
  Along thy dank and dismal shore.
Still, as we pass thy banks of dirt,
Full many a former desperate spirt
  Comes back upon my mind.
No more, no more of reminiscence,
Our steamer's paddles swiftly hiss hence—
  Soon Fulham's left behind.
The Crabtree's past, and Chiswick's bower,
And now we pull near Mortlake's tower,
And as we gain the chosen scene
A merry sight it is I ween.
Steamers are there, with jovial freight,
Rowers of various skill and weight
In pair-oar, four-oar, six, and eight;
And funnies small, and barges great
  That almost stop the way.
And horsemen on the shore are there,
And carriages with ladies fair,—
'Twere worth a morning's snooze I swear,
  One glance at their array.

And lo upon the glorious tide
  A glorious shape appearing,
The Cambridge boat in all the pride
  Of conscious swiftness steering.
As if the beauteous thing enjoyed
  The racing strife and glee,
She putteth out her light-blue oars,
  And glideth gracefully.

From Trinity her captain came,
Her number Seven did the same,
  And Two, and Three, and Four;
As Bow and Six two Johnians strive;
And Magdalen sends as number Five
  A stout and stalwart oar.

Oh, proud was every Cambridge heart
  Their sinewy frames to scan.
And blithe and hearty was the cheer,
That, as the starting-place they near,
  Along the waters ran.

And gallant was that rival bark
Whose hues of blue so deep and dark
  The Oxford colours showed.
A manlier and an abler crew,
A bark more light and fair to view
  Ne'er upon Isis rowed.

Now fairly marshalled for the strife
  The eager rivals lie;
Thrown back in row the light oars quiver
Over the surface of the river
  In keen expectancy.
Each tongue is hushed; with throbbing heart
Each watches for the sign to start:
'Tis given—the mooring lines are slipped,
With light half-stroke the blades are dipped,
Like greyhounds from the leash set free,
The boats spring simultaneously,
  And dash along the tide.
By wave and shore the shouting throng
Follows their fleet career along,
While still with hope and courage strong
  They struggle side by side.

And swift and swift, with rapid lightness
  The flashing oars dip evenly,
Alternating their feathery brightness
  With sweeping strokes—By Chiswick, see,
With unabated speed they glance;
The light-blue bows are in advance,
  And "Cambridge" is the cry.
Still pressing on with desperate burst
Through Hammersmith our men are first,
  As if in Victory.

But no—again abreast we view
The " darkly beautifully blue ;"
 The goal is full in sight ;
The Oxford holds her own once more.
Say ye who betted six to four,
 If odds like these were right ?

Speed, Cambridge, speed. Thy champion's pride
In fiercer struggle ne'er was tried :
Quick ! quicker forward on the feather !
Pull the good stroke out well together !
One effort more for honour's meed,
The bridge is near—speed, Cambridge, speed !
Again she claims her pride of place,
Again she heads the breathless race,
Close pressed by her unflinching foe,—
Gallantly to the end they go.
The arch is shot, the strife is o'er,
And Cambridge has one laurel more.

I rhyme not for the seedy elf,
Who cannot fancy for himself
How pealed the cheering from the crowd,
And little cannons thundered loud—
How, as the crews the shores regain,
The corks popp'd high ; and bright champagne
(From which as long as oarsmen train
With other things they must refrain),
Refresh'd with its immortal rain
The thirsty soul that drinks amain,
Then gasps for breath, and drinks again—
How sweetly Mrs. Avis smiled,
How some rejoiced, and some were ryled,
And how we hope as good a crew
Will come next spring from either U-
niversity for us to view,
 At Putney, Hammersmith, or Kew.
                                        EVERARD CLIVE.

THE CHISWICK FLOWER FÊTE
FOR 1846.

Ho! members, take your tickets,—
    Ho! maidens, choose your shawls!
The son looks out his waistcoats,
    The sire selects his smalls.
To-day is Flora's triumph,
    To-day great sights you view,
So, cabmen, drive your cattle,
    And drive your bargains too.

Green are the squares of London,
    And some few lanes are green,
And trees of city foliage
    Shade walks of stone between.
And green are certain gala days,
    With places known to fame—
The inner circle of the park
    That bears the Regent's name.

And green are those great glasses
    That hold Germania's wine,
That they tell you suit the vintage
    Of the clear Moselle and Rhine:
And green are those young freshmen,
    Who, to earn a gentle name,
Take credit of a tailor,
    Or give it to a dame.

But greener far than any
    Is Chiswick's shaven sward;
And gayer than all gala-days
    Are the groups that swarm abroad.
See how they muster onwards,—
    The car, the cab, the team;
My dearest friends in carriages,
    My dearer self by steam.

Bright is the first fresh show of Spring,
    When cucumbers are rare;
And bright the show of hot July,
    When Autumn's fruits are there:

Autumn that's forced beforehand,
As children oversage,
When all forestalls its season,
Like minds before their age.

But the brightest day among them,
The grandest show of three,
Is that which brings the roses,
And draws down you and me
So 'mid the great Triumvirs
Did greater Cæsar sway;
So 'mid the days of Epsom
Stands out the Derby day.

Gay are the grounds at Hackney,
And Cheam has beds in bloom;
And Mr. Epps of Maidstone
Has flowers of faint perfume.
And Bromley's stocks at nightfall
Breathe sweetly through the air,
And a thousand tulips ornament
Each Lea Bridge Road parterre.

And Ealing's glassy houses
Exclude each colder breeze;
And the air is full of odours
Of exotic orchides.
And there hang the strangest blossoms
From the strangest sorts of trees;
And Fahrenheit is standing at
A hundred hot degrees.

There steams the watery vapour;
There reek the fumes of peat;
Their Tropic heats surround your head,
And damps strike up your feet;
There cacti stand like hedges,
A long and leafless row;
Their climbers curl their tresses,
And catch the heads below.

Hot water apparatuses,
  In iron pipes, transmit
Equable sorts of atmosphere,
  For plant or fruit-tree fit.
But the youth that led the maiden
  Through the sweets of that parterre,
Would find her faint upon his arm,
  And call, like Brougham, for air.

Red are the Twick'nam strawberries,
  And Hampton boasts its vines;
And melons thrive in Battersea;
  And Chelsea vaunts its pines.
St. George loves Sheen and Richmond
  For his own immortal rose;
And Eve might envy Putney
  For the apples that it grows.

But now nor Cheam nor Maidstone
  Shine bright, as once they shone;
And all the stocks of Bromley,
  With all their scents are gone.
Save for its maids and moonshine
  Fair Bromley has no dew,
The Lea Bridge wind wafts dust enough,
  But it wafts no odours too.
Their hues, their fruits, their odours
  Are all on Chiswick showered,
And Bromley, Cheam, and Maidstone
  Are lank and disembowered.

Here stand the golden products
  Of every sun and clime,
And seem to live, like lover's vows,
  In spite of space or time.
To bring each flower to Chiswick
  Is Science sent to roam;
But the flower itself lives easy,
  And makes itself at home.

Where Suez joins the Continents,—
    Where Afric joins the line,—
Where Texas joins the Union,—
    And Indus joins the brine,
Come all the hues of Flora,—
    The blues, the reds, the greens ;
From beyond the lines of railways
    And beyond the writs of queens.

But we only feel their odours,
    And we only see their hues ;
They've esoteric meanings
    That some know how to use.
And, perhaps, as Mr. Wordsworth says,
    We transplant them to abuse.

Each orchis is an emblem
    In its own exotic land,
And telleth tale of tenderness
    That the natives understand.
Sent by mulatto Mercuries
    It may augur hope or fear ;
I wish I found the lady
    That could feel its meaning here.
                TRAVELLING BACHELOR.

A SAD CASE.

THEY say there is anguish in loving in vain ;
    But, oh ! 'tis a deeper and gloomier pain
To be ardently loved by the fond and true-hearted,
When the power of returning that love is departed.

Our feelings once faded, return not at will,
We upbraid our own coldness, but cold are we still ;
While the heart whose young love we so long were awaking,
With that love unrequited before us is breaking !
                EVERARD CLIVE.

THE DEVIL'S RACE.

'Tis of Lord Luttrèll
  Who once did dwell
By the banks of the gentle Rye:
  The Hell-fire Club
  They did him dub,
The king of their company.

  On New Year's Eve
  He was seen to grieve,
Amid the roaring cheer;
  And the reason he had
  For being so sad,
You all straightway shall hear.

  In the hour of need
  A gallant steed,
He lost in the chace that day;
  And a strange black knight
  Who sat at his right,
Had borne the brush away.

  And the knight in black
  Said "My lord, your pack,
Although they're of high degree,
  And I fain must own
  Fair sport have shown,
Don't go the right pace for me!"

  The lord's lip curled,
  And he swore, the world
Such hounds could not produce,
  And a horse he'd find
  Would leave behind
The devil himself let loose.

  Now the knight in black
  Would his dark mare back,
And darker none mote be;
  "A Tartar," he said,
  "She was born and bred,
And her name was Hecate.

" Her beauty, breed,
　And strength and speed,
Were matchless," he'd declare ;
" And whenever tried,
　She'd tame the pride
Of the hunters of Kildare."

" I scorn thy word,"
　Said the proud proud lord,
" And I'll wager down," quoth he,
　" Ten thousand pounds,
　With my Irish hounds
To ride once more with thee."

Oh, then looked at him
　That stranger grim,
With a dread, unearthly stare,—
　" Ten thousand," said he,
　" So let it be,
And double it if you dare !"

" Twice thousands ten
　We'll make it, then,"
Said the Lord Luttrell, quite free,—
　" And if I don't ride away
　From the devil that day,
May the devil ride away with me !"

Then the stranger wrote
　A red red note,
In a book as black as jet ;
　" At your own word
　I'll take you, my lord ;
Good faith ! 'tis a sporting bet !"

Then they went to bed,
　And blue flames, 'tis said,
Flashed round the black knight's curtain ;
　And no mortal dare
　Go near the black mare,
Kicking all night, and snorting.

Uprose the morn,
And the merry bugle horn
Rang thorough the woodlands clear;
And merry rode out
The Hell-fire rout
That morn to hunt the deer.

Three score and ten
Down the forest glen,—
'Twas a glorious sight to see,
As they trotted in line,
With their coursers so fine,
And their scarlet toggery.

The lord that day
Rode an iron grey;
Of all his steeds 'twas the best;
And close by his side,
In gloomy pride,
Rode out the stranger guest.

At the Hell-fire array,
With a shrill, sharp neigh,
The black mare neighed in glee;
And the stranger down low,
To his saddle bow,
Saluted them in courtesy.

Of his steed so proud
Their praise ran loud;
Of horse-flesh she was the queen;
Such paces, such points,
Such limbs and such joints,
They surely ne'er had seen.

The land, they said,
Such brave steeds that bred,
And riders brave as he,
Be it mountain or plain,
Or far across the main,
A brave brave land must be.

" 'Tis a far countree,"
The black knight said he,
" A low, dark, burning strand;
You'll see it, I swear,
And feel it, I declare ;
And I'll meet you when you land."

Oh, did it lie east,
Or south, or west,
Or yet in the north far down ?
And they asked him whether
He should meet them together,
Or meet them there one by one ?

" Oh, it lies not east,
Nor south, nor west,
Nor yet in the north far down,"
The black knight said,
" And to none but the dead
Could that land be ever known."

Then trot, trot away,
And they trotted so gay,
All singing a hunting strain,
Till Leixlip they passed,
And Castletown at last,
Tom Conolly's grand demesne.

There the Squire came out
To join the merry rout,
And the bottle and glass went round;
Then through the back gate,
With spirits elate,
And on to the hunting ground.

FYTTE THE THIRD.

Hark ! the huntsman's horn,
From the top of Ballygorn !
Hark, away ! 'tis Lord Luttrell's cry!
He cheers the brave pack
On the wild deer's track,
And waves his cap on high.

And the stranger is there,
On his bounding mare,
By the side of the lord and the gray.
Each holds down his hands,
And in his stirrups stands,—
They're off! a fair start, and away!

"Sir Knight," cried Luttrèll,
"This day shall tell
Of your boast so proud and vain!"
"My lord, ride your best,"
Said the gloomy guest,
"You may never, never ride again."

Away! away!
'Neath the glad sun's ray;
Away o'er the meadows so green!
The black mare's away,
And the iron grey
Is on her flank, I ween.

Away! away!
The Hell-fires that day
Rode at a thundering pace;
Though none could gain
The side of the twain,
In front of the Devil's race.

Through dewy copse,
Down the sunny slopes,
And they leave the vales behind;
O'er ditch, wall, and briar,
Like furze on fire,
Or the rush of a roaring wind.

Like a hailstone shower
By the old Round Tower
Of Taptoo, and the old fox cover,
They rattled amain
To Killadoon demesne
Where the stag popp'd the wall, and over.

Lord Leitrim's gate
May frown in state,
'Twill not that rout turn back, —
Crash! the Knight bursts through,
With a wild halloo;
And Luttrell's on his track.

Through Killadoon wood,
Down by the old flood,
There's nought the Hell-fires to stay;
Then to clear the back bounds
For the open grounds,
Hark forward! away! away!

Ardrass! Ardrass!
I swear by the mass,
'Twould old Nimrod cheer to see
That sight of pride
By thy heathery side,
Now bursting gloriously!

They turned, you think,
By the Liffey's brink;
But no, the high flood-tide
The brave stag bore
Down a mile or more,
E'er he reached the other side.

Lo! that headlong dash
Of the hounds' splash, splash.
'Tis the bound of black Hecatè:
The boiling spray,
As she cleaves her way,
Hisses most fearfully.

Of three score and ten,
All Hell-fire men
Who rode in chase that day,
Not one all round
Took that dreadful bound
But the lord and his bonny bonny grey.

With hand on mane,
And a loose loose rein,
And the good steed's head let free,
He steered him o'er
To the shelving shore,
Like ship through a stormy sea.

Off! off! again
Are those coursers twain,
Refreshed by the wintry tide;
First the knight in black,
Whilst the lord at his back
Some twenty lengths must ride.

'Tis all very well,
Thought Lord Luttrèll,
His pace and racing skill;
But the churchyard jump
Will somebody stump,
On the top of Lyon's hill.

Just then, they say,
The gallant grey,
In his wind looked put about,
Whilst the coal-black mare
Had as much to spare
As when she first set out.

Away! away!
For the old church grey,
Speeds the stag unerringly;
At a glorious bound
Over wall and mound,
And he's saved in the sanctuary.

Like thunder-burst
Came the black knight first,
Right at the stones went he;
But made full stop
On the old wall top
And yelled most fearfully.

"Now my bonny bonny grey,
There's the devil to pay,
And let us pay him well ;
Clear the churchyard stone
And the day's our own—
Hie over !" cried Lord Luttrèll.

Then Black Hecatè
Was a sight to see,
Rearing up higher and higher ;
Kicking the top stones
'Mongst the dead men's bones,
And her nostrils all on fire.

"Sir knight ! sir knight !
Though in strange plight,
Perched up on high you be ;
I little reck,
If you break your neck,
So you pay your bet to me.

" Beyond my bounds
Are these holy grounds,
In a hotter place to you
My debt I'll pay
Some other day,
Till then, my lo.d, adieu !"

As the Demon spoke
The thunder woke,
And flashed the lightning's flame,
With a brimstone scent
Through th' air as he went,
To the place from whence he came.

On Lyon's hill
Say the old men still,
On each New Year's Eve of grace,
A pack in full cry
Can be heard hard by,
And the noise of the Devil's Race.

GENERAL BALLADS.

THE OPENING CHAUNT.

BY DR. MAGINN.

Written on the occasion of the First Publication of 'Bentley's Miscellany.'

I.

Come round and hear, my public dear,
  Come hear, and judge it gently,—
The prose so terse, and flowing verse,
  Of us, the wits of Bentley.

II.

We offer not intricate plot
  To muse upon intently;
No tragic word, no bloody sword,
  Shall stain the page of Bentley.

III.

The tender song which all day long
  Resounds so sentimént'ly,
Through wood and grove all full of love,
  Will find no place in Bentley.

IV.

Nor yet the speech which fain would teach
  All nations eloquéntly;—
'Tis quite too grand for us the bland
  And modest men of Bentley.

V.

For science deep no line we keep,
　We speak it reverently ;—
From sign to sign the sun may shine,
　Untelescoped by Bentley.

VI.

Tory and Whig, in accents big,
　May wrangle violently :
Their party rage shan't stain the page—
　The neutral page of Bentley.

VII.

The scribe whose pen is mangling men
　And women pestilently,
May take elsewhere his wicked ware,—
　He finds no mart in Bentley.

VIII.

It pains us not to mark the spot
　Where Dan may find his rent lie ;
The Glasgow chiel may shout for Peel,
　We know them not in Bentley.

IX.

Those who admire a merry lyre,—
　Those who would hear attent'ly
A tale of wit, or flashing hit,—
　Are ask'd to come to Bentley.

X.

Our hunt will be for grace and glee,
　Where thickest may the scent lie ;
At slashing pace begins the chase—
　Now for the burst of Bentley.

THE famous periodical writer, Dr. Maginn, was born about the end of the last century, in Cork, where his father kept one of the most respectable schools in the South of Ireland. The precocity of the younger Maginn in the usual academic studies was such that he was enabled, at the early age of thirteen, to enter the Dublin University ;

and when he was scarcely twenty-one, an age at which only the minority
of university students attain their Bachelorship in Arts, he obtained
the highest degree, of Doctor of Laws. Although he distinguished
himself in Classics, and arrived at a highly critical and accurate knowledge of the ancient Greek and Latin authors of the University course,
under the careful tuition of his father, as well as from having taken his
share in the work of the school—he is reported to have " coached " the
head class when he was no more than seventeen years of age, after
having taken his Bachelor's degree—his versatility in many other
branches of knowledge, to which men apply themselves later in life,
was equally remarkable. From his earliest boyhood the study of English literature, and of the English poets especially, formed his chief
delight. Like Jerrold, he was a Shakespearian from his childhood, a
fact which is proved beyond question in his Shakespeare papers contributed to 'Bentley's Miscellany,' even at a time when his naturally
buoyant spirits had begun to feel a melancholy depression, and his fine
faculties might have been expected to be on the wane. Of many
others of our most eminent English authors in prose and verse, from
the Elizabethan age downwards, he could not only repeat leading passages, but whole pages by heart. Whether it was that his repugnance
to scientific studies, although as regards these he passed creditably to
his Bachelor's degree, prevented him from trying for a Fellowship which
in any other University his brilliant classical attainments would have
most assuredly won for him, and this too at a time when the number
of Fellowships in the Dublin University was much more limited, and
a vacancy in consequence was of rarer occurrence than at present, or
that his genius, incapable of restraint or plodding, at once took wing,
and gloried in its early flight over flowery and congenial fields of
thought, cannot, at this distance of time, and in the absence of any
well authenticated account of his early days, be ascertained. Certain
it is, however, that, like the young Etonians of the Anti-Jacobin, he
too gave early and brilliant promise ; and the best things in prose and
verse of those days in ' Bolster's Cork Magazine,' were said to be from
the pen of the precocious young Doctor. ' Blackwood's Magazine '
was commenced in 1817, when Maginn was about twenty-one years of
age, after having taken his degree of Doctor of Laws at the Dublin
University. Sympathising with its politics and its pluck, and anxious
to serve under Christopher North, he became connected with it in
about a couple of years after its commencement, his first contribution to it being a metrical Latin version of the famous old English
ballad of the Chevy Chase. Shortly afterwards appeared in it to the
great amusement of the learned world, "The Wine-Bibber's Glory,"

the English verses of which are remarkable for the easy, rhythmical, natural expression, and never-flagging humour which characterise Maginn's happiest efforts, and the Latin ones, a most marvellous performance in their way, leave all competition, in modern times, at least, behind. One can easily understand whence Prout derived the first ideas of the classic comicalities which he developed in 'Frazer's Magazine,' about a dozen years, and followed up in 'Bentley's Miscellany,' about a dozen and a half after the following had appeared in 'Blackwood.' It is the prototype beyond all question in modern times and in these countries at least, of this species of literary composition of which the 'Bentley Ballads' contain so many specimens—the writer of it himself, a Bentleian in his day—and forms a natural appendant to Prout's polyglot lay upon the Hot Wells of Clifton, and the English and Latin song, by O'Leary, and the Whiskey Drinker on 'Ireland's Mountain Dew.'

THE WINE-BIBBER'S GLORY.	POTORIS GLORIA.
Quo me Bacche rapis tui.	
Plenum.	Hor.

A melody in English and Latin, to a tune for itself, lately discovered in Herculaneum—being an ancient Roman air—or if not, quite as good.

If Horatius Flaccus made jolly old Bacchus	Si Horatio Flacco de hilari Baccho
So often his favourite theme;	Mos carmina esset cantare,
If in him it was classic to praise his old Massic	Si Massica vina vocaret divina Falernaque sciret potare.
And Falernian to gulp in a stream;	
If Falstaff's vagaries 'bout Sack and Canaries	Si nos juvat mirè Falstaffium audire
Have pleased us again and again;	Laudentem Hispanicum merum,
Shall we not make merry on Port, Claret, or Sherry,	Cor nostrum sit lætum ob Portum, Claretum,
Madeira, and sparkling Champagne?	Xerense, Campanum, Maderum.
First Port, that potation preferred by our nation	Est Portum potatio quam Anglica natio
To all the small drinks of the French;	Vinis Galliæ prætulit lautis
'Tis the best standing liquor for layman or vicar,	Sacerdote amatur, et laicis potatur
The army, the navy, the bench.	Consultis, militibus, nautis.
'Tis strong and substantial, believe me, no man shall	Si meum conclave hoc forte et suave
Good Port from my dining-room send;	Vitaverit essem iniquus,
In your soup, after cheese, every way it will please,	Post caseum, in jure, placebit secure
But most tête-à-tête with a friend.	Præsertim cum adsit amicus.

Fair Sherry, Port's sister, for years they dismissed her,
To the Kitchen to flavour the jellies—
There long she was banished, and well-nigh had vanished
To comfort the kitchen-maids' bellies;
Till his Majesty fixt, he thought Sherry when sixty
Years old, like himself, quite the thing;
So I think it but proper to fill a tip-topper,
Of Sherry to drink to the king.

Huic quamvis cognatum, Xerense damnatum,
Gelatâ culina tingebat,
Vinum exul ibique dum coquo cuique,
Generosum liquorem præbebat.
Sed a rege probatum est valde pergratum
Cum (ut ipse) sexagenarium
Largo ergo implendum regique bibendum
Opinor est nunc necessarium.

Though your delicate Claret by no means goes far, it
Is famed for its exquisite flavour;
'Tis a nice provocation to wise conversation
Queer blarney or harmless palaver;
'Tis the bond of society, no inebriety
Follows a swig of the Blue;
One may drink a whole ocean, but ne'er feel commotion
Or head-ache from Chateaux Margoux.

Claretum. oh! quamvis haud forte (deest nam vis)
Divina sapore notatur;
Hinc dulcia dicuntur, faceta nascuntur,
Leniterque philosophizatur!
Socialis potatio! te haud fregit ratio.
Purpureo decoram colore!
Tui maximum mare liceret potare
Sine mentis frontisve dolore!

But though Claret is pleasant to taste for the present,
On the stomach it sometimes feels cold;
So to keep it all clever and comfort your liver,
Take a glass of Madeira that's old;
When 't has sailed for the Indies, a cure for all wind 'tis,
And cholic 'twill put to the rout;
All doctors declare a good glass of Madeira
The best of all things for the gout.

Etsi vero in præsenti Claretum bibenti
Videatur imprimis jucundum,
Cito venter frigescat, quod ut statim decrescat,
Vetus vinum Maderum adeundum.
Indos si navigârit, vento corpus levârit
Coliceamque fugârit hoc merum;
Podagrâ cruciato vinum optimum dato,
Clamant medici docti "Maderum!"

Then Champagne, dear Champagne, ah! how gladly I drain a
Whole bottle of Oeil de perdrix;
To the eye of my charmer, to make my love warmer,
If cool that love ever could be.
I could toast her for ever; but never, oh, never
Would I her dear name so profane;
So if e'er, when I'm tipsy, it slips to my lips, I
Wash it back to my heart in Champagne!

Campanum! Campanum quo gaudio lagenam
Ocelli Perdricis sorberem!
Ad dominæ oculum exhauriam poculum
Tali philtro si unquam egerem.
Propinarem divinam—sed peream si sinam
Nomen carum ut sic profanatur,
Et si cum Bacchus urget, ad labia surget
Campano ad cor revolvetur!

Over a space of ten years from the time of his first connexion with it, the Doctor was a constant contributor in prose and verse to 'Blackwood's Magazine,' including his portions of the celebrated 'Noctes Ambrosianæ,' to the earlier numbers of which he contributed largely. The 'Noctes' began in 1822, and ended in 1835, seven years after Maginn had withdrawn from the publication. In 1823, he had given up his schoolmaster's life at Cork, and thrown himself on the world of letters in London, where he became actively employed in political literature, writing for the 'Representative,' (old John Murray's unfortunate venture for which Mr. Disraeli wrote leaders and reviews), the 'John Bull,' the 'Standard,' the 'Age,' and a short-lived Tory publication called the 'Torch.' In 1830, 'Fraser's Magazine' was commenced under the editorship of the Doctor, and Mr. Hugh Fraser, a clever man about town—not the publisher of the work, whose name was James, and no relative whatever to the editor. To this periodical he contributed amongst other remarkable papers his 'Homeric Ballads ;' and he had the merit in those days, as indeed the late Serjeant Murphy, another Cork man and a ripe scholar, had, of contributing some portions of the Prout papers. When 'Bentley's Miscellany' was commenced in 1837, Maginn wrote the 'Opening Chaunt,' and became one of its leading contributors. As allusion has been made in our preface to these portions of his literary labours, we may pass on to the sad and melancholy close of a career which had opened with such extraordinary brightness and exultation. Imprisonment for debt, an emaciated frame, consumption, and a broken heart, the result of years of unrestrained convivial enjoyment, and the most reckless improvidence, wound up at the early age of forty-six, one of the most brilliant and eccentric Irishmen of the nineteenth century. He died in the August of 1842, at Walton-on-Thames, in extremely straitened circumstances, which many of his personal friends and admirers of his splendid genius and unselfish heart would have been too happy to alleviate, had he not been too proud to appeal to their benevolence. A day or two before his death, a handsome remittance—one of the many tributes of sympathy afforded by the same noble hearted friend of genius in distress—arrived at his cottage from the late Sir Robert Peel, who had been applied to in his behalf by a literary friend—arrived in time—to pay his funeral expenses. Maginn was of singularly unaffected and most engaging manners, simple-hearted, with no reserve as to what was in him—and what treasures of knowledge were his—and with no care for even the morrow, much less the distant future. Nothing could daunt, or darken, or depress him, and he retained his boyishness and elasticity of spirit to the last. A friend of his, who gave a sketch of his life and writings

in the Dublin University Magazine shortly after his decease, speaking
of his literary and social character says—"It would be hard to name
any other writer of his time, except Sydney Smith, who was at once so
witty, so philosophical. so elegant, and earnest in political discourses.
As a conversationalist he was known for the liveliness of his fancy,
the diversity of his anecdotes, the richness and felicity of his illustra-
tions, the depth and shrewdness of his truth, the readiness of his re-
partee, and the utter absence of anything like dictation to those who
came to listen and to be instructed—'_idem lætus et præsens, jucundus et
gravis, tam copiâ, tam brevitate mirabilis._' Lastly, as a man, he pos-
sessed the most childlike gentleness and simplicity, the greatest mo-
desty, the warmest heart, the most benevolent hand, with the most
scanty means. From faults he was not free, from wild irregularities he
was not exempt. But great genius is seldom perfect; its excesses
must be forgiven when they are counterbalanced by fine qualities.
'_Summi enim,_' says Quintilian, '_sunt homines tantum !_' The rock upon
which Steel and Burns split, the sole blot upon Addison, the only
stigma upon Charles Lamb, that which exiled Fox from the cabinet of
England, and reduced Sheridan to poverty and shame, was the ruin
too of the late William Maginn." Whilst the veil of charity is let fall
over this sad feature of his memory, let the wisest and best of us all
remember that he was a man.

THE BOTTLE OF ST. JANUARIUS.

BY FATHER PROUT.

I.

IN the land of the citron and myrtle, we're told
   That the blood of a MARTYR is kept in a phial,
Which, though all the year round, it be torpid and cold,
   Yet grasp but the crystal, 'twill _warm_ the first trial.
Be it fiction or truth, with your favourite FACT,
   O, profound LAZZARONI! I seek not to quarrel;
But indulge an old priest who would simply extract
   From your legend, a lay—from your martyr, a moral.

II.

Lo! with icicled beard JANUARIUS comes!
   And the blood in his veins is all frozen and gelid,
And he beareth a bottle; but TORPOR benumbs
   Every limb of the saint:—would ye wish to dispel it?

With the hand of good-fellowship grasp the hoar sage—
Soon his joints will relax and his pulse will beat quicker;
Grasp the *bottle* he brings—'twill grow warm, I'll engage,
Till the frost of each heart he's dissolved in the LIQUOR!

PROBATUM EST.

FATHER PROUT—whose real name was MAHONY, and who assumed as his *nom de plume* the name of a worthy Roman Catholic pastor, who for many years had lived at Watergrass Hill, in the County of Cork, renowned for his unostentatious piety, mediæval lore, and patriarchal hospitality,—was a native of the southern capital of Ireland, where his family were respectable merchants for several generations back, and their remote ancestors chiefs of their sept or clan during the civil wars against the English Crown, or petty princes, previous to the invasion, when the south of Ireland alone could boast of nearly as many independent principalities as there are counties at present in the whole of the island. One of his forefathers greatly distinguished himself at the siege of Limerick, and was the Mahony afterwards ennobled by the French monarch, in whose service he led a most brilliant charge right through a numerous and compact body of the enemy. On this occasion being told by his lieutenant that the enemy had reformed, and asked what was to be done next, he replied without hesitation, whilst he clapped spurs to his horse, and waved his sword on high, "Charge them again, by J——s!" The reverend father had all the fire, and much of the untamed and untameable spirit of his race, features of his character which the Jesuits, amongst whom (see Preface) he received his education, too plainly perceived, when they declined recommending him to orders; and he must have applied himself to the study of some other profession, if a friendly Italian prelate, who hated the order of Ignatius most cordially, had not ordained him. From the day, however, on which he entered the priesthood till his death, a period of about thirty years, it may be safely said that he officiated little more than a couple of years altogether. It was his fellow-townsmen, Dr. Maginn and Serjeant Murphy, who, whilst he was attached to the chapel of the Bavarian Minister, introduced him to the literary life of London. There he made his *debut* in the pages of 'Frazer's Magazine.' The 'Prout Papers,' which were modelled on the 'Noctes Ambrosianæ' of 'Blackwood's Magazine,' appeared in the earlier numbers of Frazer, and had a brilliant success. His next appearance was in 'Bentley's Miscellany,' to which he contributed the polyglot poems, some of which have been selected for this volume. He afterwards became connected with the 'Globe' newspaper, to which he contributed for several years as foreign correspondent from Paris; and he was the holder as well of some shares in the 'Globe' property, which his family sold out after his decease. He had a small private fortune of his own, which raised him above the necessity of seeking employment in the rigorous profession he had adopted, as was generally reported, to please his family's pietistic notions much more than his own natural inclination. It also enabled him to follow at his ease the much more congenial pursuit of literary fame, and to cultivate the intercourse of the leading intellects of his time. He was a great traveller, and a most accomplished modern linguist, the facility and idiomatic perfection of his French and Italian being something extraordinary, whether in conversation or in his more studied compositions for the press. Of his eminent Latin scholarship, the reader may form some idea on referring to the remarks on that subject made in the preface to this edition of the 'Bentley Ballads.' Mahony was a brilliant conversationalist, and a most amusing, although not always, to some of his hearers, an agreeable companion. There was a strong Johnsonian element in him of consciousness, amounting at times to a contemptuous superiority, which would break into downright rudeness of discussion. He had an ungovernable propensity to break flies upon the wheel, and to smash little people who were presumptuous enough to doubt, even with the utmost courtesy, the correctness of his opinions. In the society of ladies, who petted and flattered him very much, his choleric temperament was charmed and soothed down, and "the extraordinary creature" (the name he went by amongst his fair friends), who would worry and toss up a hundred small controversialists of his own sex, in the same time that the famous dog Billy would have settled so many rats, became *tout à fait* in "my ladye's bower," a tame and most agreeable lion. He died in Paris in the year 1866, and was buried at Shandon in his native county, now rendered famous by his exquisitely touching song upon its church bells, which, if he never had written another, would have entitled him to rank amongst our first lyric writers, and which most likely will live as long not only in these countries, but wherever the English language is spoken, as even the happiest efforts of his countryman Moore.

THE JACKDAW OF RHEIMS.

BY THOMAS INGOLDSBY.

"Tunc miser Corvus adeo conscientiæ stimulis compunctus fuit, et exe-
cratio cum tantopere excarneficavit, ut exinde tabescere inciperet, maciem
contraheret, omnem cibum aversaretur, nec amplius crocitaret : pennæ
præterea ei defluebant, et alis pendulis omnes facetias intermisit, et tam
macer apparuit ut omnes ejus miserescent."   *   *   *
"Tunc abbas sacerdotibus mandavit ut rursus furem absolverent; quo
facto, Corvus, omnibus mirantibus, propediem convaluit, et pristinam, et sani-
tatem recuperavit."   *De Illust. Ord. Cisterc.*

THE Jackdaw sat on the Cardinal's chair!
  Bishop and abbot, and prior were there :
Many a monk, and many a friar,
Many a knight, and many a squire,
With a great many more of lesser degree,—
In sooth a goodly company ;
And they served the Lord Primate on bended knee.
  Never, I ween, was a prouder seen,
Read of in books, or dreamt of in dreams,
Than the Cardinal Lord Archbishop of Rheims !

  In and out through the motley rout,
That little Jackdaw kept hopping about ;
Here and there like a dog in a fair,
Over comfits and cakes, and dishes and plates,
Cowl and cope, and Rochet and pall,
Mitre and crosier ! he hopp'd upon all !
  With saucy air, he perch'd on the chair
Where, in state, the great Lord Cardinal sat
In the great Lord Cardinal's great red hat ;
  And he peer'd in the face of his Lordship's Grace,
With a satisfied look as if he would say,
"We two are the greatest folks here to-day !"

And the priests, with awe, as such freaks they saw,
Said, " the Devil must be in that little Jackdaw !"

The feast was over, the board was clear'd,
The flawns and the custards had all disappear'd,
And six little Singing-boys,—dear little souls !
In nice clean faces, and nice white stoles,
  Came, in order due, two by two,
Marching that grand refectory through !
A nice little boy held a golden ewer,
Emboss'd and fill'd with water, as pure
As any that flows between Rheims and Namur,
Which a nice little boy stood ready to catch
In a fine golden hand-basin made to match.
Two nice little boys, rather more grown,
Carried lavender-water, and eau de Cologne ;
And a nice little boy had a nice cake of soap,
Worthy of washing the hands of the Pope.
  One little boy more a napkin bore,
Of the best white diaper, fringed with pink,
And a Cardinal's Hat, mark'd in " permanent ink."

The great Lord Cardinal turns at the sight
Of these nice little boys dress'd all in white:
  From his finger he draws his costly turquoise ;
And, not thinking at all about little Jackdaws,
  Deposits it straight by the side of his plate,
While the nice little boys on his Eminence wait ;
Till, when nobody's dreaming of any such thing,
That little Jackdaw hops off with the ring !

  There's a cry and a shout, and a deuce of a rout,
And nobody seems to know what they're about,
But the monks have their pockets all turn'd inside out ;
  The friars are kneeling, and hunting, and feeling
The carpet, the floor, and the walls, and the ceiling.
  The Cardinal drew off each plum-colour'd shoe,
And left his red stockings exposed to the view ;
  He peeps, and he feels in the toes and the heels ;

They turn up the dishes,—they turn up the plates,—
They take up the poker and poke out the grates,
 —They turn up the rugs, they examine the mugs ;—
 But, no !—no such thing ;—they can't find THE RING !
And the Abbot declar'd that " when nobody twigg'd it,
Some rascal or other had popp'd in and prigg'd it !"
The Cardinal rose with a dignified look,
He called for his candle, his bell, and his book !
 In holy anger, and pious grief,
 He solemnly cursed that rascally thief !
He cursed him at board, he cursed him in bed ;
From the sole of his foot to the crown of his head ;
He cursed him in sleeping, that every night
He should dream of the devil, and wake in a fright ;
He cursed him in eating, he cursed him in drinking,
He cursed him in coughing, in sneezing, in winking ;
He cursed him in sitting, in standing, in lying;
He cursed him in walking, in riding, in flying,
He cursed him in living, he cursed him in dying !—
Never was heard such a terrible curse !
 But what gave rise to no little surprise,
Nobody seem'd one penny the worse !

  The day was gone, the night came on,
The Monks and the Friars they search'd till dawn ;
 When the Sacristan saw, on crumpled claw,
Come limping a poor little lame Jackdaw !
 No longer gay, as on yesterday ;
His feathers all seem'd to be turn'd the wrong way ;—
His pinions droop'd—he could hardly stand,—
His head was as bald as the palm of your hand ;
 His eye so dim, so wasted each limb,
That, heedless of grammar, they all cried, " THAT'S HIM !—
That's the scamp that has done this scandalous thing !
That's the thief that has got my Lord Cardinal's Ring !"
 The poor little Jackdaw, when the monks he saw
Feebly gave vent to the ghost of a caw ;
And turn'd his bald head, as much as to say ;
" Pray be so good as to walk this way !"

Slower and slower he limp'd on before,
Till they came to the back of the belfry door,
    Where the first thing they saw, midst the sticks and straw,
Was the RING in the nest of that little Jackdaw!

Then the great Lord Cardinal call'd for his book,
And off that terrible curse he took;
    The mute expression served in lieu of confession,
And, being thus coupled with full restitution,
The Jackdaw got plenary absolution!
    —When those words were heard, that poor little bird
Was so changed in a moment, 'twas really absurd.
    He grew sleek, and fat: in addition to that,
A fresh crop of feathers came thick as a mat!

His tail waggled more even than before;
But no longer it wagged with an impudent air,
No longer it perched on the Cardinal's chair.
    He hopp'd now about with a gait devout;
At Matins, at Vespers, he never was out;
And, so far from any more pilfering deeds,
He always seem'd telling the confessor's beads.
If any one lied, or if any one swore,
Or slumber'd in prayer-time and happened to snore,
    That good Jackdaw would give a great "caw!"
As much as to say, "don't do so any more!"
While many remark'd, as his manners they saw,
That they never had known such a pious Jackdaw!
    He long lived the pride of that country side,
And at last in the odour of sanctity died;
    When, as words were too faint, his merits to paint,
The conclave determined to make him a saint;
And on newly-made saints and popes, as you know,
It's the custom, at Rome, new names to bestow,
So they canonized him by the name of Jim Crow!

RICHARD HARRIS BARHAM was born December the 6th, 1788, at Canterbury. He inherited from a long line of gentle ancestors reaching back to the Conquest a moderate estate, a portion of which consisted of the Manor of Tappington or Tapton Wood often alluded to in the 'Ingoldsby or Golden Legends,' of which he was the author. The estate when it came to him was somewhat curtailed and encumbered, as stated by his son in the entertaining biography he gives of his father appended to the larger editions of the Legends. He met with an accident coming up to London to enter at St. Paul's School, owing to the overturning of a mail coach, which shattered one of his arms, rendering it weak for life. Amongst the friendships which he formed at this famous public school was that of Mr. Bentley, his connexion with whom in after life was the means of giving to the world those wonderful tales of mirth and marvel in verse, on which his brilliant literary reputation is founded. He went up Captain of St. Paul's to Oxford, and entered Brazenose as a gentleman commoner. A desultory reader from his boyhood, an early scribbler of prose and verse, and a well prepared classic when he matriculated at the age of nineteen, he seems to have given himself no trouble to attain University honours and emoluments, and was satisfied to come out second class, respectably, at the end of his undergraduate career. After going through the usual divinity course, he was admitted to orders, and got appointed to the curacy of Ashford in Kent. In 1814, after his marriage to Caroline, daughter of Captain Smart of the Royal Engineers, he was presented by the Archbishop of Canterbury to the living of Snargate in Romney Marsh, and at the same time to the curacy of Warehorn, a couple of miles distant, at which latter place he took up his residence. The principal bulk of his parishioners were a wild smuggling race, but not bad Christians or church goers, their fiscal irregularities notwithstanding, and parson and flock too, were very good friends, and got on very harmoniously together. In 1821, he was elected, somewhat unexpectedly, to a minor canonry in Saint Paul's, which was the turning point of his literary fate, as he came up shortly after the election to reside in London. In 1824, he received the appointment of a priest in ordinary of his Majesty's Chapel Royal, and was almost immediately afterwards presented to the incumbency of St. Mary Magdalene, and St. Gregory by St. Paul. About this time he contributed to 'Blackwood's Magazine,' and the 'John Bull,' and was a conservative in politics, as may be inferred from his connexion with those publications—a connexion which brought about an intimate friendship between him and the celebrated wit and light littérateur, Theodore Hook, which lasted for many years, and

5

was only interrupted by the death of the latter. In 1837, Mr. Bentley having beat up for the most brilliant contributors he could enlist for his now periodical, the 'Miscellany,' was fortunate enough to secure the invaluable aid of his old Pauline schoolfellow and friend; and Mr. Barham, hitherto an anonymous, and, unless to a few intimate friends, an unknown contributor to the periodical press, commenced the 'Golden Legends' under the *nom de plume* of Ingoldsby. This incognito however, as is generally the case where the production takes the town by storm, was soon pierced through, and he was hailed by his assumed name in literary and fashionable circles as often as by his own. Mr. Barham was a member of the Garrick, and for many years previously to his death he was on the managing committee of that famous club. He also took a great interest in the affairs of the Literary Fund, and was ever attentive and kind in obtaining its assistance for distressed authors.

The following brief summary, at once able and just, of the powers displayed by the author of 'The Golden Legends,' is extracted from the Biography by his son, to which allusion has been already made :—

"As respects the poems, remarkable as they have been pronounced for the wit and humour which they display, their distinguishing attraction lies in the almost unparalleled flow and facility of the versification. Popular phrases, sentences, the most prosaic, even the cramped technicalities of legal diction, and snatches from well nigh every language, are wrought in with an apparent absence of all art and effort that surprises, pleases, and convulses the reader at every turn ; the author triumphs with a master's hand over every variety of stanza, however complicate or exacting ; not a word seems out of place, not an expression forced ; syllables the most intractable find the only partners fitted for them throughout the range of language, and couple together as naturally as those kindred spirits, which poets tell us were created pairs, and dispersed in space to seek out their particular mates. A harmony pervades the whole, a perfect modulation of numbers never perhaps surpassed, and rarely equalled in compositions of this class. This was the *forte* of Thomas Ingoldsby ; a harsh line or untrue rhyme grated like the Shandæan hinge upon his ear ; no inviting point or alluring pun would induce him to entertain either for an instant; sacrifice or circumlocution were the only alternatives. At the same time, scarcely any vehicle could be better adapted for the development of his peculiar powers, than that unshackled metre which admits of no laws save those of rhyme and melody; but which also from the very want of definite regulations, presents no landmark to guide the poet, and demands a thorough knowledge of rhythm to prevent his becoming lost among a succession of confused and unconnected stanzas.

"Of the unflagging spirit of fun which animates these productions, there can be but one opinion; Mr. Barham was, unquestionably, an adept in the mysteries of mirth, happy in his use of anachronism, and all the means and appliances of burlesque; he was skilled, moreover, to relieve his humour, however broad, from any imputation of vulgarity by a judicious admixture of pathos and antiquarian lore. There are, indeed, passages in his writings, 'The Execution' for example, and the battle field in 'The Black Mousquetaire,' standing out in strong contrast from the ludicrous imagery which surrounds them, and affording evidence of powers of a very opposite and far higher order."

By every competent judge who reads but one or two of 'The Golden Legends,' the above critique on their chief merits—for they have many minor ones—will not be taken *cum grano salis*, as coming from a partial and over affectionate source, the son praising the father, the pupil upholding the master, the painter of 'The Temptations of Saint Anthony' descanting upon the beauties displayed in the tableaux of St. Dunstan, St. Odille, St. Cuthbert, St. Nicholas, and St. Aloys, the models and exemplars which he himself had studied and imitated so successfully. The eulogium, however unqualified, is simply the verdict of the literary world given five-and-twenty years back, and never since reversed or questioned.

Mr. Barham was subject to a bronchial and lung affection for little more than half a year before his decease, in consequence of a cold which he caught in sitting too near an open window, through which an autumnal east wind blew bitterly on him. It was on the occasion of Her Majesty's visit to the City to open the Royal Exchange towards the end of 1844. He seems, contrary to the injunctions of his medical advisers, to have more or less neglected the malady, which at last became so serious in the May of 1845, that he was obliged to remove with Mrs. Barham, then also a great invalid, to Clifton, for change of air and scene, as well as to be removed for a season, effectually from the wear and tear of body and mind, which is easily understood by those who have had any experience of the never ending day work, and the social evenings of a London literary lion. It was during the few weeks of his sojourn at Clifton, where he seemed to derive some benefit, and where, not improbably, he might have effectually baffled the attack upon his constitution, had he remained the entire summer, that in a moment of superior inspiration, he composed those prophetic lines—the most exquisitely beautiful of all his productions, and his last,—'As I lay a-thynkynge.' It was the memory of his children who had gone before which came over him in that beautiful vision; and the spirit of filial piety in that bird of heaven soaring upwards beckoned him to follow! He died shortly after his return to London on the 17th, and his funeral took place on the 21st of June, 1845, in the fifty-seventh year of his age.

"Conscious," says his biographer, "as his family could not fail to be, of the very high esteem in which he was held by those with whom he had been professionally connected, they were not prepared for the unanimous demonstration of respect which they thought good to exhibit on this occasion. The windows of the streets situated in the parishes of St. Faith and St. Gregory, through which the funeral procession passed, were closed. Both churches were hung with black cloth, and the officers of the latter one, in deep mourning received his remains at the porch, and, together with many of his old parishioners, witnessed their consignment to the rector's vault, beneath that altar at which he had ministered so long."

A quarter of a century has passed away since the 'Ingoldsby Ballads or Golden Legends' stood in front of the foremost light literature of their day; and the fame which they enjoyed, so far from decreasing, would appear to be increasing with the demands of a new generation which cannot produce any work of mirth and marvel equal or even second to it. Issues of the work which affords the most pure enjoyment to every class of English readers, have just now been announced, of every size and price, from the *edition de luxe* at a guinea to the half-crown railway volume, the latter the most beautiful thing of the kind and for the money that can be well imagined; and Mr. Bentley has the satisfaction of feeling that the tribute which he thus pays to the memory and merits of his old schoolfellow and friend is neither uncalled for nor inopportune—a tribute which may be revived from time to time, after he too shall have closed the evening of his days, and for generations whilst the old name and publishing house shall stand, an *immortelle* and golden garland, one of the fairest in all the garden of our literary dead, its native perfume as rich as of yore, and its amaranthine leaves unfaded.

OLD MORGAN AT PANAMA.

BY G. E. INMAN.

I.

IN the hostel-room we were seated in gloom, old Morgan's trustiest crew;
No mirthful sound, no jest went round, as it erst was wont to do.
Wine we had none, and our girls were gone, for the last of our gold was spent;
And some swore an oath, and all were wroth, and stern o'er the table bent;
Till our chief on the board hurl'd down his words, and spake with his stormy shout,
"Hell and the devil! an' this be revel, we had better arm and out.
Let us go and pillage old Panama,
We, the mighty Buccaneers!"

II.

Straight at the word each girt on his sword, five hundred men and
    more ;
And we clove the sea in our shallops free, till we reach'd the
    mainland shore.
For many a day overland was our way, and our hearts grew weary
    and low,
And many would back on their trodden track, rather than farther go ;
But the wish was quell'd, though our hearts rebell'd, by old Mor-
    gan's stormy roar,—
" The way ye have sped is farther to tread, than the way which
    lies before."
        So on we march'd upon Panama,
          We, the mighty Buccaneers !

III.

'Twas just sunset when our eyes first met the sight of the town of
    gold ;
And down on the sod each knelt to his God, five hundred warriors
    bold ;
Each bared his blade, and we fervent pray'd (for it might be our
    latest prayer),
" Ransom from hell, if in fight we fell,—if we lived, for a booty
    rare !"
And each as he rose felt a deep repose, and a calm o'er all within ;
For he knew right well, whatever befell, his soul was assoil'd
    from sin.
        Then down we march'd on old Panama,
          We, the mighty Buccaneers !

IV.

The town arose to meet us as foes, and in order beheld us come,—
They were three to one, but warriors none,—traders, and such like
    scum,
Unused to wield either sword or shield ; but they plied their new
    trade well.
I am not told how they bought and sold, but they fought like
    fiends of hell.

They fought in despair for their daughters fair, their wives, and
their wealth, God wot !
And throughout the night made a gallant fight,—but it matter'd
not a jot.
> For had we not sworn to take Panama,
> We, the mighty Buccaneers ?

V.

O'er dying and dead the morn rose red, and o'er streets of a redder
dye ;
And in scatter'd spots stood men in knots, who would not yield
or fly.
With souls of fire they bay'd our ire, and parried the hurl and
thrust ;
But ere the sun its noon had won they were mingled with the dust.
Half of our host in that night we lost,—but we little for that had
care ;
We knew right well that each that fell increased the survivor's share
> Of the plunder we found in old Panama,
> We, the mighty Buccaneers !

VI.

We found bars of gold, and coin untold, and gems which to count
were vain ;
We had floods of wine, and girls divine, the dark-eyed girls of
Spain.
They at first were coy, and baulk'd our joy, and seem'd with their
fate downcast,
And wept and groan'd, and shriek'd and swoon'd ; but 'twas all
the same at last.
Our wooing was short, of the warrior's sort, and they thought it
rough, no doubt ;
But, truth to tell, the end was as well as had it been longer about.
> And so we revell'd in Panama,
> We, the mighty Buccaneers !

VII.

We lived in revel, sent care to the devil, for two or three weeks or so,
When a general thought within us wrought that 'twas getting
time to go.

So we set to work with dagger and dirk to torture the burghers hoar,
And their gold conceal'd compell'd them to yield, and add to our
common store.
And whenever a fool of the miser school declared he had ne'er a
groat,
In charity due *we* melted a few, and pour'd them down his throat.
This drink we invented at Panama,
We, the mighty Buccaneers!

VIII.

When the churls we eased, their bags well squeezed, we gave
them our blessing full fain,
And we kiss'd our girls with the glossy curls, the dark-eyed girls
of Spain;
Our booty we shared, and we all prepared for the way we had to
roam,
When there rose a dispute as to taking our route by land or by
water home.
So one half of the band chose to travel by land, the other to travel
by sea:
Old Morgan's voice gave the sea the choice, and I follow'd his for-
tunes free,
And hasten'd our leaving old Panama,
We, the mighty Buccaneers!

IX.

A bark we equipp'd, and our gold we shipp'd, and gat us ready
for sea;
Seventy men, and a score and ten, mariners bold were we.
Our mates had took leave, on the yester-eve, their way o'er the
hills to find,
When, as morning's light pierc'd through the night, we shook her
sails to the wind.
With a fresh'ning breeze we walk'd the seas, and the land sunk
low and low'r;
A dreary dread o'er our hearts there sped we never should see
land more—
And away we departed from Panama,
We, the mighty Buccaneers!

X.

For a day or two we were busy enow in setting ourselves to rights,
In fixing each berth, our mess, and so forth, and the day's watch
and the night's;
But when these were done, over every one came the lack of aught
to do,
We listless talk'd, we listless walk'd, and we pined for excitement
new.
Oh! how we did hail any shift in the gale, for it gave us a sail to
trim!
We began to repent that we had not bent our steps with our com-
rades grim.
And thus we sail'd on from old Panama,
We, the mighty Buccaneers!

XI.

Day after day we had stagger'd away, with a steady breeze abeam;
No shift in the gale; no trimming a sail; how dull we were, ye
may deem!
We sung old songs till we wearied our lungs; we push'd the
flagon about;
And told and re-told tales ever so old, till they fairly tired us out.
There was a shark in the wake of our bark took us three days to
hook;
And when it was caught we wish'd it was not, for we miss'd the
trouble it took.
And thus we sail'd on from old Panama,
We, the mighty Buccaneers!

XII.

At last it befell, some tempter of hell put gambling in some one's
head;
The devil's device, the cards and the dice, broke the stagnant life
we led:
From morn till night, ay, till next morn's light, we plied the bones
right well;
Day after day the rattle of play clatter'd through the caravel.
How the winners laugh'd, how the losers quaff'd! 'twas a mad-
ness, as it were.
It was a thing of shuddering to hark to the losers swear.
And thus we sail'd on from old Panama,
We, the mighty Buccaneers!

XIII.

From morn till night, ay, till next morn's light, for weeks the
　play kept on :
'Twas fearful to see the winners' glee, and the losers haggard and
　wan ;
You well might tell, by their features fell, they would ill brook
　to be crost ;
And one morn there was one, who all night had won, jeer'd some
　who all night had lost.
He went to bed—at noon he was dead—I know not from what,
　nor reck ;
But they spake of a mark, livid and dark, about the dead man's neck !
　　　And thus we sail'd on from old Panama,
　　　　We, the mighty Buccaneers !

XIV.

This but begun : and those who had won lived a life of anxious
　dread ;
Day after day there was bicker and fray ; and a man now and then
　struck dead.
Old Morgan stern was laugh'd to scorn, and it worried his heart
　I trow ;
Five days of care, and his iron-grey hair was as white as the
　winter's snow :
The losers at last his patience o'erpast, for they drew their sword
　each one,
And cried, with a shout, " Hell take you ! come out, and fight for
　the gold ye have won—
　　　The gold that our blood bought at Panama,
　　　　We, the mighty Buccaneers !"

XV.

We never were slow at a word and a blow, so we cross'd our irons
　full fain ;
And for death and life had begun the strife, when old Morgan
　stopp'd it amain,
And thunder'd out with his stormy shout,—" Dogs, ye have had
　your day !
To your berths !" he roar'd. " Who sheaths not his sword,
　Heaven grant him its grace, I pray !

For I swear, by God, I will cleave him like wood!" There was
    one made an angry sign ;
Old Morgan heard, and he kept his word ; for he clove him to the
    chine.

So ended *his* exploits at Panama:
He, the mighty Buccaneer!

XVI.

At this we quail'd, and we henceforth sail'd, in a smouldering
    sort of truce ;
But our dark brows gloom'd, and we inward fumed for a pretext
    to give us loose :
When early one morn—"A strange sail astern!" we heard the
    look-out man hail ;
And old Morgan shout, "Put the ship about, and crowd every
    stitch of sail!"
And around went we, surging through the sea at our island wild
    buck's pace ;
In wonderment what old Morgan meant, we near'd to the fated
    chase—

We, the pillagers of old Panama,
We, the mighty Buccaneers!

XVII.

She went right fast, but we took her at last. 'Twas a little brig-
    antine thing ;
With four men for crew, and a boy or two—a bark built for
    trafficking ;
Besides this crew were three women, too: her freight was salt-
    fish and oil :
For the men on board, they were put to the sword ; the women we
    spared awhile.
And all was surmise what to do with the prize, when old Morgan,
    calling us aft,
Roar'd, "Ye who have fool'd yourselves out of your gold take
    possession of yonder craft,

And go pillage some other Panama,
Ye, the mighty Buccaneers!"

XVIII.

We were reckless and rude, we had been at feud till 'twas war to
the very knife ;
But it clove each heart when we came to part from comrades in
many a strife :
Over one and all a gloom seem'd to fall, and in silence they pack'd
their gear,
Amid curses and sighs, and glistening eyes, and here and there
a tear.
Then each of each band shook each old mate's hand, and we
parted with hearts full sore ;
We all that day watch'd them lessen away. They were never
heard of more !
We kept merrily on from old Panama,
We, the mighty Buccaneers !

XIX.

Their sufferings none know, but ours, I trow, were very, oh ! very
sore ;
We had storm and gale till our hearts 'gan fail, and then calms,
which harass'd us more ;
Then many fell sick ; and while all were weak, we rounded the
fiery cape ;
As I hope for bliss in the life after this, 'twas a miracle our escape !
Then a leak we sprung, and to lighten us, flung all our gold to the
element :
Our perils are past, and we're here at last, but as penniless as we
went.
And such was the pillage of Panama
By the mighty Buccaneers !

THE BUCCANEERS.

Buccan was the name given to the primitive gridiron of the Caribbee
Islands, or Lesser Antilles, lying between Puerto Rico and the Gulf
of Paria. It was made of the hard wood of the country, and was
placed high above the sacrificial fire by the natives, who smoked as
well as roasted upon it the flesh of the prisoners whom they took in
war. It was adopted from their earliest arrival in those regions by
the European settlers in their hunting expeditions through the islands,

as well as on the shores of the South American Continent, where also the aboriginal Carib had flourished and hunted the bison before them. From the name of the cooking apparatus, *buccan*, came that of the cooking process *buccaning*, until in the course of natural derivation the hunters themselves became better known as *buccaneers* than *monteros*, the ancient name of the Spanish hunters. The cruelties exercised by Spanish jealousy against the early adventurers from the various coun- tries of Europe in quest of the treasures of the Eldorado, left numbers of these latter no alternative but the chase and the *buccan*, with piratical excursions in open boats, not capable of holding more than twenty men, upon the waters of the Gulf, to supply their additional wants, at the expense of Spanish traders. These earlier adventurers, driven to this wild mode of life by land and sea, were the original Buccaneers of the sixteenth century. Shortly after the first quarter of the seventeenth century, however, had passed away, a universal enthusiasm against the Spanish name began to spread throughout Eng- land, France, the Low Countries, Denmark, &c., in consequence of the accounts which reached Europe of the cruelties practised upon the emigrants from those countries, who, in spite of all prohibitions and threatened terrors, would still make their way to the land of the gold. It appears to have mattered little what relations, whether of peace or war, Spain was under with the other European governments, these latter would not, or could not, restrain their seafaring subjects from fitting out privateering expeditions against her possessions in the New World. This, the second, and by far the more formidable era of the buccaneers, continued for considerably more than half a century, and beheld in its course not alone the plunder and destruction of their powerful enemy's vessels upon the ocean, but of her richest and largest colonial cities, and the massacre of myriads of her inhabitants. It was of this class of freebooters, "the Mighty Buccaneers," as our poet calls them, that Morgan, the son of a Welsh farmer, was one of the most re- doubted captains. There were others who gained equal fame and riches in the same desperate career, and who had equal influence over their wild followers, such as Montbars, who had such a thirst for Spanish blood as to have obtained the name of the Exterminator, L'Olonais, Michael del Basco, Pointis, Van Horn, Peter of Dieppe, called Peter the Great, Mansvelt, &c.; and besides Henry Morgan, we hear of the names of such English captains as Richard Sawkins, John Watling, William Damper, and Lionel Wafer, the two last men- tioned of whom wrote marvellous descriptions on their return home to England of their adventures as well as of the countries which had been the scene of their depredations. At one time or other, and in some cases more than once, from the fourth to the last decade of the seventeenth century, those freebooters, in different bodies, following one or other of the above-mentioned leaders, took and plundered not only such important cities on the Atlantic sea-board of the Spanish possessions as Maracaybo, Campeachy, Porto Bello, Carthagena, Vera Cruz, but Guayaquill, Panama, and other places of equal consequence on the coasts of the South ; and not satisfied with capturing them, and taking possession of their wealth, they massacred their male, and outraged their female inhabitants. The stern and relentless brutality of the Spaniards, who pursued the English and French like wild beasts, murdering them wherever they could hunt them down in small parties, disentitled them to mercy, according to the wild law of the time, whenever it came to their own turn to fall under the power of the sea-robbers. The small island of Tortuga, one of the Lesser Antilles, which they fortified very strongly, was the stronghold of the Buccaneers. Here they organised and fitted out their expeditions, and revelled in all sorts of licentiousness after the sale of their plunder, which was chiefly effected at Jamaica and San Domingo. The Buccaneers attacked the large Spanish merchantmen, who were all well armed, with their light, sharp prows, coming down rapidly with a favouring wind upon their gigantic opponents' broadsides, and their marksmen picking off the gunners at their portholes with the most extraordinary precision. Then came the pitching of their network and boarding tackle, the rush up the side, the brief massacre, and all was over.

The picture drawn by the poet so vividly in the third stanza of the ballad, is far from an imaginary one. There are one or two fine paintings, by old masters, of Italian banditti praying before the altar of the Madonna and Child. Cahir na Cappul, Frency, and others of the "Irish Rogues and Rapparees" "who robbed the rich to give to the poor," were careful to attend mass on the Sunday. Sawkins, one of the Buccaneer captains already mentioned, threw the dice overboard when he found his men throwing them on a Sunday ; and another of those worthies, Watling, sternly impressed upon his followers the necessity of keeping holy the Sabbath-day.

The free-booting chiefs looked upon themselves as petty potentates, each making war upon his own hook against the Spaniard, considered at the time the common enemy of mankind ; and his sea-warriors thought they had as good a right to fight for his black flag, as the free-lances of the middle ages had to follow on shore the most blazoned banner in Christendom.

After their return from any signal success by land or sea, our heroes invariably offered up thanks to Heaven at Tortuga or the first island at which they landed, in the old pietistic jargon, for having crowned their arms with victory, with as much pretensions, (the ragamuffins), as if they were Christian emperors, ordering their archiepiscopal ministers to offer up *Te Deums* to the God of Christian Peace after so many head of Christian game had been shot down, and so many Christians' throats had been cut so victoriously. And to carry out the matter logically (Locke's madman theory of wrong premises and right conclusion) they gave a tenth of the *spolia opima* to the clergy with a *modicum quid* to be distributed amongst the poor, and not unfrequently an additional sum towards the building of churches and the endowment of religious institutions. Such is the power of the supernatural even in the wildest and most desperate of human careers, a power which is called superstition where small robbers and cut-throats have the audacity beyond all conventional rules to mix up Heaven with their quarrels, and orthodoxy where the Alexanders and Napoleons of the world do the same thing as a matter of course. Another of the spiritualities of the Buccaneers was equally singular; namely, that they never went on an expedition without having first implored Heaven to allow them to return home again laden with booty, or to save them from the infernal fire of the other world, which they were so conscious of having so richly deserved.

In the year 1668, eight years after the Restoration, when Morgan's sovereign, Charles the Second, was at peace with Spain by the Treaty of the Triple Alliance, which Sir William Temple had concluded at the opening of the year between England, Holland, and Sweden, to assist Spain against the ambition of the French King, and when a general peace reigned throughout Europe, Spain and Portugal having made up their quarrel through the mediation of England, and France and Spain having shaken hands by the Treaty of Aix la Chapelle, the great English freebooter, caring little about the relations between the Great Powers of Europe, or whether his country was at peace or war with any or all of them, made his celebrated attack upon Portobello. Here he surprised the sentinels, and took the outworks in a rush. The small garrison, however, defended the interior of the town for a short space so well that they were enabled, with the chief inhabitants, who took with them their gold and silver, and the plate of the churches, to retreat to the citadel. Morgan having got a number of captive monks and nuns together, ordered them to advance with scaling ladders, and place them against the walls of the fortress, thinking that the defenders, from religious scruples, would not fire at them. He was mistaken, however, for the governor ordered the garrison to fire at every living thing that approached the walls. The chief of the Buccaneers then

commanded, and headed the assault, which was successful. The place
was taken by storm, and all inside put to the sword, with the exception
of the women, who were subjected to the brutal law of the conquerors.
The bullion alone taken by Morgan and his followers on this occasion
amounted to upwards of £100,000 sterling, and the rich merchandize
of various kinds carried off by his sea robbers, was said to have sold
for half a million in Jamaica. His last and most daring deed was when
he marched across the Isthmus to the capture of Panama. Having
assembled at a small island opposite the Mosquito coast, one of the
largest flotillas and bodies of men ever commanded by a pirate chief in
those waters, he steered direct for Chagres, between which and Panama
on the opposite side of the Isthmus, there was a good trade by means of
the river Chagres. The latter was navigable by large barges and sailing
vessels of light draught as far as the small town of Cruces, standing
about forty miles inland from the mouth, whence the goods were for-
warded on mules or men's backs. A small fortress at the entrance of
that river, which forms the port of Chagres, stopped the expedition for
some hours. An Indian of the garrison, who was a good archer, let
fly a shaft at Morgan as he stood at some distance from the walls in
the centre of a small reconnoitring party, but not being as good a
marksman as Bertram de Gurdun, who killed our first Richard under
similar circumstances when besieging the fortress of Chaluz, he only
pierced the eye of one of the staff. Morgan, instantly plucking the
arrow from the wound, bound the head of it round with tow, and fired
it from his musket into the town, where it fell upon the roof of one of
the wooden houses and set that side in a blaze in a few minutes. Pro-
fiting by the terror and confusion which reigned inside for the moment,
the Buccaneers, headed by their redoubted chief, stormed and carried
the place, the governor and the garrison perishing sword in hand.
Proceeding up the river, they met with equally stubborn resistance at
Cruces, which they took by a similar *coup de main.* After having
sacked those towns, and butchered and outraged their unfortunate inhabitants, Morgan marched his men, laden as they were with plunder,
over-land to Panama. Numbers of them, like Alexander's followers
when sated with the conquest and plunder of India, thinking they had
gone quite far enough, and expressing their wishes pretty loudly along
the line of march to retrace their steps, Morgan's voice, more powerful
than the Macedonian's, stilled the incipient mutiny. As the ballad
truly has it, he told them with his stormy roar, at which all who ever
heard it trembled, " The way ye have sped is farther to tread than the
way which lies before!"
Panama was taken after a day and a half's desperate fighting on

both sides, and when the freebooters got in, the inhabitants who did not escape by flight on board the vessels in the harbour, or to the mountains, were all put to the sword, the conquerors only reserving, as was their wont in such cases, the women. The amount of the plunder of this most flourishing mart of the Pacific can be well imagined when Morgan received for his own share, after the proceeds of the entire had been realized at Jamaica, no less a sum than £100,000 sterling. It was after the capture of the place, and when the female captives had been disposed of, the most beautiful of them all falling to the lot of the commander, that one of the most singular and interesting events of his life occurred to him, and one which it may be well supposed had not been noticed in the account of this passage of his adventures, from which the author of the Bentley Ballad drew his inspiration, or he would have celebrated it. Morgan, it appears, did not feel inclined to show the same delicate consideration to the Spanish lady who had fallen into his power, which Scipio had shewn to her beautiful countrywoman under similar circumstances upwards of two thousand years before, either as regarded her fortune or her honour. Having taken possession of the one, he proceeded to deprive her forcibly of the other. His captive, however, being more of the Maid of Saragossa, than the Donna Inez type, burst from his arms, exclaiming, "Ruffian, forbear to ravish from me my honour, as thou hast wrested from me my fortune and my liberty! No, be assured that my soul shall sooner be separated from my body, than you shall carry out your nefarious purpose!" She then, with the bound of a tigress, sprung at him, poniard in hand, and would have reached his heart, if he had not jumped aside from the blow, and dexterously seizing her, before she could recover herself, held her down till she became exhausted. He did not murder her on the spot, but had her thrown into the darkest and most loathsome dungeon in Panama, determined to subdue her proud spirit by severities. His followers, however, became clamourous, after a day or two, at his detaining them for nothing more important than a hopeless love affair, after the great work had been done which they came to accomplish. The idea, moreover, that they might be made to pay dearly for any unnecessary delay, if a force from Portobello were allowed time to come down upon them, was not distant from the thoughts of even the most reckless and abandoned amongst them at the moment, when it behoved them for the sake of their lives as well as their booty to retreat by land or water as speedily as possible. They took their departure, therefore, from Panama, as narrated in Inman's ballad, the great majority by land to Chagres, where they had left their flotilla in charge of a picked number of their comrades, and a small number by sea, to sail round

Cape Horn before they could reach the *rendezvous* on the Atlantic side, where the general distribution of the proceeds of the expedition was to take place. The poor lady, who had so nobly combated the most unmitigated and formidable ruffian of his day, was liberated from her perilous position by her returning countrymen, and lived, it was said, to an age at which, if she could no longer inspire romance, she could at least challenge respect, when she told the story of how the terrible English freebooter chief stormed the bravely defended works of Panama, but failed in carrying the citadel of her virtue.

We next hear of Morgan's return to England with his enormous wealth, where he easily managed to get presented at the Court of the Merry Monarch. It was not from pure admiration of his exploits, that Charles the Second, whose expensive private pleasures compelled him to be a pensioner, to the amount of a couple of hundred thousand pounds sterling a year, of the Grande Monarque, bestowed upon Morgan the dignity of knighthood, and appointed him Governor of Jamaica. All was fish, from whatever quarter, that fell into the royal net, and the gold fish was the most precious of any. And so long as it was good coin of the realm, he thought, with the wise Roman Emperor of old, that no money could have a bad smell about it. As the chief wealth of the capital of the West of England was once derived from the slave trade, so that of the commercial entrepôts of the chief West India islands arose from the traffic carried on, and the enormous sums recklessly spent therein by the plunderers of the Spanish Main. Indeed, as was once said of Bristol, so it might have been said of those places, that the walls of their houses were cemented with human blood. It was the infamous traffic of the Buccaneers of the seventeenth century which formed beyond doubt the foundation of the wealth not only of the English but of the French possessions in the West Indies. The close of that century saw the last of the most extraordinary association of pirates since the days of the Northern Sea-Kings, when, after the peace of Ryswick, the maritime powers of Europe agreed to put them down. As an earnest of their determination, an English and Dutch fleet meeting a flotilla of the Buccaneers, under the leadership of Pointis, on its return to Tortuga, from the sacking of Carthagena, laden with booty, dealt with it in the most summary manner, sinking it, vessels and crews, with a few exceptions, consisting of some half dozen of the smallest and swiftest vessels, which escaped out of the affair to Jamaica.

Sir Henry Morgan died at the seat of his government, full of years and honours, another instance in the history of worldly success of the mysterious ways of Providence to men.

G

Mr. Inman, the writer of the ballad to which the above observations have reference, was little known in the literary world of London. 'The Buccaneers,' and a couple of other poems of similar rough power, contributed to 'Bentley's Miscellany,' were the only productions of his we ever heard of. He was a wine merchant in the City of London, and came to a melancholy and untimely end. Returning late one night through Hyde Park from a convivial party, he fell into the Serpentine, and was drowned.

OLD AGE AND YOUTH.

BY THOMAS HAYNES BAYLEY.

Old Age sits bent on his iron-grey steed :
　Youth rides erect on his courser black ;
And little he thinks in his reckless speed
　Old Age comes on, in the *very same track.*

And on Youth goes, with his cheek like the rose
　And his radiant eyes, and his raven hair ;
And his laugh betrays how little he knows,
　Of AGE and his sure companion CARE.

The courser black is put to his speed,
　And Age plods on, in a quieter way,
And little youth thinks that the iron-grey steed
　Approaches him nearer, every day !

Though one seems strong as the forest tree,
　The other infirm, and wanting breath ;
If ever YOUTH baffles OLD AGE, 'twill be
　By rushing into the arms of DEATH !

On his courser black, away Youth goes,
　The prosing sage may rest at home ;
He'll laugh and quaff, for well he knows
　That years must pass ere Age *can come.*

And since too brief are the daylight hours
　For those who would laugh their lives away ;
With beaming lamps, and mimic flowers,
　He'll teach the night to mock the day !

Again he'll laugh, again he'll feast,
His lagging foe he'll still deride,
Until—when he expects him the least—
Old Age and he stand side by side!

He then looks into his toilet-glass,
And sees Old Age reflected there!
He cries, " Alas! how quickly pass
Bright eyes, and bloom, and raven hair!"

The lord of the courser black must ride,
On the iron-grey steed, sedate and slow!
And thus to him who his power defied,
Old Age must come like a conquering foe.

Had the prosing sage not preach'd in vain,
Had Youth not written his words on sand,
Had he early paused, and given the rein
Of his courser black to a steadier hand:

Oh! just as gay might his days have been,
Though mirth with graver thoughts might blend;
And when at his side Old Age was seen,
He had been hail'd as a timely friend.

THOMAS HAYNES BAYLEY

WAS born at Bath, 13th of October, 1797, and died at Boulogne-sur-
Mer, 22nd of April, 1839. He was the son of Nathaniel Bayley, Esq.,
of Mount Beacon House, near Bath. He began his poetic career very
early, and like Ovid almost lisped in numbers. He received his
primary education at Winchester School, went thence to Leyden, and
later in life to St. Mary's Hall, Oxford. He first fancied theology,
then law; read for both; gave them up, before reaching the high altar
of the one, or entering the vestibule of the other; took unto himself a
wife, (Miss Hayes, the belle of Bath), at a very early age; and gave
himself up to love and the Muses. His numerous comediettas, farces,
and pieces of all kinds, which were produced on the stage over twenty
years of his life, have gone out of fashion long since, and almost out of
the memory of those who enjoyed them in their younger days; but
some of his beautiful ballads, — 'Oh no! we never mention her!'
'I'd be a butterfly,' 'Gaily the Troubadour,' 'Round my own
pretty rose,' 'Oh leave me to my sorrow,' &c., &c., so light and
rhythmical, and with such charms of grace and sentiment about them,
will long remain popular amongst our English upper classes.

THE SABINE FARMER'S SERENADE.

BARNEY BRALLAGHAN.

BY FATHER PROUT.

BY TOM HUDSON.

I.

ERAT turbida nox
  Horâ secundâ mane
Quando proruit vox
  Carmen in hoc inané;
Viri misera mens
  Meditabatur hymen,
Hinc puellæ flens
  Stabat obsidens limen;

  Semel tantum dic
Eris nostra LALAGE;
  Ne recuses sic
Dulcis Julia Callage.

II.

Planctibus aurem fer,
  Venere tu formosior;
Dic, hos muros per,
  Tuo favore potior!
Voce beatum fac;
  En, dum dormis, vigilo,
Nocte obambulans hâc
  Domum planctu stridulo.
  Senel tantum dic
Eris nostra LALAGE;
  Ne recuses sic,
Dulcis Julia Callage.

III.

Est mihi prægnans sus,
  Et porcellis stabulum;
Villula, grex, et rus*
  Ad vaccarum pabulum;

I.

'TWAS on a windy night,
  At two o'clock in the morning,
An Irish lad so tight,
  All wind and weather scorning.
At Judy Callaghan's door,
  Sitting upon the palings,
His love tale he did pour,
  And this was part of his wailings:—

  Only say
You'll be Mrs. Brallaghan;
  Don't say nay,
Charming Judy Callaghan.

II.

Oh! list to what I say,
  Charms you've got like Venus;
Own your love you may,
  There's but the wall between us.
You lie fast asleep
  Snug in bed and snoring;
Round the house I creep,
  Your hard heart imploring.
  Only say
You'll have Mr. Brallaghan;
  Don't say nay,
Charming Judy Callaghan.

III.

I've got a pig and a sow,
  I've got a sty to sleep 'em;
A calf and a brindled cow,
  And a cabin too, to keep 'em;

---

* 1° in voce *rus.* Nonne potiùs legendum *jus,* scilicet, *ad vaccarum pabulum?* De hoc *jure* apud Sabinos agricolas consule *Scriptores de re rustica* passim. Ita *Bentleius.*

Feriis cerneres me
 Splendido vestimento,
Tunc, heus! quàm benè te
 Veherem in jumento!*
Semel tantum dic
Eris nostra LALAGÉ
Ne recuses sic,
Dulcis Julia Callage.

Sunday hat and coat,
 An old grey mare to ride on.
Saddle and bridle to boot,
 Which you may ride astride on.
Only say
You'll be Mrs. Brallaghan;
Don't say nay,
Charming Judy Callaghan.

IV.

Vis poma terræ? sum
 Uno dives jugere;
Vis lac et mella,† cùm
 Bacchi succo,‡ sugere?
Vis aquæ-vitæ vim?§
 Plumoso somnum sacculo?‖
Vis ut paratus sim
 Vel annulo vel baculo?¶

IV.

I've got an acre of ground,
 I've got it set with praties;
I've got of 'baccy a pound,
 I've got some tea for the ladies;
I've got the ring to wed,
 Some whisky to make us gaily;
I've got a feather-bed
 And a handsome new shilelagh.

Jus imo antiquissimum, at displicet vox æquivoca; jus etenim *a mess of pottage* aliquando audit, ex. gr.

Omne suum fratri Jacob *jus* vendidit Esau,
 Et Jacob fratri *jus* dedit omne suum.

Itaque, pace Bentleii, stet lectio prior.—*Prout.*

* *Veherem in jumento.* Curriculo-ne? an ponè sedentem in equi dorso? dorsaliter planè. Quid enim dicit Horatius de uxore sic vectà? Nonne "*Post equitem sedet atra cura?*"—*Porson.*

† *Lac et mella.* Metaphoricè pro *tea:* muliebris est compotatio Græcis non ignota, teste Anacreonte,—

ΟΙ.ΗΝ, θεαν θεαινην,
 θελω λεγειν εταιραι, κ. τ. λ.
 Brougham.

‡ *Bacchi succo.* Duplex apud poetas antiquiores habebatur hujusce nominis numen. Vineam regebat prius; posterius cuidam herbæ exoticæ præerat quæ *tobacco* audit. Succus utrique optimus.—*Coleridge.*

§ *Aquæ-vitæ vim,* Anglo-Hybernicè, "*a power of whisky,*" ισχυς scilicet, vox pergræca.—*Parr.*

‖ *Plumoso sacco.* Plumarum congeries certè ad somnos invitandos satis apta; at mihi per multos annos laneus iste saccus, Ang. *woolsack,* fuit apprimè ad dormiendum idoneus. Lites etiam *de lana* ut aiunt *caprini,* soporiferas per annos xxx. exercui. Quot et quam præclara somnia!—*Eldon.*

¶ Investitura "*per annulum et baculum*" satis nota. Vide P. Marca de

Semel tantum dic	*Only say*
Eris nostra LALAGÉ	*You'll have Mr. Brallaghan ;*
Ne recuses sic,	*Don't say nay,*
Dulcis Julia Callage.	*Charming Judy Callaghan.*

V.

Litteris operam das ;
　Lucido fulges oculo ;
Dotes insuper quas
　Nummi sunt in loculo,
Novi quod apta sis*
　Ad procreandam sobolem !
Possides (nesciat quis ?)
　Linguam satis mobilem.†
　Semel tantum dic
Eris nostra LALAGÉ ;
　Ne recuses sic,
Dulcis Julia Callage.

V.

You've got a charming eye,
　You've got some spelling and
　reading ;
You've got, and so have I,
　A taste for genteel breeding :
You're rich, and fair, and young,
　As everybody's knowing ;
You've got a decent tongue
　Whene'er 'tis set a-going,
　Only say
You'll be Mrs. Brallaghan ;
　Don't say nay,
Charming Judy Callaghan.

VI.

Conjux utinam tu
　Fieres, lepidum cor, mi !
Halitum perdimus, heu,
　Te sopor urget.　Dormi !
Ingruit imber trux—
　Jam sub tecto pellitur
Is quem crastina lux‡
　Referet huc fideliter.

VI.

For a wife till death
　I am willing to take ye ;
But, och ! I waste my breath,
　The devil himself can't wake ye.
'Tis just beginning to rain,
　So I'll get under cover ;
To-morrow I'll come again,
　And be your constant lover.

Concord.　Sacerdotii et Imperii : et Hildebrandi Pont. Max. bullarium.—
Prout.

　Baculo certè dignissim. pontif.—*Maginn.*

　* *Apta sis.*　Quomodo noverit ?　Vide Proverb. Solomonis cap. xxx. v. 19.
Nisi forsan tales fuerint puellæ Sabinorum quales impudens iste balatro Cornelius mentitur esse nostrates.—*Blomfield.*

　† *Linguam mobilem.*　Prius enumerat futuræ conjugis bona *immobilia*,
postea transit ad *mobilia,* Anglice, *chattel property.*　Præclarus ordo
sententiarum !—*Car. Wetherall.*

　‡ Allusio ad distichon Maronianum, "Nocte pluit totâ, *redeunt spectacula
manè.*"—*Prout.*

κ. τ. λ.

Semel tandem dic	*Only say*
Eris nostra LALAGÉ;	*You'll be Mrs. Brallaghan;*
Ne recuses sic,	*Don't say nay,*
Dulcis Julia Callage.	*Charming Judy Callaghan.*

Tom HUDSON (Hibernicis Hibernior) was born within the classic precincts of Saint Giles, where his father kept a public house to which he succeeded. He was one of the best singers of Irish and English drolleries of his day; and was professionally engaged for many years at the 'Coal Hole' and 'Cider Cellar.' He also used to sing "for love" on special occasions, at 'The Peacock' in Maiden Lane, a favourite resort, like 'Offley's' and 'The Eccentrics,' of the wits of town, to oblige his friend, Ben Morgan, the landlord, who was himself the best Irish singer of the same pre-eminently convivial period. Tom drank in his incomparable Irish fun with his mother's milk, although on the wrong side of the Irish Channel, and in his 'Barney Brallaghan' succeeded in producing the most perfect Irish love ditty of the humourous class perhaps ever written, with the exception of Lover's 'Molly Carew.' Prout, no bad judge of such matters, selected both songs for metrical translation into the language of the learned of all nations.

THE LEGEND OF MANOR HALL.

BY THOMAS LOVE PEACOCK.

OLD Farmer Wall, of Manor Hall,
     To market drove his wain:
Along the road it went well stowed
     With sacks of golden grain.

His station he took, but in vain did he look
     For a customer all the morn;
Though the farmers all, save Farmer Wall,
     They sold off all their corn.

Then home he went, sore discontent,
     And many an oath he swore,
And he kicked up rows with his children and spouse,
     When they met him at the door.

Next market-day he drove away
     To the town his loaded wain:
The farmers all, save Farmer Wall,
     They sold off all their grain.

No bidder he found, and he stood astound
  At the close of the market-day,
When the market was done, and the chapmen were gone
  Each man his several way.

He stalked by his load along the road ;
  His face with wrath was red ;
His arms he tossed, like a good man crossed
  In seeking his daily bread.

His face was red, and fierce was his tread,
  And with lusty voice cried he,
" My corn I'll sell to the devil of hell,
  If he'll my chapman be."

These words he spoke just under an oak
  Seven hundred winters old ;
And he straight was aware of a man sitting there
  On the roots and grassy mould.

The roots rose high, o'er the green-sward dry,
  And the grass around was green,
Save just the space of the stranger's place,
  Where it seemed as fire had been.

All scorched was the spot, as gipsy-pot
  Had swung and bubbled there :
The grass was marred, the roots were charred,
  And the ivy stems were bare.

The stranger up-sprung : to the farmer he flung
  A loud and friendly hail,
And he said, " I see well, thou hast corn to sell,
  And I'll buy it on the nail."

The twain in a trice agreed on the price ;
  The stranger his earnest paid,
And with horses and wain to come for the grain
  His own appointment made.

The farmer cracked his whip, and tracked
  His way right merrily on ;
He struck up a song as he trudged along,
  For joy that his job was done.

His children fair he danced in the air;
His heart with joy was big;
He kissed his wife; he seized a knife,
He slew a sucking pig.

The faggots burned, the porkling turned
And crackled before the fire;
And an odour arose that was sweet in the nose
Of a passing ghostly friar.

He twirled at the pin, he entered in,
He sate down at the board;
The pig he blessed, when he saw it well dressed,
And the humming ale out-poured.

The friar laughed, the friar quaffed,
He chirped like a bird in May;
The farmer told how his corn he had sold
As he journeyed home that day.

The friar he quaffed, but no longer he laughed,
He changed from red to pale:
"Oh, helpless elf! 'tis the fiend himself
To whom thou hast made thy sale!"

The friar he quaffed, he took a deep draught;
He crossed himself amain:
"Oh, slave of pelf! 'tis the devil himself
To whom thou hast sold thy grain!

"And sure as the day, he'll fetch thee away,
With the corn which thou hast sold,
If thou let him pay o'er one tester more
Than thy settled price in gold."

The farmer gave vent to a loud lament,
The wife to a long outcry;
Their relish for pig and ale was flown;
The friar alone picked every bone,
And drained the flagon dry.

The friar was gone; the morning dawn
Appeared, and the stranger's wain
Came to the hour, with six-horse power,
To fetch the purchased grain.

The horses were black : on their dewy track
   Light steam from the ground up-curled ;
Long wreaths of smoke from their nostrils broke,
   And their tails like torches whirled.

More dark and grim, in face and limb,
   Seemed the stranger than before,
As his empty wain, with steeds thrice twain,
   Drew up to the farmer's door.

On the stranger's face was a sly grimace,
   As he seized the sacks of grain ;
And, one by one, till left were none,
   He tossed them on the wain.

And slily he leered as his hand up-reared
   A purse of costly mould,
Where, bright and fresh, through a silver mesh,
   Shone forth the glistering gold.

The farmer held out his right hand stout,
   And drew it back with dread ;
For in fancy he heard each warning word
   The supping friar had said.

His eye was set on the silver net ;
   His thoughts were in fearful strife ;
When, sudden as fate, the glittering bait
   Was snatched by his loving wife.

And, swift as thought, the stranger caught
   The farmer his waist around,
And at once the twain and the loaded wain
   Sank through the rifted ground.

The gable-end wall of Manor Hall
   Fell in ruins on the place :
That stone-heap old the tale has told
   To each succeeding race.

The wife gave a cry that rent the sky
   At her goodman's downward flight :
But she held the purse fast, and a glance she cast
   To see that all was right.

'Twas the fiend's full pay for her goodman gray,
And the gold was good and true ;
Which made her declare, that " his dealings were fair,
To give the devil his due."

She wore the black pall for Farmer Wall,
From her fond embraces riven :
But she won the vows of a younger spouse
With the gold which the fiend had given.

Now, farmers, beware what oaths you swear
When you cannot sell your corn ;
Lest, to bid and buy, a stranger be nigh,
With hidden tail and horn.

And with good heed, the moral a-read,
Which is of this tale the pith,—
If your corn you sell to the fiend of hell,
You may sell yourself therewith.

And if by mishap you fall in the trap,
Would you bring the fiend to shame,
Lest the tempting prize should dazzle her eyes,
Lock up your frugal dame.

THOMAS LOVE PEACOCK was a vigorous and scholarly writer of prose
and verse, one of a brilliant class for the last few years gradually passing
away, and little appreciated or understood by the bulk of the present
generation. He was a refined and far-seeing philosopher, who did not
allow his keen relish for the ridiculous to outstrip his good nature—

" Whose humour, as gay as the firefly's light,
    Played round every object, and shone as it played ;
  Whose wit in the combat, as gentle as bright,
    Ne'er carried a heart-stain away on its blade."

He was born at Weymouth, in 1785, and died in 1866, at his retreat
on the banks of his favourite Thames, near London, in the eighty-first
year of his age. Having lost his father, a London merchant, when yet
a child, our author's education fell to the care of his mother, who sent
him to one of the best private schools in England in those days, Mr.
Dix's Academy, at Englefield Green. He never went up to either
University, but such was the enthusiastic love and assiduity which he
evinced in the study of classical literature, not only during his school
career, but throughout the course of his long life, that he lived to be

considered even in academic circles one of the ripest scholars of his age and country. His novels were written during his more mature manhood, with one exception, published when he was past seventy, and considered by many of the best judges as his *chef d'œuvre*. His first production, published in 1806, when he was twenty-one years of age, and received most favourably by the literary world, was a poem, the subject of which was 'Palmyra.' In 1812 he brought out another, entitled 'The Genius of the Thames.' Shelley, who became acquainted with him soon after the publication of the latter, although differing from its main principles that "commerce is prosperity," or that "the glory of the British flag is the happiness of the British people," expressed his admiration of the genius, power, and information in both of the poems, whilst with respect to the conclusion of 'Palmyra,' he considered it "the finest piece of poetry he had ever read." In the early part of 1816 came out 'Headlong Hall,' the first in order of time and the smallest of his prose fictions. Then appeared 'Nightmare Abbey' in 1818, 'Maid Marian' in 1822, 'Crotchet Castle' the same year, and 'Melincourt' some half-dozen years afterwards. 'Gryll Grange' was first published towards the close of his life in 'Frazer's Magazine,' and subsequently in a collected form. As pictures of the humours and follies of English society fifty years ago, those works are unrivalled. They have little of plot, less of counterplot, and nothing whatever of the sensational in their composition. Their literary charms are of a much higher order. Carried along by his descriptive powers, and the brilliancy of his dialogue, you forget all about his fiction, and now and then a song comes in, which you find a most agreeable distraction. Those songs were in Thackeray's opinion among the best of their age. One of the happiest of them, is the *Three Times Three*, given at the banquet in 'Headlong Hall.'

> "In his last binn Sir Peter lies,
>   Who knew not what it was to frown;
>   Death took him mellow by surprise,
>   And in his cellar stopped him down.
>   Through all our land we could not boast
>   A knight more gay, more prompt than he,
>   To rise and fill a bumper toast,
>   And pass it round with Three Times Three.
>
> "None better knew the feast to sway
>   Or keep mirth's boat in better trim;
>   For nature had but little clay
>   Like that of which she moulded him.
>   The meanest guest that graced his board
>   Was there the freest of the free;
>   His bumper toast when Peter poured
>   And passed it round with Three Times Three.

> " He kept at true good humour's mark,
>   The social flow of pleasure's tide ;
> He never made a brow look dark,
>   Nor caused a tear but when he died.
> No sorrow round his tomb should dwell :
>   More pleased his gay old ghost would be,
> For funeral song, and passing bell,
>   To hear no sound but THREE TIMES THREE."

The exquisitely tender idea of not having "caused a tear but when he died," occurs in Beranger's celebrated *Roi d'Yvetot*, the song which first made him famous. It may well be doubted, however, if Peacock had seen it before he composed *Sir Peter ;* although the French Emperor laughed heartily at it when it was first repeated to him by his Minister, De Fontaines, in whose department of the public service the poet held an humble position : "En voyant," as M. Mirecourt in his 'Life of Beranger' has it, "cette douce et joyeuse critique de ses conquêtes et de son regne," it scarcely enjoyed general circulation, and was not regularly published during Napoleon's time. The gentle satire amused him, and he used to hum the refrain "entre ses dents" of—

>   "Oh ! oh ! oh ! oh ! ah ! ah ! ah ! ah !
>   Quel bon petit roi c'etait la !
>   Ah ! ah !"

Nevertheless he did not choose that all France should laugh at it. It was published in the first edition of 'Beranger's Songs' *(Chansons morales et autres)* a few months after the final restoration of the Bourbon dynasty. 'Headlong Hall,' as already stated, came out about the same time, early in 1816.

Peacock was appointed to a lucrative situation in the Examiners' Office in the old India House, in his thirty-fifth year, which he held till the end of his life. He contributed to the 'Examiner' in its best days, during the editorship of Albany Fonblanque, and to the 'Westminster Review' in the most brilliant period of its career. He was also an occasional contributor to 'Bentley's Miscellany' when that periodical was worthy of his pen, and before it had passed out of the hands of the New Burlington Street house. 'The Legend of Manor Hall,' one of the best of our English *diablerie* ballads, is an admirable specimen of his narrative style : simple, straightforward, and complete, whilst the rhythmical flow of his verse, and his quaint, although not over-strained old English expression stamps him at once a master of this class of metrical composition, the seeming simplicity of which makes its achievement so rare, and constitutes its chief difficulty.

The following graceful remarks at the close of an excellent review of his life and writings, in the 'North British,' for September, 1866, may not inappropriately conclude our own brief notice of one of the most brilliant humourists of our age and country :—

"After what has been quoted and said about Peacock, the reader will readily believe that he was an old-fashioned scholar and gentleman of the old school to the last. Such was indeed the case. He told Mr. Thackeray, to whom we are indebted for the anecdote, that he now read nothing but Greek. He was heretical on the subject of Tennyson and living poets generally. His favourite wine was Madeira. He consorted chiefly, out of his own private circle, with men of the past,—dining, we believe, nowhere, except now and then at Lord Broughton's. He lived near the Thames, and delighted in going on its waters, and he cherished an intention—never, unfortunately, carried out—of editing ' Sophocles.' In these simple, old-world pursuits he passed a vigorous old age, and his portrait, by Wallis, shows us a veteran with a fine massive brow, crowned with white hair, strong, regular features, and a rather large mouth, instinct with character, the whole tinged with the reddish tints of a lusty, English autumn. He died at Shepperton, near his favourite river, early in 1866, having reached his eighty-first year."

THE "ORIGINAL" DRAGON.

A LEGEND OF THE CELESTIAL EMPIRE.

Freely translated from an undeciphered MS. of Con-fuse-us,* and dedicated to Colonel Bolsover, of the Horse Marines.

BY C. J. DAVIDS.

I.

A DESPERATE dragon, of singular size,—
  (His name was *Wing-Fang-Scratch-Claw-Fum*,)—
Flew up one day to the top of the skies,
  While all the spectators with terror were dumb.
The vagabond vow'd as he sported his tail,
  He'd have a *sky lark*, and some glorious fun :
For he'd nonplus the natives that day without fail,
  By causing a *total eclipse of the sun !†*
He collected a crowd by his impudent boast,
  (Some decently dress'd—some with hardly a rag on,)
Who said that the country was ruin'd and lost,
  Unless they could compass the death of the *dragon*.

---

* " Better known to illiterate people as *Confucius*."—WASHINGTON IRVING.

† In *China* (whatever European astronomers may assert to the contrary) an *eclipse* is caused by a *great dragon eating up the sun.*

To avert so shocking an outrage, the natives frighten away the monster from his intended *hot* dinner, by giving a morning concert, *al fresco ;* consisting of drums, trumpets, cymbals, gongs, tin-kettles, &c.

II.

The emperor came with the whole of his court,—
    (His Majesty's name was *Ding-Dong-Junk*)—
And he said—to delight in such profligate sport,
    The monster was mad, or disgracefully drunk.
He call'd on the army : the troops to a man
    Declared—though they didn't feel frighten'd the least—
They never could think it a sensible plan
    To go within reach of so ugly a beast.
So he offer'd his daughter, the lovely *Nan-Keen*,
    And a painted pavilion, with many a flag on,
To any brave knight who could step in between
    The *solar eclipse* and the dare-devil *dragon*.

III.

Presently came a reverend bonze.—
    (His name, I'm told, was *Long-Chin Joss*,)—
With a phiz very like the complexion of bronze ;
    And for suitable words he was quite at a loss.
But, he humbly submitted, the orthodox way
    To succour the *sun*, and to bother the foe,
Was to make a new church-rate without more delay,.
    As the clerical funds were deplorably low.
Though he coveted nothing at all for himself,
    (A virtue he always delighted to brag on,)
He thought, if the priesthood could pocket some pelf,
    It might hasten the doom of this impious *dragon*.

IV.

The next that spoke was the court buffoon,—
    (The name of this buffer was *Whim-Wham-Fan*,)—
Who carried a salt-box and large wooden spoon,
    With which, he suggested, the job might be done.
Said the jester, " I'll wager my rattle and bells,
    Your pride, my fine fellow, shall soon have a fall :
If you make many more of your horrible yells,
    I know a good method to make you sing small !'"
And when he had set all the place in a roar,
    As his merry conceits led the whimsical wag on,
He hinted a plan to get rid of the bore,
    By putting some *salt* on the *tail* of the *dragon !*

V.

At length appear'd a brisk young knight,—
(The far-famed warrior, *Bam-Boo-Gong,*)—
Who threaten'd to burke the big blackguard outright,
And have the deed blazon'd in story and song.
With an excellent shot from a very *long bow*
He damaged the dragon by cracking his crown ;
When he fell to the ground (as my documents show)
With a smash that was heard many miles out of town.
His death was the signal for frolic and spree—
They carried the corpse, in a common stage-waggon ;
And the hero was crown'd with the leaves of green tea,
For saving the *sun* from the jaws of the *dragon.*

VI.

A poet, whose works were all the rage,—
(This gentleman's name was *Sing-Song-Strum,*)—
Told the terrible tale on his popular page :
(Compared with *his* verses, *my* rhymes are but rum !)
The Royal Society claim'd as their right
The spoils of the vanquish'd—his wings, tail, and claws ;
And a brilliant bravura, describing the fight,
Was sung on the stage with unbounded applause.
" The valiant *Bam-Boo*" was a favourite toast,
And a topic for future historians to fag on,
Which, when it had reach'd to the Middlesex coast,
Gave rise to the legend of " *George and the Dragon.*"

SAPPHO.

BY C. HARTLEY LANGHORNE.

" If she could sleep, she says, she should do well."—*Faithful Shepherdess.*

SHE sat upon Himertè's shore,
    Upon a glowing height;
The thyme that grew beneath her feet
    Was bath'd in living light;
Was never seen in western clime
    So beautiful a sight !

She look'd upon a beauteous land,
　A witching land, I ween;
Below, the happy swains and girls
　Were tripping o'er the green;
Their laughter was as clear and loud
　As care had never been.

To that fair cheek and snowy arm,
　E'en Venus' self might bow;
Her laughing locks of sunny hair
　Flow o'er her marble brow;
She lifts her hazel eye and smiles—
　She is a goddess now!

But evanescent is that smile;
　She sighs adown the breeze;
　　She slowly stoops,
　　And humbly droops
　Her head upon her knees,
And thrilling sobs upheave her breast;
　Sure she is ill at ease.

She breathes her plaint in bitter words,
　With many a bitter groan;
A sea-nymph heard it in her cave,
　That melancholy moan;
She travell'd on a dolphin's back,
　And told it me alone.

"Ah! Phaon, whither hast thou fled
　Across the ocean brine?
The happy heart of other days
　Can never more be mine;
Rhodopis has Charaxus' love,—
　Why should her mistress pine?

"I ever spoke but of thy name,
　I would not be denied;
And when they said thy lance was good,
　I wept with joy and pride;
But when they spoke of broken vows,
　I thought I should have died.

7

" My violet locks and honey'd smile
   You once could fondly praise ;
You used to think no other maid
   Could trill such pleasant lays,
Or strike the harp with such a hand
   To witch the woodland fays.

" There was a lily grew within
   My plane-tree shaded bower,
And when my head was on your breast,
   As oft at moonlit hour,
You ever said that I was like
   That gentle lily flower.

" The scorching sun has scath'd my plant.
   The genial dews have fled,
And wither'd stem and drooping flower ·
   Show it is sore bested ;
Yes ! I am like that lily now,
   That hangs its broken head !"

Her plaint was echoed overhead,
   And echoed underground ;
The dryads heard it in their glades,
   And murmur'd it around ;
And every leaf on every tree
   Took up the dreary sound.

A sea-nymph heard it in her cave,
   That melancholy moan,—
She travell'd on a dolphin's back,
   And told it me alone.

CHARLES HARTLEY LANGHORNE was born at Berwick-upon-Tweed,
on the 20th of June, 1818, and was the second son of John Langhorne, Esq., banker, of that place, and his wife, Mary Susan, only
daughter of John Bailey, Esq., of Chillingham and Hazelrigg, in the
county of Northumberland. He was educated at the New Academy,
Edinburgh, where he was six years head of his class, and ultimately of
the whole school. From there he went to Glasgow University, where
he carried off its chief classical distinction—Lord Jeffery's gold medal
as the best Grecian—and he finally graduated at Exeter College, Ox-

ford. When at the latter University, he was most distinguished for his classical attainments, which were of a description now rarely met with. He was a most indefatigable reader, and few indeed were the Greek or Roman authors with whose works he was not intimately acquainted. He loved English poetry with equal enthusiasm ; but for logic and mathematics he cared so little, that, in consequence of deficiency in this respect, to the disappointment of his friends and himself, he only obtained a second class, instead of the anticipated first.

On leaving Oxford, he entered himself at Lincoln's Inn, and was pursuing his studies for the Bar, when his career was cut short by an attack of inflammation of the lungs, caused by getting wet in the hunting field, when on a visit to a friend. He died at his chambers, on the 26th, and was interred at Highgate Cemetery on the 29th of April, 1845.

THE TEMPTATIONS OF ST. ANTHONY.

BY R. H. DALTON BARHAM.

" He would have passed a pleasant life of it, in despite of the devil and all his works, if his path had not been crossed by a being that causes more perplexity to mortal man than ghosts, goblins, and the whole race of witches put together, and that was—a woman."—*Sketch-Book.*

St. Anthony sat on a lowly stool,
    And a book was in his hand ;
Never his eye from its page he took,
Either to right or left to look,
But with steadfast soul, as was his rule,
    The holy page he scanned.

" We will woo," said the imp, " St. Anthony's eyes
    Off from his holy book :
We will go to him all in strange disguise,
And tease him with laughter, whoops, and cries,
    That he upon us may look."

The devil was in the best humour that day
    That ever his highness was in :
And that's why he sent out his imps to play,
And he furnished them torches to light their way,
Nor stinted them incense to burn as they may,—
    Sulphur, and pitch, and rosin.

So they came to the Saint in a motley crew,
    A heterogeneous rout:
There were imps of every shape and hue,
And some looked black, and some looked blue,
And they passed and varied before the view,
    And twisted themselves about:
And had they exhibited thus to you,
I think you'd have felt in a bit of a stew,—
    Or so should myself, I doubt.

There were some with feathers, and some with scales,
    And some with warty skins;
Some had not heads, and some had tails,
And some had claws like iron nails;
And some had combs and beaks like birds,
And yet, like jays, could utter words;
    And some had gills and fins.

Some rode on skeleton beasts, arrayed
    In gold and velvet stuff,
With rich tiaras on the head,
Like kings and queens among the dead;
While face and bridle-hand, displayed,
In hue and substance seemed to cope
With maggots in a microscope,
And their thin lips, as white as soap,
    Were colder than enough.

And spiders big from the ceiling hung,
    From every creek and nook:
They had a crafty, ugly guise,
And looked at the Saint with their eight eyes;
And all that malice could devise
Of evil to the good and wise
    Seemed welling from their look.

Beetles and slow-worms crawled about,
    And toads did squat demure;
From holes in the wainscoting mice peeped out,
Or a sly old rat with his whiskered snout;
And forty-feet, a full span long,
Danced in and out in an endless throng:
There ne'er has been seen such extravagant rout
    From that time to this, I'm sure.

But the good St. Anthony kept his eyes
   Fixed on the holy book ; —
From it they did not sink nor rise ;
Nor sights nor laughter, shouts nor cries
   Could win away his look.

A quaint imp sat in an earthen pot,
   In a big-bellied earthen pot sat he :
Through holes in the bottom his legs outshot,
And holes in the sides his arms had got,
And his head came out through the mouth, God wot !
   A comical sight to see.

And he drummed on his belly so fair and round,
   On his belly so round and fair ;
And it gave forth a rumbling, mingled sound,
'Twixt a muffled bell and a growling hound,
   A comical sound to hear :
And he sat on the edge of a table-desk,
   And drummed it with his heels ;
And he looked as strange and as picturesque
As the figures we see in an arabesque,
Half hidden in flowers, all painted in fresque,
   In Gothic vaulted ceils.

Then he whooped and hawed, and winked and grinned,
   And his eyes stood out with glee ;
And he said these words, and he sung this song,
And his legs and his arms, with their double prong,
Keeping time with his tune as it galloped along,
Still on the pot and the table dinned
   As birth to his song gave he.

" Old Tony, my boy ! shut up your book,
   And learn to be merry and gay.
You sit like a bat in his cloistered nook,
Like a round-shoulder'd fool of an owl you look ;
But straighten your back from its booby crook,
   And more sociable be, I pray.

" Let us see you laugh, let us hear you sing ;
   Take a lesson from me, old boy !

Remember that life has a fleeting wing,
And then comes Death, that stern old king,
  So we'd better make sure of joy."

But the good St. Anthony bent his eyes
  Upon the holy book:
He heard that song with a laugh arise,
But he knew that the imp had a naughty guise,
And he did not care to look.

Another imp came in a masquerade,
  Most like to a monk's attire:
But of living bats his cowl was made,
Their wings stitched together with spider thread:
And round and about him they fluttered and played;
And his eyes shot out from their misty shade
  Long parallel bars of fire.

And his loose teeth chattered like clanking bones,
  When the gibbet-tree sways in the blast:
And with gurgling shakes, and stifled groans,
He mocked the good St. Anthony's tones
  As he muttered his prayer full fast.

A rosary of beads was hung by his side,—
  Oh, gaunt-looking beads were they!
And still, when the good Saint dropped a bead,
He dropped a tooth, and he took good heed
To rattle his string, and the bones replied,
  Like a rattle-snake's tail at play.

But the good St. Anthony bent his eyes
  Upon the holy book ;
He heard that mock of groans and sighs,
And he knew that the thing had an evil guise,
  And he did not dare to look.

Another imp came with a trumpet-snout,
  That was mouth and nose in one:
It had stops like a flute, as you never may doubt,
Where his long lean fingers capered about,
As he twanged his nasal melodies out,
  In quaver, and shake, and run.

And his head moved forward and backward still
  On his long and snaky neck ;
As he bent his energies all to fill
His nosey tube with wind and skill,
And he sneezed his octaves out, until
  'Twas well-nigh ready to break.

And close to St. Anthony's ear he came,
  And piped his music in :
And the shrill sound went through the good Saint's frame,
With a smart and a sting, like a shred of flame,
Or a bee in the ear,—which is much the same,—
  And he shivered with the din.

But the good St. Anthony bent his eyes
  Upon the holy book ;
He heard that snout with its gimlet cries,
And he knew that the imp had an evil guise,
  And he did not dare to look.

A thing with horny eyes was there,
  With horny eyes like the dead ;
And its long sharp nose was all of horn,
And its bony cheeks of flesh were shorn,
And its ears were like thin cases torn
From feet of kine, and its jaws were bare ;
And fish-bones grew, instead of hair,
  Upon its skinless head.

Its body was of thin birdy bones,
  Bound round with a parchment skin ;
And when 'twas struck, the hollow tones
That circled round like drum-dull groans,
  Bespoke a void within.

Its arm was like a peacock's leg,
  And the claws were like a bird's :
But the creep that went, like a blast of plague,
To loose the live flesh from the bones,
And wake the good Saint's inward groans,
As it clawed his cheek, and pulled his hair,
And pressed on his eyes in their beating lair,
  Cannot be told in words.

But the good St. Anthony kept his eyes
   Still on the holy book;
He felt the clam on his brow arise,
And he knew that the thing had a horrid guise,
   And he did not dare to look.

An imp came then like a skeleton form
   Out of a charnel vault:
Some clingings of meat had been left by the worm,
Some tendons and strings on his legs and arm,
And his jaws with gristle were black and deform,
   But his teeth were as white as salt.

And he grinned full many a lifeless grin,
   And he rattled his bony tail;
His skull was decked with gill and fin,
And a spike of bone was on his chin,
And his bat-like ears were large and thin,
   And his eyes were the eyes of a snail.

He took his stand at the good Saint's back,
   And on tiptoe stood a space:
Forward he bent, all rotten-black,
And he sunk again on his heel, good lack!
And the good Saint uttered some ghostly groans,
For the head was caged in the gaunt rib-bones,--
   A horrible embrace!
And the skull hung o'er with an elvish pry,
And cocked down its India-rubber eye
   To gaze upon his face.

Yet the good St. Anthony sunk his eyes
   Deep in the holy book:
He felt the bones, and so was wise
To know that the thing had a ghastly guise,
   And he did not dare to look.

Last came an imp,—how unlike the rest!
   A beautiful female form:
And her voice was like music, that sleep-oppress'd
Sinks on some cradling zephyr's breast;

And whilst with a whisper his cheek she press'd,
Her cheek felt soft and warm.

When over his shoulder she bent the light
Of her soft eyes on to his page,
It came like a moonbeam silver bright,
And relieved him then with a mild delight,
For the yellow lamp-lustre scorched his sight,
That was weak with the mists of age.

Hey! the good St. Anthony boggled his eyes
Over the holy book:
Ho ho! at the corners they 'gan to rise,
For he knew that the thing had a lovely guise,
And he could not choose but look.

There are many devils that walk this world,—
Devils large, and devils small;
Devils so meagre, and devils so stout;
Devils with horns, and devils without;
Sly devils that go with their tails upcurled,
Bold devils that carry them quite unfurled.
Meek devils, and devils that brawl;
Serious devils, and laughing devils;
Imps for churches, and imps for revels;
Devils uncooth, and devils polite;
Devils black, and devils white;
Devils foolish, and devils wise;
But a laughing woman, with two bright eyes,
Is the worsest devil of all.

A TALE OF GRAMMARYE.

BY R. H. DALTON BARHAM.

THE Baron came home in his fury and rage,
He blew up his Henchman, he blew up his Page;
The Seneschal trembled, the Cook looked pale,
As he ordered for supper grilled kidneys and ale,
Vain thought! that grill'd kidneys can give relief,
When one's own are inflamed by anger and grief.

What was the cause of the Baron's distress?
Why sank his spirits so low?—

The fair Isabel, when she should have said "Yes,"
  Had given the Baron a "No."
He ate, and he drank, and he grumbled between:
First on the viands he vented his spleen,—
The ale was sour,—the kidneys were tough,
And tasted of nothing but pepper and snuff!
—The longer he ate, the worse grew affairs,
Till he ended by kicking the butler downstairs.

All was hushed—'twas the dead of the night—
   The tapers were dying away,
  And the armour bright
  Glanced in the light
   Of the pale moon's trembling ray;
Yet his Lordship sat still, digesting his ire,
With his nose on his knees, and his knees in the fire,—
All at once he jump'd up, resolved to consult his
Cornelius Agrippa de rebus occultis.

   He seized by the handle
   A bed-room flat candle,
  And went to a secret nook,
   Where a chest lay hid
   With so massive a lid,
  His knees, as he raised it, shook,
Partly, perhaps, from the wine he had drunk,
Partly from fury, and partly from funk;
For never before had he ventured to look
In his Great-Great-Grandfather's conjuring-book.

   Now Lord Ranulph Fitz-Hugh,
   As lords frequently do,
Thought reading a bore,—but his case is quite new;
   So he quickly ran through
   A chapter or two,
For without Satan's aid he knew not what to do,—
When poking the fire, as the evening grew colder,
   He saw with alarm,
   As he raised up his arm,
An odd-looking countenance over his shoulder.

  Firmest rock will sometimes quake,
  Trustiest blades will sometimes break,

Sturdiest hearts will sometimes fail,
Proudest eye will sometimes quail ;—
No wonder Fitz-Hugh felt uncommonly queer
Upon suddenly seeing the Devil so near,
Leaning over his chair, peeping into his ear.

    The stranger first
    The silence burst,
And replied to the Baron's look : —
    "I would not intrude,
    But don't think me rude
If I sniff at that musty old book.
    Charms were all very well
    Ere Reform came to Hell ;
But now not an imp cares a fig for a spell.
    Still I see what you want,
    And am willing to grant
The person and purse of the fair Isabel.
Upon certain conditions the maiden is won ;—
You may have her at once, if you choose to say ' Done !'

    " The lady so rare,
    Her manors so fair,
Lord Baron I give to thee :
    But when once the sun
    Five years has run,
Lord Baron, thy soul's my fee !"
Oh ! where wert thou, ethereal Sprite ?
    Protecting Angel, where ?
Sure never before had noble or knight
    Such need of thy guardian care !
No aid is nigh—'twas so decreed ;—
The recreant Baron at once agreed,
And prepared with his blood to sign the deed.

    With the point of his sword
    His arm he scored,
And mended his pen with his Misericorde ;
    From his black silk breeches
    The stranger reaches
A lawyer's leathern case,

Selects a paper,
And snuffing the taper,
The Baron these words mote trace :—
" Five years after date, I promise to pay
My soul to old Nick, without let or delay,
For value received."—" There, my Lord, on my life,
Put your name to the bill, and the lady's your wife."

*   *   *   *   *

All look'd bright in earth and heaven,
And far through the morning skies
Had Sol his fiery coursers driven,—
That is, it was striking half-past eleven
As Isabel opened her eyes.

All wondered what made the lady so late,
For she came not down till noon,
Though she usually rose at a quarter to eight,
And went to bed equally soon.
But her rest had been broken by troublesome dreams :—
She had thought that, in spite of her cries and her screams,
Old Nick had borne off, in a chariot of flame,
The gallant young Howard of Effinghame.
Her eye was so dim, and her cheek so chill,
The family doctor declared she was ill,
And muttered dark hints of a draught and a pill.

All during breakfast to brood doth she seem
O'er some secret woes or wrongs ;
For she empties the salt-cellar into the cream,
And stirs up her tea with the tongs.
But scarce hath she finished her third round of toast,
When a knocking is heard by all—
" What may that be ?—'tis too late for the post,—
Too soon for a morning call."
After a moment of silence and dread,
The court-yard rang
With the joyful clang
Of an armed warrior's tread.
Now away and away with fears and alarms,—
The lady lies clasped in young Effinghame's arms.

She hangs on his neck, and she tells him true,
How that troublesome creature, Lord Ranulph Fitz-Hugh,
Hath vowed and hath sworn with a terrible curse,
That, unless she will take him for better for worse,
    He will work her mickle rue!

"Now, lady love, dismiss thy fear,
Should that grim old Baron presume to come here,
We'll soon send him home with a flea in his ear;—
    And, to cut short the strife,
    My love! my life!
Let me send for a parson, and make you my wife!"

No banns did they need, no licence require,—
    They were married that day before dark:
The Clergyman came,—a fat little friar,
    The doctor acted as Clerk.

But the nuptial rites were hardly o'er,
Scarce had they reached the vestry door,
    When a knight rushed headlong in;
    From his shoes to his shirt
    He was all over dirt,
    From his toes to the tip of his chin;
But high on his travel-stained helmet tower'd
The lion-crest of the noble Howard.

By horrible doubts and fears possest,
The bride turned and gaz'd on the bridegroom's breast—
    No Argent Bend was there;
    No Lion bright
    Of her own true knight,
    But his rival's Sable Bear!
The Lady Isabel instantly knew
'Twas a regular hoax of the false Fitz-Hugh;
And loudly the Baron exultingly cried,
"Thou art wooed, thou art won, my bonny gay bride!
Nor heaven nor hell can our loves divide!"

This pithy remark was scarcely made,
When the Baron beheld, upon turning his head,
    His Friend in black close by;

He advanced with a smile all placid and bland,
Popp'd a small piece of parchment into his hand,
 And knowingly winked his eye.

  As the Baron perused,
  His cheek was suffused
With a flush between brick-dust and brown;
  While the fair Isabel
  Fainted, and fell
In a still and death-like swoon.
Lord Howard roar'd out, till the chapel and vaults
Rang with cries for burnt feathers and volatile salts.

"Look at the date!" quoth the queer-looking man,
 In his own peculiar tone;
"My word hath been kept,—deny it who can,—
 And now I am come for my own."
Might he trust his eyes?—Alas! and alack!
'Twas a bill ante-dated full five years back!
  'Twas all too true—
  It was over due—
The term had expired!—he wouldn't "renew,"—
And the Devil looked black as the Baron looked blue.

  The Lord Fitz-Hugh
  Made a great to-do,
And especially blew up Old Nick,—
  "'Twas a stain," he swore,
  "On the name he bore
To play such a rascally trick!"—
"A trick?" quoth Nick, in a tone rather quick,
"It's one often played upon people who 'tick.'"
  Blue flames now broke
  From his mouth as he spoke,
They went out, and left an uncommon thick smoke,
  Which enveloping quite
  Himself and the Knight,
The pair in a moment were clean out of sight.
  When it wafted away,
  Where the dickens were they?
Oh! no one might guess—Oh! no one might say,—

But never, I wis,
From that time to this,
In hall or in bower, on mountain or plain,
Has the Baron been seen, or been heard of again.

As for fair Isabel, after two or three sighs,
She finally opened her beautiful eyes.
 She coughed, and she sneezed
 And was very well pleased,
After being so rumpled, and towzled, and teased,
To find when restored from her panic and pain,
My Lord Howard had married her over again.

MORAL.

Be warned by our story, ye Nobles and Knights,
Who're so much in the habit of "flying of kites;"
And beware how ye meddle again with such Flights:
At least, if your energies Creditors cramp,
Remember a Usurer's always a Scamp,
And look well at the Bill, and the Date, and the Stamp
Don't Sign in a hurry, whatever you do,
Or you'll go to the Devil, like Baron Fitz-Hugh.

THE RED-BREAST OF AQUITANIA.

AN HUMBLE BALLAD.

BY FATHER PROUT.

" *Are not two sparrows sold for a farthing? yet not one of them shall
fall to the ground without your Father.*"—St. Matthew, x. 29.

" Gallos ab Aquitanis Garumna flumen dividit."—Julius Cæsar.

" Sermons in stones, and good in everything."—Shakspeare.

 " Genius, left to shiver
 On the bank, 'tis said,
 Died of that cold river."—Tom Moore.

I.

River trip
from Thou-
louse to
Bourdeaux.

Oh, 'twas bitter cold
 As our steam-boat roll'd
Down the pathway old

Of the deep GARONNE,—
And the peasant lank,
While his *sabot* sank
In the snow-clad bank,
  Saw it roll on, on.

Thermome-
ter at ·0.
Snow 1½ foot
deep. Use of
wooden shoes.

II.

And he hied him home
To his *toit de chaume;*
And for those who roam
  On the broad bleak flood
Cared he? Not a thought;
For his beldame brought
His wine-flask fraught
  With the grape's red blood.

Yᵉ Gascon
farmer hieth
to his cot-
tage, and
drinketh a
flaggonne.

III.

And the wood-block blaze
Fed his vacant gaze
As we trod the maze
  Of the river down.
Soon we left behind
On the frozen wind
All farther mind
  Of that vacant clown.

He warmeth
his cold
shins at a
wooden fire.
Good b'ye to
him.

IV.

But there came anon,
As we journey'd on
Down the deep GARONNE,
  An acquaintancy,
Which we deem'd, I count,
Of more high amount,
For it oped the fount
  Of sweet sympathy.

Yᵉ Father
meeteth a
stray ac-
quaintance
in a small
bird.

V.

'Twas a stranger drest
In a downy vest,
'Twas a wee RED-BREAST,

Not yᵉ
famous alba-
tross of that
ancient ma-

(Not an "*Albatross*,")
But a wanderer meek,
Who fain would seek
O'er the bosom bleak
 Of that flood to cross.

riner olde Coleridge, but a poore robin.

VI.

And we watch'd him oft
As he soar'd aloft
On his pinions soft,
 Poor wee weak thing,
And we soon could mark
That he sought our bark
As a resting ark
 For his weary wing.

Ye sparrow crossing ye river maketh hys half-way house of the fire-ship.

VII.

But the bark, fire-fed,
On her pathway sped,
And shot far a-head
 Of the tiny bird,
And quicker in the van
Her swift wheels ran,
As the quickening fan
 Of his winglets stirr'd.

Delusive hope. Ye fire-ship runneth 10 knots an hour: 'tis no go for ye sparrow.

VIII.

Vain, vain pursuit!
Toil without fruit!
For his forkèd foot
 Shall not anchor there,
Tho' the boat meanwhile
Down the stream beguile
For a bootless mile
 The poor child of air!

Ye byrle is led a wilde goose chace adown ye river.

IX.

And 'twas plain at last
He was flagging fast,
That his hour had past

Symptomes of fatiguo. 'Tis melan-cholie to fall

S

*between
2 stools.*

In that effort vain ;
Far from either bank,
Sans a saving plank,
Slow, slow he sank,
Nor uprose again.

X.

Mort of y
birde.

And the cheerless wave
Just one ripple gave
As it oped him a grave
In its bosom cold,
And he sank alone,
With a feeble moan,
In that deep GARONNE,
And then all was told.

XI.

*Y^e old man
at ye helm
weepeth for
a sonne lost
in ye bay of
Biscaye.*

But our pilot grey
Wiped a tear away ;
In the broad BISCAYE
He had lost his boy !
And that sight brought back
On its furrow'd track
The remember'd wreck
Of long perish'd joy !

XII.

*Condoleance
of ye ladies ;
eke of 1
chasseur
d'infanterie
légère.*

And the tear half hid
In soft BEAUTY's lid
Stole forth unbid
For that red-breast bird ;—
And the feeling crept,—
For a WARRIOR wept ;
And the silence kept
Found no fitting word.

XIII.

*Olde Father
Prontte
sadly
moralizeth.*

But *I* mused alone,
For I thought of one
Whom I well had known

In my earlier days,
Of a gentle mind,
Of a soul refined,
Of deserts design'd
   For the Palm of Praise.

anent y
birde.

XIV.

And well would it seem
That o'er Life's dark stream,
Easy task for Him
   In his flight of Fame,
Was the SKYWARD PATH,
O'er the billow's wrath,
That for GENIUS hath
   Ever been the same.

Y streame*
of Lyfe. A
younge man
of fayre
promise.

XV.

And I saw him soar
From the morning shore,
While his fresh wings bore
   Him athwart the tide,
Soon with powers unspent
As he forward went,
His wings he had bent
   On the sought-for side.

Hys earlie
flyght across
y streame.*

XVI.

But while thus he flew,
Lo! a vision new
Caught his wayward view
   With a semblance fair,
And that new-found wooer
Could, alas! allure
From his pathway sure
   The bright child of air.

A newe ob-
ject calleth
his eye from
y maine*
chaunce.

XVII.

For he turn'd aside,
And adown the tide
For a brief hour plied

Instabilitie
of purpose a
fatall evyl
in lyfe.

His yet unspent force,
And to gain that goal
Gave the powers of soul,
Which, unwasted, whole,
    Had achieved his course.

XVIII.

This is y*
morall of
Father
Prout's
humble
ballade.

A bright SPIRIT, young,
Unwept, unsung,
Sank thus among
    The drifts of the stream ;
Not a record left,—
Of renown bereft,
By thy cruel theft,
    O DELUSIVE DREAM!

THE MONKS OF OLD.

BY WILLIAM JONES.

MANY have told of the monks of old,
    What a saintly race they were ;
But 'tis more true that a merrier crew
    Could scarce be found elsewhere ;
        For they sung and laugh'd,
        And the rich wine quaff'd,
    And lived on the daintiest cheer.

And some they would say, that throughout the day
    O'er the missal alone they would pore ;
But 'twas only, I ween, whilst the flock were seen
    They thought of their ghostly lore ;
        For they sung and laugh'd,
        And the rich wine quaff'd
    When the rules of their faith were o'er.

And then they would jest at the love confess'd
    By many an artless maid ;
And what hopes and fears they have pour'd in the ears
    Of those who sought their aid.
        And they sung and laugh'd,
        And the rich wine quaff'd
    As they told of each love-sick jade.

And the Abbot meek, with his form so sleek,
  Was the heartiest of them all,
And would take his place with a smiling face
  When refection bell would call ;
    And they sung and laugh'd,
    And the rich wine quaff'd,
  Till they shook the olden wall.

In their green retreat, when the drum would beat,
  And warriors flew to arm,
The monks they would stay in their convent grey,
  In the midst of dangers calm,
    Where they sung and laugh'd,
    And the rich wine quaff'd,
  For none would the good men harm.

Then say what they will, we'll drink to them still,
  For a jovial band they were ;
And 'tis most true that a merrier crew
  Could not be found elsewhere ;
    For they sung and laugh'd,
    And the rich wine quaff'd,
  And lived on the daintiest cheer.

THE FROG.

BY THE IRISH WHISKEY DRINKER.

I THINK the frog*
  A jolly dog,
He drinks through the live-long day ;
  He never need think
  Where to go for his drink,
And he's never a chalk to pay.
  The summer night long
  He sings his hoarse song,†
By the side of the streamlet blue,
  And he pipes his bassoon
  To the ladye moon,
And he drinks her health in dew !

---

* Ευκτος ο τω βατριχω, παιδες, βιος, ου μελεδαινει
Του τυ πιειν εγχουντα, παρεσι γαρ αφθονον αυτω·
            THEOCRITUS, *Idyll* X.

Βρεκεκεκεξ κουξ κουξ.—ARISTOPHANES, *Ranæ.*

CHORUS.
Drink to the frog,
He's a jolly dog;
He drinks through the live-long day;
He never need think
Where to go for his drink,
And he's never a chalk to pay.

The fish may swim,
And the wild bird skim
The earth, the sea, and the air;
And the hound pursue,
So swift and true,
The game to the forest lair.
Toil, prey, and strife!
What boots such life?
I like the frog's the best;
The blithe summer through
He has nothing to do,
And in winter he takes his rest.
Drink to the frog, &c.

AD MOLLISSIMAM PUEL- LAM E GETICÂ CARU- ARUM FAMILIÂ.

OVIDIUS NASO LAMENTATUR.

MOLLY CAREW.

BY SAM LOVER.

I.

Heu! heu!
Me tœdet, me piget o!
Cor mihi riget o!
Ut flos sub frigido...
Et nox ipsa mî, tum
Cum vado dormitùm,
Infausta, insomnis,
Transcurritur omnis...

I.

Och hone!
Oh! what will I do?
Sure my love is all crost,
Like a bud in the frost...
And there's no use at all
In my going to bed;
For 'tis dhrames, and not sleep,
That comes into my head...

Hoc culpâ fit tuâ
Mi, mollis Carùa,
Sic mihi illudens,
Nec pudens.—
  Prodigium tu, re
Es, verâ, naturæ,
Candidior lacte ;—
Plus fronte cum hâc te,
Cum istis ocellis,
Plus omnibus stellis
Mehercule vellem.—
Sed heu, me imbellem !
A me, qui sum fidus,
Vel ultimum sidus
Non distat te magis...
Quid agis !
  Heu ! heu ! nisi tu
Me ames,
Pereo ! pillaleu !

And 'tis all about you,
My sweet Molly Carew,
And indeed 'tis a sin
And a shame.—
  You're complater than nature
In every feature ;
The snow can't compare
With your forehead so fair :
And I rather would spy
Just one blink of your eye
Than the purtiest star
That shines out of the sky ;
Tho'—by this and by that !
For the matter o' that—
You're more distant by far
Than that same.
  Och hone, wierasthrew !
I am alone
In this world without you !

II.

Heu ! heu !
  Sed cur sequar laude
Ocellos aut frontem
Si NASI, cum fraude,
Prætereo pontem ?...
  Ast hic ego minùs
Quàm ipse LONGINUS
In verbis exprimem
Hunc nasum sublimem...
  De floridâ genâ
Vulgaris camœna
Cantaret in vanum
Per annum.—
  Tum, tibi puella !
Sic tument labella
Ut nil plus jucundum
Sit, aut rubicundum ;
Si primitùs homo
Collapsus est pomo,

II.

Och hone !
  But why should I speak
Of your forehead and eyes,
When your nose it defies
Paddy Blake the schoolmaster
  To put it in rhyme ?—
Though there's one BURKE,
He says,
Who would call it *Snublime*...
  And then for your cheek,
Throuth 'twould take him a week
Its beauties to tell
As he'd rather :—
  Then your lips, O machree !
In their beautiful glow
They a pattern might be
For the cherries to grow.—
'Twas an apple that tempted
Our mother, we know ;

Si dolor et luctus
Venerunt per fructus,
Proh! ætas nunc serior
Ne cadat, vereor,
Icta tam bello
Labello:
  Heu! heu! nisi tu
Me ames,
Pereo! pillaleu!

III.
Heu! Heu!
  Per cornua lunæ
Perpetuò tu ne
Me vexes impunè? . . .
  I nunc choro salta
(Mac-ghius nam tecùm)
Plautâ magis altâ
Quàm sueveris mecùm! . . .
  Tibicinem quando
Cogo fustigando
Ne falsum det melus,
Anhelus.—
  A te in sacello
Vix mentem revello,
Heu! miserè scissam
Te inter et Missam;
Tu latitas vero
Tam stricto galero
Ut cernere vultum
Desiderem multùm.
Et dubites jam, nùm
(Ob animæ damnum)
Sit fas hunc deberi
Auferri?
  Heu! heu! nisi tu
Coràm sis,
Cæcus sim: eleleu!

IV.
Heu! heu!
  Non me provocato,

For apples were scarce
I suppose long ago:
But at this time o' day,
'Pon my conscience I'll say,
Such cherries might tempt
A man's father!
  Och hone, wierasthrew!
I'm alone
In this world without you!

III.
Och hone!
  By the man in the moon!
You teaze me all ways
That a woman can plaze;
  For you dance twice as high
With that thief Pat Maghee
As when you take share
In a jig, dear, with me;
  Though the piper I bate,
For fear the ould chate
Wouldn't play you your
Favourite tune.
  And when you're at Mass
My devotion you crass,
For 'tis thinking of you
I am, Molly Carew;
While you wear on purpose
A bonnet so deep,
That I can't at your sweet
Pretty face get a peep.
Oh! lave off that bonnet,
Or else I'll lave on it
The loss of my wandering
Sowl!
  Och hone, like a howl,
Day is night,
Dear, to me without you!

IV.
Och hone!
  Don't provoke me to do it,

Nam virginum sat, o!
Stant mihi amato...
  Et stuperes planè
Si aliquo manè
Me sponsum videres;
Hoc quomodo ferres?
  Quid diceres, si cum
Triumpho per vicum,
Maritus it ibi,
Non tibi!
  Et pol! Catherinæ
Cui vacca, (tu, sine)
Si proferem hymen
Grande esset discrimen;
Tu quamvis, hìc aio,
Sis blandior Maio,
Et hæc calet rariùs
Quam Januarius;
Si non mutas brevi,
Hanc mihi decrevi
(Ut sic ultus forem)
Uxorem;
  Tum posthâc diù
Me spectrum
Verebere tu...elelcu!

For there's girls by the score
That loves me, and more.
  And you'd look very queer,
If some morning you'd meet
My wedding all marching
In pride down the street.
  Throth you'd open your eyes,
And you'd die of surprise
To think 'twasn't you
Was come to it.
  And 'faith! Katty Naile
And her cow, I go bail,
Would jump if I'd say,
"Katty Naile, name the day."
  And though you're fair and fresh
As the blossoms in May,
And she's short and dark
Like a cold winter's day,
Yet if *you* don't repent
Before Easter,—when Lent
Is over—I'll marry
For spite.
  Och hone; and when I
Die for you,
'Tis my ghost that you'll see every
    night!

LOVER was born in 1797 in Dublin, and died in Jersey in the summer of this year, 1868. He was the son of a stock-broker and insurance agent in that city, and receiving a plain, mercantile education, he was transferred to a desk in his father's office at a very early age. His leisure hours would seem to have been employed in the study of painting and music, for he was enabled to resign his original occupation, and give himself up to miniature painting, from which he derived a competent income, and married before he reached his thirtieth year. He became popular about this time in Dublin society by the publication of some exceedingly pretty drawing-room songs, of which 'The dark-haired Girl,' and 'Under the Rose,' were the chief, and a volume of very humourous tales and sketches of humble Irish life. His lyrics he set very cleverly to his own music; and he illustrated his prose works with his own etchings, which were in some instances worthy of Leech or

Cruikshank. He moreover sang his songs with a tiny, but tuneful voice, by no means unlike Tom Moore's, and like him, to his own pianoforte accompaniment. He recited also his prose tales and sketches at evening parties with such success, that his volume went through several editions. He came to London as he was approaching his fortieth year, when his reputation as a clever writer of Irish songs, and humourous Irish prose fiction had travelled before him. He had then commenced the publication of his very beautiful lays of the Irish peasant superstitions, 'The Angel's Whisper,' 'The Fairy Boy,' 'The Four-leaved Shamrock,' &c., and had become equally celebrated for another class of Irish songs, in which his essentially humourous genius was equally at home: amongst these were 'Molly Carew,' 'Rory O'Moore,' 'The Birth of St. Patrick,' and 'Molly Bawn.' Lover published at one time or other, after his arrival in London, some prose works of fiction, novels, and dramas, which had not by any means the same success as his lyrics, with the single exception of 'The White Horse of the Peppers,' which owed not the least portion of its popularity to the unrivalled acting of Tyrone Power. His chief contribution to 'Bentley's Miscellany' was the Irish story of 'Handy Andy,' which spread over several months of the periodical, and was afterwards republished in a collected form. The cleverest of Lover's intellectual performances was achieved a few years before he left Ireland, when he illustrated the famous and most formidable 'Parson's Horn Book,' the letter-press portion of which, in prose and verse, was contributed by a number of clever anti-tithe agitators, with Mr. Thomas Browne, a miller and farmer of the Queen's County, at their head, who subsequently published the 'Comet' newspaper in Dublin. This weekly journal after a two years' desperate fight with the Anglesey and Stanley administration, was crushed by Crown prosecutions, but not before the writings and caricatures of 'Comet and Horn Book' had produced such a state of feeling throughout Ireland, as compelled the Whig government of the day to abolish the collection of tithe at the point of the bayonet, from the occupier of the land, and transferred it into a rent charge upon the landlord. Lover kept the fact of his having caricatured the Irish tithe system in his younger days, from his English friends, to the last day of his life; and it is probable if he had not done so, that his name would not have been placed on the pension list for a hundred a year, which he enjoyed for a few years before his death, and which has been very considerately continued to his widow.

The exceedingly clever and witty Latin version of his comic *chef d'œuvre* is from the master hand of Father Prout.

THE GRAND CHAM OF TARTARY,

AND

THE HUMBLE-BEE.

Abridged from the voluminous Epic Poem by Beg-beg, formerly a mendicant ballad-singer, afterwards Principal Lord Rector of the University of Samarcand, and subsequently Historiographer and Poet Laureate to the Court of Balk.

BY C. J. DAVIDS.

I.

THE great Tartar chief, on a festival day,
  Gave a spread to his court, and resolved to be gay ;
But, just in the midst of their music and glee,
The mirth was upset by a humble-bee—
          A humble-bee—
They were bored by a rascally *humble-bee !*

II.

This riotous bee was so wanting in sense
As to fly at the Cham with malice prepense ;
Said his highness, "My fate will be *felo-de-se,*
If I'm thus to be teas'd by a humble-bee—
          A humble-bee—
How *shall* I get rid of the humble-bee !"

III.

The troops in attendance, with sabre and spear,
Were order'd to harass the enemy's rear :
But the brave body-guards were forced to flee—
They were all so afraid of the humble-bee—
          The humble-bee—
The soldiers were scar'd by the humble-bee.

IV.

The solicitor-general thought there was reason
For indicting the scamp on a charge of high-treason ;
While the chancellor *doubted* if any decree
From the woolsack would frighten the humble-bee—
          The humble-bee—
So the lawyers fought shy of the humble-bee.

V.

The Cham from his throne in an agony rose,
While the insect was buzzing right under his nose :—
"Was ever a potentate plagued like me,
Or worried to death by a humble-bee !
       A humble-bee—
Don't let me be stung by the humble-bee !"

VI.

He said to a page, nearly choking with grief,
"Bring hither my valiant commander-in-chief:
And say that I'll give him a liberal fee,
To cut the throat of this humble-bee—
       This humble-bee—
This turbulent, Jacobin, humble-bee !"

VII.

His generalissimo came at the summons,
And, cursing the courtiers for cowardly *rum-uns,*
"My liege," said he, "it's all fiddle-de-dee
To make such a fuss for a humble-bee—
       A humble-bee—
I don't care a d—n for the humble-bee !"

VIII.

The veteran rush'd sword in hand on the foe,
And cut him in two with a desperate blow.
His master exclaim'd, " I'm delighted to see
How neatly you've settled the humble-bee !"
       The humble-bee—
So there was an end of the humble-bee.

IX.

By the doctor's advice (which was prudent and right)
His highness retired very early that night:
For they got him to bed soon after his tea,
And he dream'd all night of the humble-bee—
       The humble-bee—
He saw the grim ghost of the humble-bee.

MORAL.

Seditious disturbers, mind well what you're *arter*—
Lest, humming a prince, you by chance catch a *Tartar*.
Consider, when planning an impudent spree,
You may get the same luck as the humble-bee—
    The humble-bee—
Remember the doom of the humble-bee !

HAROUN ALRASCHID.

BY G. E. INMAN.

O'ER the gorgeous room a luxurious gloom,
 Like the glow of a summer's eve, hung :
From its basin of stone, with rose-leaves bestrown
 The fountain its coolness flung ;
Perfumes wondrously rare fill'd the eunuch-fann'd air,
 And on gem-studded carpets around
The poets sung forth tales of glory or mirth
 To their instruments' eloquent sound ;
On a throne framed of gold sat their monarch the bold,
 With coffers of coin by his side,
And to each, as he sung, lavish handfuls he flung,
 Till each in his gratitude cried,
"Long, long live great Haroun Alraschid, the Caliph of Babylon
  old !"

Disturbing the feast, from the Rome of the East
 An embassage audience craves ;
And Haroun, smiling bland, cries, dismissing the band,
 " We will look on the face of our slaves !"
Then the eunuchs who wait on their Caliph in state
 Lead the messenger Lords of the Greek.
Proud and martial their mien, proud and martial their sheen,
 But they bow to the Arab right meek ;
And with heads bending down, though their brows wear a frown,
 They ask if he audience bestow.
" Yea, dogs of the Greek, we await ye, so speak !—
 Have ye brought us the tribute you owe ?
Or what lack ye of Haroun Alraschid, the Caliph of Babylon old ?"

Then the Greek spake loud, " To Alraschid the Proud
   This message our monarch doth send:
While ye play'd 'gainst a Queen, ye could mate her, I ween—
   She could ill with thy pieces contend;
But Irene is dead, and a Pawn in her stead
   Holds her power and place on the board:
By Nicephorus stern is the purple now worn,
   And no longer he owns thee for lord.
If tribute ye claim, I am bade in his name
   This to tell thee, O King of the World,
With these, not with gold, pays Nicephorus bold !"—
   And a bundle of sword-blades he hurl'd
At the feet of stern Haroun Alraschid, the Caliph of Babylon old.

Dark as death was his look, and his every limb shook,
   As the Caliph glared round on the foe—
" View my answer !" he roar'd, and unsheathing his sword,
   Clove the bundle of falchions right through.
"Tell my slave, the Greek hound, that Haroun the Renown'd,
   Ere the sun that now sets rise again,
Will be far on the road to his wretched abode,
   With many a myriad of men.
No reply will he send, either spoken or penn'd ;
   But by Allah, and Abram our sire,
He shall read a reply on the earth, in the sky,
   Writ in bloodshed, and famine, and fire !
Now begone !" thundered Haroun Alraschid, the Caliph of Baby-
   lon old.

As the sun dropt in night by the murky torchlight,
   There was gathering of horse and of man ;
Tartar, Courd, Bishareen, Persian, swart Bedoween,
   And the mighty of far Khorasan—
Of all tongues, of all lands, and in numberless bands,
   Round the Prophet's green banner they crowd,
They are form'd in array, they are up and away,
   Like the locusts' calamitous cloud ;
But rapine or spoil, till they reach the Greek soil,
   Is forbidden, however assail'd.
A poor widow, whose fold a Courd robb'd, her tale told,
   And he was that instant impaled
By the stern wrath of Haroun Alraschid, the Caliph of Babylon old !

On o'er valley and hill, river, plain, onwards still,
  Fleet and fell as the desert-wind, on!
Where was green grass before, when that host had pass'd o'er,
  Every vestige of verdure was gone!
On o'er valley and hill, desert, river, on still,
  With the speed of the wild ass or deer,
The dust of their tread, o'er the atmosphere spread,
  Hung for miles like a cloud in their rear.
On o'er valley and hill, desert, river, on still,
  Till afar booms the ocean's hoarse roar,
And amid the night's gloom, o'er tower, temple, and tomb,
  Heraclea, that sits by the shore!
Doom'd city of Haroun Alraschid, the Caliph of Babylon old.

There was mirth at its height in thy mansions that night,
  Heraclea, that sits by the sea!
Thy damsels' soft smiles breathed their loveliest wiles,
  And the banquet was wild in its glee!
For Zoe the fair, proud Nicephorus' heir,
  That night was betrothed to her mate,
To Theseus the Bold, of Illyria old,
  And the blood of the Island-kings great.
When lo! wild and lorn, and with robes travel-torn,
  And with features that pallidly glared,
They the Arab had spurn'd from Damascus return'd,
  Rush'd in, and the coming declared
Of the armies of Haroun Alraschid, the Caliph of Babylon old.

A faint tumult afar, the first breathing of war,
  Multitudinous floats on the gale:
The lelie shout shrill, and the toss'd cymbals peal,
  And the trumpet's long desolate wail,
The horse-tramp of swarms, and the clangour of arms,
  And the murmur of nations of men.
Oh woe, woe, and woe, Heraclea shall know—
  She shall fall, and shall rise not again;
The spiders' dusk looms shall alone hang her rooms,
  The green grass shall grow in her ways,
Her daughters shall wail, and her warriors shall quail,
  And herself be a sign of amaze,
Through the vengeance of Haroun Alraschid, the Caliph of
  Babylon old.

'Tis the dawn of the sun, and the morn-prayer is done,
    And the murderous onset is made ;
The Christian and foe they are at it, I trow,
    Fearfully plying the blade.
Each after each rolls on to the breach,
    Like the slumberless roll of the sea.
Rank rolling on rank rush the foe on the Frank,
    Breathless, in desperate glee ;
The Greek's quenchless fire, the Mussulman's ire
    Has hurled over rampart and wall.
And 'tis all one wild hell of blades slaughtering fell,
    Where fiercest and fellest o'er all
Work'd the falchion of Haroun Alraschid, the Caliph of Babylon old.

But day rose on day, yet Nicephorus grey,
    And Theseus, his daughter's betrothed,
With warrior-like sleight kept the town in despite,
    Of the Moslem insulted and loathed.
Morn rose after morn on the leaguers outworn,
    Till the Caliph with rage tore his beard ;
And, terribly wroth, sware a terrible oath—
    An oath which the boldest ev'n fear'd.
So his mighty Emirs gat around their compeers,
    And picked for the onslaught a few.
Oh ! that onslaught was dread,—every Moslem struck dead !
    But, however, young Theseus they slew,
And that gladdened fierce Haroun Alraschid, the Caliph of
    Babylon old.

Heraclea, that night in thy palaces bright
    There was anguish and bitterest grief.
"He is gone ! he is dead !" were the words that they said,
    Though the stunn'd heart refused its belief :
Wild and far spreads the moan, from the hut, from the throne,
    Striking every one breathless with fear.
"Oh ! Theseus the bold, thou art stark,—thou art cold,—
    Thou art young to be laid on the bier."
One alone makes no moan, but with features like stone,
    In an ecstasy haggard of woe,
Sits tearless and lorn, with dry eyeballs that burn,
    And fitful her lips mutter low
Dread threatenings against Haroun Alraschid, the Caliph of
    Babylon old.

The next morn on the wall, first and fiercest of all,
    The distraction of grief cast aside,
In her lord's arms arrayed, Zoe plied the death-blade,—
    Ay, and, marry, right terribly plied.
Her lovely arm fair, to the shoulder is bare,
    And nerved with a giant-like power
Where her deadly sword sweeps fall the mighty in heaps;
    Where she does but appear the foe cower.
Rank on rank they rush on,—rank on rank are struck down,
    Till the ditch is choked up with the dead.
The vulture and crow, and the wild dog, I trow,
    Made a dreadful repast that night as they fed
On the liegemen of Haroun Alraschid, the Caliph of Babylon old.

This was not to last.—The stern Moslem, downcast,
    Retrieved the next morning their might;
For Alraschid the bold, and the Barmecide old,
    Had proclaimed through the camp in the night,
That whoso should win the first footing within
    The city that bearded their power,
Should have for his prize the fierce girl with black eyes,
    And ten thousand zecchines as her dower.
It spurred them right well; and they battled and fell,
    Like lions, with long hunger wild.
Ere that day's set of sun Heraclea was won,
    And Nicephorus bold, and his child,
Were captives to Haroun Alraschid, the Caliph of Babylon old.

To his slave, the Greek hound, roared Haroun the Renowned,
    When before him Nicephorus came,
"Though the pawn went to queen, 'tis checkmated, I ween.
    Thou'rt as bold as unskilled in the game.
Now, Infidel, say, wherefore should I not slay
    The wretch that my vengeance hath sought?"—
"I am faint,—I am weak—and I thirst," quoth the Greek,
    "Give me drink." At his bidding 'tis brought;
He took it; but shrank, lest 'twere poison he drank.
    "Thou art safe till the goblet be quaffed!"
Cried Haroun. The Greek heard, took the foe at his word,
    Dashed down on the pavement the draught,
And claimed mercy of Haroun Alraschid, the Caliph of Babylon old.

9

Haroun never broke word or oath that he spoke,
  So he granted the captive his life,
And then bade his slaves bear stately Zoe the fair,
  To the warrior who won her in strife ;
But the royal maid cried in the wrath of her pride,
  She would die ere her hand should be given,
Or the nuptial caress should be lavished to bless
  Such a foe to her house and to Heaven.
Her entreaties they spurned, and her menace they scorned ;
  But, resolute, spite of their power,
All food she denied, and by self-famine died ;
  And her father went mad from that hour.
Thus triumph'd stern Haroun Alraschid, the Caliph of Babylon old !

TO THE HOT WELLS OF CLIFTON.

IN PRAISE OF RUM-PUNCH.

A TRIGLOT ODE, VIZ.

1° Πινδαρου περι ρευματος ῳδη.
2° Horatii in fontem Bristolii carmen.
3° A Relick (unpublished) of the "unfortunate Chatterton."

BY FATHER PROUT.

PINDAR.	HORACE.	CHATTERTON.
a.	I.	1.
Πηγη βριστολιας	O fons Bristolii	E ken your worth
Μαλλον εν υαλῳ	Hoc magis in vitro	"Hot wells" of Bristol,
Λαμπουσ' ανθεσι συν	Dulci digne mero	That bubble forth
Νεκταρος αξιη	Non sine floribus	As clear as crystal ;
Σ' αντλω	Vas impleveris	In parlour snug
Ρευματι πολλῳ	Undâ	I'd wish no holter
Μισγων	Mel solvento	To mix a jug
Και μελιτος πολυ.	Caloribus.	Of Rum and Water.
β	II.	2.
Ανηρ καν τις εραν	Si quis vel venerem	Doth Love, young chiel,
βουλεται η μαχην	Aut praelia cogitat,	One's bosom ruffle
Σοι Βακχου καθαρον	Is Bacchi calidos	Would any feel
Σοι διαχρωννυσει	Inficiet tibi	Ripe for a scuffle ?

Φοινῳ	Rubro sanguine	𝕿𝖍𝖊 simplest plan
Θ' αιματι νᾶμα·	Rivos,	𝕴𝖘 just to take a
Προθυμος τε	Fiet protinus	𝖂𝖊𝖑𝖑 stiffened can
Ταχ' εσσεται.	Impiger!	𝕺𝖋 old 𝕵amaica.

γ.	III.	3.
Σε φλεγμ' αιθαλοεν	Te flagrante bibax	𝕭eneath the zone
Σειριου αστερος	Ore canicula	𝕲rog in a pail or
Αγμοζει πλωτορι·	Surgit navita : tu	𝕽um – best alone—
Συ κρυος ηδυν εν	Frigus amabile	𝕯elights the sailor.
Νησοις	Fessis romere	𝕿he can he swills
Αντιλεσαισι	Mauris	𝕬lone gives vigour
Ποιεις	Præbes ac	𝕴n the 𝕬ntilles
Κ' αιθιοπων φυλῳ.	Homini nigro.	𝕿o white or nigger.

δ.	IV.	4.
Κρηναις εν τε καλαις	Fies nobilium	𝕿hy claims, 𝕺 fount,
Εσσεται αγλαη	Tu quoque fontium	𝕯escive attention :
Σ' εν κοιλῳ κυλακι	Me dicente ; cavum	𝕭enceforward count
Ενθεμενην εως	Dum calicem reples	𝕺n classic mention.
Υμνησω,	Urnamque	𝕽ight pleasant stuff
Λαλον εξ ου	Unde loquaces	𝕿hine to the lip is ;
Σον δε ρευμα καθαλλεται.	Lymphae	𝖂e've had enough
	Desiliunt tuae.	𝕺f 𝕬ganippe's.

WHO ARE YOU?

BY SAM LOVER AND FATHER PROUT.

" Who are you?—Who are you?
    Little boy that's running after
Ev'ry one up and down,
    Mingling sighs amidst your laughter?"
"I am Cupid, lady belle,
    I am Cupid, and no other."
"Little boy, then pr'ythee tell
    How is Venus? How's your mother?
Little boy, little boy,
    I desire you tell me true :
Cupid, oh! you're altered so,
    No wonder I cry *Who are you?*

II.

"Who are you?—Who are you?
  Little boy, where is your bow?
You had a bow, my little boy."
  "So had you, m 'am, long ago."
"Little boy, where is your torch?"
  "Madam, I have given it up:
Torches are no use at all;
  Hearts will never now *flare up*."
"Naughty boy, naughty boy,
  Words like these I never knew;
Cupid, oh, you're altered so,
  No wonder I cry *Who are you?*"

METASTASIO   AND   FONTENELLE.

I.

La Signora.

Chi sei tu?   Chi sei tu?
  Dimi piccolo fanciullo
Sempr' andante sù et giù
  Sospirando fra 'l trastullo.
Cupido.
Son Cupido in verità
  Rè do' burle leggiadre.
La Sig.
Dunque di per carità,
  Come stia, tua madre?
Senj' arco cosl, perchè?
  Dove sono le saiette?
La faretra poi dov' è?
  Sembianze son sospette—
  CHI SEI TU?

I.

La Dame.

Qui es tu?   Qui es tu?
  Bel enfant aux gais sourires,
Toi qui cours tout devetu,
  Et ris parfois, parfois soupires?
Cupidon.
Dame, je suis Cupidon,
  Dieu d'amour, fils à CITHERE.
La Dame.
Bel enfant, eh, dis moi donc
  Comment va, VENUS, la mere?
Cette fois, sans carquois
  Je te vois, avec surprise,
Cupidon, est il donc
  Etonnant que l'on te dise,
  QUI ES TU?

II.

La Sig.

Chi sei tu?   Chi sei tu?
  Arme c'eran altre volte.
Cupido.
Giovan' ELLA non è più
  Mi furon' allora tolte.
La Sig.
E la torcia, perchè dl,
  Hai voluto tu lasciare?

II.

La Dame.

Qui es tu?   Qui es tu?
  Qu'a tu donc fait de tes armes,
De tes traits de fer pointu . . .?
  Cupidon.
De *vos* traits . . où sont les charmes?
  La Dame.
Vous votre beau, moi mon flambeau
  Ensemble nous lâchâmes :

<table>
<tr><td>

Cupido.

Cuori signor' oggidì
  Più non vogliono bruciare.
    La Sig.
Tu rispondermi così
  Fanciulletto ! che vergogna !
O ! sci cambiato, sì,
  Ate dunque dir' bisogna
    "Chi sei tu ?"

</td><td>

Cupidon.

Or, plus d'espoir helas ! de voir
  Pour nous les cœurs en flammes !
    La Dame.
Petit enfant, c'est peu galant
  D'user pareil langage ;
Pas étonnant que maintenant
  Chacun dise au village
    "Qui es tu ?"

</td></tr>
</table>

SONG OF JANUARY.

BY FATHER PROUT.

"Ille ego qui quondam," &c., &c.—*Æneid.*

I.

In the month of Janus,
  When Boz* to gain us,
Quite "Miscellaneous,"
  Flashed his wit so keen,
One, (Prout they call him,)
In style most solemn,
Led off the volume
  Of his magazine.

II.

Though MAGA, 'mongst her
Bright set of youngsters,
Had many songsters
  For her opening tome ;
Yet she would rather
Invite "the Father,"
And an indulgence gather
  From the Pope of Rome.

III.

And such a beauty
From head to shoe-tie,
Without dispute we
  Found her first boy,

---

* Alluding to Dickens's appearance in the opening number of the 'Bentley's Miscellany,' January, 1837.

That she detarmined,
There's such a charm in't,
The Father's *sarmint*
   She'd again employ.

IV.

While other children
Are quite bewilderin',
'Tis joy that fill'd her in
   This bantling ; 'cause
What eye but glistens,
And what ear but listens,
When the clargy christens
   A babe of Boz ?

V.

I've got a scruple
That this young pupil
Surprised its parent
   Ere her time was sped ;
Else I'm unwary,
Or, 'tis she's a fairy,
For in January
   She was brought to bed.

VI.

This infant may be
A six months' baby,
But may his cradle
   Be blest ! say I ;
And luck defend him !
And joy attend him !
Since we can't mend him,
   Born in July.

VII.

He's no abortion,
But born to fortune,
And most opportune.
   Though before his time ;

Him, Muse, O! nourish,
And make him flourish
Quite Tommy Moorish
 Both in prose and rhyme!

VIII.

I remember, also,
That this month they call so,
From Roman JULIUS
 The " *Cæsarian* " styled ;
Who was no gosling,
But, like this Boz-ling,
From birth a dazzling
 And precocious child !

  GOD SAVE THE QUEEN.

THE OLD BELL.

" In an old village, amid older hills,
 That close around their verdant walls to guard
 Its tottering age from wintry winds, I dwell
 Lonely, and still, save when the clamorous rooks
 Or my own fickle changes wound the ear
 Of Silence in my tower."—ANON.

FOR full five hundred years I've swung
 In my old grey turret high,
And many a different theme I've sung
 As the time went stealing by !
I've peal'd the chaunt of a wedding morn ;
 Ere night I have sadly toll'd,
To say that the bride was coming, love-lorn,
 To sleep in the church-yard mould !
  Ding dong,
    My careless song ;
   Merry and sad,
    But neither long !

For full five hundred years I've swung
 In my ancient turret high,
And many a different theme I've sung
 As the time went stealing by !

I've swell'd the joy of a country's pride
  For a victory far off won,
Then changed to grief for the brave that died
  Ere my mirth had well begun !
        Ding-dong,
                My careless song,
          Merry or sad,
                But neither long !
For full five hundred years I've swung
  In my breezy turret high,
And many a different theme I've sung
  As the time went stealing by !
I have chimed the dirge of a nation's grief
  On the death of a dear-loved king,
Then merrily rung for the next young chief ;
  As *told*, I can weep or sing !
        Ding-dong,
                My careless song ;
          Merry or sad,
                But neither long !
For full five hundred years I've swung
  In my crumbling turret high ;
'Tis time my own death-song were sung,
  And with truth before I die !
I never could love the themes they gave
  My tyrannized tongue to tell :
One moment for cradle the next for grave—
  They've worn out the old church bell !
        Ding-dong,
                My changeful song ;
          Farewell now,
                And farewell long !

OLD MOUNTAIN DEW.

BY CHARLES MACKAY.

AWAY with your port and your fine-flavour'd sherry,
  And fill up with toddy as high as you please ;
We men of the Northland should know ourselves better
  Than pledge her in liquors so paltry as these !

In whiskey, perfumed by the peat of the heather,
 We'll drink to the land of the kind and the true,—
  Unsullied in honour,
  Our blessings upon her!
 Scotland for ever! and old mountain dew!
   Neish! neish! neish! hurra!

Mountain dew! *clear* as a Scot's understanding,
 Pure as his conscience wherever he goes,
Warm as his heart to the friend he has chosen,
 Strong as his arm when he fights with his foes!
In liquor like this should old Scotland be toasted;
 So fill up again, and the pledge we'll renew—
  Long flourish the honour
  Her children have won her—
 Scotland for ever! and old mountain dew!
   Neish! neish! neish! hurrah!

May her worth, like her lowland streams, roll on unceasing,—
 Her fame, like her highland hills, last evermore,—
And the cold of her glens be confined to the climate,
 Nor enter the heart, though it creep through the door.
And never may we, while we love and revere her,
 As long as we're brave, and warm-hearted, and true,
  Want reason to boast her,
  Or whiskey to toast her—
 Scotland for ever! and old mountain dew!
   Neish! neish! neish! hurra!

THE PHANTOM SHIP.

BY ELLEN PICKERING.

" My child! my child! come down to rest
  The day has long been past:
 Sleep in thy mother's blessing blest,
  The night is waning fast."

" Dear mother, let us linger here,
  The moon shines forth so bright:
 The starry sky is all so clear,
  It does not look like night;

" And all around the waveless sea
  In glassy smoothness lies,
And on it flows so silently,
  It bids no murmur rise.

" And as I bend me o'er the side,
  Methinks I trace below
The ocean's depths, their jewel'd pride,
  A fair and goodly show;

" The beauties that the Mighty One
  Hath lavish'd there from old;
The treasures that from earth have gone,
  The diamond and the gold;

" The glitt'ring and the sighed-for things
  Man seeks 'mid care and strife,
And ocean from him hardly wrings
  With wreck or loss of life;

" The silver fish that gently glide,
  Or glance in gladsome play,
Filling with life the crystal tide,
  How fair and bright are they!

" And see! and see! approaching now,
  A ship of pride and cost;
The weary crew asleep below,
  The helmsman at his post.

" No rushing wind compels her course,
  No tempest raves around;
She moves as by some unseen force,
  Whilst all is still around.

" She ruffles not the glassy tide,
  Bends not her stately mast,
No fretful billows chafe her side,
  No foam is round her cast.

" She leaves no track upon the sea,
  No furrow in her wake;
But on, and on unerringly
  Her silent way doth take."

" Come down to rest, my gentle child !
　　Thou dost not see aright :
　Thy words are as a sleeper's wild ;
　　There is no ship in sight."

" Yes, yes, the stately ship is near,
　　And all my words are true :
　A child looks on her mother dear,
　　As I look up at you.

" And now I hear the soften'd tone,
　　And gentle words of love ;
　And now they sound as though mine own,
　　And now as thine they move."

" Hush ! hush, my child ! no ship is nigh,
　　No voices canst thou hear :
　A shadowy cloud is in thine eye,
　　The breeze is in thine ear."

"No shadowy cloud is in mine eye ;
　　No breeze is in mine ear ;
　The stately ship is passing by,
　　And gentle tones I hear.

" One walks the deck with weary pace,
　　As though he sighed for sleep ;
　The steersman turns an anxious face
　　Across the waveless deep.

" And two beside the steersman stand,
　　A mother and her child :
　One holds, as now I hold your hand,
　　One smiles as late you smiled."

" My child ! my child ! it cannot be !"
　　Thus forth the mother broke ;
　And yet she answer'd shudd'ringly,
　　And trembled as she spoke.

" My child ! my child ! it cannot be !
　　Vessel save ours is none.
　Look ! o'er the still unbounded sea
　　We take our way alone."

" Her words are true," the steersman said,
    To youth it has been given
To speak, without deceit or dread,
    The changeless will of Heav'n.

" Your child the phantom ship hath seen!
    Ere set to-morrow's sun,
No trace will rest where we have been,
    Our mortal course be run."

Before the morrow's sun went down,
    There was nor trace nor mark,
To show where o'er the sea had gone
    That strong and gallant bark.

No shatter'd spars, no riven mast
    Were floating o'er the waves :
None knew when those from life had past,
    Who slept in wat'ry graves.

Yet all she bore across the waves
    Had passed from human sight,
With none to weep above their graves,
    Or read the funeral rite.

A MERRY DITTY ON THE MOUNTAIN DEW.

BY JOSEPH O'LEARY.

Whiskey—drink divine !
    Why should driv'llers bore us
With the praise of wine,
    Whilst we've thee before us ?
Were it not a shame,
    Whilst we gaily fling thee
To our lips of flame,
    If we would not sing thee !

CHORUS.

Whiskey—drink divine !
    Why should drivellers bore us
With the praise of wine,
    Whilst we've thee before us ?

AD ROREM MONTANUM. DITHYRAMBUS.

BY THE IRISH WHISKEY DRINKER.

Vitæ Ros divine !
    Vinum quis laudaret
Te præsente—quis
    Palmam Vino daret ?
Proh pudor ! immemores
    Tui, dum te libamus,
Ore flammato tuos
    Honores non canamus ?

CHORUS.

Vitæ Ros divine !
    Vinum quis laudaret
Te præsente—quis
    Palmam vino daret ?

Greek and Roman sung
  Chian and Falernian;
Shall no harp be strung
  To thy praise Hibernian?
Yes; let Erin's sons,
  Generous, brave, and frisky,
Tell the world at once
  They owe it to their whiskey!
    Whiskey—drink divine! &c.

If Anacreon, who
  Was the grapes' best poet,
Drank the Mountain Dew,
  How his verse would show it!
As the best then known,
  He to wine was civil;
Had he Innishowen,
  He'd pitch wine to the devil!
    Whiskey—drink divine! &c.

Bright as Beauty's eye
  When no sorrow veils it;
Sweet as Beauty's sigh
  When Young Love inhales it;
Come thou, to my lip!
  Come, oh, rich in blisses!
Every drop I sip
  Seems a shower of kisses!
    Whiskey—drink divine! &c.

Could my feeble lays
  Half thy virtues number,
A whole grove of bays
  Should my brows encumber.
Be his name adored
  Who summed up thy merits
In one little word,
  When he called thee " SPERRITS!"
    Whiskey—drink divine! &c.

Veteres Falernum
  Chiumque laudavêre;
De te nefas filios
  Hibernice silere!
Nam fortes et protervi
  Hibernici habentur;
Tibique has virtutes
  Debere confitentur.
    Vitæ Ros divine! &c.

Teius Lyæi
  Cecinit honorem;
Cecinisset dulcius
  Montanum ille Rorem!
HORDEARIUM si
  Forte libavisset!
Ad inferos Lyæum
  Anacreon misisset!
    Vitæ Ros divine! &c.

Clarior ocello
  Veneris ridente;
Suavior suspirio
  Cupidine præsente!
Liceat beatis
  Te labris applicare,
Imbrem et basiorum
  Guttatim delibare!
    Vitæ Ros divine! &c.

Versibus pusillis
  Si satis te laudarem,
Lauro Apollinari
  Hæc tempora celarem.
Faustus ille semper
  Sit, et honoratus,
A quo "SPIRITUS" tu
  Meritò vocatus!
    Vitæ Ros divine! &c.

Send it gaily round ;
  Life would be no pleasure
If we had not found
  This immortal treasure.
And when tyrant Death's
  Arrows shall transfix you,
Let your latest breaths
  Be "Whiskey! whiskey! whiskey!!!"

Ordine potemus
  Festivo recumbentes,
Cur vivere optemus
  Hoc munere egentes ?
Cum te Libitina
  Telo vulnerabit,
"Nectar! nectar!" spiritus
  Deficiens clamabit!

CHORUS.

Whiskey—drink divine!
Why should driv'llers bore us
With the praise of wine,
Whilst we've thee before us ?

CHORUS.

Vitæ Ros divine!
Vinum quis laudaret
Te præsente—quis
Palmam vino daret ?

JOSEPH O'LEARY, the author of the English portion of this song, one of the best ever written in praise of Ireland's ' Mountain Dew', was a native of Cork, and a Parliamentary reporter on the staff of the ' Morning Herald.' In his latter days he was " told off" to the easier duty of an occasional visit to one or other of the metropolitan police offices, where his racy sketches, when the subject was worthy of his pen, equalled if not surpassed those of the once celebrated ' Mornings in Bow Street,' the production of another Irishman of a former generation. O'Leary was the type of a clever class of young Irishmen who came up to London about thirty years ago, after they had had a little training on one or other of the Irish newspapers for whi h they had reported and scribbled in various ways. By far the greater number of them were Roman Catholics, who, being poor and warmly attached to the faith of their fathers, were completely shut out from the s zarships, scholarships, and other emoluments of the exclusively Protes ant University of Dublin.

The same class of men born in En land within the pale of the national religion, that is the religion of the majority, would have gone up with exhibitions and scholarships from one or other of the numerous endowed schools of their country to Oxford and Cambridge, there to win additional scholarships during their under-graduate course, and in the ordinary run of probabilities to rise to their share of the numerous fellowships, professorships, masterships, &c., of those two ancient universities which hold forth of all our glorious institutions the noblest and richest prizes of life to the sons of the English middle classes. To say nothing of the vast opening presented by the Church with its rich rewards for successful scholarship, one of those fellowships held by a layman for seven years enables him to devote himself during that time to one or other of the lay professions without being obliged to have recourse to desultory literary efforts to help him in his finance, whilst enticing him too often from the straight and steady course which leads to the professional goal. This most unfair and most un-natural state of things was long felt in Ireland before the establishment of the Queen's Colleges by the class from which O'Leary and the Irish reporters of the Parliamentary gallery sprung, and was often spoken of as a leading grievance amongst themselves, without a hope being entertained by any of those whom it galled and pressed of a Parliamentary remedy for it. The Roman Catholic prelates at all times and under all circumstances had set their faces against opening Trinity College, Dublin, which they called "a den of iniquity," to Roman Catholics, preferring an exclusive university of their own as at present; and Mr. O'Connell would not move in the matter at any time subsequent to the Emancipation Act, being afraid, for obvious reasons, to offend the heads of his church, and indeed sympathising very little in the matter, as with all his unquestionably brilliant genius and com-manding talents he had not an academic instinct in his composition. If after the great victory of Civil and Religious liberty of 1829 he had addressed himself to practical reforms, including this very question of middle-class education, and thrown the weight of his great powers and popularity into the scale for the material benefit of Ireland and her people, how many more victories might he not have added to the only great one with which his name will be associated by the calm and un-prejudiced verdict of after times! If he had retired to enjoy the emoluments and honours of his profession which were waiting to be showered on him, and left the practical questions of his country's material improvement to men more accurately trained to and better ac-quainted with them in all their details and bearings, what a happier history would Ireland's have been, what a nobler fate would have been his own, since that day of patriotic hope which was destined before many years—years of broken promise and wasted energy—to end in the sorrow of the old and the middle-aged, the indignation of the young, and the lost confidence of all, followed up by the melancholy Young Ireland outbreak, and afterwards by the far more lamentable outspread of Fenianism over an unhappy and distracted country! If even, after having been drawn in triumph through the streets of Dublin, on his return to it, covered with political glory, he had descended from that magnificent car fabricated for him by the united Trades' Union of that city, and followed by myriads of willing captives—if he had descended from it but to pass away shortly and for ever, who of Ireland's proud-est sons, her Grattans, her Currans, her Floods, her Charlemonts, who had nobly contended in the same great cause of civil and religious liberty, could have been compared with him?

" Quid illo eive tulisset
Natura in terris, quid Roma beatius unquam,
Si, circumducto captivorum agmine et omni
Bellorum pompâ, animam exhalassat opimam,
Quum de Teutonico vellet descendere curru ?'

If some of those reforms, which appeared but paltry and common-
place to Mr. O'Connell and the Irish patriotic school of his latter
days had been carried out, a career would have been opened to the
sons of the poorer ranks of the Irish Roman Catholic middle-class,
whose education entitled them to aspire beyond the counter and the
workshop, far more profitable and far worthier of their deserts than
that of being the hewers of wood and drawers of water, in a literary
sense, to the English newspapers. Sooth to say, their connexion with
these latter scarcely afforded them a decent bagman's allowance to
support wives and families in the great metropolis, with little re-
source left but to drown their disappointment, pottle-deep, in such
taverns as the Cider Cellar, the Coal Hole, and the Codger's Hall, where
good, easy, and prosperous citizens used to drop in at night, after they
had counted their gains and sent wives and children to bed, to hear
those clever and most amusing poor fellows flash about their wit and
humour, and to enjoy their quaint stories and capital songs, many of
which they composed themselves, like the famous Whiskey Song of
Joseph O'Leary.

POETICAL EPISTLE TO BOZ.

FROM FATHER PROUT.

I.

A RHYME! a rhyme! from a distant clime,—from the gulph of
the Genoese :
O'er the rugged scalps of the Julian Alps, dear Boz! I send you
these,
To light the *Wick* your candlestick holds up, or, should you list,
To usher in the yarn you spin concerning Oliver Twist.

II.

Immense applause you've gained, oh, Boz! through continental
Europe :
You'll make Pickwick œcumenick ; of fame you have a sure hope :
For here your books are found, gadzooks ! in greater *luxe* than any
That have issued yet, hotpress'd or wet, from the types of GALIG-
NANI.

III.

But neither when you sport your pen, oh, potent mirth-compeller !
Winning our hearts "in monthly parts," can Pickwick or Sam
    Weller
Cause us to weep with pathos deep, or shake with laugh spasmodical,
As when you drain your copious vein for Bentley's periodical.

IV.

Folks all enjoy your Parish Boy,—so truly you depict him ;
But I, alack ! while thus you track your stinted poor-law's victim,
Must think of some poor nearer home, poor who, unheeded perish,
By squires despoiled, by " patriots" gulled,—I mean the starving
    Irish.

V.

Yet there's no dearth of Irish mirth, which to a mind of feeling,
Seemeth to be the Helot's glee before the Spartan reeling ;
Such gloomy thought o'ercometh not the glee of England's humour,
Thrice happy isle ! long may the smile of genuine joy illume her !

VI.

Write on, young sage ! still o'er the page pour forth the flood of
    fancy ;
Wax still more droll, wave o'er the soul Wit's wand of necromancy.
Behold ! e'en now around your brow th' immortal laurel thickens ;
Yea, SWIFT or STERNE might gladly learn a thing or two from
    DICKENS.

VII.

A rhyme ! a rhyme ! from a distant clime,—a song from the sunny
    south !
A goodly theme, so Boz but deem the measure not uncouth.
Would, for thy sake, that " PROUT " could make his bow in
    fashion finer,
" *Partant* " (from thee) " *pour la Syrie,* " for Greece and Asia
    Minor.

SARDANAPALUS.

SARDANAPALUS was Nineveh's king ;
    And, if all be quite true that the chroniclers sing,
      Loved his song and his glass,
      And was given, alas !

10

Not only to bigamy,
Nor even to trigamy,
But (I shudder to think on't) to rankest polygamy:
For his sweethearts and wives were so vast in amount,
They'd take you a week or two *only* to count!

One morning his Majesty jumped out of bed,
And hitting his valet a rap on the head,
By way of a joke, " Salamenes," he said,
    " Go, proclaim to the court,
    'Tis our will to resort,
    By way of a lark,
    To our palace and park
On the banks of Euphrates, and there, with our wives,
Sing, dance, and get fuddled, for once in our lives ;
So, bid our state-rulers and nobles, d'ye see,
Hie all to our banquet not later than three,
And prepare for a long night of jollity."
" Very good," said the valet ; then eager and hot
On his errand, ducked thrice, and was off like a shot.

When the court heard these orders, with rapture elate,
They adjourn'd all the business of church and of state,
    And hurried off, drest
    Each man in his best ;
    While the women, sweet souls,
    Went with them by shoals,
Some in gigs, some in cabs, some on horseback so gay,
And some in an omnibus hired for the day.—
(If busses in those days were not to be seen,
All I can say is, they *ought* to have been.)—
    Like a torrent, the throng
    Roll'd briskly along,
Cheering the way with jest, laughter, and song,
To the Banquetting Hall, where the last of the group
Arrived, by good luck, just in time for the soup.

The guests set to work in superlative style,
And his Majesty, equally busy the while,
Encouraged their efforts with many a smile.
    The High Priest was the first,
    Who seemed ready to burst ;

(For the ladies so shy,
They swigged on the sly !)
But, proud of his prowess, he scorn'd to give o'er,
'Till at length with a hiccup he fell on the floor,
Shouting out, 'mid his qualms,
That verse in the Psalms,
Which saith (but it surely can't mean a whole can !)
That " Wine maketh merry the heart of a man."

While thus they sate tippling, peers, prelates, and all,
And music's sweet voice echoed light through the Hall;
His Majesty rose,
Blew his eloquent nose,
And exclaiming, by way of exordium, " Here goes !"
Made a speech which produced a prodigious sensation,
Greatly, of course, to the King's delectation ;
One courtier, o'erpower'd by its humour and wit,
Held both his fat sides, as if fearing a fit !
While another kept crying, " Oh, God, I shall split !"
(So when a great publisher cracks a small joke,
His authors at table are ready to choke.)
And all, with the lungs of a hurricane, swore
They had ne'er heard so droll an oration before,
With the single exception of one silly fellow,
Who not being, doubtless, sufficiently mellow,
Refused to applaud, or to join in the laughter,
And was hang'd for a traitor just ten minutes after.

By this time Dan Phœbus in ocean had sunk,
And the guests were all getting exceedingly drunk,
When, behold ! at the door
There was heard a loud roar,
And in rush'd a messenger covered with gore,
Who bawl'd out, addressing the Head of the State,
"If your Majesty pleases, the Foe's at the gate,
And threaten to kick up the Devil's own din,
If you do not surrender, and bid them come in ;
The mob, too, has risen,
And let out of prison,
With the jailor's own keys (but it's no fault of *his'n*),

Some hund..ds of burglars, and fences, and prigs,
Who are playing all sorts of queer antics and rigs;
Already they've fir'd up one church for a beacon,—
Hocussed a bishop, and burked an archdeacon,
And swear, if you don't give them plenty of grog,
They'll all become Chartists, and go the whole hog!"

Scarce had he ended, when hark! with a squall,
A second grim Herald pops into the Hall,
          And, " Woe upon woe!
          The desperate foe,"
Quoth he, " Have forced open the gates of the town,
And are knocking hy scores the rich citizens down;
          As I pass'd with bent brow,
          By the Law Courts just now,
Lo, sixty attorneys lay smash'd in a row,
Having just taken wing for the regions below,
(When lawyers are dead, none can doubt where they go,)
'Mid the cheers of each snob, who sung out, as he past,
' So, the scamps have gone home to their father at last!'"

Oh! long grew the face of each guest at this tale,
The men they turn'd red, and the women turn'd pale;
But redder and paler they turn'd when they heard
The more terrible tidings of herald the third!—
In he bounced with a visage as black as a crow's,
And a mulberry tinge on the tip of his nose;
          He'd a rent in his breeches,
          A tergo, the which is
(As Smollett has taught us long since to believe*)
Not the pleasantest sight for the daughters of Eve;
And he shook like a leaf, as thus hoarsely he spake
In the gruff and cacophonous tones of a drake —
          The town's all on fire,
          Hut, palace and spire
Are blazing as fast as the foe can desire:
          Such crashing and smashing,
          And sparkling and darkling!
Such squalling, and bawling, and sprawling,
And jobbing, and robbing, and mobbing!

---

* *Vide* Miss Tabitha Bramble, in Smollett's ' Humphrey Clinker.'

Such kicking and licking, and racing and chasing,
Blood-spilling and killing, and slaughtering and quartering!
You'd swear that old Nick, with Belphegor his clerk,
And Moloch his cad, were abroad on a lark!"

" Here's a go!" said the King, staring wild like a bogle
At these tidings, and wiping his eyes with his fogle ;
" 'Tis vain now to run for
Our lives, for we're done for ;
So, away with base thoughts of submission or flight,
Let's all, my brave boys, die like heroes to-night ;
Raise high in this Hall a grand funeral pile,
Then fire it, and meet our death-doom with a smile!"
He ceased, when a courtier replied in low tone,
" If your Majesty pleases, I'd rather live on ;
For, although you may think me as dull as a post,
Yet I can't say I've any great taste for a roast ;
'Tis apt to disorder one's system ; and so,
Good-night to your Majesty—D.I.O. !"
So saying, he made for the door and rushed out,
While quick at his heels rushed the rest of the rout,
Leaving all alone,
The King on his throne,
With a torch in one hand which he waved all abroad,
And a glass in the other, as drunk as a Lord !

That night, from the Hall, late so joyous, there broke,
Spreading wide in 'mid air, a vast column of smoke ;
While, higher and higher,
Blazed up the red fire,
As it blazed from Queen Dido's funeral pyre!—
Hark to the crash, as roof, pillar, and wall
Bend—rock—and down in thunder fall !
Hark to the roar of the flames, as they show
Heaven and earth alike in a glow !
The hollow wind sobs through the ruins, as though
'Twere hymning his dirge, who, an hour ago,
Was a King in all a King's array ;
But now lies, a blackened clod of clay,
In that Hall whose splendours have past away,
Save in old tradition, for ever and aye !

ERINNA.*

BY C. HARTLEY LANGHORNE.

GENTLE Erinna!
   Sweet primrose, appear!
Gentle Erinna!
   Be here; oh, be here!

Come, when sweet twilight
   Steals over the earth;
Come, when the fairest
   Of visions have birth;

Come, when soft silence
   Enthrals the wrapt mind,
When the chains of the world
   Lose their power to bind.

Come, when the glow-worms
   Glance gay in the lane;
Come, when the village-maid,
   Lists to her swain.

Come, when the night stock
   Flings odours around;
Come, when the balmy dews
   Kiss the glad ground.

Come, when Selene
   Sheds mildly her rays,
When the meadows are veiled
   In a dim silver haze.

Come, when the nightingale
   Sings to her fere;
Gentle Erinna!
   Be here! oh, be here!

---

* Erinna was a Greek poetess, the contemporary and countrywoman of
Sappho. Meleager, in his Garland, assigns to her the crocus as her emblem,
on account of its maiden paleness, as in Cymbeline,—
      "The flower that's like thy face,—pale primrose."
When but sweet seventeen, Erinna—
      "Left this world of sorrow and pain,
      And returned to the land of thought again."

Tell me how Sappho
  And you walked of yore,
To list to the ripple
  On Lesbos' old shore.

Tell how you lay
  'Neath the green myrtle boughs;
Tell how you whispered
  Each other your vows.

Tell of the loved one,
  The auburn-haired youth;
Tell of Abrocomas,—
  Tell me the truth.

How Eros saw you,
  And bent his swift bow;
Tell me the whispers
  Of long, long ago.

Sing me the songs
  That you then used to trill,
Murm'ring as soft
  As some reed-haunted rill;

Strains that charmed silence,
  Enthrilling the ear,
While the Lesbian maidens
  Hung round you to hear.

Tell how your marriage song
  Welcomed the day;
Tell how it changed
  To the sad well-a-way!

Brightest! you fled
  From this dark world of pain,
To the " marled seas" above
  You have mounted again.

Yet stoop, sweet Erinna,
  Oh! stoop from thy sphere!
Gentle Erinna!
  Be here! oh, be here!

FOR A' THAT.

BY ROBERT BURNS.

I.

Is there,
  For honest poverty,
That hangs his head
  And a' that?
The coward slave
We pass him by,
  We dare be poor for a' that:
  For a' that, and a' that,
Our toils obscure,
  And a' that;
The rank is but
The guinea's stamp,
  The MAN's the gowd for a' that.

II.

What! though
On homely fare we dine,
Wear hodden grey,
  And a' that;
Give fools their silks,
And knaves their wine,
  A man's a MAN for a' that:
  For a' that, for a' that,
Their tinsel show,
  And a' that;
The honest man,
Though e'er so poor,
  Is king o' men for a' that.

III.

Ye see
Yon birkie, ca'd a lord,
Wha struts and stares,
  And a' that;

QUOI! PAUVRE HONNETE!

BY FATHER PROUT.

I.

Quoi! Pauvre honnête
  Baisser la tête?
Quoi! rougir de la sorte?
Que l'âme basse
S'éloigne et passe
Nous—soyons gueux! n'importe
Travail obscur—
  N'importe!
Quand l'or est pur
  N'importe!
Qu'il ne soit point
Marqué au coin
D'un noble rang—qu'importe!

II.

Quoiqu'on dût faire
Bien maigre chère
Et vêtir pauvre vêtement;
  Aux sots leur soie,
  Leur vin, leur joie;
Ça fait-il L'HOMME? eh, nulle-
  ment!
Luxe et grandeur—
  Qu'importe!
Train et splendeur—
  Qu'importe!
Cœurs vils et creux!
Un noble gueux
Vaut toute la cohorte!

III.

Voyez ce fat—
Un vain éclat
L'entoure, et on l'encense,
Mais après tout

Though hundreds worship
At his word,
  He's but a coof for a' that:
  For a' that, for a' that,
His riband, star,
  And a' that;
The man of
Independent mind
  Can look and laugh at a' that.

Ce n'est qu'un fou,—
Un sot, quoiqu'il en pense:
Terre et maison,
  Qu'il pense—
Titre et blazon,
  Qu'il pense—
Or et ducats,
Non! ne font pas
  La vraie indépendence!

IV.

A king
Can make a belted knight,
A marquis, duke,
  And a' that;
But an HONEST MAN
's aboon his might,
  Guid faith he manna fa' that.
For a' that, for a' that,
Their dignities,
  And a' that;
The pith o' sens,
And pride o' warth
  Are higher ranks than a' that.

IV.

Un roi peut faire
Duc, dignitaire,
Comte et marquis, journellement;
Mais ce qu'on nomme
Un HONNETE HOMME,
Le peut-il faire? eh, nullement!
Tristes faveurs!
  Réellement;
Pauvres honneurs!
  Réellement;
Le fier maintien
Des gens de bien
Leur manque essentiellement.

V.

Then let us pray
That come it may—
As come it will
  For a' that—
That sense and warth,
O'er all the earth,
  May bear the gree, and a' that!
For a' that, and a' that,
It's coming yet,
  For a' that,
That man to man,
The warld a' o'er,
Shall brothers be, for a' that.

V.

Or faisons vœu
Qu'à tous, sous peu,
Arrive un jour de jugement;—
Amis, ce jour
Aura son tour,
J'en prends, j'en prends, l'en-
  gagement.
Espoir et en-
  couragement,
Aux pauvres gens
  Soulagement;
'Lors sur la terre
Vivrons en frères,
Et librement, et sagement!

THE VOICES OF THE NIGHT.

BY H. W. LONGFELLOW.

WHEN the hours of day are number'd,
   And the voices of the night
Wake the better soul, that slumber'd,
   To a holy calm delight.

Ere the evening lamps are lighted,
   And, like phantoms grim and tall,
Shadows from the fitful fire-light
   Dance upon the parlour wall,

Then the forms of the departed
   Enter at the open door!
The beloved ones, the true-hearted,
   Come to visit me once more.

He, the young and strong, who cherish'd
   Noble longings for the strife!
By the road-side fell, and perish'd,
   Weary with the march of life!

They, the holy ones, and weakly,
   Who the cross of suffering wore,
Folded their pale hands so meekly,
   Spake with us on earth no more!

And with them the being beauteous,
   Who unto my youth was given,
More than all things else to love me,
   And is now a saint in heaven.

With a slow and noiseless footstep
   Comes that messenger divine,
Takes the vacant chair beside me,
   Lays her gentle hand in mine.

And she sits and gazes at me,
   With those deep and tender eyes,
Like the stars, so still and saint-like,
   Looking downward from the skies.

Utter'd not, yet comprehended,
   Is the spirit's voiceless prayer ;
Soft rebukes, in blessings ended,
   Breathing from those lips of air.

Oh ! though oft depress'd and lonely,
   All my fears are laid aside,
If I but remember only
   Such as they have lived and died.

LONGFELLOW was born in 1807, at Portland in Maine, U. S. He took his degree with high honours, at B wdoin College, in 1825. He studied law under his father, the Hon. Stephen Longfellow, one of the most eminent of the American lawyers. Not taking earnestly to the profession marked out for him, he travelled for three years through the chief countries of Europe, to qualify himself for the Professorship of Modern Languages, which had been offered him by his *Alma Mater*, and which he took on his return home. In 1835 he was offered the same chair, with higher emoluments attached to it, in Harvard College, Cambridge, Massachusetts, which he accepted, on condition of being allowed to travel a year through Germany and Scandinavia, in order to perfect himself in the languages and literature of northern Europe. This being agreed to by the Harvard authorities, Professor Longfellow performed his professional tour, and returned in 1836 to assume the duties of the professorship of modern languages, which he fulfilled with the most distinguished ability and success during the space of eighteen years, after which he retired into private life, taking up his residence at a short distance from the scene of his professional labours. He may be said, with Tennyson and the Brownings, to be at the head of our new school of poetry, so strongly distinguished by its irregularity and confusion of metres and extreme metaphysical tendencies from the Georgian school voted out of fashion with Byron, Moore, Scott, Campbell, and other masters of the English lyre who had formed themselves on the classic models of the reign of Queen Anne. Certainly of all the living poets of the United States none is so popular in his own country, in England, and wherever our language is read and spoken, as Longfellow. He has published over a number of years a great many short lyrics, lays, and ballads, which have been all received with more or less favour on both sides of the Atlantic ; but his longer ones, such as 'Evangeline,' 'The Golden Legend,' 'Hiawatha,' and 'The Tales of a Wayside Inn,' have won him his chief laurels, and are more likely to insure him a permanent reputation with the present and future generations. Some of the best of his minor poems he sent originally to 'Bentley's Miscellany.' In addition to his poetic productions, he has contributed many valuable prose papers to 'The United States Literary Gazette,' and 'The North American Review,' and has written a couple of small novels or romances, 'Hyperion,' and 'Kavanagh,' which are very easy and agreeable reading, if not very startling or sensational.

RICHELIEU.

CARDINAL RICHELIEU was Premier of France ;
    He was keen as a fox, and you read at a glance,
In his phiz so expressive of malice and trick,
That he'd much of the nature ascribed to Old Nick ;
If a noble e'er dared to oppose him, instead
Of confuting his lordship, he whipped off his head :
        He fixed his grim paw
        Upon church, state, and law,
With as much cool assurance as ever you saw ;
        With his satire's sharp sting
        He badgered the King,
          Bullied his brother,
          Transported his mother,
And (what is a far more astonishing case)
Not only pronounced him an ass to his face,
But made love to his Queen, and because she declined
His advances, gave out she was wrong in her mind !

Now the nobles of France, and still more the poor King,
Disliked, as was natural, this sort of thing ;
The former felt shocked that plebeian beholders
Should see a peer's head fly so oft from his shoulders,
And the latter was constantly kept upon thorns
By the Cardinal's wish to endow him with horns ;
        Thus rankling with spite,
        A party one night
Of noblemen met, and determined outright
        (So enraged were the crew)
        First, to murder Richelieu,
And, if needful, despatch all his partizans too :

Next to league with the foes
Of the King, and depose
The fat-pated monarch himself, for a fool
Rebellion ne'er uses, except as a tool.

On the night that Richelieu was thus marked out for slaughter,
He chanced to be tippling cold brandy and water
With one Joseph, a Capuchin priest—a sly dog,
And by no means averse to the comforts of grog,
As you saw by his paunch, which seemed proud to reveal
How exactly it looked like a fillet of veal.
They laughed and they quaffed, 'till the Capuchin's nose
('T was a thorough-bred snub) grew as red as a rose ;
And, whenever it chanced that his patron, Richelieu,
Cracked a joke, even though it was not very new,
And pointed his smart conversational squibs,
By a slap on Joe's back, or a peg in his ribs ;
The priest, who was wonderfully shrewd as a schemer,
Would bellow with ecstacy, "'Gad, that's a *screamer !*"
Thus they chatted away, a rare couple well met,
And were just turning up for a pious duet,
When in rushed a spy,
With his wig all awry,
And a very equivocal drop in his eye,
Who cried (looking blue
As he turned to Richelieu)
"Oh, my lord, lack-a-day !
Here's the devil to pay,
For a dozen fierce nobles are coming this way ;
One of whom, an old stager, as sharp as a lizard,
Has threatened to stick a long knife in your gizzard ;
While the rest of the traitors, I say it with pain,
Have already sent off a despatch to Spain,
To state that his Majesty's ceased to reign,
And order the troops all home again."

When his Eminence heard these tidings, "Go,"
He said, in the blandest of tones, to Joe,
"And if you can catch
The traitors' despatch,

I swear—no matter how rich it be—
You shall have, dear Joe, the very next see !"—
(*Nota bene*, whenever Old Nick is wishing
To enjoy the prime sport of parson-fishing,
He always, like Richelieu, cunning and quick,
Baits with a good fat bishoprick !)

No sooner had Joe turned his sanctified back—
I hardly need add he was off in a crack—
Than up the grand stairs rushed the murderous pack,
Whereon the sly Cardinal, tipping the wink
To the spy, who was helping himself to some drink
   At a side-table, said,
   "Tell 'em I'm dead !"
Then flew to his chamber, and popped into bed.
"What, dead ?" roared the traitors. "I stuck him myself,
With a knife which I snatched from the back-kitchen shelf,"
   Was the ready reply
   Of the quick-witted spy,—
Who in matters of business ne'er stuck at a lie.
"Huzza, then, for office !" cried one, and cried all,
"The government's ours by the Cardinal's fall,"
   And, so saying, the crew
   Cut a caper or two,
Gave the spy a new four-penny piece and withdrew.

Next day all the papers were full of the news,
Little dreaming the Cardinal's death was a *ruse ;*
In parliament, too, lots of speeches were made,
And poetical tropes by the bushel displayed ;
The deceased was compared to Ulysses and Plato,
To a star, to a cherub, an eagle, and Cato ;
And 't was gravely proposed by some gents in committee
To erect him a statue of gold in the city ;
But when an economist, caustic and witty,
   Asked, "Gentlemen, pray,
   Who is to pay ?"
The committee, as if by galvanic shock jolted,
Looked horrified, put on their castors, and bolted!
Meanwhile the shrewd traitors repaired in a bevy,
All buoyant with hope, to his Majesty's levee,

When, lo! as the King with anxiety feigned,
Was beginning to speak of the loss he'd sustained,
    In strutted Richelieu,
    And the Capuchin too,
Which made each conspirator shake in his shoe;
One whispered a by-stander, looking him through,
" By Jove, I can scarcely believe it! can you?"
Another cried, " Dam'me, I thought 't was a *do !*"
And a third muttered faintly, o'ercome by his fear,
" Talk of the devil, and he's sure to appear?"

When the King, who at first hardly trusted his eyes,
Had somewhat recovered the shock of surprise,
    He shook his thick head
    At the Cardinal, and said,
In tones in which something of anger still lurked,
" How's this? Why, God bless me, I thought you were burked!"
" Had such been my fate," quickly answered Richelieu,
" Had they made me a *subject*, the rascally crew,
My liege, they'd have soon made another of you.
Look here!" and he pulled out the nobles' despatch,
Who felt that for once they had met their match,
    And exclaiming, " 'Od rot 'em,
    The scoundrels, I've got 'em!"
Read it out to the King from the top to the bottom.

Next morning twelve scaffolds, with axes of steel,
Adorned the fore-court of the sprightly Bastille;
And at midnight twelve nobles, by way of a bed,
Lay snug in twelve coffins, each *minus* a head—
A thing not uncommon with nobles, 'tis said.
    Priest Joe got his see,
    And delighted was he,
For the bishoprick suited his taste to a T ;
And Richelieu, the stern, unforgiving, and clever,
Bullied king, church, and people, more fiercely than ever!
And the moral is this—if, conspiring in flocks,
Silly geese will presume to play tricks with a fox,
And strive by finesse to get rid of the pest,
They must always expect to come off second best!

"NOT A DRUM WAS HEARD."

FRENCH TRANSLATION BY FATHER PROUT.

I.

Ni le son du tambour... ni la marche funebre...
　Ni le feu des soldats... ne marqua son depart.—
Mais du BRAVE, à la hâte, à travers les tenebres,
　Mornes... nous portûmes le cadavre au rempart !

II.

De Minuit c'était l'heure, et solitaire et sombre—
　La lune à peine offrait un debile rayon ;
La lanterne luisait peniblement dans l'ombre,
　Quand de la bayonette on creusa le gazon.

III.

D'inutile cercueil ni de drap funeraire
　Nous ne daignâmes point entourer le HEROS;
Il gisait dans les plis du manteau militaire,
　Comme un guerrier qui dort son heure de repos.

IV.

La prière qu'on fit fut de courte durée :
　Nul ne parla de deuil, bien que le cœur fut plein !
Mais on fixait du MORT la figure adorée...
　Mais avec amertume on songeait au demain.

V.

Au demain ! quand ici on sa fosse s'apprête,
　Ou son humide lit on dresse avec sanglots,
L'ennemi orgueilleux marchera sur sa tête,
　Et nous, ses veterans, serons loin sur les flots!

VI.

Ils terniront sa gloire... on pourra les entendre,
　Nommer l'illustre MORT d'un ton amer... ou fol ;—
Il les laissera dire.—Eh ! qu'importe à sa cendre,
　Que la main d'un BRETON a confiée au sol ?

VII.

L'œuvre durait encor, quand retentit la cloche,
    Au sommet du Befroi :—et le canon lointain,
Tiré par intervalle, en annonçant l'approche,
    Signalait la fierté de l'ennemi hautain.

VIII.

Et dans sa fosse alors le mîmes lentement . . .
    Près du champ où sa gloire a été consommée :
Ne mîmes à l'endroit pienc ni monument,
    Le laissant seul à seul avec sa Renommèe !

THE ABBESS AND THE DUCHESS.

BY THOMAS HAYNES BAYLEY.

ABBESS.

WHO is knocking for admission
    At the convent's outer gate ?
Is it possible a lady
    Can be wandering here so late ?
Let me see her through the lattice,
    And her story let me hear ;
—Oh ! your most obedient, madam ;
    May I ask what brings you here ?

DUCHESS.

You will very much applaud me,
    When you hear what I have done :
I've been naughty,—I'm a peni-
    tent, and want to be a nun.
I've been treated most unfairly,
    Though 'tis said I am most fair ;
I am rich, ma'am, and a duchess,
    And my name's La Vallière.

ABBESS.

Get along, you naughty woman,
    You'll contaminate us all ;
When you touch'd the gate, I wonder
    That the convent did not fall !

11

Stop ! I think you mention'd money,—
   That is—penitence, I mean :
Let her in,—I'm *too* indulgent ;—
   Pray how are the King and Queen ?

DUCHESS.

Lady Abbess, you delight me,—
   Oh ! had Louis been as kind !
But he used me ungenteelly,·
   To my fondness deaf and blind.
Oh ! methinks that now I view him,
   With his feathers in his hat,
Hem ! beg pardon—I'm aware, ma'am,
   That I mustn't speak of *that.*

ABBESS.

Not by no means, madam, never ;'
   No—you mustn't even *think ;*
(Put your feet upon the fender,
   And here's something warm to drink :
Is it strong enough ? pray stir it :)
   What on earth *could* make you go
From a palace to a convent ?
   Come,—I'm curious to know ?

DUCHESS.

Can you wonder, Lady Abbess ?
   At the change *I* should rejoice,—
I of vanities was weary,
   And a convent was my choice.
I have had a troubled conscience,
   And court manners did condemn,
Ever since I saw King Louis
   Making eyes at Madame *M.*

ABBESS.

Oh ! I think I comprehend you :
   But take care what you're about ;
Though 'tis easy to get *in* here,
   'Taint so easy to get *out :*

You'll for beads resign your jewels,
.And your robes for garments plain ;
Ere you cut the world, remember
'Tis not cut and come again !

DUCHESS.

I am willing in a cloister,
That my days and nights should pass ;
—(This is very nice indeed, ma'am ;
If you please, another glass)—
As for courtiers, I'll hereafter
Lay the odious topic by ;
Oh! their crooked ways enough are,
For to turn a nun awry !

ABBESS.

Very proper: to the sisters
'Twould be wrong to chatter thus ;
Now and then, when snug and cosy,
'Twill do very well for *us*.
It is strange how tittle-tattle
All about the convent spreads,
When the barber from the village
Comes to shave the sisters' heads.

DUCHESS.

Do you really mean to tell me
I must lose my raven locks ?
Then I'll tie 'em up with ribbon,
And I'll keep 'em in my box :
Oh! how Louis used to praise 'em !
Hem !—I think I'll go to bed.—
Not another drop, I thank you,—
It would get into my head.

ABBESS.

Benedicite ! my daughter,
You'll be soon used to the place ;
Though at meals our only duchess,
You will have to say your *grace:*

And when none can interrupt us,
  You of courtly scenes shall tell,
When I bring a drop of comfort
  From my cellar to my cell!

DEAR WOMAN.

BY THE OLD SAILOR.

Drink, drink to dear woman, whose beautiful eye,
  Like the diamond's rich lustre, or gem in the sky,
Is beaming with rapture, full, sparkling and bright—
Here's woman, the soul of man's choicest delight.

CHORUS.

Then fill up a bumper, dear woman's our toast,
Our comfort in sorrows—in pleasure our boast.

Drink, drink to dear woman, and gaze on her smile ;
Love hides in those dimples his innocent guile :
'Tis a signal for joy, 'tis a balm for all woe ;
Here's woman, dear woman, man's heaven below.
              Then fill up a bumper, &c.

Drink, drink to dear woman, and look on her tear ;—
Is it pain ? is it grief ? is it hope ? is it fear ?
Oh ! kiss it away, and believe whilst you press,
Here's woman, dear woman ! man's friend in distress.
              Then fill up a bumper, &c.

Drink, drink to dear woman, whose exquisite form
Was never design'd to encounter the storm,
Yet should sickness assail us, or trouble o'ercast,
Here's woman, dear woman ! man's friend to the last,
              Then fill up a bumper, &c.

LOVE AND POVERTY.

LITTLE Cupid, one day, being wearied with play,
  Or weary of nothing to do,
Exclaimed with a sigh, " Now why should not I
  Go shoot for a minute or two ?"
Then snatching his bow, though Venus cried "No,"
  (Oh! Love is a mischievous boy!)
He set up a mark, in the midst of a park,
  And began his nice sport to enjoy.
Each arrow he shot—I cannot tell what'
  Was the reason—fell short by a yard,
Save one with gold head, which far better sped,
  And pierced through the heart of the card.

MORAL.

My story discovers this lesson to lovers :
  They will meet a reception but cold,
And endeavour in vain Beauty's smiles to obtain,
  Unless Love tip his arrows with gold.

PHELIM O'TOOLE'S NINE MUSE-INGS ON HIS NATIVE COUNTRY.

Tune—" Cruiskeen Lawn."

I.

LET others spend their time,
  In roaming foreign clime,
To furnish them with rhyme
    For books :
They'll never find a scene
Like Wicklow's valleys green,
Wet-nursed, the hills between,
    With brooks,
    Brooks, brooks,
Wet-nursed, the hills between,
    With brooks!

Oh! if I had a station
In that part of creation,
I'd study the first CAWS *like rooks—*
        Rooks, rooks—
I'd study the first CAWS *like rooks!*

II.

Oh! how the morning loves
To climb the Sugar-Loaves,*
And purple their dwarf groves
        Of heath!
While cottage smoke below
Reflects the bloomy glow,
As up it winds, and slow,
        Its wreath—,
        Wreath, wreath—
As up it winds, and slow,
        Its wreath!
Oh! how a man does wonder him,
When he has the big CONE-UNDER-HIM,
And asked to guess his home beneath—
        'Neath, 'neath—
And asked to guess his home beneath!

III.

And there's the Dargle deep,
Where breezeless waters sleep,
Or down their windings creep
        With fear;
Lest, by their pebbly tread,
They shake some lily's head,
And cause, untimely shed,
        A tear—
        Tear, tear—
And cause, untimely shed,
        A tear.

---

* Two hills in the county of Wicklow, so called from their conical shape.

Oh ! my native Dargle,
Long may you rinse and gargle
Your rocky throat with stream so clear—
    Clear, clear—
Your rocky throat with stream so clear !

IV.

And there is Luggelaw,
A gem without a flaw,
With lake, and glen, and straw,
    So still ;
The new moon loves to sip
Its dew with her young lip,
Then takes a ling'ring trip
    O'er hill—
    Hill, hill—
Then takes a ling'ring trip
    O'er hill !
Oh ! hungry bards might dally,
For ever in this valley,
And always get their fancy's fill—
    Fill, fill,
And always get their fancy's fill !

V.

And there's the " *Divil's Glin,*"
The Devil ne'er was in,
Nor anything like sin,
    To blight :
The morning hurries there
To scent the myrtle air ;
She'd stop if she might dare,
    Till night—
    Night, night—
She'd stop if she might dare,
    Till night !
Oh ! ye glassy streamlets,
That bore the rocks like gimlets,
There's nothing like your crystal bright,
    Bright, bright,
There's nothing like your crystal bright !

VI.

And there's Ovoca's vale,
And classic Annadale,
Where Psyche's gentle tale
    Was told :
Where MOORE'S fam'd waters meet,
And mix a draught more sweet
Than flow'd at Pindus' feet
    Of old—
      Old, old,—
Than flow'd at Pindus' feet
    Of old !
Oh ! all it wants is whiskey,
To make it taste more frisky ;
Then ev'ry drop would be worth gold,—
    Gold, gold,—
Then ev'ry drop would be worth gold !

VII.

And there's the Waterfall,
That lulls its summer hall
To sleep with voice as small
    As bee's :
But when the winter rills
Burst from the inward hills,
A rock-rent thunder fills
    The breeze,—
      Breeze, breeze,—
A rock-rent thunder fills
    The breeze !
Oh ! if the LAND *was taught her*
To FALL *as well as* WATER,
How much it would poor tenants please,—
    Please, please,—
How much it would poor tenants please !

---

* The residence of the late Mrs. Henry Tighe, the charming authoress
of " Psyche."

VIII.

And if you have a mind
For sweet, sad thoughts inclined,
In Glendalough you'll find
    Them nigh :
Kathleen and Kevin's tale
So sorrows that deep vale,
That birds all songless sail
    Its sky,—
    Sky, sky,—
That birds all songless sail
    Its sky !
Oh ! cruel Saint was Kevin
To shun her eyes' blue heaven,
Then drown her in the lake hard by,—
    By, by,—
Would I have sarved her so ?—not I !

IX.

And there's—But what's the use
Of praising Scalp or Douce ?*—
The wide world can't produce
    Such sights :
So I will sing adieu
To Wicklow's hills so blue,
And green vales glittering through
    Dim lights,—
    Lights, lights,—
And green vales glittering through
    Dim lights !
Oh ! I could from December
Until the next November
MUSE *on this way both days and nights,—*
    Nights, nights,—
MUSE *on this way both days and nights !*

---

* Famous features of the mountain scenery of Wicklow.

INVITATION TO AN EVENING WALK.

BY J. A. WADE.

"There is hardly anything gives me a more sensible delight than the enjoyment of a cool still evening, after the uneasiness of a hot sultry day."—
SPECTATOR.

COME up the hill, to meet the moon—
    She'll leave her daylight slumber soon,
And over mountain, over dale,
Weep her dewy lustre pale!

Come up the hill, and hear the flowers
Rustling in their heathy bowers;
Closing some, with close of day,
Waking more to moonlight ray!

Come up the hill, and list the breeze,
Full of mingled melodies,
Rising from the glens below,
Faintly sweet, as up we go!

Come up the hill, and smell the breath
Of the purple mountain-heath,
Sweeter than the painted flowers
Rear'd in artificial bowers!

Come up the hill, and joy with me,
In the mazy scenery
That below is sleeping calm,
Smiling beauty, breathing balm!

Come up the hill, and gaze with me
On the moon-besilver'd sea,
That so gently rocking moves
To cradle the young light it loves!

Come up the hill,—'tis nearer to
The fields of Heav'n, azure blue,
Where the spheral minstrels play
Music wild and sweet, for aye!

Come up the hill,—'t will give to thee
A view of deep eternity,
That in the valley's shorten'd ken
Is never known to minds of men!

Come up the hill—the waterfall
Is emblem, true to thee, of all:
'T is tranquil where it flows near Heaven—
'T is down, with Man,—its peace is riven!

WADE was an Irishman, well known at the time he contributed to ' Bentley's Miscellany ' as the author of the words and music of the celebrated drawing-room song of ' Meet me by Moonlight,' and joint author with Doctor Crotch, of Oxford, of an elaborate historical and critical work on English Music, published by Chapple, of Bond Street. He has been dead about twenty years.

THE EVENING STAR.

BY H. W. LONGFELLOW.

THE night is come, but not too soon;
    And sinking silently,—
All silently,—the little Moon
    Drops down behind the sky.

There is no light in earth or heaven
    But the pale light of stars;
And the first watch of night is given
    To the red planet Mars.

Is it the tender star of love?
    The star of love and dreams?
Oh no! from that blue tent above
    A hero's armour gleams.

And earnest thoughts within me rise
    When I behold afar,
Suspended in the evening skies,
    The shield of that red star.

O star of strength! I see thee stand
   And smile upon my pain ;
Thou beckonest with thy mailed hand,
   And I am strong again.

Within my soul there shines no light
   But the pale light of stars ;
I give the first watch of the night
   To the red planet Mars !

The star of the unconquer'd will,
   He rises in my breast,—
Serene and resolute, and still,
   And calm, and self-possess'd.

And thou, too, whosoe'er thou art,
   That readest this brief psalm,
As one by one thy hopes depart,
   Be resolute and calm.

O! fear not in a world like this,
   And thou shalt know ere long,
Know how sublime a thing it is
   To suffer and be strong!

THE FOREST TREE.

BY J. B. T.

Hail to the lone old forest tree,
   Though past his leafy prime !
A type of England's past is he,—
   A tale of her olden time.
He has seen her sons, for a thousand years,
   Around him rise and fall ;
But well his green old age he wears,
   And still survives them all.
      Then long may his safeguard the pride and care
         Of our children's children be ;
      And long may the axe and tempest spare
         The lone old forest tree !

The Norman baron his steed has rein'd,
   And the pilgrim his journey stay'd,
And the toil-worn serf brief respite gain'd
   In his broad and pleasant shade :
The friar and forester loved it well ;
   And hither the jocund horn,
And the solemn tone of the vesper bell,
   On the evening breeze were borne.

Friar and forester, lord and slave,
   Lie mouldering, side by side,
In the dreamless sleep of a nameless grave,
   Where revelling earthworms hide :
And Echo no longer wakes at the sound
   Of bugle or vesper chime ;
For castle and convent are ivy-bound
   By the ruthless hand of Time.

But gentle and few, with the stout old tree,
   Have the spoiler's dealings been ;
And the brook, as of old, is clear and free,
   And the turf beneath as green.
Thus Nature has scatter'd on every hand
   Her lessons, since earth began,
And long may her sylvan teacher stand,
   A check to the pride of man.
      And long may his safeguard the pride and care
        Of our children's children be ;
      Long, long may the axe and tempest spare
        The lone old forest tree !

KUBLAI KHAN; OR, THE SIEGE OF KINSAI.

CANTO I

I.

YOU'VE heard, no doubt, of Kublai Khan,
That terrible man,
Who overran
The Eastern world in days of yore,
With steps of steel, in paths of gore ?
Could there be brought together but all
The bones of those his armies slew,
They would vie in bulk with the China wall,
Or fill up the great canal of Yu.

II.

He swore the Chinese realm should fall,
So he came at the head of his Tartar hordes,
Who all carried besoms as well as their swords ;
And he pitched his tents before the wall.
As soon as the following morn had birth,
He led them along in their war array ;
A part of the wall was formed of earth,
So they plied their besoms and swept it away.
Then Kublai Khan gave the word of command,
And they all poured into the Central Land.

III.

What deeds were done, is it need I say,
As on their course they wound ?
What roofs were fired, what fields laid waste,
What armies slain, what hearths disgraced,
What lovely dames were borne away,
What plainer dames were drowned ?
Oh ! woe in the rear, and death in the van,
Were ever attendant on Kublai Khan.

IV.

Fierce Kublai came to great Kinsai,
Where the Emperor dwelt, and his wives and kin,
In a beautiful palace, with rich inlay
Of gold without and of pearls within ;

And with terrible groups of his Tartar troops
He blackened the hills and the plains around;
And he vowed a vow, that its towers should bow
And its walls be scattered along the ground.

V.

But when the Emperor saw
    Proud Kublai's banners flaunting,
He was struck with amaze and awe,
    And felt that his heart was wanting;
And slipping his ribs, so august and imperial,
Into a jacket of common material,
That none might suppose him a person of note,
He got from the city by night in a boat.
But he left his queen and wives behind,
    And bade them take good care
That the insolent Tartar hordes should find
    A warm reception there.

VI.

Now it's fit you be told, that this Emperor bold,
    Besides his Empress fair,
Had twenty wives, of properest lives,
As blithe and busy as bees in hives,
    Endeavouring still,
    His hours to fill
With frolic and merriment fit to kill
The hollow-eyed phantom Care.
    There were An, and Nan, and Fan,
        And Jin, and Din, and Sin, too,
    With names that I neither can,
        Nor would wish to enter into.
And again, and besides these beautiful brides,
Who sat in due order at both of his sides,
    Furthermore he possessed,
    So might count himself blessed,
More than any that dwelt in the East or the West;
A regiment of ladies, all chosen and pick'd,
Whose hearts were brave, whose discipline strict;

All mounted on steeds of superior breeds,
And furnished with bows and brass-pointed reeds,
And swords ever ready for martial deeds.

VII.

The Empress was colonel of this gallant troop,
And the wives were the majors, the captains, lieutenants,
And ensigns that bore the invincible pennants,
       To which every foe,
       It seemed to be so,—
Was in gallantry bound to stoop.
So Sergeant Shug called over the names,
And the Empress harangued her regiment of dames:
Set out before them, in learned display,
The danger that threatened the city Kinsai;
       The myriads of Tartars
       Prepared to be martyrs,
       Rather than yield
       An inch of the field,
       Or move from the wall
       Till the town should fall.

VIII.

"So you see, my girls," said the beautiful colonel,
       "We go forth in strong quest
       Of difficult conquest:
Should they beat women the shame is infernal,
But, if they be beaten, our glory eternal.
       So let us be drest
       In our holiday best,
       With silks of bright hues,
       All embroidered, for nails,
       With the smallest of shoes,
       And the longest of nails;
       With patches of pink
       On our lips and our cheeks,
       And eye-brows of ink
       Laid in delicate streaks;
       These charms as I think,
       And the swords we shall hold,
       Will make the foe shrink,
       Be they never so bold."

IX.

"Now Major Slo, as your charger is fleet,
You shall lead the advance when we go forth to meet
The foe in the field, and Major Van
Shall bring up the rear as well as she can.
  There is work for you, fair Captain Slae,
And for Captain Shi, so forward still;
We have many to capture, and many to kill;
  But let not numbers our hearts dismay."

X.

Thus the Empress spoke to her female bands,
And the male troops also received her commands;
The male bands answered with warlike whoops,
But the hope of the town was the female troops.

CANTO II.

I.

I do not say how the siege begun,
What works were tried, what deeds were done,
What engines used, what flags upborne,
What breaches made, what trousers torn,
What throats were cut, what limbs were hack'd,
What bodies were crushed, what skulls were crack'd,
Because I don't know, and that's the fact.
But deeds of hand, and deeds of heart,
Valorous deeds upon either part,
Countless losses of lords and wives;
Walls in ruins, and silks in rags,
Terrible engines, flouting flags,
And all that belongs to a fearful fray,
You may understand without my say.
The walls though battered, were not thrown down;
And the Empress yet retained the town.

II.

Oh, ne'er had a general yet been seen
    In all the Central Land,
        Who in skill or in luck,
        Or in plenty of pluck,

Was at all to compare
With that Empress so fair.
Nor there, as I ween, had a troop ever been,
That might vie with her beautiful band.
She gallantly held the great Kinsai,
And harassed the foe both night and day;
They scarce could remain in the neighbouring plain,
Nor were safe in the hills and the valleys;
For in her defence there was so much of sense,
And so much keen wit in her sallies.

III.

Let us declare it if nobody knows,
Ladies are not such contemptible foes:
A thousand at once, and all of them chattering,
'Mid horses' hoofs clattering, pattering, spattering,
Like tilters of Eglintown all running at a ring,
Killing and scattering,
Bruising and battering,
Maiming and shattering—
Not to be flattering,
Of primal confusion they teach you a smattering.

IV.

Daily were prisoners brought into the city,
Tied by their pigtails together in pairs;
The handsome ones won on the empress's pity,
The plain ones were hung in the crescents and squares.
She offered rewards for the heads of the lords,
And the commoners, too, of the Tartar hordes.
And her soldiers oft brought them by twos and by twos,
Slung over their shoulders thus tied by their queues;
Or, sometimes a lady, with little remorse,
Arranged them in pairs o'er the neck of her horse.

V.

Now months had passed on in storming and sallying,
Fancy-phlebotomy, running, and rallying;
In hurling stones,
And in throwing darts;
In breaking bones,
And in piercing hearts:

The troops of the Timour,
  By hands and by knees,
Endeavouring to climb o'er
  The walls of the Chinese!
And the brave Chinese band,
  Ensconced in snug quarters,
Hurling hot pitch and sand
  On the heads of the Tartars:
Till the Tartars confessed, at least there in the thick of it,
That the siege of Kinsai they were heartily sick of it;
And it made Kublai Khan very fierce and splenetic,
To find it thus act as a Tartar emetic.

VI.

So the terrible Kublai swore
  That by storm he would take the city;
And wash the streets with the inmates' gore
  Without remorse or pity.
That lord nor page, that youth nor age
  Should meet with a moment's quarter:
And that proud Kinsai should be all laid low,
  And the share of the plough should over it go,
    To bury its bricks,
    Its stones and sticks,
  Its marble, mud, and mortar.

VII.

As Kublai pronounced his decree so proudly,
His blood-hungry Tartars applauded him loudly;
They clattered their swords, they struck their gongs,
The air was griped with the crudest songs;
It was beaten with shouts, and shattered with laughter,
And the echoes were ill for a month thereafter!
The broad river quaked as it rolled on its way,
And the red flags were wind-shaken over Kinsai.

VIII.

The Empress heard the clatter and jar,
As 'twas borne by the breath of the breeze from afar,
  Like a peal of tipsy thunder;

So, knowing that something must be in the wind,
With her beautiful lips she most wrathfully grinned ;
She seized her silk buckler, her breastplate she pinned,
 With a china-crape shawl doubled under;
In an elegant bow tied the string of her helmet,
And swore when the Tartars came they should be well met:
Then with eloquent speech to her ladies appealed,
And rode at the head of them forth to the field.

IX.

So on went the ladies, till, meeting the Tartars,
 They poured forth upon them a volley of arrows,
 As thick as small shot on a regiment of sparrows :
And then they turned round, and made back to their quarters.
   The Khan greatly marvelled ;
    " Oh, none of them *are* veiled,"
Cried he, " and what beauties they are every soul of them !
    Draw not a bow—
    Lay not one of them low ;
    For the moon and the sun,
    I would not part with one ;
But forward, my Tartars, and capture the whole of them.
 Seize me alive every dear little beauty;
 Yours is Kinsai if you do me this duty ;
 These shall alone be my share of the booty."

X.

Then onward they all hurried, (O for quick metre !)
The Tartars were fleet, but the ladies were fleeter ;
If those seemed to fly along, these seemed to shoot,
And they got to the city in spite of pursuit.

XI.

Now first in the chase was the amorous Khan ;
No thoughts from the moment the flight began
   Had entered his brain,
   Except to obtain
The prize upon which he had fixed his mind.
His passion and eagerness made him so blind
That he did not perceive how his troops fell behind.

And being well mounted,
   He rode quite alone;
And recklessly counted
   The quarry his own,
As he dashed through the gate
Very proud and elate.
But he found his mistake in another half minute,
When the guards shut the portal, and closed him within it.
Then the ladies came back very joyous and gay,
And the Khan was their prisoner there in Kiusai.

CANTO III.

I.

The Empress sat on the Emperor's throne,
   And the Emperor's sceptre swayed:
She had slipped on his trousers, too, over her own,
And she gave her commands in the despot's tone;
      And every vassal
      Within the castle
   Her delegate voice obeyed.
Oh! a delicate voice was her delegate voice,
And every one made it a matter of choice
   To do her behest as soon as 'twas spoken,
      With an eagerness owing
      In part to his knowing
That else every one of his bones would be broken,
   Say naught of his being flayed.

II.

The Empress sat on the Emperor's throne,
   And sent six ladies the Khan to call;
" For, tell him," said she, " I've a bit of a bone
   I would pick with him here in my audience hall."
The Khan was pleased when he heard that say,
For he'd tasted nothing since break of day.
   And he went to the chamber to find the bone;
      But when he came there
      The table was bare,
And so the poor Khan had none.

III.

He strode through the room nowise forlorn,
  His step was bold and free ;
Although he was not in America born,
  Yet a-merry-Khan was he.
Round his ankles, and waist, and neck he bore
Chain-cable enough for a seventy-four ;
    Yet proudly he paced along :
And as all such Eastern heroes do
When they find themselves in a bit of a stew,
      To keep up his pluck
      In spite of ill luck,
    Consoled himself with a song.

IV.

But whilst the Khan in his fetters,
  Marched up the hall with pride,
Where the ladies, who proved his betters,
  Were ranged upon either side ;
If his little red eyes stood out from his head,
It was not with rage, it was not with dread,
It was not with hate, it was not with scorn,
    It was only with joy and a large surprise
At the beautiful sight, such as since he was born
  Had never before met his little red eyes ;
And he smiled as he glanced, with his eyes full of flames,
At beautiful Empress and beautiful dames.

V.

The Empress so bold, and her ladies so fair,
  Were exceedingly taken with Kublai Khan ;
They liked his person, they liked his air,
  And, to tell it in brief, they liked the man.
His jaws were wide, his forehead narrow,
He seemed a person of pith and marrow ;
And with eyes so red, and beard so yellow,
They thought him a very delectable fellow.

VI.

Yet the Empress thought it fit and right
To look very grave at the Tartar knight,

Because, by-and-by, by way of a finis,
She purposed to hang his Tartar highness.
She meant he should hang, his neck reposing
In a silken twist of her own composing ;
And so she considered the way to behave
Would be, for the present, to look very grave.

VII.

"Kublai Khan," the Empress said,
　　In a very impressive and solemn manner,
"Over our fertile land you've sped,
　　With bloody sword and flouting banner :
You have seized our maidens, you've slaughter'd our youth,
　　You have cut off the heads of our aged sires,
　　You've spoiled our cities and fields with fires ;
Nor infants in arms could move ye to ruth :
　　You have poisoned our rivers, and drained our vats,
　　And made short work of our rice and rats.
The punishment, then, the law requires,
　　Is burning to death with red-hot wires ;
But since you are brave, we all agree
Only to hang you on yonder tree.
Is there anything, Khan, you can urge, of force
To hinder the law in its simple course ?"

VIII.

Kublai Khan he stroked his beard,
And said, very quietly, "Who's afeard ?"
He swelled up his cheek before he could speak,
And scratched his nose, so knowing and sleek ;
To seem at his ease he made an endeavour,
　　But felt Kinsai was a comical place ;
His eyes looked redder and harder than ever,
　　And stood rather further out from his face.
His case was queer ; however 'twas good
To put the best face on it he could ;
Nor had he just then a better at hand
　　Than that with his two little hard red eyes,
And a thick, long beard, so yellow and grand,
　　Which gave him a look very fierce and wise.

IX.

"Dear lady," at last he thus began,
    And seemed by his smile to be free from fear,—
"We oftentimes put the beer in a can,
    But I see you're for putting the Khan in a bier.
You must do as you please, most lovely flower,
For Kublai Khan is in your power.
      It was rather unwise
      To be caught by those eyes,
So green in their hue, and so small in their size;
      No doubt on't :—but there,—
      I fell into the snare,
And it's often our lot to be killed by the fair;
      So—thus in Kinsai—
      I have only to say
That if you adjudge me death my due,
I am proud, dear lady, to die for you;
But an' if you had not so fierce a will,
To live for you I'd be prouder still.

X.

"That I've wasted your fields and towns with fires,
    And filled your streams with a sanguine dye,
That I've cut the throats of your youths and sires,
    And eaten your rats, I can't deny :
But never, believe it, most beautiful elf,
Would Kublai Khan hurt such as yourself."

XI.

Now how could it be but the Empress fair,
    Now how could it be but her ladies bright,
Now how could it be but each one there,
    Should be touched at these words of the Tartar knight?
So they talked for awhile in an under breath,
      And to do what they could
      For his comfort and good,
Agreed to accord him his choice of a death.
Whether to die by maiming and mangling,
Drowning, burning, or choking and dangling.

And when the Khan bold answer made,
  And honestly owned that, if he might,
(Since fighting e'er had been his trade,)
  He'd rather prefer to fall in fight.
The ladies acceded to this proposition,
And choosing three heroes of noble condition,
To slaughter Khan Kublai they gave them commission.

XII.

These heroes were tall and terrible chaps,
  Of warlike fame untarnished ;
Two peacock's feathers in each of their caps,
  And their helms were of pasteboard varnished ;
Their shoulder-guards and breast-plates fair
Were made of cotton, and stuffed with hair ;
Their steps were fleet, and their arms were strong,
Their eyes were fierce, and their beards were long ;
And each, besides a bow and a mace,
  Carried a terrible silken shield,
Pictured whereon was a hideous face,
  To fright the foeman out of the field.
Each at his back a banneret bore ;
  Through a hollow bamboo its staff was thrust ;
And of two placards, behind and before,
  That called him " Brave," and *this* " Robust."

XIII.

The chosen ground was the palace lawn ;
The fence was framed, and the swords were drawn :
The three from the East, the Khan from the West,
To meet in the middle their steps addressed.
  Side by side advanced the three,
    All heroes of one stamp ;
  Side by side, and knee by knee,
    With very deliberate tramp.
When they almost met their Tartar foe,
  Who towards them came at swifter pace,
They stopped at once in a fearful row,
  And held their shields out towards his face ;
Then, working secret wires within,
  Made the terrible faces squint and grin ;

And they trusted by this decisive plan
To frighten away the Tartar Khan.

XIV.

But lo! and behold! the Tartar Khan
  Was not prepared to take the hint;
He looked at the shields, that fearless man!
  And "Ho!" said he, "you may grin and squint!"
Then in both his hands his sword raised he,
To shatter the shields of the warlike three.
This showed a heart on the Tartar's part,
  For which the three were not prepared:
They stepped in a crack some paces back,
  And opened their mouths and eyes, and stared.
"Why stay we here?" cried valiant Fli,
  "Oh, fly we hence!" cried dauntless Flee,
    And in mighty dismay
    Shun-Fo ran away;
I know not which might soonest hie,
  Or which was the fleetest of all the three.

XV.

Their flags were all to ribbons torn,
  By the current of air, so fast their flight;
The peacock plumes from their caps were borne,
  And they showed no feather except the white.
And as they ran, the bold placard
That proclaimed them "brave" was their shield and guard.
Their flight had turned it towards the Khan,
Who never perceived they were brave till they ran.

XVI.

The Tartar bold pursued their flight,
  And cleft them down from crown to heel;
And his eyes gleamed bright with his grim delight,
  As then on his queue he wiped his steel,
He bowed to the Queen and her ladies fair;
  His face was flecked with spirts of gore:
"We'll leave these three to the doctor's care,
  And now, sweet Queen, I am ready for more!"

XVII.

Three more were brought, and he slaughtered them,
  And then came five, and those he slew ;
As you with a knife cut a floweret's stem,
  As easily he chopped men in two.
Then seven, and nine, came against him all ;
  He hack'd the whole of them limb from limb :
And dwarfs so strong, and giants so tall ;
  But giants and dwarfs were alike to him.
The blood of his foes dripped down from his nose,
  And made his beard in a gory trim ;
And at every blow as he killed a foe,
  He bowed to the ladies, and smiled so grim.

XVII.

Then the sons and sires, the brothers and cousins
  Of those sweet ladies came into the lists,
And he slaughtered them all by tens and dozens ;
  You'd think that the work would have sprained his wrists.
But Kublai Khan was stout and willing,
And not to be easily tired of killing :
He cut off their heads, spare time to amuse,
And roped them, like onions, up by their queues.

XIX.

When the Queen and her troop of China-roses
  Beheld the fate of the lords and masters,
  Those stars of fight, those China-asters,
Thus snipped by the Khan, and bound in posies,
They were filled with a measureless admiration,
Of the terrible chief of the Tartar nation.
And the Empress spoke, and said, " O Khan,
Since you've shown yourself such a valorous man,
And slain the prime of our warriors thus,
You will not be afraid of a match with us.
So whet you your sword on the edge of your shield,
Till I and my ladies come into the field."

XX.

Kublai bowed with infinite grace,
　　Smiled in a very bewitching way,
Wiped the blood from off his face,
　　And made reply to the Empress gay :
" O lady bold, O lady bright,
　　To slaughter men I have little care ;
Send more of such if you think it right :
　　But I draw not sword on dames so fair.
A match with you and your ladies sweet,
Is what would make my bliss complete ;
But that which thus would sweeten life
Is a match in love, and not in strife."

XXI.

The Queen and her beautiful ladies laughed ;
　　Should the Khan be killed, they would all be sorrier :
They ever had loved the warrior-craft,
　　And it made them love the crafty warrior.
They whispered some blame of the Emperor's flight,
And declared that that ought to have kindled their spite ;.
So the Empress bowed low, with most ladylike ease,
And answered, " Brave Khan, be it just as you please."

XXII.

Then he danced them by fours, by tens, and by scores,
Over charcoal pots that were set at the doors ;
　　The town of Kinsai was full of delight ;
　　　　Oh ! a wonderful man
　　　　Was the Tartar Khan,
And he conquered in love when he couldn't in fight.

LINES TO MY DOUBLE-BARRELLED GUN, BROWN BESS.

I HAVE a sweet friend, and her name is Brown Bess !
　　Who often in raptures I ardently press,
And as on my shoulder she'll rest or recline,
I glory to think that I can call her mine.

Her voice how it echoes through valley and grove,
When I make her repeat the fond fire of her love,
It comes from her bosom in one noble strain,
Where, save to please me, it would ever remain.

She's tall, and she's slender, with scarce any waist,
And, what is most curious, she hath *but one breast;*
If *there* I should touch her in play or in sport,
It is strange, she's the *first* one to *spread the report.*

And, oddly enough, she is not flesh and blood!
How could she? for sulphur and nitre's her food!
Her body is iron, her head it is wood!
But she does as I bid her, she's *true* and she's *good.*

If she's well-directed, how lofty's her aim,
Objects most exalted she will for you claim,
Whatever you wish for she'll bring down with death,
Though she *wastes* all her *strength,* and *gives up her last breath.*

Her soul is for pleasure, dull life's her disgust,
If idle she's kept she will spoil and will rust,
She seeks not the banquet, or mirth-swelling hall,
Still—*there's none more adapted, or fit for a ball.*

She's most temperate, too, e'en to a moral,
Although she doth keep both a *flask* and a *barrel.*
Ay, *barrels;* but she, like the publican knaves,
Keeps these for *the pigeons, that come for their graves.*

Miss Steam has an appetite always so large,
Whilst each meal for Bessy, is but a *small charge;*
Then *drink* costs her nothing, she loves to be *dry,*
Whilst steam must have *pipes, and a constant supply.*

Then Steam is so *flighty,* and Bess so docile.
With Steam you can't travel in surety one mile:
With Bess you may go through the land, far and wide,
With her under your arm, the same as a bride.

Again, as a bride, should you *movingly press*
My Bess—the soft pressure—will *swiftly confess*
The *warmth of her feelings;* her *sensitive frame*
Will *quickly* evince in *the strength of her flame.*

The young lordling's plaything, the gamekeeper's pride!
The night-watcher's friend, and the freebooter's bride!
The smuggler's *chere amie*, the bushranger's wife,
Who would part with her only on parting with life.

Sweet nymph! she would coax the "birds off the bushes,"
As oft she hath done both blackbirds and thrushes.
Then why should you wonder at my tender love,
When a *cock* or a *cap-on*, she also *can move?*

Forgive this long story, but I had my cue,
In laying down all her perfections—for you,
There's two I forgot, she's *allied* to famed *Lock(e)*,
And *doth really belong to an excellent stock.*

Good reader! I bow, and exhausted retire,
And hope you will think that I have not missed fire,
But brought *down my game*, and each time *hit the mark*,
And *handled* my *gun well*—albeit on a *lark.*

J. ST. L. MC. C.

THE ASCENTS OF MONT BLANC.

BY ALBERT SMITH.

WHEN Jacques Balmat from his party was thrown,
He found out the summit untaught and alone,
And when he returned to his doctor with glee,
He said, "For your care you shall go up with me,"
With your baton so sharp, tra la!

The next who tried was De Saussure, we're told,
Who climbed in a full suit of scarlet and gold:
Whilst poor M. Bourrit, four times driven back,
In dudgeon returned to Geneva—good lack!
With his baton so sharp, tra la!

Woodley, Clissold, and Beaufoy, each thought it no lark,
And were followed by Jackson, and Sherwell and Clarke.
Then Fellowes and Hawes by a new passage went,
And avoided the dangers of Hamel's ascent,
With their batons so sharp, tra la!

Brave Auldjo next was pulled over a bridge
Of ice-poles laid on the glacier's ridge ;
You will see all his wonderful feats, if you look
At the views drawn by Harding, and placed in his book,
   And his baton so sharp, tra la!

Full forty gentlemen, wealthy and bold,
Have climbed up in spite of the labour and cold ;
But of all that number there lives not one
Who speaks of the journey as very good fun.
   With their batons so sharp, tra la!

ALBERT SMITH, one of the most famous light litterateurs of his time, was born on the 24th May, 1816, and died 23rd May, 1860. He was buried at Brompton Cemetery. He was originally brought up to the medical profession, and took a regular London degree. In preparation for the latter he studied a couple of years in Paris, lived in the Quartier Latin, and became acquainted with all the peculiarities of the French student life, and perfected himself in the French language. He was one of the original contributors to *Punch*, his first paper in that successful publication having been the ' Physiology of the Medical Student.' His first dramatic venture was ' Aladdin,' a burlesque or extravaganza, in conjunction with Mr. Charles Kenny. In his next piece of the same description, he had for his collaborateurs Mr. T. Taylor and Mr. C. Kenny. His third, ' The Enchanted Horse,' was his joint production with Mr. Taylor. He was also the author, or associated author, of ' Puss in Boots,' ' Whittington and his Cat,' ' Novelty Fair,' ' Esmeralda,' ' Cinderella,' and other similar dramatic extravaganzas, all of which, without exception, had a great run in their day. He wrote five novels, the chief of which appeared first in ' Bentley's Miscellany,'— ' The Adventures of Mr. Ledbury,' ' The Scattergood Family,' ' Christopher Tadpole,' ' The Pottleton Legacy,' and ' The Marchioness of Brinvilliers.' Besides his ' Physiology of the Medical Student,' which was considered one of the best things in the early numbers of *Punch*, he wrote brief physiologies of ' London Evening Parties,' ' The Gent,' ' The Ballet Girl,' ' The Flirt,' &c., which amused the town as much as any of his more elaborate productions. The greatest successes, however, of his rapid and versatile genius and most indefatigable industry, were his ' Ascent of Mont Blanc,' his ' Overland Mail,' and his ' Chinese Exhibition,' which entertainments he brought out successively at the Egyptian Hall, sustaining them himself, sole author and actor of their wonderfully humourous medleys of prose and verse, and realizing by them a large fortune. He had previously seen everything which he described, having ascended Mont Blanc, and made rapid journeys to Cairo, Alexandria, Constantinople, and the Celestial Empire. He married a short time before his death, the beautiful and talented Miss Keeley, eldest daughter of Mr. and Mrs. Keeley, the celebrated comic actor and actress, by whom he had no issue. The marriage took place in August, 1859, nine months before his decease, which latter occurred but one day before the forty-fourth anniversary of his birthday.

A LETTER FROM AN OLD COUNTRY HOUSE.

Dear Arthur,

'Tis so very slow,
I can't tell what to do,
And so I've got a pen and ink,
And mean to write to *you!*
You know how intervening space
I reckon'd, bit by bit,
Until this time arrived : and now
It has not proved a hit!

'Tis very well. The house is old,
With an enormous hall ;
I think what learned architects
Elizabethan call.
With mullion'd windows, shutters vast,
And mystic double floors,
And hollow wainscots, creaking stairs,
And four-horse-power doors.

And authors who could write a book
Might subjects find in hosts—
Of civil wars, and wrongful heirs,
And murders, bones, and ghosts.
And this you know 's all very well
'Neath a bright noontide sun ;
But when the dismal nightfall comes,
'Tis anything but fun.

I'll own,—but this is *entre nous*,—
   I was in such a fright
At my gaunt bed-room, that my eyes
   I never closed all night
When first I lay there : for each thing
   Associations brought
Of bygone crimes, and mouldy deeds,
   With frightful interest fraught.

'Twas like the room where Tennyson
   Made Mariana stay—
A chamber odorous with time,
   And damp, and chill decay.
The moon look'd in with ghastly stare
   On those who haply slept :
And 'gainst the casement all night long
   Some cypress branches swept.

And tapestry was on the walls—
   Dull work that did engage
Fair fingers, fleshless long ago,—
   Now dim and black with age.
And when I trod upon the floor,
   It groan'd and wheezed and creak'd,
And made such awful noises that
   One's very temples reck'd.

And in the middle of the night,
   Half dozing in my bed,
Although beneath the counterpane
   I buried deep my head,
I saw most ghastly phantom forms
   Of mildew'd men and girls;
With axe-lopp'd heads, and steel-pierced breasts,
   And long gore-dabbled curls.

I was so glad when morning came,
   For then all fear was o'er.
I slept 'till Fox had three times changed
   The water at my door.

13

And when I reach'd the breakfast-room,
  The eggs and game were gone,
And I was tied to marmalade
  And haddock all alone.

Now nothing can make up for this,
  Nor horse, nor game, nor gun;
Nor yet charades, night after night,
  Until they lose their fun.
Nor Emily's contralto voice,
  And dark and floating eyes:
Nor that young Countess—*belle de nuit?*
  Nor Julia's smart replies.

I long to be in town again,
  For all the word recalls
The raptures of a private box,
  Or comfort of the stalls.
Those cozy dinners at the club;
  Those rich *Regalia* fumes;
A whirl at Weippert's; or perchance
  A supper at our rooms.

So tell the boys I'm coming back,
  No more this year to roam,
(Don't send the birds to Collingwood;
  He never dines at home).
The second dinner-bell has rung,
  I'll finish then forthwith,
And so
      Believe me to remain,
          Yours always,
              ALBERT SMITH.

THE MAN WITH A TUFT.

BY THOMAS HAYNES BAYLEY.

I.

I EVER at college
  From commoners shrank,
Still craving the knowledge
  Of people of rank:

In my glass my lord's ticket
 I eagerly stuffed ;
And all called me " Riquet,"
 The man with the Tuft.

II.

My patron ! most noble !
 Of highest degree !
Thou never canst probe all
 My homage for thee !
Thy hand—oh ! I'd lick it,
 Though often rebuff'd ;
And still I am " Riquet,"
 The man with the Tuft !

III.

Too oft the great, shutting
 Their doors on the bold,
Do deeds that are cutting,
 Say words that are cold !
Through flattery's wicket
 My body I've stuff'd
And *so* I am " Riquet,"
 The man with the Tuft !

IV.

His lordship's a poet,
 Enraptured I sit ;
He's dull—(and I know it)—
 I call him a wit !
His fancy, I nick it,
 By me he is puff'd,
And still I am " Riquet,"
 The man with the Tuft !

A MODERN ECLOGUE.

" —— Non tu in triviis, indocte, solebas,
Stridenti miserum stipulâ dispendere carmen ?"

VIRG., Ecl. 3.

ON a stout bench that faced " The Pig and Friar,"
Sat Jemmy Doubletouch and Pat Maguire :
Long tubes of clay, with dark Virginian weed,
Crowned the rude board to serve their present need ;
While, placed by Tapps, the host, between each man
Best double stout o'erflowed the polish'd can.
And who were Pat and Jemmy ? some will cry :
" Arcades ambo," is our sage reply,—
" Cantare pares," and if not too weary,
Or else too drunk, " parati respondere."
In fact they both were chaunters—up and down—
Highways and byways—country and in town—
Traversed the land while loud their ditties rung,
And oft composed the sonnets which they sung ;
And now by chance had met beneath the shade
That Thomas Tapps' wide-spreading beech tree made.
What glees were troll'd, how many clouds were blown,
What cans were filled and emptied is not known,
(Save by the host,) until, as time flew past,
Though friends at first, they had a tiff at last,
And on this point in anger took their stand—
Who in his craft was deemed the better hand.
" I'll bet," quoth Doubletouch, " four quarts of stout,
To one of punch (but stiff,) I'll serve you out.
But, hark ! my daisy, nothing old won't do ;
So mind your stops, and strike up summat new."
" Agreed !" said Paddy ; " Done !" cries Jem, " that's flat !
But for a judge?—here's Tapps—now go it, Pat !"

PAT.

Och ! whiskey's the life and the sowl of a man,
So I'll sing its praise first, and as long as I can :
If the *says* were made of it—good luck to the sight !
It's myself 'ud be swimmin' from mornin' till night.

JEMMY.

Oh! ale is the stuff that will make a dog jolly,
What cures them is sick and is got melancholy:
It runs through our gammut than quicksilver quicker—
I'm bless'd if it ain't the most primest of licker!

PAT.

St. Patrick's the boy that could turn topsy-turvy
Great Britain and Scotland—so says Father Murphy;
He bothers the world with his divil-may-care, O!
St. Patrick for ivir, the comical *hayro!*

JEMMY.

And where is the chap for St. George that won't cheer
Nor swig in his honour a gallon of beer ?
St. Georgy's the one as a body may brag on ;
Hurrah for the fellor as walloped the dragon!

PAT.

I'll sing next of praytees, the boast of ould Erin,
What dainty compared wid 'em 's worth a red herrin',
You may walk from Coleraine to that place they call Hayti,
Bad luck to the thing you will find like a praty.

JEMMY.

Let the Mounseer go boast of his soup made of herbs—
Of his garlic the Don, vich some stomachs disturbs ;
I knows vot is vot, and I'm wastly mistaken,
If they're equal to cabbage, when biled with good bacon.

PAT.

Was there iver a boy on the 'arth or the air
Who's not daunced a jig at great Donnybrook Fair?
The blissed remimbrance e'en now makes me frisky,
Such crackin' of heads, and such lashiu's of whiskey!

JEMMY.

Vot a sight as is Bartle'my!—not any part in
Of England collected sich wonders for sartin'.
Here's the man as will swallow a sword, if he's let ;
Vot a hungry old cove, and uncommon sharp-set!

PAT.

In love I'm all over wid Katty O'Flanaghan,
For a glance of whose eye often back have I ran again;
Aisy death to me then, but she hates human natur,
The sweet little, nate little, iligant cratur!

JEMMY.

Oh! dear Molly Muggins, vot love is between us!
You're a regular, no-mistake, out-and-out Wenus!
Sich beauty to pieces would lather the world,
When your hair's out of paper and dapperly curled.

PAT.

Och, musha! then sure it's myself that must pity
The spalpeen that never saw dear Dublin city.
They may talk of their Constantinople—shoot aisy!—
Whooo! we could bate them with Ballinacrasy.

JEMMY.

Faix! Lunnon's a town vot is desperate fine,
And from all other cities will take out the shine.
There's the great Leaden Hall, and an acre vot's long,
And the Parliament House, where they chaffs it so strong.

PAT.

By this and by that, but a wager I'd howld,
No plant's like the Shamrouge, so purty and bowld,
Which, stuck in our hats, on our Saints' day is seen,—
But we steep it, your sowl! all the night in potteen.

JEMMY.

Your Sawney may chatter and boast of his Thistle,
Taffy talk of his Leek—but I care not a whistle,—
Odd rat it! what fellor in country or town
As would not give a cheer for the Rose—and the Crown?

"Hold, hold, my masters!" Tapps exclaim'd, "have done!
I thinks as how both bets are fairly won;
For both have chaunted prime and come it strong.
Jemmy the punch is your'n for that 'ere song:
To you I judges, Pat, four quarts of stout,
And, if you please, will help to drink it out;
So now to your work:—but ere you goes away,
Gemmen, I hopes you won't forget to pay."

THE LASS OF ALBANY *

BY ROBERT BURNS.

MY heart is wae, and unco wae,
  To think upon the raging sea,
That roars between her gardens green,
  And the bonnie lass of Albany.

This lovely maid's of royal blood,
  That ruled Albion's kingdoms three;
But oh! alas! for her bonnie face!
  They've wrang'd the lass of Albany.

In the rolling tide of spreading Clyde
  There sits an isle of high degree;
And a town of fame, whose princely name
  Should grace the lass of Albany.

But there's a youth, a witless youth,
  That fills the place where she should be:
We'll send him o'er to his native shore,
  And bring our ain sweet Albany.

Alas the day, and woe the day,
  A false usurper wan the gree;
Who now commands the tower and lands,
  The royal right of Albany.

We'll daily pray, we'll nightly pray,
  On bended knees most fervently,
The time may come, with fife and drum
  We'll welcome home fair Albany.

---

* Hitherto unpublished and contributed to the 'Miscellany' for the year
1837.

HEAVY WET.

FYTTE THE FIRST.

The Poet assert-
eth the surpass-
ing excellence of
nectareous porter
over all other
drinks *ejusdem
generis,*

O HEAVY Wet! thine excellence*
   I sing, O Heavy Wet!
Nectar of man,† who, having beer,
Need envy not Olympian cheer—
   On thee my soul is set!

whereof he enu-
merateth the
chiefest in esti-
mation, viz.,
Guinness's stout,

Let other British bacchanals
   Imbibe the fuscous stream,
Which Guinness from Elbana sends‡
To Christendom's remotest ends,
   Turban'd with mantling cream ;

---

* *O Heavy Wet! thy excellence.*] An apostrophe far more spirited and soul-sprung than that wherewith Byron opens his celebrated lyric, " The isles of Greece ! the isles of Greece," inasmuch as the object is in the one case addressed directly in the second person singular; in the other indirectly in the third plural.

† *Nectar of man.*] As nectar is the beverage of the supernal gods, so is porter the drink of those mortals who seek to approximate the felicity of the Olympians, " to make of earth a heaven." Who ever heard of a man metamorphosed into a fiend by potations of *porter*, whereas (not to mention the daily frightful effects of spirituous liquor), the savage Saxons, and those ferocious pirates, the Danes, considered it the height of enjoyment to swill deep and frequent potations of *ale.*

‡ *Which Guinness from Elbana sends.*] Guinness, the famous brewer of Dublin, (Elbana), whose stout is to be met with among every civilized people throughout the globe.

The poet frequently, when upholding the superiority of porter in convivial circles, used to quote the following lines from 'An Idyl on the Battle,' as affording a comprehensive catalogue of beverages much in vogue, but all of which he maintained hid their diminished heads when placed in juxta-position with his idolized drink. The versification being unfamiliar to many, I shall take the liberty of facilitating its scansion by making each verso into its several feet.

" Ales from the | famous | towns of | Burton, | Marlboro', | Taunton ;
  Porter from | lordly | Thames, and | beer of | various descriptions :
  Brandy of | Gallic | growth, and | rum from the | isle of Ja | maica;
  Deadly, and | heavy | wet, blue | ruin, | wax, and Ge | neva;
  Hollands that | ne'er saw | Holland, rum, | brown-stout, | perry, and |
    cyder ;
  Spirit in all | ways pre | pared, stark | naked, | hot or cold | water'd ;
  Negus, or | godlike | grog, flip, | lamb's-wool, | syllabub, | rumbo,
  Toddy, or | punch, or | shrub, or the | much snug | stingo of | gin-twist."

Or, fraught with Oriental floods,
  Of Hodgson's bitter brewin',
Of Burton, Edinbro', or Crew,
Consign dull care and devils blue
  To utter rout and ruin;

Hodgson's pale Indian ale, the ales of Burton and Edinbro', and the Cambrian Crew,

The fittest drink I stout maintain,
  For coppers cool or hot,
Is porter—by the Thames's side
From Barclay's vasty vats supplied,
  Pull'd from a pewter-pot!

the most perfect of all being Barclay's porter, especially when quaffed from 'the native pewter.'

FYTTE THE SECOND.

When noontide Phœbus* from my couch
  Invites me to arouse,
Recruited by the balmy charms
Of genial Somnes' downy arms
  From yesternight's carouse,

Getting out of bed at 12 o'clock, nothing the worse for the jollities of the past night,

No vile infusion of Cathay,†
  I femininely sip,
With muffin, or if toast a bite,—
No gas-and-water bottled tight,
  Pollutes my waking lip;

he escheweth matutinal quackeries, such as tea and toast, or soda-water;

* *When noontide Phœbus.*] In the opening stanza, the "regular irregularity" of his daily life is set forth in terms of mythological embellishment, which invest the subject with a singular poetic grace. Two facts regarding his habits are clearly deducible; the one that he indulged without fail in a nocturnal carousal, the other, that he never rose earlier than twelve o'clock. As it takes eight, or at least seven hours sleep to "recruit" a person properly, we may likewise conclude that his couch-seeking hour was not later than five, or earlier than four in the morning.

† *Cathay.*] China. The patriotism of the poet is here manifest in his denunciation of that unnatural beverage, tea, for which so many millions are annually abstracted from our pockets to fill those of the pig-eyed and pig-headed, rat-eating, and rat-tailed Chinese. Were the money so thrown away expended at home in the consumption of porter; and, taking it for granted that, even as it is one Englishman is a match for any three Frenchmen, how many frog-fed Mounseers could we not then dispose of?

A similar spirit of contempt for the effeminacy of tea-drinking is evinced by O'Dogherty in his ninety-seventh maxim. "Of tea I have on various occasions hinted my total scorn. It is a weak, nervous affair, adopted for the digestion of boarding-school misses, whose occupation is painting roses

but breakfasts substantially on slices of York-shire or West-phalia ham, fried,

But rasher from the brawny thigh
   Of porker, deftly fried,
Which Yorkshire unexceeded yields,
Or acorn-fed from forest-fields
   Of Westphaly supplied;

whose passage downward he facilitateth with reviving draughts of Bar-clay's porter.

Whose savoury *catabasis**
   I momentar'ly cheer
With fresh'ning streams, (as summer rains
Invigorate the sitient plains)
   Of Barclay's blessed beer.

---

from the life, practising quadrilles, strumming on the instrument, and so forth."

On the use of soda-water here condemned, as on that of bacon lauded in the following stanza, I allow that many opinions exist. I have more than once heard the father of the Irish bar boast his utter innocence of two acts, which he held in deepest abhorrence, viz., drinking soda-water, or tasting swine's flesh. And I fully appreciate the soundness of his self-gratulation; for the first I have ever regarded as an abominable compost, ever since the day that some of it being spilled on one of my boots, speedily burned a hole through the leather; and, as to hog's-flesh, with the exception of Westpha-lian ham, it is fit food only for the great unwashed. On soda-water, as it has its patrons, one word more. Its use is disapproved of by the ladies. If you *must* have some gaseous waking-drink, let it be *ginger-beer*, qualified with rum or brandy, the former (*crede experto*) is the better.

* *Whose savoury catabasis.*] For the benefit of such readers as do not profess an acquaintance with the Greek tongue, I beg to maintain that the word *catabasis* signifies *descent*, in the same manner as *anabasis* does *ascent*. The derivation of these words is curious, and was, I confess, unknown to me, until lately communicated by an eminent philologist. There lived at Athens, in the time of Pisistratus, a wealthy and powerful man of Scythian ex-traction, whose name was Abasis. He had two daughters of singular beauty and accomplishments, the objects of universal admiration, and on his death he bequeathed to them immense fortunes. The one, by a virtuous and pru-dent bearing, rose higher and higher every year in the estimation of the Athenians till she finally attained to unexampled influence in the city. But the other, through extravagancies and improprieties, retrograded in a like proportion, till she sunk into the depths of indigence and ignominy. Hence their names became " household words;" that of Ann Abasis, the elder and discreeter of the two, being used to personify a progressive exaltation in good; and that of the other sister, Catherine, or Cat Abasis, a fall into the abyss of evil. The words, in course of time, came to be employed in a more unrestricted sense, e.g., Xenophon's Anabasis, &c. &c.

FYTTE THE THIRD.

There's many a worthy customer,
   Who, when he sits to smoke
(To counteract aridity),
Betimes his physiognomy
   Doth in a measure poke

> Many smokers
> of fair repute
> are wont to
> moisten their
> lips from time
> to time

Of whiskey, rum, or shrub-baptiz'd
   Schiedam, or *eau-de-vie;*
Whilst Mocha's slop by some is prized,
And soda'd sherry not despis'd,
   Sherbet, or sangaree.

> with brandy-and-
> water, hollands-
> and-co., sherry-
> and-soda, coffee,
> &c., &c., &c.;

But I my snowy yard of clay
   Fill'd skilfully, and fired,
With longing thirst, as vain to tell
As pilgrims for the desert well,
   For Porter am inspired.

> but he, having
> lit his clay pipe,
> is seized with
> inexpressible
> longing for por-
> ter;

The yard of clay I calmly draw,
   The pewter-pot I drain,
Whilst visions beatifical,
In reverie extatical,
   Send ripe athwart my brain.

> and to the pipe
> and pot con-
> signed, giving
> full scope to
> the flights of
> reverie,

FYTTE THE FOURTH.

Anathema maranatha
   Be every French *ragoût,*
Hors d'œuvre, entremets, bouilli,
Potage of griping herb, *roti,*
   And witch-concocted stew.

> he execrateth
> the multifarious
> abominations
> of outlandish
> cookery,

Where founder'd, broken-down old hacks,
   As sav'ry meat are prized,
And victims of the feline horde
Are oft presented on the board
   Right *concyningly* disguised.

> wherein the
> flesh of horses
> and cats is oft-
> times subtlely
> employed;

but, on arrival
of the dinner-
hour, repasteth
on domestic fare,
(making especial
mention of cer-
tain fishes, and
concluding with
cheese,)

When summon'd to the table by*
    "The tocsin of the soul,"
A cutlet, rump, or fowl with gammon,
Preceded by a cut of salmon,
    Or turbot, or fried sole,

diluted with
floods of porter.

With Stilton's crumbling mass wound up,
    In guileless, solid pride,
Adown mine unsuspecting throat
In brotherhood congenial float
    With porter's mellow tide.

---

* *When summoned to the table, &c.*]

"That tocsin of the soul, the dinner-bell."—BYRON.

Among a host of excellences it is difficult to make a selection; but perhaps of the entire poem this and the succeeding stanza are more pregnant
with exquisite matter than any other. While the poet, led away by the
warmth of his feelings, enters into a wide and varied field, replete with the
choicest flowers and sweetest thoughts, it is to be remarked how beautifully
he has preserved the harmony of design by making them all subservient to
his great object, the praise of porter, without which all the excellences he
has introduced would be shorn of their effect. This, as Horace tells us, is
the true art of poetry. What a throng of moving images appear in a small
space! rising in rapid succession like the apparitions in Macbeth, a scene
which the poet must have had in mind; for, like them, they are seven in
number, and, like them, each overpowering, in a separate and peculiar way,
the senses of the beholder. 'Cutlet,' 'rump,' 'fowl,' 'gammon,' 'salmon,'
'turbot,' 'sole.' Here he stops for a moment, as if fearful of the effects he
might produce on the excited imagination of the reader, did he not, by
bringing the stanza to a close at this peculiar spot, give breathing-time to
observe how gracefully he descends from his circling height in the ensuing
line:—

"With Stilton's crumbling mass wound up."

And then the finishing of the fytte with the glorious picture of all things
floating in harmony upon the mellow tide. What is there in Byron's apostrophe to the ocean that equals this? Nothing.

N.B. "Never take lobster-sauce to salmon; it is mere 'painting of the
lily.' The only true sauce for salmon is vinegar, mustard, cayenne pepper,
and parsley."—O'DOGHERTY'S TWENTY-SIXTH MAXIM.

FYTTE THE FIFTH.

Oh, Toby Mathew, wondrous wight!
Thou very reverend friar!
Despite the fame illumes thy path,
My soul against thy watery wrath,
Is fill'd with righteous ire.

For though great good thou hast achiev'd
'Mongst men who mock'd the law,
But now are turn'd to peaceful mood,
From tongue of flame and hand of blood,
By scouting Usquebaugh,—

It needed not to interdict
All reasonable cheer,
And leave the shamrock to expire
Of utter drought, in land of Ire,*
Denouncing wholesome Beer!

---

* *Land of Ire.*] Poeticé for Ireland. Hannibal is now proved to have understood the use of gunpowder, and the ancient Egyptians that of steam-engines, and the art of brewing. It is also beyond doubt that brewing was well known to the Scythians, with a colony of whom, the ancient Irish, perished the knowledge of one of the sublimest mysteries ever known to man—the art of making heath-beer from the blossoms of the heath-plant. And this was the manner of its loss.—The Danes, on their invasion, found (to use the words of the chronicler) "amonge the famylys of the chiefetaynes a most sweete-savoured and cunnynge drinke." The secret of its manufacture was so highly prized, that it was kept strictly confined to the chief of one particular tribe and his eldest son, the persons employed in making it being invariably put to death on the completion of their task, like the slaves who performed the office of sextons for Alaric. Phelim Olladh Oge, who was the possessor of the secret shortly before the reign of Brian Boru, was one of the most warlike and strenuous adversaries of the Danes, but was at length defeated in a bloody battle, and taken prisoner, together with his only son. On being brought before the Danish leader, they were offered their lives on condition of revealing the mystery of the heath-beer. For many days they stedfastly refused to do so; but at length, as narrated by Dalton in his records, "the sayde Phelim did fayne to consento unto theyre wishes, on condition that they wolde fyrste putte hys sonne to dethe before hys eyes, whiche beying presently done, he clapped hys handis with delite, and mockit them gratcly, saying, 'Doo unto me as ye liste; lo, the yuthe is dedde, and there is none that remayns to tell;' whereatto the kynge, chokeynge with rage, did slaye hym strutely with hys own handc."

FYTTE THE SIXTH.

He rapturously apostrophizeth porter, the true source of Paradisaical felicity ;

Oh, Porter ! stream of Paradise !
　　By thee to man is given
Delight more rare than bearded Turk,
When rushing to the deathful work,
　　Aspires to taste in Heaven.

its virtuous influences are more potent than the Elysian spells of the Enchantress,

Thy virtues on the moral frame,
　　And physical alike,
With influence beyond the power
Of fam'd Armida's fairy bower,
　　Do magically strike ;

conferring the blessing of robust health on the body,

For whilst on pious votaries
　　They bounteously bestow
A prize far 'bove *rouleaus* of wealth,
Of muscular and lusty health
　　The ripe and ruddy glow,—

That the ancient Germans also knew how to produce this liquor is proved by Tacitus. "Potui humor ex hordeo aut frumento in quamdam similitudinem vivi corruptus."—*De moribus Germanorum,* sec. xxiii.　See also Pliny, lib. xiv. c. 22.

The Egyptians (of whose acquaintance with the art of brewing mention has been made above) ascribed the invention of beer to Osiris, whom they venerated nearly as much as Bacchus.　They called it 'zethum,' and considered it little inferior to wine.　See Diodorus, lib. i. pp. 17 and 31; Herodotus, lib. ii. c. 77.

The classical reader will recollect the passage in the Anabasis, in which Xenophon encounters a race of beer-drinkers in Armenia.　"Their houses were underground, the entrance like the mouth of a well, but spacious below. The inhabitants entered by means of ladders; but the way for their cattle was dug down, so as to enable them to walk in as on an inclined plane.　In these abodes were goats, oxen, birds, and their young.　The cattle were fed on fodder; and we found among them wheat, and barley, and pulse, and a *wine made from barley,* which is kept in jars; and there were reeds at hand, large and small, and when they would drink they applied the reeds to the jars and sucked up the liquor, which was of great strength, unless when mixed with water.　We found it a most delightful drink.　Their tables were covered with lamb, pork, kid, and veal, with great plenty of wheaten bread; and when the health of a friend was to be drunk they repaired to a jar, and applying their mouths to the reeds, sucked in a bending posture like as the ox drinketh, and thus satisfied their desire."

With like beneficence they shed
  On th' elevated mind,
From all anxiety secure,
" Making assurance doubly sure,"
  Felicity refined.

and raising the
mind to the
purest felicity.

Then let us sing God save the Queen !
  And Barclay—Perkins eke,
And may we never know regret
For lack of pots of heavy wet
  One day throughout the week.

He concludeth in
the pious spirit
of loyalty and
universal philan-
thropy.

THE SNAIL.

" TRAVELLING by tardy stages,
    Carrying thy house with ease,
Like the wisest of the sages,
  Excellent Diogenes !
Snail, I greet thee,—why so gloomy ?
  Tell me where thy sorrow lies ;
Thou hast mansion snug and roomy,
  That a naked slug would prize.
Dost thou creep to herbage shady,
  Badger'd by a scolding spouse ?
Art thou jealous that thy lady
  Occupies another house ?"—

" Stranger, I have cause to cavil,
  Reason good to grieve, alack !
I am doomed for life to travel
  With a load upon my back.
O'er my journey slowly creeping,
  (Watch me as I wander near,)
It is water'd by my weeping,
  Moisten'd by a slimy tear !
Even Sinbad, on my credit,
  Suffer'd less than hapless me ;
His adventure,—have you read it ?—
  With the ' Old Man of the Sea.'

After making efforts many,
  Vainly toiling night and day,
Sinbad made him drunk, and then he
  Shook him off, and—walk'd away.
Gladly would I burthens barter
  With thee, Sinbad,—honest Jack!
Tho' thy rider proved 'a Tartar,'
  Wondrous fond of ' pick-a-back.'
Marvel not at my depression—
  I can never respite have,
Victim to my indiscretion,
  Sadly sinking to the grave.
This abode has dwindled greatly ;
  Yes, believe it, if you can,
It was once a mansion stately,
  I was once a handsome man.
Mothers in a thousand quarters
  Calculated on my pelf,
While their less designing daughters
  Loved me for my humble self.
Flatter'd by their kind advances,
  I was giddy with delight ;
Going out to balls and dances,
  Turning morning into night.
Early hours thus despising,
  You may well suppose that I
Never slept, till, Phœbus rising,
  Warn'd me in the Eastern sky.
All the morning friends unnumber'd
  To my dwelling used to come,
And my servant (whilst I slumber'd)
  Told them I was not at home.
Conscience sometimes made me suffer,
  But that quickly pass'd away ;
It became a great deal tougher,
  And I lied from day to day.
Anger'd by this conduct shocking,
  Death advanced with hasty stride :
At my habitation knocking,
  And *he* would not be denied.

Warning take and wisely ponder—
Ponder for the time to come ;
I (for ever doom'd to wander)
Now am always found ' at home.' "

TO A FOUNTAIN IN HYMETTUS.

BY EDWARD KENEALY.

"These infantine beginnings gently bear,
Whose best desert and hope must be your bearing."
PHINEAS FLETCHER.

O PURE and limpid fountain,
    What snow on Alpine mountain,
  Sparkles like thee ?
While on thy turf reclining,
Our features soft and shining
  In thee we see.
The zephyrs flitting o'er thee,
O fount, methinks adore thee,
  And linger still,
With winglets light and tender
O'er thine eyes of splendour,
  And drink their fill.

A thousand sunny flowers
Their fragrance, like rich dowers,
  Around thee shed ;
And through the woodbine branches
No breeze its coldness launches
  On thy calm bed.
Sunshine upon thee slumbers,
As if thy rills' sweet numbers
  Lull'd it to rest ;
The stars of night and morning
For ever are adorning
  Thy crystal breast.

14

About thy banks so fragrant,
That little rose-winged vagrant,
  Cupid, is seen;
And in thy silv'ry waters
Bathe the mild Goddess-daughters,
  In Beauty's sheen.
The Dryads rob'd in brightness,
With feet of fawn-like lightness,
  The Graces Three,
Beneath the golden glances
Of Hesper weave their dances,
  O fount! round thee.

Pan leaves his rosy valleys,
And by thy brightness dallies
  All day,—and wakes
Echo—the forest haunting—
Up with the notes enchanting
  His wild pipe makes.
Here, too, at times resorted,
Fair Venus, when she sported
  With am'rous Mars.
Their hearts with passion beating,
And none to view their meeting,
  But the lone stars.

Play on, thou limpid fountain
Eternal as yon mountain
  Olympus-crown'd:
Gush on—in light Elysian,
As Poet's shape-fill'd vision,
  Or Apollo's round.
The smiles of Heaven above thee,
And the stars to love thee,
  Fount, thou shalt glide
From thy crystal portal,
Strong, beauteous, and immortal,
  Whate'er betide.

COUNT CASKO' WHISKY AND HIS THREE HOUSES.

A TEMPERANCE BALLAD.

THERE is a demon in the land,
  A demon fierce and frisky,
Who steals the souls of mortal men,
  His name is Casko' Whisky.

Lo! mounted on a fiery steed,
  He rides through town and village,
And calls the workman from his shop,
  The farmer from his tillage.

Clutched in his lanky red right hand
  He holds a mighty bicker,
Whose polished sides run daily o'er,
  With floods of burning liquor.

Around him press the clamorous crowds,
  To taste his liquor greedy;
But chiefly come the poor and sad—
  The suffering and the needy.

All those oppressed by grief and debts
  The dissolute, the lazy,
Draggle-tail'd sluts, and shirtless men,
  And young girls lewd and crazy.

"Give! give!" they cry, "give, give us drink!
  Give us your burning liquor,
We'll empty fast as you can fill,
  Your fine capacious bicker.

"Give, give us drink to drown our care,
  And make us light and frisky,
Give! give! and we will bless thy name,
  Thou good Count Casko' Whisky!"

And when the demon hears them cry,
  Right merrily he laugheth,
And holds his bicker out to all,
  And each poor idiot quaffeth.

14—2

The first drop warms their shivering skins,
  And drives away their sadness,
The second lights their sunken eyes
  And fills their souls with gladness.

The third drop makes them shout and roar,
  And play each furious antic.
The fourth drop boils their very blood,
  The fifth drop drives them frantic!

And still they drink the burning draught,
  Till old Count Casko' Whisky
Holds his bluff sides with laughter fierce,
  To see them all so frisky.

'More! more!" they cry, "come, give us more!
More of that right good liquor!
Fill up, old boy, that we may drain
  Down to the dregs your bicker!"

The demon spurs his fiery steed,
  And laughs a laugh so hollow,
Then waves his bicker in the air,
  And beckons them to follow.

On! on! he rides, and onwards rush
  The heedless thousands after,
While over hill and valley wide
  Resounds his fiend-like laughter.

On! on! they rush through mud and mire,
  On! on! they rush, exclaiming;
"O Casko' Whisky, give us more,
  More of thy liquor flaming!"

At last he stops his foaming steed,
  Beside a rushing river,
Whose waters to the palate sweet,
  Are poison to the liver.

"There!" says the demon, "drink your fill—
Drink of these waters mellow,
They'll make your bright eyes blear and dull,
  And turn your white skins yellow.

"They'll cause the little sense you have
By inches to forsake you,
They'll cause your limbs to faint and fail,
And palsies dire to shake you!

"They'll fill your homes with care and grief,
And clothe your back with tatters,
They'll fill your hearts with evil thoughts,
But never mind! what matters?

"Though virtue sink, and reason fail,
And social ties dissever,
I'll be your friend in hour of need,
And find you homes for ever!

"For I have built three mansions high,
Three strong and goodly houses,
To lodge at last each goodly soul
Who all his life carouses!

"The first it is a goodly house,
Black are its walls, and high,
And full of dungeons deep and fast,
Where death-doomed felons lie.

"The second is a lazar-house,
Rank, foetid, and unholy;
Where, fettered by diseases foul,
And hopeless melancholy,

"The victims of potations deep
Pine on their couch of sadness;
Some calling death to end their pain,
And some imploring madness.

"The third house is a spacious house,
To all but sots appalling;
Where by the parish bounty fed,
Vile in the sunshine crawling,

"The worn-out drunkard ends his days,
And eats the dole of others,
A plague and burden to himself,
An eye-sore to his brothers!

" So drink the waters of this stream,
   Drink deep the cup of ruin!
Drink, and, like heroes, madly rush
   Each man to his undoing!

" One of my mansions high and strong,
   One of my goodly houses,
Is sure to lodge each jolly soul
   Who to the dregs carouses!"

Into the stream his courser plunged,
   And all the crowd plunged after
While over hill and valley wide
   Resounded peals of laughter.

For well he knew this demon old,
   How vain was all his preaching;
The ragged crew that round him flocked
   Were too far gone for teaching.

Even as they wallow in the stream,
   They cry aloud quite frisky,
" Here's to thy health, thou best of friends!
   Kind generous Casko' Whisky.

" We care not for thy houses three,
   We live but for the present,
And merry will we make it yet,
   And quaff these waters pleasant!"

Loud laughs the fiend to hear them speak,
   And lifts his brimming bicker,
" Drink, fools!" quoth he, " you'll pay your scot;
   I'll have your souls for liquor."

THE LOVER'S LEAP.*

BY J. A. WADE.

Oh! have you not heard of that dark woody glen,
    Where the oak-leaves are richest and rarest,
Where CONNAL, the chief and the foremost of men,
    Lov'd EILY, of maidens the fairest ?
She plighted her faith, but as quickly withdrew,
    At a story that slander'd her lover :—
She left him in wrath, but how little she knew
    That her peace at their parting was over!

He met her in vale, and he met her in grove,—
    At midnight he roam'd by her dwelling;
But he said not a word of the truth of his love,
    For his cheek the sad story was telling!
He found her one eve, by the rock in the glen,
    Where she once vow'd to love him for ever,—
He gaz'd, till she murmur'd "Dear Connal," and then
    He leap'd from the rock to the river!

The summer pass'd on, and the chief was forgot,
    But one night, when the oak leaves were dying,
There came a sad form to that desolate spot,
    'Neath which the brave Connal was lying.
She gaz'd on the brown swelling stream 'mid the rocks,
    As she lean'd the wild precipice over:
She look'd a farewell to the glen of the oaks,
    And Eily was soon with her lover!

WRECK OF THE HESPERUS.

BY H. W. LONGFELLOW.

It was the schooner Hesperus
    That sail'd the wintry sea ;
And the skipper had ta'en his little daughter
    To bear him company.

---

* A romantic spot in the Dargle, County Wicklow, so named from numerous traditions resembling the present subject.

Blue were her eyes as the fairy-flax,
    Her cheeks like the dawn of day,
And her bosom sweet as the hawthorn buds
    That ope in the month of May.

The skipper he stood beside the helm,
    With his pipe in his mouth,
And watch'd how t e veering flaw did blow
    The smoke now west, now south.

Then up and spake an old sailór,
    Had sail'd the Sp nish Main,
"I pray thee put in o yonder port,
    For I fear a hurricane.

"Last night the moon had a golden ring,
    And to-night no n oon we see!"
The skipper he blew a whiff from his pipe,
    And a scornful la gh laugh'd he.

Colder and louder b ew the wind,
    A gale from the north-east;
The snow fell hissing in the brine,
    And the billows f oth'd like yeast.

Down came the storm, and smote amain
    The vessel in its strength;
She shudder'd and aused, like a frighted steed,
    Then leap'd her cable's length.

"Come hither! come hither! my little daughter,
    And do not tremtle so :
For I can weather the roughest gale
    That ever wind did blow."

He wrapp'd her warm in his seaman's coat
    Against the stin ing blast;
He cut a rope from a broken spar,
    And bound her to the mast.

"O father! I hear the church-bells ring—
    Oh! say, what may it be?"
"'Tis a fog-bell on a rock-bound coast!"
    And he steer'd for the open sea.

"Oh father! I hear the sound of guns—
  Oh! say, what may it be?"
"Some ship in distress, that cannot live
  In such an angry sea!"

"O father! I see a gleaming light—
  Oh! say, what may it be?"
But the father answer'd never a word,
  A frozen corpse was he.

Lash'd to the helm, all stiff and stark,
  With his face to the skies,
The lantern gleam'd through the gleaming snow
  On his fix'd and glassy eyes.

Then the maiden clasp'd her hands, and pray'd
  That savéd she might be;
And she thought of Christ, who still'd the wave
  On the lake of Galilee.

And fast through the midnight dark and drear,
  Through the whistling sleet and snow,
Like a sheeted ghost the vessel swept
  Toward the reef of Norman's Woe.

And ever the fitful gusts between
  A sound came from the land;
It was the sound of the trampling surf
  On the rocks and the hard sea-sand.

The breakers were ri ht beneath her bows,
  She drifted a dreary wreck,
And a whooping billow swept the crew
  Like icicles from h r deck.

She struck where the white and fleecy waves
  Look'd soft as card d wool;
But the cruel rocks they gored her side
  Like the horns of an angry bull.

Her rattling shrouds, all sheathed in ice,
  With the masts we t by the board,
Like a vessel of glass she stove and sank,
  Ho! ho! the breakers roar'd!

At daybreak, on the bleak sea-beach,
  A fisherman stood aghast
To see the form of a maiden fair
  Lash'd close to a drifting mast.

The salt sea was frozen on her breast,
  The salt tears in her eyes ;
And he saw her hair, like the brown sea-weed,
  On the billows fall and rise.

Such was the wreck of the Hesperus,
  In the midnight and the snow !
Christ save us all from a death like this
  On the reef of Norman's Woe!

THE WINE GOD.

BY C. HARTLEY LANGHORNE.

COME along, come along, to the voice of our song,
  And list to our carol the vintage-night long !
The maid will be there with her bright sunny hair,
And the pard and the lion will soon quit their lair ;
And the tiger as well will bow to thy spell,
And couch at our feet in our violet dell ;
And all that is beauteous, and brilliant, and gay,
Will greet thee, Psilas ! Come away ! come away !
  Then fill, fill, fill to him still,
  By the lentisk copse, and the vine-cover'd hill,
  The sweet lily beds, and the dancing rill,—
      Fill, fill !

Let the smiles of thy face, with their wild lovely grace,
Cast joy and contentment on all in the place ;
Let the vineyard be blest where thou takest thy rest,
And the corn-field and garden thy foot may have prest ;
Come, God of the Wine, with the aspect divine,
And Helios himself will forget how to shine ;
Come, sport with us here 'neath the welkin so clear,
And Selenè will soon jilt her Latinian fere,
And fly to us here, and fly to us here.

Then fill, fill, fill to him still,
By the lentisk copse, and the vine-cover'd hill,
The sweet lily beds, and the dancing rill,—
    Fill, fill!

Greatest, omnipotent, mightiest power!
This is the moment, this is the hour,—
Visit thy son in his own Chian bower,
Where, crown'd with the myrtle, and ivy, and vine,
He holdeth high rites to the God of the Wine;
Revel, and song, and proud festive glee,
Such as is meet for a god like thee.
Then leave the cliffs on the Noxian stand,
And bless with thy presence Oenoplon's land!
    Then fill, fill, fill to him still,
    By the lentisk copse, and the vine-cover'd hill,
    The sweet lily beds, and the dancing rill,—
        Fill, fill!

A TRUE LOVE SONG.

BY ALFRED CROWQUILL.

TELL me, charmer, tell me, pray,
    Have you sisters many, say?
One sweet word, ay, yet another,
Have you got a single brother?
Have you got an aunt or two,
Very much attached to you?
Or some uncles very old,
Willing you their lands and gold?

Have you money in your right
That in case we take to flight,
And your ma and pa be cross,
We should never feel the loss?
Gold indeed 's a fleeting thing,
But when in a wedding-ring,
There 'tis endless round and round—
Settlements should thus be found.

Are your parents young or not;
Have they independence got?
Believe me, as your love true,
'Tis alone my care for you
Makes me thus particular,
As regards your pa and ma.
Sisters, love, are very well,
But the truth I'll frankly tell.

When a man intends to fix,
He doesn't like to marry six!
Brothers, too, are very well
To escort a sister belle;
But they stand much in the way
When the dowry is to pay:
Then, sweet, I freely own,
You I love, and you alone.

At your feet I humbly kneel,
I have nothing—to reveal,
Fortune's been unkind to me
'Till she kindly proffered thee.
Speak! and let me know my fate;
Speak! and alter your estate;
If you are, what I suppose,
I'll take a cab, love, and propose.

WHITE BAIT.*

"Inest sua gratia parvis."

Aspice quâ juxta Thamesim regalia surgunt
     Mœnia, et Hospitii nobilis aula patet:
Scilicet emeritis hic nautis otia fecit
     Securam præbes Anglia grata domum.
Stat vicina domus, minus haud celebranda, Trafalgar,
     Ad quam convivas atria celsa vocant.

---

* The above verses are the production of one of Westminster's most gifted
sons.

Huc longos cupiens urbis vitare labores
Turba ruit variis luxuriosa modis.
Nunc Aldermannos, pisces consumere natos,
Per fluvium lentè civica pompa trahit.
Nunc regni proceres, ferro viâ strata, senatûs
Elapsos strepitu fert, populique duces
Qualescunque sint, omnes coquuntur eodem,
Omnes quippe gulæ suscitat unus amor.
Nec mora, quin dubiam videas apponere cœnam
Servos, et lauto pondere mensa gemit.
Hic pinguis Salmo, et boreali ex æquore Rhombus,
Hic Soleæ et Mulli, luscius atque vorax.
Attamen haud Salis est, frustra fluviique marisque
Thesauros, habiles apposuêre coqui :
Convivæ quiddam proprium notumque requirant,
Nempe sua est albis gratia pisciculis.

WESTMONASTERIENSIS.

SAINT PATRICK.

(AUTHOR UNKNOWN.)

Saint Patrick was a gentleman,
　And came of decent people ;
He built a church in Dublin town,
　And on it put a steeple.
His father was a Hoolagan,
　His sister an O'Grady,
His mother was a Mulligan,
　And his wife the Widow Brady.

CHORUS.

Success attend St. Patrick's fist,
　He was a saint so clever ;
He gave the snakes and toads a twist,
　And bothered them for ever!

The Wicklow hills are very high,
　And so's the hill of Howth, sir ;
But there's a hill that's higher still
　And bigger than them both, sir.

SANCTUS PATRICIUS.

(IRISH WHISKEY DRINKER.)

De gente natus inclytâ
　Patricius, Ierne,
Urbem donavit cathedrâ,
　Pyramide superne.
Cui pater erat Hoolagan,
　Et soror erat Greda,
Et pia mater Mulligan
　Viduaque conjux Breda.

CHORUS.

Sic faustus sit Patricius
　Dextram in angues jecit ;
Torsit bufones fortiter,
　In sæclaque confecit !

Dant oscula sideribus
　Hotha Glucklovioque ;
Assurgit collis alibi,
　Præcelsior utroque.

Twas from the top of that same hill,   Patricius è vertice
    Saint Patrick preached the *sarmint*   Dulci sermone rudes
That drove the frogs into the bogs,   Demersit vermes Tartaro,
    And banished all the *varmint!*   Ranasque in paludes.

Success attend St. Patrick's fist, &c.   Sic faustus sit Patricius, &c.

Nine hundred thousand vipers blue,   Angues blanditos vocibus
    He charmed with his sweet discourses,   Quas edidit jucundis,
And *sarved* them up at Killaloo   In jusculum decoquit ut
    In soups and second courses.   Mensas ornent secundas.
The blind worms crawling on the grass,   Dolere mitte Killalu,
    Disgusted all the nation,   Virctis inquinatis,
Till he opened their eyes and their   Qua viperis aperuit
    hearts likewise,   Ocellos occæcatis!
    To a sense of their situation!

Success attend St. Patrick's fist, &c.   Sic faustus sit Patricius, &c.

There's not a mile, through Ireland's   Quacunque in Apostolum
    Isle,   Catervas explicaret
    Where the dirty creatures musters!   Calcatur Pestis ungulâ
But there he put his dear fore foot,   Dilectâ ubi staret.
    And murdered them in clusters.   Heus Bufo! Heus Ranuncule.
The toads went pop, the frogs went slop,   Dum licet, denatato!
    Slap dash into the water,   Quo caudam serves, Coluber,
And the snakes committed suicide   Te ipsum jugulato!
    To save themselves from slaughter!

Success attend St. Patrick's fist, &c.   Sic faustus sit Patricius, &c.

No wonder that the Irish boys   Ut fortis sis, Hibernice,
    Are all so brave and frisky,   Ut semper sis in flore,
For sure Saint Pat he taught them that,   *Patriciorum* Pater te
    And the way of making whiskey.   Conspersit VITÆ RORE!
No wonder that the Saint himself   Expressit Hordearium
    Was handy at distilling,   Manu Beatus bonâ,
For his mother kept a shebeen house   Vendeditque pia genetrix
    In the town of Enniskillen!   Cyathatim in cauponâ!

Success attend St. Patrick's fist,   Sic faustus sit Patricius!
    He was a saint so clever;   Dextram in angues jecit;
He gave the toads and snakes a twist,   Torsit bufones fortiter,
    And banished them for ever!   In sæclaque confecit!

CROFTON CROKER asserts, and Lover seems to have been of the same opinion, that this famous Irish song was a mosaic work put together at different times by different hands, the first portion of it having been sung a great many years ago at a masquerade in Cork, by a couple of gentlemen in the character of ballad singers, each taking most probably (I should think) the alternate lines, which would have given it a much droller effect than if both had sung it in first and second parts, as a regular duet, or in unison. In some parts of Ireland—and of England as well—this mode of ballad singing, especially where a married couple are the performers, is still adopted. Mr. Croker, speaking only from tradition, may be mistaken, and in the absence of more positive proof, I should be more inclined to think that the 'Praises of St. Patrick' emanated from one poetic source, the once famous Dick Milligan, of Cork, the acknowledged author of the 'Groves of Blarney,' who, according to some accounts, had at least a hand in the production. As in the praises of Venus, Diana, Minerva, Hercules, Bacchus, Theseus, &c., by one or other of the ancient poets, we have in the Irish hymn the birth, genealogy, and achievements of the Patron Saint of Ireland, all heroic in their way, as became a demigod, whether he wielded club or crosier, and supernatural to the highest point of the sublime, whether man or woman performed them. We have also, as an appropriate *finale*, a delicate touch about the chief virtues of his descendants, whose valour and vivacity are derived from the sacred fount of inspiration which he opened for their especial comfort and civilization, and which has ever since enjoyed a classic reputation equal at least to the waters of Helicon themselves, and superior to those of any other fountain of ancient or modern times, from Arethusa or Ammon to Blandusium or Vaucluse. There is an unmistakable homogeneity about the song of 'St. Patrick,' with a beginning, a middle, and an end, conceived by the one mind, and executed by the one hand, a characteristic more observable in the lyrics of the old school than in those of the new. In transferring its native beauties to the language of the educated of all nations, I have adopted the metre of the original, and without sacrificing the spirit to the letter, have adhered in all other aspects as closely as possible to the poet's conceptions. The air, for the information of the English reader, is nearly alike to the popular one on both sides of St. George's Channel, of Miss Bayley, with the exception of the chorus, which in the Irish song is a *da capo*, or repetition of the first part of the air itself.

THE FISHERMAN'S DWELLING.

FROM THE GERMAN OF HENRICH HEINE,

BY MARY HOWITT.

WE sate by the fisher's dwelling,
    And looked upon the sea;
The evening mists were gathering,
    And rising up silently.

Forth from the lofty lighthouse
    Streamed softly light by light,
And in the farthest distance
    A ship hove into sight.

We spoke of storm and shipwreck;
    Of seamen, and how they lay
Unsafe 'twixt heaven and water,
    'Twixt joy and fear each day.

We spoke of lands far distant;
    We took a world-wide range,
We spoke of wondrous nations,
    And manners new and strange.

Of the fragrant, glittering Ganges,
    Where giant trees uptower,
And handsome, quiet people,
    Kneel to the lotus flower.

Of Lapland's filthy people,
    Flat-headed, wide-mouthed, we spake;
How they squat round their fires and jabber,
    And shriek o'er the fish they bake.

The maidens listened so gravely;
    At length no more was said;
The ship was in sight no longer,
    And night over all was spread.

THE VILLAGE BLACKSMITH.

BY H. W. LONGFELLOW.

UNDER a spreading chestnut tree
  The village smithy stands;
The smith a mighty man is he,
  With large and sinewy hands,
And the muscles of his brawny arms
  Are strong as iron bands.

His hair is crisp, and black, and long,
  His face is like the tan,
His brow is wet with honest sweat,
  He earns whate'er he can,
And looks the whole world in the face,
  For he owes not any man.

Week out, week in, from morn till night,
  You can hear his bellows blow,
You can hear him swing his heavy sledge
  With measured beat and slow,--
Like a sexton ringing the old kirk-chimes,
  When the evening sun is low.

And children coming home from school
  Look in at the open door;
They love to see the flaming forge,
  And hear the bellows roar,
And catch the burning sparks that fly
  Like chaff from a threshing-floor.

He goes on Sunday to the church,
  And sits among his boys;
He hears the parson pray and preach,
  He hears his daughter's voice,
Singing in the village choir,
  And it makes his heart rejoice.

It sounds to him like her mother's voice,
  Singing in Paradise!
He needs must think of her once more,
  How in her grave she lies,

15

And with his hard, rough hand he wipes
A tear from out his eyes.

Toiling, rejoicing, sorrowing,
Onward through life he goes ;
Each morning sees some task begin,
Each evening sees it close ;
Something attempted, something done,
Has earned a night's repose.

Thanks! thanks to thee my worthy friend
For the lesson thou hast taught!
Thus at the sounding forge of Life
Our fortunes must be wrought,
Thus on its sounding anvil shaped,
Each burning deed and thought.

CUPID IN LONDON.

BY R. MORE.

Young Cupid, grown tired of his wild single life
And the pranks he had long been pursuing,
Determined to marry a sweet little wife,
So in earnest he set out a-wooing.

But disdaining to win her by magic or art,
Or aught save his beauty and merit,
Away with contempt threw his bow and his dart,
No longer their pow'r to inherit.

Then to London he came one fine morning in May,
When the full tide of fashion was flowing ;
His purse was brim-full, his heart light and gay,
And his cheeks with fresh roses were glowing.

As a fine handsome youth he was soon known in town,—
All the ladies his manner delighted ;
Not a ball or a rout with the world would go down
Unless Mr. Love were invited.

His cab was "*perfection*," his horse "*quite a love*,"
  And his *Tiger* "*the least of the little;*
No one else ever wore such a hat or a glove,
  And his *Stultz* was a fit to a tittle.

The bride that he sought for was easy to find
  In the midst of such dazzling attraction ;
And soon a fair maiden he met to his mind,
  Whom he loved at first sight to distraction.

'Twas at *Almack's* he met with the dear lovely girl,
  She was called "*the prize flower of the season;*"
And her exquisite form in the waltz to entwirl
  Was enough to deprive him of reason.

So he told her his love, and she whispered "Oh fie!"
  As she blushed and looked round for her mother ;
And Cupid inquired, with a tremulous sigh,
  If her heart ever beat for another.

But her mind was as pure as her beauty was bright ;
  And she told him no one e'er could win her
Who in frivolous pastime alone took delight—
  The *beau* of a ball or a dinner.

Ashamed and dejected, poor Cupid retired,
  Resolving to *cut*—cutting capers,—
And chambers next day in *the Temple* he hired,
  And filled them with law-books and papers.

Then to study the Law, like a man he went down,
  No scholar could ever be apter,
For he bought an arm-chair, with a wig and a gown,
  And in BLACKSTONE he read *a whole chapter*.

At the end of a fortnight he grew thin and pale,
  And he thought he should die without jesting ;
So he dressed all in black, which he thought must prevail,
  For it made him look quite interesting.

In a cavalry reg'ment to battle he went,
  And he said not a word of his going ;
But resolved that in action his life should be spent,
  Or at least that his blood should be flowing.

And soon in a charge which he gallantly led
   At the enemy's troops in platoon,
He got a sad cut (while defending his head)
   In the arm from a heavy dragoon.

Disabled from duty, he homeward returned,
   The news of a victory bringing;
And now with affection his loved maiden burned,
   And the town with his praises was ringing.

One morning he called with his arm in a sling,
   And attired as a dashing young lancer;
To refuse him this time was a difficult thing,
   For she loved him, indeed,—when a dancer.

When he talked of his passion, she listened with pride,
   And her heart by assault was soon carried;
And she shortly appeared as the young soldier's bride,
   For in less than a month *they were married.*

THE MISLETOE.

BY FATHER PROUT.

I.

A PROPHET sat in the Temple gate,
   And he spoke each passer by
In thrilling tones—with words of weight—
   And fire in his rolling eye.

" *Pause thee, believing Jew!*
 " *Nor make one step beyond*
 " *Until thy heart hath conned*
 " *The mystery of this wand.*"

And a rod from his robe he drew;—
   'Twas a withered bough
   Torn long ago
From the trunk on which it grew.
   But the branch long torn
   Showed a bud new born,
That had blossomed there anew;—

That wand was " JESSE'S rod,"
  Symbol, 'tis said,
  Of HER, the Maid—
Yet mother of our GOD !

II.

A priest of EGYPT sat meanwhile
  Beneath his palm tree hid,
On the sacred brink of the flowing Nile,
  And there saw mirror'd, 'mid
Tall obelisk and shadowy pile
  Of ponderous pyramid,
One lowly, lovely, LOTUS plant,
  Pale orphan of the flood ;
And long did that aged hierophant
  Gaze on that beauteous bud ;
For well he thought, as he saw it float
  O'er the waste of waters wild,
On the long-remember'd cradle boat,
  Of the wond'rous Hebrew child :—
Nor was that lowly lotus dumb
Of a mightier Infant still, to come,
    If mystic skiff
    And hieroglyph
Speak aught in LUXOR'S catacomb.

III.

A GREEK sat on Colonna's cape,
  In his lofty thoughts alone,
And a volume lay on PLATO'S lap,
  For *he* was that lonely one ;
    And oft as the sage
    Gaz'd o'er the page
His forehead radiant grew,
    For in Wisdom's womb
    Of the WORD to come
A vision blest his view.—
He broached that theme in the ACADEME
  Of the teachful olive grove—
And a chosen few that secret knew
  In the PORCH'S dim alcove.

IV.

A SYBIL sat in Cumæ's cave
  In the hour of infant ROME,
And her vigil kept and her warning gave
  Of the HOLY ONE to come.
'Twas she who culled the hallowed branch
  And silent took the helm
When he the Founder-Sire would launch
  His bark o'er Hades' realm :
But chief she poured her vestal soul
Thro' many a bright illumined scroll,
    By priest and sage,
    Of an after age,
Conned in the lofty CAPITOL.

V.

A DRUID stood in the dark oak wood
  Of a distant northern land,
And he seem'd to hold a sickle of gold
  In the grasp of his withered hand,
And he moved him slowly round the girth
  Of an aged oak, to see
If an orphan plant of wondrous birth
  Had clung to the old oak tree.
And anon he knelt and from his belt
  Unloosened his golden blade,
Then rose and culled the MISLETOE
Under the woodland shade.

VI.

O blessed bough ! meet emblem thou
  Of all dark EGYPT knew,
Of all foretold to the wise of old,
  To ROMAN, GREEK, and JEW.
And long, God grant, time-honor'd plant,
  Live we to see thee hung
In cottage small as in baron's hall
  Banner and shield among !
Thus fitly rule the mirth of Yule
  Aloft in thy place of pride,
Still usher forth in each land of the North
  The solemn CHRISTMAS TIDE !

THE GREEK POET'S DREAM.

BY EDWARD KENEALY.

Siate presenti . . . .
Tu madre d'Amor col tuo giocondo
E lieto aspetto, e 'l tuo figliol veloce
Co' dardi sol possente à tutto 'l mondo.

BOCCACCIO.

I DREAM'D a dream
    As fair—as bright
As the star's soft gleam,
    Or eyes of light.
At the midnight hour
    The Queen of Love,
From her fairy bower
    Of smiles above,
        With Cupid came,
        And, with grace Elysian,
Yielded the god
    To the bard's tuition.
"This child hath come
    To learn from thee,
In thine own dear home
    Thy minstrelsy:
Teach him to sing
    The strains thou hast sung;
Like a bird of spring
    O'er its callow young."
She vanish'd in light,—
    That witching one,
Like a meteor of night,
    That shines, and is gone.
The Sprite of the skies
    Remain'd by me,
His deep-blue eyes
    Radiant with glee.
His looks were bright
    As roses wreathed.
A wild delight
    From his features breathed.

Legends I taught him
  Of nymph and swain;
Of hearts entangled
  In Love's sweet chain.
Fables that charm
  The soul from sadness;
Stories that warm
  The coldest to gladness:
Songs all glowing
  With passion and mirth,
Like music flowing
  From heaven to earth.
Such were the treasures
  Of wit and thought
I gave: yet dream'd not
  My task was nought.
Cupid listened,
  And clapp'd his hands,
And his wild eyes glistened
  Like burning brands.
Fanning the air
  With snow-white wings,
He seized my lyre,
  He swept the strings:
He look'd—he glitter'd
  Like golden morn,
As he chanted the loves
  Of the Heaven-born.
His voice was sweet
  And perfume-laden,
And light as the feet
  Of dancing maiden.
"Hearts there are
  In Heaven above
Of wild desires,
  Of passionate love.
Hearts there are
  Divinest of mould,
Which love hath among
  His slaves enroll'd;—

Love hath been,
  And ever will be:
The might of Heaven
  Shall fade ere he."
Then the Boy,—
  Nearer advancing,
The Spirit of Joy
  In his blue eyes dancing,
Told me such secrets
  Of Heaven as ne'er
Were before reveal'd
  But to poet's ear,
Revealings of beauty
  That make the soul
Like the stars, that on wings
  Of diamond roll.
In song—in splendour
  The god departed;
The spell was o'er,
  From sleep I started.
Thoughts like sunbeams
  Around me hung,
And my heart still echoed
  What Love had sung.
Oh! what could Heaven
  Deny to us,
To whom it hath given
  Its secrets thus?

MY SOLDIER BOY.

BY DR. MAGINN.

I GIVE *my soldier-boy a blade,*
  In fair Damascus fashioned well;
Who first the glittering falchion swayed,
  Who first beneath its fury fell,
I know not, but I hope to know,
  That for no mean or hireling trade,
To guard no feeling base or low,
  I give my soldier-boy a blade.

Cool, calm, and clear, the lucid flood,
  In which its tempering work was done,
As calm, as clear, as cool of mood,
  Be thou whene'er it sees the sun.
For country's claim, at honour's call,
  For outraged friend, insulted maid,
At mercy's voice to bid it fall,
  I give my soldier-boy a blade.

The eye which marked its peerless edge,
  The hand that weighed its balanced poise,
Anvil and pincers, forge and wedge,
  Are gone, with all their flame and noise—
And still the gleaming sword remains.
  So when in dust I low am laid,
Remember by these heart-felt strains
  I gave my soldier-boy a blade.

ENDYMION.

BY H. W. LONGFELLOW.

THE rising moon has hid the stars;
  Her level rays, like golden bars,
    Lie on the landscape green,
    With shadows brown between.

And silver-white the river gleams,
As if Diana, in her dreams,
    Had dropt her silver bow
    Upon the meadows low.

On such a tranquil night as this,
She woke Endymion with a kiss,
    When, sleeping in the grove,
    He dreamed not of her love.

Like Dian's kiss, unasked, unsought,
Love gives itself, but is not bought;
    Nor voice nor sound betrays
    Its deep, impassioned gaze.

It comes,—the beautiful, the free,—
The crown of all humanity,—
   In silence and alone,
   To seek the elected one.

It lifts the boughs, whose shadows deep
Are life's oblivion,—the soul's sleep,—
   And kisses the closed eyes
   Of him who slumbering lies.

O, weary hearts! O, slumbering eyes!
O, drooping souls, whose destinies
   Are fraught with fear and pain!
   Ye shall be loved again!

No one is so accursed by fate,
No one so wholly desolate,
   But some heart, though unknown,
   Responds unto his own.

Responds, as if with unseen wings
A breath from heaven had touched its strings;
   And whispers in its song,
   " Where hast thou stay'd so long ?"

THE WAR SONG OF THE GALLANT EIGHTY-EIGHTH.

BY THE IRISH WHISKEY DRINKER.

COME now, brave boys, we're on for marching,
For Ireland's glory and divarsion :
Where cannons roar, and men are dying,
March, brave boys, there's no denying!
   Love, farewell !

Hark ! 'tis the Colonel gaily crying,
" March, brave boys, there's no denying,
Colours flying, drums are baying,
March, brave boys, there's no retrayting !"
   Love, farewell !

The major cries, " Boys, are you ready ?"
" Yes, your honour, firm and steady ;

PÆAN MILITARIS LEGIONIS LXXXVIII HIBERNICÆ.

JUVERNÆ decus et tutamen !
   Nos Patria vocat in certamen !
Gemitus quà tristè sonant !
Quà tormenta sæva tonant !
   Vale carissima !

Audin ! ait Dux jocosè
" Signa vocant bellicosè
Tympanumque ! Corda sursum !
Nulla via est retrorsum !"
   Vale carissima !

" An parati ?" (Sic Legatus)
Nullus, ecce, non paratus !

Give every man his flask of powdher,
And his firelock on his shouldher!"
    Love, farewell!

    Suum cuique en scloppetum!
    Sacculisque pulvis detur!
    Vale carissima!

The mother cries, "Boys, do not wrong me,
Do not take my daughters from me!
If you do, I will tormint you!
After death my ghost will haunt you!"
    Love, farewell!

    Mater inde "O tenellis,
    Præcor, parcite puellis!
    Vos viva usque objurgabo,
    Umbra pœnas flagitabo!"
    Vale carissima!

"Oh, Molly, dear, you're young and tinder,
And when I'm gone you won't surrinder,
Howld out like an auncient Roman,
And live and die an honest woman."
    Love, farewell!

    O Maria, mei lepores,
    Dum revertar, scortatores
    Pelle, seu vivas, seu relicta,
    Romanâ fide sis invicta!
    Vale carissima!

"Oh, Molly, darling, grieve no more, I
'M going to fight for Ireland's glory;
If I come back, I'll come victorious;
If I die, my sowl in glory is!"
    Love, farewell!

    Quid fles—quid trepidas dolore?
    En Patriæ vocor amore!
    Victor, si redeam, redibo;
    Ad astra moriturus ibo!
    Vale carissima!

MANY popular song writers from time to time, when fortunate enough to light upon a lyrical idea, or stray fragment of some primitive song, handed down from generation to generation, until it had all but passed away, have happily adopted, added to, and remodelled it, without being in any way open to the charge of plagiarism. The air to which the quaint Anglo-Irish words of 'Love, Farewell,' are sung, is one of the most perfect of its kind, at once wild and beautiful, and much better suited for the Highland bagpipe, or the fife and drum, than the regular band of a regiment. The fond and sad adieu at the end of each quatrain, like the *Ochone-a-ree* of the Scotch coronach or the *Wirrasthrew* of the Irish funeral keen, has no rhythmical connexion, strictly speaking, with the melody, forming as it does a ninth irregular bar to the eight regular ones, of which the air is composed.

Shortly after the battle of Culloden, and the breaking up of the Scottish clans, some thousands of the Highland peasants were thrown on the world by the utter defeat of the Stuart cause, and the ruin of their chiefs. Unlike King James's Irish soldiers, after the siege of Limerick, whose simple notions of honour and fealty to an unfortunate dynasty led them to bid an eternal farewell to their native country, and seek an asylum in foreign armies, Charles Edward's followers, entertaining less political scrupulosity, made the most of the situation, and took service under the actual English government of the day. The Dalgety *provenant* was all and everything to men whose only alternative was to die of honour and starvation in their native hills. For it must not be forgotten that whilst Louis the Fourteenth was ready to receive the unfortunate Irish Jacobites with open arms, and incorporate them into his army as a distinct and privileged brigade, his successor was not disposed to go the same friendly length with the Scotch who survived the battle of Culloden. The latter he thought, most probably, more decisive of the fate of the Stuarts than his great-grandfather did the battle of the Boyne. A proof of how little Louis the Fifteenth cared for the utterly fallen house, may be seen in the short and unceremonious notice served on the Pretender whilst at the theatre, in obedience to which he was obliged to leave France to satisfy the demand of the British Ambassador.

Agreeing to serve the House of Hanover, the *debris* of the Scottish clans were formed into four regiments, each of which went by the name of the Highland Watch—first, second, third, and fourth, according to the date of its formation.—One of these regiments was sent to Canada, one to Virginia, one to Gibraltar, and one to Ireland. They proved thoroughly loyal to their adopted colours, and better soldiers never served the British Crown. It is to the pipers of the Highland regiment which was thus introduced to garrison duty in different parts of Ireland about the middle of the last century that she is indebted for the origin at least of this popular *chant de depart*, in the same way as she is said to be under a similar obligation to some early English regiment for the renowned fife-and-drum air of 'The Girl I left behind me.' This latter is the old English air of 'Brighton Camp,' the words of which are also English, most unquestionably ("I'm lonesome since I crossed the hill," &c.), the only Irish association to which it could lay claim, as far as I could ever see, being that Julian gave it amongst his Irish Quadrilles on the strength of Moore's having put to it his beautiful words —

> " As slow our ship her foamy track
> Against the wind was cleaving—"

The Irish often accuse the Scotch of borrowing their airs without acknowledgment. They would not be accused of knowingly doing the same thing themselves to the English, who have an ancient school of native melody, of rare and exquisite beauty, better known and appreciated—strange to say — in Ireland than amongst themselves, or at least amongst their own fashionable circles.

The oldest inhabitant of the other side of St. George's Channel can only remember two stanzas of 'Love, farewell!' as it was sung about fifty years ago by an old regiment called *The Black Bells*, " marching to death with military glee," along the Dublin Quay, where they embarked at the Pigeon House for England, to join the unfortunate Walcheren expedition. These were the first and fourth of the present version. The second line of the first ran—

> "First for France and then for Holland."

The other stanza, in which the mother appeals to the virtuous feelings (*quantum valeant*) as well as to the fears of the retiring troops on behalf of the family honour, remains unchanged—happily so, we may still be permitted to think, as a type of simple manners, bearing the antique stamp of a bold, broad faith, in the supernatural, even to the extent of divine justice permitting an outraged parent to return from beyond the tomb and wreak vengeance upon the perpetrator of the wrong.

The fifth stanza contemplates a higher *morale* and more satisfactory arrangement for all parties concerned, than the melancholy and disreputable order of things so feelingly and *fearfully* deprecated by the old lady in the fourth. Dibdin's naval heroes absent, or on the point of being so, took a broader view of the situation, their implorations to Nan and Sue to be constant and true being of a more conventional character—the constancy and truth of the winds and waves, according to sailors' notions, in general.

Paddy's alternative, the apotheosis of his "sowl in glory," in case that his body should be laid low, is superior to any picture which our great naval poet has given us of the British tar soaring aloft. Poor Jack's spirit, emancipated from its mortal coil, and rising above the sulphurous clouds and din of battle, would be satisfied with getting in anyhow and anywhere in the upper regions, of which, sooth to say, he has ever entertained rather mystic notions. Any quiet little nook or corner in the skies would be hailed as a post of refuge and rest by the brave and honest fellow, who felt he had simply done his duty. Pat's idea of the glory which awaited the soul of the Irish warrior soaring upwards from the arms of victory, is eminently Celtic, and in all respects a much higher conception—

> "Ille deûm vitam accipiet, divisque videbit
> Permixtos heroas, et ipse videbitur illis."

THE RAINY DAY.

BY H. W. LONGFELLOW.

THE day is cold, and dark and dreary;
    It rains, and the wind is never weary;
The vine still clings to the mouldering wall,
But at every gust the dead leaves fall,
    And the day is dark and dreary.

My life is cold, and dark, and dreary;
It rains, and the wind is never weary;
Memory clings to the mouldering past,
But the hopes of youth fall thick in the blast,
    And the days are dark and dreary.

Be still, sad heart, and cease repining;
Above the dark clouds is the sun still shining;
Thy fate is the common fate of all;
Into each life some rain must fall,
    Some days must be dark and dreary.

MY NORA!

BY T. J. OUSELEY.

MY NORA—dear NORA, is dreaming,
    The moon on her fair cheek is gleaming;
    Whilst the fairies unseen,
    Kiss her forehead serene,
As her eyes—through their lashes are beaming.

My NORA—sweet NORA is weeping,
The pearls through those lashes are peeping;
    Oh, the fairies, I fear,
    Have just breath'd in her ear
That my love from her bosom is creeping.

My NORA—loved NORA is waking,
Her heart with its anguish is breaking;
    NORA, come to thy rest
    On my fond, faithful breast—
Of thy soul's grief, love, mine is partaking.

EXCELSIOR

BY H. W. LONGFELLOW.

THE shades of night were falling fast,
  As through an Alpine village passed
A youth, who bore, 'midst snow and ice,
A banner with the strange device—*Excelsior!*

His brow was sad; his eye beneath
Flashed like a falchion from its sheath,
And like a silver clarion rung
The accents of that unknown tongue—*Excelsior!*

In happy homes he saw the light
Of household fires gleam clear and bright;
Above the spectral glaciers shone,
And from his lips escaped a groan—*Excelsior!*

"Try not the pass!" the old man said;
"Dark lowers the tempest overhead;
The roaring torrent is deep and wide!"
And loud that clarion voice replied—*Excelsior!*

"O stay," the maiden said, "and rest
Thy weary head upon this breast!"
A tear stood in his bright blue eye,
But still he answered with a sigh—*Excelsior!*

"Beware the pine-tree's wither'd branch!
Beware the awful avalanche!"
This was the peasant's last good-night;
A voice replied, far up the height—*Excelsior!*

At break of day, as heavenward
The pious monks of Saint Bernard
Uttered the oft repeated prayer,
A voice cried through the frosty air—*Excelsior!*

A traveller, by the faithful hound,
Half buried in the snow was found,
Still grasping in his hand of ice
That banner with the strange device—*Excelsior!*

There, in the twilight cold and grey,
Lifeless, but beautiful, he lay,
And from the sky, serene and far,
A voice fell, like a falling star—*Excelsior!*

HON. MR. SUCKLETHUMBKIN'S STORY.
THE EXECUTION.

A SPORTING ANECDOTE.

BY THOMAS INGOLDSBY.

MY Lord Tomnoddy got up one day;
 It was half after two, he had nothing to do,
So his lordship rang for his cabriolet.

Tiger Tim was clean of limb,
His boots were polish'd, his jacket was trim;
With a very smart tie in his smart cravat,
And a smart cockade on the top of his hat;
Tallest of boys, or shortest of men,
He stood in his stockings just four foot ten;
And he ask'd, as he held the door on the swing,
'Pray, did your Lordship please to ring?'

My Lord Tomnoddy he raised his head,
And thus to Tiger Tim he said,
 'Malibran's dead, Duvernay's fled,
Taglioni has not yet arrived in her stead;
Tiger Tim, come tell me true,
What may a nobleman find to do?'

Tim look'd up, and Tim look'd down,
He paus'd, and he put on a thoughtful frown,
And he held up his hat, and he peep'd in the crown;
He bit his lip, and he scratch'd his head,
He let go the handle, and thus he said,
As the door, released, behind him bang'd;
'An't please you, my Lord, there's a man to be hang'd.'

My Lord Tomnoddy jump'd up at the news,
 'Run to M'Fuze, and Lieutenant Treegooze,
And run to Sir Carnaby Jenks, of the Blues.

16

Rope-dancers a score I've seen before—
Madame Sacchi, Antonio, and Master Black-more ;
 But to see a man swing at the end of a string,
With his neck in a noose, will be quite a new thing.'

My Lord Tomnoddy stept into his cab—
Dark rifle-green, with a lining of drab ;
 Through street and through square,
 His high-trotting mare,
Like one of Ducrow's, goes pawing the air.
Adown Piccadilly and Waterloo Place
Went the high-trotting mare at a very quick pace ;
 She produced some alarm, but did no great harm,
Save frightening a nurse with a child on her arm,
 Spattering with clay two urchins at play,
Knocking down—very much to the sweeper's dismay—
An old woman who wouldn't get out of the way,
 And upsetting a stall near Exeter Hall,
Which made all the pious Church-Mission folks squall.
 But eastward afar through Temple Bar,
My Lord Tomnoddy directs his car ;
 Never heeding their squalls,
 Or their calls or their bawls,
He passes by Waithman's Emporium for shawls,
And, merely just catching a glimpse of St. Paul's,
 Turns down the Old Bailey,
 Where in front of the gaol, he
Pulls up at the door of the gin-shop, and gaily
Cries, ' What must I fork out to-night, my trump,
For the whole first-floor of the Magpie and Stump ?

The clock strikes Twelve—it is dark midnight—
Yet the Magpie and Stump is one blaze of light.
 The parties are met ; the tables are set ;
There is ' punch,' ' cold *without*,' ' hot *with*,' heavy wet,
 Ale-glasses and jugs, and rummers and mugs,
And sand on the floor, without carpets or rugs,
 Cold fowl and cigars, pickled onions in jars,
Welsh rabbits and kidneys—rare work for the jaws :—
And very large lobsters, with very large claws ;

And there is M'Fuze, and Lieutenant Tregooze;
And there is Sir Carnaby Jenks, of the Blues,
All come to see a man 'die in his shoes!'

The clock strikes One! supper is done,
And Sir Carnaby Jenks is full of his fun,
Singing 'Jolly companions every one!'
My Lord Tomnoddy is drinking gin toddy,
And laughing at ev'ry thing, and ev'ry body.—

The clock strikes Two! and the clock strikes Three!
—'Who so merry, so merry as we?'
Save Captain M'Fuze, who is taking a snooze,
While Sir Carnaby Jenks is busy at work,
Blacking his nose with a piece of burnt cork.

The clock strikes Four!—round the debtors' door
Are gather'd a couple of thousand or more;
As many await at the press-yard gate,
Till slowly its folding doors open, and straight
The mob divides, and between their ranks
A waggon comes loaded with posts and with planks.

The clock strikes Five! the Sheriffs arrive,
And the crowd is so great that the street seems alive;
But Sir Carnaby Jenks blinks and winks,
A candle burns down in the socket, and stinks.
Lieutenant Tregooze is dreaming of Jews,
And acceptances all the bill-brokers refuse;
My Lord Tomnoddy has drunk all his toddy,
And just as the dawn is beginning to peep,
The whole of the party are fast asleep.

Sweetly, oh! sweetly, the morning breaks,
    With roseate streaks,
Like the first faint blush on a maiden's cheeks;
Seem'd as that mild and clear blue sky
Smiled upon all things far and high,
On all—save the wretch condemn'd to die!
Alack! that ever so fair a Sun,
As that which its course has now begun,

Should rise on such a scene of misery!—
Should gild with rays so light and free
That dismal, dark-frowning Gallows-tree!

And hark!—a sound comes, big with fate;
The clock from St. Sepulchre's tower strikes—Eight!—
List to that low funereal bell:
It is tolling, alas! a living man's knell!—
And see!—from forth that opening door
They come—HE steps that threshold o'er
Who never shall tread upon threshold more!
—God! 'tis a fearsome thing to see
That pale wan man's mute agony,—
The glare of that wild, despairing eye,
Now bent on the crowd, now turn'd to the sky
As though 'twere scanning, in doubt and in fear,
The path of the Spirit's unknown career.
Those pinion'd arms, those hands that ne'er
Shall be lifted again,—not even in prayer;
That heaving chest!—enough—'tis done!
The bolt has fallen!—the spirit is gone—
For weal or for woe is known but to One!—
—Oh! 'twas a fearsome sight!—Ah me!
A deed to shudder at,—not to see.

Again that clock! 'tis time, 'tis time!
The hour is past: with its earliest chime
The chord is severed, the lifeless clay
By ' dungeon villains' is born away:
Nine!—'twas the last concluding stroke!
And then—my Lord Tomnoddy awoke!
And Tregooze and Sir Carnaby Jenks arose,
And Captain M'Fuze, with the black on his nose.
And they stared at each other, as much as to say
' Hollo! hollo! here's a rum go!
Why, Captain!—my Lord!—here's the devil to pay!
The fellow's been cut down and taken away!

What's to be done? we've miss'd all the fun!—
Why, they'll laugh at and quiz us all over the town,
We are all of us done so uncommonly brown.

What *was* to be done?—'twas perfectly plain
That they could not well hang the man over again:
What *was* to be done?—the man was dead !
Nought *could* be done—nought could be said ;
So—my Lord Tomnoddy went home to bed !

THE EXPEDITION TO PONTARLIN.

BY W. COOKE TAYLOR.

Oh long, very long Winter lengthens his day;
  We hear not the song of the birds from the spray ;
They are silent and sad in the groves and the bowers,
Awaiting the coming of spring-time and flowers!

But when the first birds on the branches were seen,
And the hedge changed its brown for a mantle of green,
The trumpet of war blew its blast o'er the land,
And summon'd the brave to the patriot band!

There was arming and bustling, confusion and haste,
Ere battalions were form'd, and line-of-march traced ;
But when once in the field, the proud duke we defied :—
At peasants no longer he laugh'd in his pride.

We came on so proudly through Burgundy's states,
That we soon forced Pontarlin to open its gates ;
And the women, at morn dress'd in colours so bright,
Were making the dark weeds of widows ere night.

The foreigners, frantic, came forward in force ;
They number'd twelve thousand of foot and of horse:
They assaulted us fiercely to gain back the town,
But their vaunts and their boastings were soon cloven down !

Our Swiss sprung upon them with blow upon blow,
Till never was seen such a wide overthrow ;
From the ramparts their banners and pennons were thrust,
And lay all unheeded, defiled in the dust !

The Wild Bear of Berne put forth his sharp claws,
And bristled his mane up, and grinded his jaws ;
He came with his cubs, who of thousands were four,
And the foreigners trembled on hearing his roar!

Be warn'd, duke of Burgundy! timely beware,
Nor venture to mate thee with Berne's fierce Bear;
See his teeth, see his claws, his cubs eager for prey;
Haste! haste! save your lives, and get out of his way.

They would not take warning; the Bear rose in wrath,
And soon through their ranks forc'd a terrible path,
And, though the Burgundians were full four to one,
The Bear and his cubs soon compell'd them to run!

And still the Bear roar'd, until, borne on the gale,
Its echo had reach'd the brave burghers of Basle;
And they said, since the Bear is come out of his den,
We must go and assist him with all of our men.

Then prais'd be the warriors of Basle and of Berne,
Nor pass we in silence Soleure and Lucerne!
They came without summons our dangers to share,
And bravely they fought by the side of the Bear!

Thus strengthen'd, to Grandson our armies were led,
As the knights and the nobles of Burgundy fled.
We girdled the town, and our musketry's din
Never ceas'd night or day, the proud fortress to win!

On the morning of Sunday the place we assail'd;
Its gates were forced open, its ramparts were scal'd;
The banner of freedom soon stream'd from its towers,
And announc'd to the duke that proud Grandson was ours!

WILLIAM COOKE TAYLOR, a native of Ireland, and LL.D. of the University of Dublin, was well known in the political and literary circles of the metropolis about twenty years ago, when such notabilities as Cobden, Pelham Villiers, Forbes, Owen, Latham, Lankester, Carter Hall, Lover, &c., used to meet at his hospitable table in Arlington Street, Camden Town. He was for a long period amongst the leading contributors of the 'Athenæum,' and was the author of 'Romantic Biographies of the Age of Elizabeth,' 'The Revolutions and Conspiracies of Europe,' and 'Memoirs of the House of Orleans.' He brought out through the publishing house of John William Parker, in the Strand, a host of useful manuals on educational and other subjects; and was for some years a contributor of prose and verse to 'Bentley's

Miscellany.' During the stormy year of the Young Ireland troubles, he acted as private secretary to Lord Clarendon, and was carried off the year following, (1849) at his residence in Dublin, by an attack of cholera. His talents were of a versatile character. Besides being a good classic, he knew most European and some of the Oriental languages; and in some of the leading branches of science his attainments were respectable. He was a member of the Athenæum Club for many years; and was one of the sixty *savans* who, discontented with the invidious arrangements made by the dinner committee of the British Association the year they met at Birmingham, left the banqueting hall in a body, and dining at 'The Red Lion,' a tavern in the immediate neighbourhood, established then and there the famous 'Red Lion dining club of literary and scientific men, who met monthly for several years afterwards at Anderton's in Fleet Street, London.

THE SIEGE OF HENSBURGH.

BY JOHN RYAN.

BRAVE news! brave news! the Emperor
   Hath girded on his sword,
And swears by the rood, in an angry mood,
   And eke by his knightly word,
That humbled Hensburgh's towers shall be,
With all her boasted chivalry.

The brazen clarion's battle note
   Hath sounded through the land;
And brave squire and knight, in their armour dight,
   Ay, many a gallant band,
Have heard the summons far and near,
And come with falchion and with spear.

" Ho! to the rebel city, ho!
   Let vengeance lead the way!"
And anon the sheen of their spears was seen,
   As they rushed upon the prey.
Beneath where Hensburgh's turrets frown'd,
Great Conrade chose his vantage ground.

Far stretching o'er the fertile plain
His snow-white tents were spread ;
And the sweet night air, as it linger'd there,
Caught the watchful sentry's tread.
Then o'er the city's battlement
The tell-tale breeze its echo sent.

Day after day the leaguer sat
Before that city's wall,
And yet, day by day, the proud Guelph cried " *Nay,*"
To the herald's warning call ;
Heedless, from morn to eventide,
How many a famish'd mother died.

Weak childhood, and the aged man,
Wept—sorely wept for bread ;
And pale Hunger seem'd, as his wild eye gleam'd
On the yet unburied dead,
As if he longed, alas ! to share
The night dog's cold, unhallow'd fare.

*   *   *   *   o

*   *   *   *   o

No longer Hensburgh's banner floats ;
Hush'd is her battle-cry,
For a victor waits at her shatter'd gates,
And her sons are doom'd to die.
But Hensburgh's daughters yet shall prove
The saviours of the homes they love !

All glory to the Emperor,
The merciful and brave ;
Sound, clarions, sound, tell the news around,
And ye drooping banners wave !
Hensburgh's fair daughters, ye are free;
Go forth, with all your " *braverie !*"

" Bid them go forth," the Emperor cried,
  " Far from the scene of strife,
Whether matron staid, or the blushing maid,
  Or the daughter, or the wife ;
For ere yon sun hath left the sky,
Each rebel-male shall surely die.

" Bid them go forth," the Emperor said,
  " We wage not war with *them ;*
Bid them all go free, with their ' *braverie,*'
  And each richly valued gem ;
Let each upon her person bear
That which she deemed her *chiefest* care."

The city's gates are open'd wide ;
  The leaguer stands amaz'd ;
'Twas a glorious deed, and shall have its meed,
  And by minstrel shall be praised,
For each had left her *jewell'd tire ;*
To bear a *husband* or a *sire.*

With faltering step each laden'd one
  At Conrade's feet appears ;
In amaze he stood, but his thirst for blood
  Was quench'd by his falling tears ;
The victor wept aloud to see
Devoted woman's constancy.

All glory to the Emperor,—
  All glory and renown !
He hath sheath'd his sword, and his royal word
  Hath gone forth to save the town ;
For woman's love is mightier far
Than all the strategics of war.

BRYAN O'LYNN.

BY THE IRISH WHISKEY DRINKER.

IN Dalkey a king of great weight,
 Though his deeds are not *blarney'd* in
  story,
For he rose, and he *row'l'd* to bed late,
 Lived Bryan O'Lynn in his glory.
With a nate spanchel'd* cawbeen† so gay,
He was crown'd by Queen Sheelah each
  day
   They say.
Bryan's praise let us sing!
 What a jolly good king
Was rattling bowld Bryan O'Lynn!
  Hurroo!!

His palace was thatched with straw;
 There he took all his meals and his glass;
And all his dominions he saw,
 When he sauntered along on his ass;
Hearty, simple, and free, to confide,
With no guard but "Dog Tray" would
  he ride
   By his side.
Bryan's praise let us sing, &c.

The nation ne'er groan'd for his table,
 Though he drank rather fast, it is true;
Says Bryan, "If my people are able
 To drink, sure I'll drink whiskey, too.
An income-tax, then, at each door,
A pint to each keg he would score,
   No more.
Bryan's praise let us sing, &c.

'Mongst the darlings of gentle degree
 He was mighty polite; and 'twas rather
Suspected his subjects could see
 Many reasons to call him their father.

LE ROI D'YVETOT.

(BERANGER.)

IL était un roi d'Yvetot,
 Peu connu dans l'histoire,
Se levant tard, se couchant tôt,
 Dormant fort bien sans gloire;
Et couronné par Jeanneton
D'un simple bonnet de cotton,
  Dit on.
 Oh, oh, oh, oh!
 Ah, ah, ah, ah!
Quel bon petit roi c'était là!
  La, la!

Il faisait ses quatre repas
 Dans son palais de chaume,
Et sur un âne, pas a pas,
 Parcourrait son royaume.
Joyeux, simple, et croyant le
 bien,
Pour tout guarde il n'avait rien
  Qu'un chien.
 Oh, oh, oh, oh, &c.

Il n'avait de goût onereux,
 Qu'une soif un peu vive;
Mais en rendant son peuple heu-
 reux,
Il faut bien qu'un roi vive.
Lui même à table et sans suppôt,
Sur chaque muid levait un pot
  D'impôt.
 Oh, oh, oh, oh! &c.

Aux filles de bonnes maisons
 Comme il avait su plaire,
Ses sujets avaient cent raisons
 De le nommer leur père :

---

 * *Spanchel*, noun substantive,—a hay or straw rope, chiefly used for tying
the legs together of cows or pigs, to hinder them, not from trespassing on
their neighbour's property, but from roaming too far from home. *Spanchel*,
verb,—to tie or fasten with a hay or straw rope.
 † A felt hat of no particular shape.

Four days in the year, sometimes six,
To manœuvre the boys, he would fix,
    And their sticks.
Bryan's praise let us sing, &c.

With the neighbours most friendly lived
    he,
  And sighed not his power to increase;
If with Bryan all our kings would agree,
  The world would have comfort and
    peace!
When on high he was called to appear,
Sad Dalkey then shed its first tear
    On his bier.
  For his death let us cry,
  Let us cry, "Arrah, why,
Bryney, jewel, och! why did you die?
    Wirrasthrew!!!"

Bryan's phiz is preserved to this day,
  Hung out o'er a sheebeen-shop door,
Where those that are able to pay
  May drink of good whiskey galore.
The house is in Tandragee,
And it 's kept by one Widow Magee,—
    D' ye see?
  Bryan's praise let us sing,
  What a jolly good king
Was rattling ould Bryan O'Lynn!
    Hurroo!

D'ailleurs il ne levait de ban,
Que pour tirer quatre fois l'an,
    Au blanc.
Oh, oh, oh, oh! &c.

Il n'aggrandit point ses états,
  Fut un voisin commode,
Et modèle des potentats,
  Prit le plaisir pour code.
Ce n'est que lorsqu'il expira
Que le peuple qui l'enterra,
    Pleura.
Oh, oh, oh, oh! &c.

On conserve encor le portrait
  De ce digne et bon prince;
C'est l'enseigne d'un cabaret
  Fameux dans la province.
Les jours de fête bien souvent
Le foule s'écrie en buvant,
    Devant:
  Oh, oh, oh, oh!
  Ah, ah, ah, ah!
Quel bon petit roi o'était là!
    La, la!

THEOCRITUS.

BY C. H. LANGHORNE.

"And with a tale, forsooth he cometh to you—with a tale which holdeth children from play, and old men from the chimney corner."
SIR PHILIP SIDNEY.

THEOCRITUS! Theocritus! ah! thou hadst pleasant dreams,
  Of the crystal spring Burinna, and the Haleus' murm'ring
    streams;
Of Physcus, and Neaethus, and fair Arethusa's fount,
Of Lacinion's beetling crag, and Latymnus' woody mount;

Of the fretted rocks and antres hoar that overhang the sea,
And the sapphire sky and thymy plains of thy own sweet Sicily ;
And of the nymphs of Sicily, that dwelt in oak and pine—
Theocritus! Theocritus! what pleasant dreams were thine!

And of the merry rustics who tend the goats and sheep,
And the maids who trip to milk the cows at morning's dewy peep,
Of Clearista with her locks of brightest sunny hair,
And the saucy girl Eunica, and sweet Chloe kind and fair ;
And of those highly favoured ones, Endymion and Adonis,
Loved by Selena the divine, and the beauteous Dionis ;
Of the silky-haired caprella, and the gentle lowing kine—
Theocritus! Theocritus! what pleasant dreams were thine !

Of the spring time, and the summer, and the zephyr's balmy breeze ;
Of the dainty flowers, and waving elms, and the yellow humming
          bees ;
Of the rustling poplar and the oak, the tamarisk and the beech,
The dog-rose and anemone,—thou had'st a dream of each !
Of the galingale and hyacinth, and the lily's snowy hue,
The couch-grass, and green maiden-hair, and celandine pale blue,
The gold-bedropt cassidony, the fern, and sweet woodbine—
Theocritus! Theocritus! what pleasant dreams were thine!

Of the merry harvest-home, all beneath the good green tree,
The poppies and the spikes of corn, the shouting and the glee
Of the lads so blithe and healthy, and the girls so gay and neat,
And the dance they lead around the tree with ever twinkling feet;
And the bushy piles of lentisk to rest the aching brow,
And reach and pluck the damson down from the overladen bough,
And munch the roasted bean at ease, and quaff the Ptelean wine—
Theocritus! Theocritus! what pleasant dreams were thine !

And higher dreams were thine to dream—of Heracles the brave,
And Polydeukes good at need, and Castor strong to save ;
Of Dionysus and the woe he wrought the Theban king ;
And of Zeus the mighty centre of Olympus' glittering ring ;
Of Tiresias, the blind old man, the famed Aonian seer ;
Of Hecatè, and Cthonian Dis, whom all mankind revere ;
And of Daphnis lying down to die beneath the leafy vine—
Theocritus! Theocritus! what pleasant dreams were thine!

But mostly sweet and soft thy dreams—of Cypris' loving kiss,
Of the dark-haired maids of Corinth, and the feasts of Sybaris;
Of alabaster vases of Assyrian perfume,
Of ebony, and gold, and pomp, and softly-curtained room;
Of Faunus piping in the woods to the Satyrs' noisy rout,
And the saucy Panisks mocking him with many a jeer and flout;
And of the tender-footed Hours, and Pieria's tuneful Nine—
Theocritus! Theocritus! what pleasant dreams were thine!

SPRING.
A RELIC OF PROVENÇAL LITERATURE.
BY W. C. TAYLOR.

ANGELIC choirs in upper air chaunt with their golden tongues
  The praises of that mighty king to whom the world belongs;
Who bade the stars to shine in heaven; who severed land from sea;
Who gave the fishes to the deep, the cattle to the lea.
The beauteous Spring begins its reign; the woods are in their
  bloom;
The verdant trees put forth their leaves, the flow'rets shed perfume;
The birds commence their twittering songs, and of the feather'd
  crowd,
The smallest has the notes that are the sweetest and most loud.
'Tis Philomel, who in the grove has sought the highest spray,
And thence pours forth sweet melody from eve to dawn of day.
Ah, gentle bird! incessantly why dost thou thus bewail?
Wouldst quell the sounds of lyre and harp by thy more plain-
  tive tale?
The maid who strikes the timbrel stops to lend a willing ear,
And princes in attention stand thy thrilling song to hear.
Cease, gentle bird, to strain thy throat with notes so wild and
  deep,
And let the weary world at last resign itself to sleep.
Ah! wretched bird, thou wilt not cease, but through the livelong
  night,
Neglecting food, wilt persevere the listeners to delight.
All hear with joy, but in return none succour will afford,
Save he who gave the power of song, the all-preserving Lord.
But summer comes, the bird is hush'd, by parent's care engross'd,
Forgotten then, unknown he dies by chill of winter's frost.

OWED TO MY CREDITORS.

BY ALFRED CROWQUILL.

In vain I lament what is past,
    And pity their woe-begone looks;
Though they grin at the credit they gave,
    I know I am in their best books.
To my *tailor* my *breaches* of faith,
    On my conscience but now lightly sit,
For such lengths in *his measures* he's gone,
    He has given me many *a fit.*
My bootmaker finding *at last,*
    That my *soul* was too stubborn to suit,
Waxed wroth when he found he had got
    Anything but *the length of my foot.*
My hatmaker cunningly *felt*
    He'd seen many like me before,
So *brimful* of insolence vowed
    On credit he'd crown me no more.
My baker was crusty, and burnt,
    When he found himself quite overdone
By a *fancy-bred* chap like myself—
    Ay, as *cross* as a *Good Friday's bun.*
Next my laundress, who wash'd pretty clean,
    In behaviour was dirty and bad;
For into *hot water* she popp'd
    All the shirts and the dickies I had.
Then my butcher who'd little *at stake,*
    Most surlily opened his *chops,*
And swore my affairs out of *joint,*
    So on to my *carcase* he pops.
In my lodgings exceedingly *high,*
    Though *low* in the rent to be sure,
Without warning my landlady seized,
    Took my things, and the key of the door.
Thus cruelly used by the world,
    In the Bench I can smile at its hate;
For a time I must alter my *stile,*
    For I cannot get out of the *gate.*

RAILWAY DACTYLS.

BY G. D.

Here we go off on the " London and Birmingham,"
   Bidding adieu to the foggy metropolis!
Staying at home with the dumps, is confirming 'em ;—
   Motion and mirth are a fillip to life.
Let us look out! Is there aught that is *see*-able?
   Presto!—away !—what a vanishing spectacle!
Well! on the whole, it is vastly agreeable—
   " Why, sir, perhaps it is all very well,"—
      Tricketty, tracketty, tricketty, tracketty!
   " *Barring* the noise, and the smoke, and the smell."

Now, with the company pack'd in the carriages,
   Strange is the medley of voluble utterings,—
Comings and goings, deceases and marriages,—
   Oh, what a clatter of matters is *there!*
History, politics, letters, morality,
   Heraldry, botany, chemistry, cookery,
Poetry, physic, the stars, and legality,—
   All in a loud opposition of tongues!
      Tricketty, tracketty, tricketty, tracketty!
   Never mind *that*—it is good for the lungs.

" All that 's remarkable; now, we may *stir* and see ;
   Free circulation—how huge are its benefits !"—
" Yet, sir, with all the improvement in *currency,*
   Great is the dread of *a run on the banks.*"—
" *Fight* with *America!* Do but the folly see !
   Since unto *both*, sir, belongs the same *origin.*"—
" What's your opinion of Peel and his policy ?"—
   " What of the weather ?—and how is the wind ?"
      Tricketty, tracketty, tricketty, tracketty !
   " Oh! that that *whistle* were far off as Ind!"

On, like a hurricane! on, like a water-fall !
   Steam away ! scream away ! hissing and spluttering !'
" Madam, beware lest your out-leaning daughter fall !"
   " Yes, sir, I will; but her *life* is *insured.*"—

" Cobden's a-coming to mob and to rabble us !"—
" Zounds ! sir, my *corn !* Do you think I'm of adamant ?".—
" Oh, what an appetite ! Heliogabalus !
    That little fellow will eat himself *ill !*"
       Tricketty, tracketty, tricketty, tracketty !
" When you're at home again, give him a pill."

Oh, Mr. Hudson ! Macadam's extinguisher !
    Men are as boys in the grasp of thy *schoolery !*
Those who love England can no better *thing* wish her
    Than to have *thee* for her *Ruler of Lines !*
Praised as thy course is, to heighten the fame of it,
    I'll give you a hint, without fee or expectancy :—
Write us a *book*—and let *this* be the name of it,
     " *Rail*-ways and *Snail*-ways ; or, Roads New and Old."
       Tricketty, tracketty, tricketty, tracketty !
Won't such a volume in thousands be sold ?

Here we go on again, every link of us !
    Oh, what a chain ! what a fly-away miracle !
Birds o' the firmament ! what do ye think of us ?
    Minutes ! be steady, as *markers of miles !*
Well ! of new greatness we now have the germ in us !
    But the *collector*, I see, coming hither is.
" Ladies and gentlemen—this is the *terminus*—
    Ticket, sir ! ticket, sir !—end of the line !"
       Ricketty, racketty, ricketty, racketty !
" Friends of velocity ! now let us *dine !*"

THE NORMAN PEASANT'S HYMN TO THE VIRGIN.

BY WILLIAM JONES.

Hope of the faithful ! behold us now bending,
    Submissive, contrite, at thy footstool of love ;
The tears of thy children repentant are blending,
    Oh ! plead for their help in thy kingdom above !
       Thou canst each bosom see,
       May it more sinless be,
       Ave Maria,
       To glorify thee !

We are defenceless without thy protection,
To watch o'er our night, and to shield us by day;
And 'tis to the warmth of thy care and affection
Our thoughts are more hallow'd, our feet less astray.
Thou canst each bosom see,
May it more sinless be,
Ave Maria,
To glorify thee!

Be thou our comfort, when shaded by sorrow,
For weak are the tendrils we cling to below;
As night is subdued in the dawn of a morrow,
Illume with thy brightness the depths of our woe!
Thou canst each bosom see,
May it more sinless be,
Ave Maria,
To glorify thee!

Through the dim valley our vespers are pealing,
Borne on the winds to a sunnier sphere;
While yon star that lonely the skies are revealing
Doth tell in its beaming thou hearest our prayer.
Thou canst each bosom see,
May it more sinless be,
Ave Maria,
To glorify thee!

WELLINGTON.

BY H. W. LONGFELLOW.

A MIST was driving down the British Channel,
The day was just begun,
And through the window-panes, on floor and panel,
Streamed the red Autumn sun.

It glanced on flowing flag and rippling pennon,
And the white sails of ships;
And, from the frowning rampart, the black cannon
Hailed it with feverish lips.

Sandwich and Romney, Hastings, Hythe, and Dover
 Were all alert that day,
To see the French war-steamers speeding over,
 When the fog cleared away.

Sullen and silent, and like couchant lions,
 Their cannon, through the night,
Holding their breath, had watched in grim defiance
 The sea-coast opposite.

And now they roared at drum-beat from their stations
 On every citadel;
Each answering each, with morning salutations,
 That all was well!

And down the coast, all taking up the burden,
 Replied the distant forts,
As if to summon from his sleep the Warden
 And Lord of the Cinque Ports.

Him shall no sunshine from the fields of azure,
 No drum-beat from the wall,
No morning gun from the black fort's embrazure
 Awaken with their call!

No more surveying with an eye impartial
 The long line of the coast,
Shall the gaunt figure of the old Field-Marshal
 Be seen upon his post!

For in the night, unseen, a single warrior,
 In sombre harness mailed,
Dreaded of man, and surnamed the destroyer,
 The rampart wall has scaled.

He passed into the chamber of the sleeper,
 The dark and silent room;
And as he entered, darker grew and deeper
 The silence and the gloom.

He did not pause to parley or dissemble,
 But smote the Warden hoar;
Ah! what a blow! that made all England tremble
 And groan from shore to shore.

Meanwhile, without the surly cannon waited,
The sun rose bright o'erhead ;
Nothing in Nature's aspect intimated
That a great man was dead !

GATHER THE ROSE-BUDS WHILE YOU MAY !

BY GEORGE DANIEL.

LIFE is short, the wings of time
Bear away our early prime,
Swift with them our spirits fly,
The heart grows chill, and dim the eye.
Seize the moment ! snatch the treasure !
Sober haste is wisdom's leisure.
Summer blossoms soon decay ;
" *Gather the rose-buds while you may !*"

Barter not for sordid store
Health and peace ; nor covet more
Than may serve for frugal fare
With some chosen friend to share !
Not for others toil and heap,
But *yourself* the harvest reap ;
Nature smiling, seems to say,
" *Gather the rose-buds while you may !*"

Learning, science, truth sublime,
Fairy fancies, lofty rhyme,
Flowers of exquisite perfume !
Blossoms of immortal bloom !
With the gentle virtues twin'd,
In a beauteous garland bind
For your youthful brow to-day,—
" *Gather the rose-buds while you may !*"

Life is short—but not to those
Who early, wisely pluck the rose.
Time he flies—to us 'tis given,
On his wings to fly to Heaven.

Ah ! to reach those realms of light,
Nothing must impede our flight ;
Cast we all but *Hope* away !
" *Gather the rose-buds while we may !*"

<hr />

THE ILLUMINATION.

A TALE OF ALMA MATER.

BY A. R. W.

" Pulsatus rogat, et pugnis concisus adorat,
Ut liceat paucis cum dentibus inde reverti."
JUVENAL, iii., Sat. 300 v.

PREFACE.

THE subject of the following tale is matter now of history,
    But shrouded, to avoid offence, in due poetic mystery ;
And I assure my readers all, in cottage, hall, or palace, sirs,
That, though I " nought *exterminate,*" I " nought set down in
    malice," sirs.

Air—" Guy Faux."

A tragi-comedy I sing ; three " grave and *Reverend* signors,"
Who sallied forth one luckless night, with dignified demeanours,
To send home all *their* college men, on pain of rustication,
Whom they found joining in the *row* at last Illumination !

For sundry graceless undergrads, with wine somewhat " *promis-
    cuous,*"
From flooring bumpers to " the Queen," (such power good port
    or whisky has !)
A *Gown-and-town* row had got up to testify their loyalty !
By " *milling*" well all *Rads* and *Cads* and other foes to royalty !

At length the streets, " at noon of night," had grown a little
    quieter,
For one by one had dropped off home each capless, gownless rioter,
On which our heroes, satisfied with this consoling knowledge, sirs,
And thinking all their labours o'er, were hastening back to col-
    lege, sirs !

When, just as they had turned into the lane of classic* " Simmary,"
They fell among a mob of *cads,* assembled there in grim array,

<hr />

* St. Mary Hall.

Who set upon them, blacked their eyes, and mauled them so
confoundedly,
That one of them, "*intirely kilt*" and bleeding on the ground did
lie!

As he lay groaning o'er his wounds, in sad and doleful *barytones*,
There chanced to be among the crowd some modern "*good Sa-
maritans,*"
Who pitying saw his hapless plight, with love quite *Demiurgical*,*
Conveyed him home, where he was forced to send for aid chirurgical!

The "*Sawbones*" came, with visage long, and shook his head
mysteriously,
Says he, "The patient has, I fear, been damaged very seriously,
But trust my skill—(on frailer hopes doth oft the life of man
turn, sirs,)—
They haven't quite put out the *light*, though they've sorely
smashed the *lantern*, sirs!"

Some drugs were sent *instanter* by this son of Æsculapius;
"Hanc *lotionem* applices, et huncce *haustum* capias!"
But, through his stupid *scout's* mistake, being *addled* most infer-
nally,
He swallowed up the *lotion* and applied the *draught* externally!!

By gnawing pains, ere long, was rack'd his stomach *magisterial*,
Which made him dread his latter end and inquest *coronerial;*
"Quick, fetch a stomach-pump!" he groan'd, "with strong eme-
tics cram me well!
I've *been and done it*—'tis a case of—pison yourself, Samiwel!"

A stomach-pump was quickly brought, and *all hands* set to work
at it,
And speedily they *clean'd him out!*—let no one smile or smirk at it!
His life was saved; but to this day, (of that night's row the last
trophy),
That stomach-pump *sticks in his throat!* Thus ended this catas-
trophe!

---

* For the enlightenment of my *unlearned* readers, I have the honour to
inform them that the *Demiurgus* was the deity of the Platonists, and by
them regarded as a being of pure love and benevolence.

MORAL.

Be warned, ye *Dons*, for *Gown-town rows*, like matrimonial
  quarrels, sirs,
Produce for those who interfere more broken heads than laurels,
  sirs,
But if you *will* thus waste the health, which was to *cool your por-
  ridge* meant,
You'll meet with many a *heavy blow, and very sad discourage-
  ment!*

Sage counsel would I likewise give to each bold under-graduate—
" Experto crede"—brothers all, when in a *row* a *cad* you hit,
The chances are, that, *though you win*, you'll find it bad economy
To carry home a tattered gown and battered physiognomy !

Oxford, 19th of February, 1840.

THE MARQUIS WELLESLEY'S ADDRESS TO ETON.

ME, when thy shade and Thames's meads and flowers,
  Invite to soothe the cares of waning age,
May memory bring to me my long-past hours,
  To calm my soul, and troubled thoughts assuage.

Come, parent Eton ! turn the stream of time
  Back to thy sacred fountain crown'd with bays,
Recall my brightest, sweetest days of prime,
  When all was hope and triumph, joy and praise.

Guided by thee, I raised my youthful sight
  To the steep solid heights of lasting fame,
And hail'd the beams of clear ethereal light
  That brighten round the Greek and Roman name.

O blest Instruction ! friend to generous youth !
  Source of all good ! you taught me to intwine
The Muse's laurel with eternal truth,
  And woke her lyre to strains of faith divine.

ONE HOUR WITH DEATH.

SUGGESTED BY A PICTURE BY SIR JOSHUA REYNOLDS IN THE DULWICH GALLERY.

THE sun has gone in from this world of sin,
    The gaunt wolf roams the fell—
" Now whither dost speed on thy tall white steed !
    Strange rider, pause and tell."

" Mount, mount with me, and thou shalt see
    A boon to thee I give:
The terrible power for a single hour,
    To ride with me—and LIVE !"

" By the thrilling tone, and the eye of stone,
    And the blue and vapouring breath,
By the hard, cold brow, I know thee now,--
    Dread rider ! thou art DEATH !

" Oh ! might I refuse—but I dare not choose—
    My spirit is not free ;
Thy gift is a doom, and, though not to the tomb,
    I feel I must go with thee !"

Away ! away ! through mire and clay,
    The riders two are sped,
Death first drew rein on a battle plain,
    'Mid heaps of festering dead.

He gazed all around, and no longer he frown'd,
    But he laugh'd with fiend-like glee—
" The fires of hell burn wondrous well
    When man does my work for me !"

And on and on, o'er clod and stone,
    Are sped those riders twain,
Towards a glimmering light through the darksome night,
    Which beam'd from a cottage pane.

And a lovely sight did that glimmering light
    Show to the gazers there ;
In the twilight gloom of a lonely room
    Sat a lady pale and fair.

In heavy unrest, on her gentle breast,
    Its young brow knit with pain,
Lay the fever'd check of an infant weak,
    Too feeble to complain.

The tear-drop was dry in the mother's eye,
    Her cold lips spoke no word :
Her will she had given to the will of Heaven—
    She was waiting on the Lord!

Yet ever a glance she cast askance
    Of strange distrust and fear,
Through the doubtful gloom of that silent room,
    As she felt that Death was near.

He has passed the door, he treads the floor,
    His arm is raised to slay,
But a bright form was seen to rush between,
    And a stern voice cried, " Away !

" Destroyer, flee ! oh, not to thee,
    Through many a peaceful year,
Is it given to split the bonds which knit,
    That fond and faithful pair.

" And in thy brief hour of impotent power,
    When I may not bid thee fly ;
Not to them shalt thou bring or terror or sting,
    Nor to thee shall be victory !

" Back, wretch !" o'erpowered the grim shape cowered,
    And winced like a chidden boy,
Then again on its course he urged his pale horse,
    Still eager to destroy.

At a lordly hall was his next stern call,
    Where 'neath silken canopy,
Afraid to pray, a rich man lay,
    Who knew that he must die.

His failing ear, it could not hear
    One blessing from the poor ;
But he knew whose steed had slack'd its speed,
    Whose hand was on the door.

His straining eye could nought descry
    O'er his couch of sculptured gold,
Save the gloating stare of some eager heir,
    Or the glance of some menial cold.

Oh! he would have given for one hope of Heaven,
    And one of Love's true tears,
All his wealth and his lands, and have toiled with his hands
    Forward through a thousand years.

But he turned his face from the Spirit of Grace,
    He scoffed at the orphan's cry ;
His god it was pelf, his love it was self ;
    He must godless, loveless, die!

TO A LADY SINGING.

BY J. A WADE.

THERE is a light about those eyes,
    Warm, rich, but tender, like the hue
That's left upon the vesper skies
    When day has turn'd to misty blue:
A mild repose, as if the sun
    Of joy had not been long departed ;
And twilight thoughts had just begun
    Half blissfully, half broken-hearted!
        Oh! lady look but thus,
        And I could gaze for ever!

Within thy voice there is a tone,
    Soft, sweet, and trembling, like the sighs
That night-birds through the valleys moan,
    Thinking they sing gay melodies!
A tranquil sound, as if the tide,
    The noisy tide of mirth and laughter,
Had fall'n adown youth's green hill-side,
    To flow in quiet ever after!
        Oh! lady sing but thus,
        And I could hear for ever!

JARL ROLLO.

BY G. E. INMAN.

THE winds are in motion to favour the brave,
 And the steeds of the ocean are cleaving the wave;
Of a thousand wild warriors, the mighty, the free,
Those steeds are the carriers across the dark sea:
The Berserkers, howling, stand ranged on each prow,
And their frantic eyes, scowling, gleam death to the foe;
Now, this was the host of Jarl Rollo, the Northman.

Loud shouted the heroes, and bared was each brand,
As forth from the sea rose the cloud of the land;
And wild was the wrestle, each fierce to be first,
As down from each vessel the ravagers burst;
And fierce was the onset, and fiercely repell'd;
But, ere it was sunset the landsmen were quell'd;
And the Jarl burnt the town for a light to march on by!

To Rouen, with ravage, the sea-monarch goes,
With merriment savage, destroying the foes;
Church, city, and village, they all fared the same,
First given to pillage, then given to flame;
The monks by the halter or cross were all kill'd,
And even on the altar the nuns they defiled,—
All but two or three old ones, whose good saints preserved them.

To Charles, the French monarch, his nobles in rule
Told the march of this anarch:—now Charles was a fool,
Recked nought what was doing, folks did as they please,
Nor whatever was brewing while he had his ease.
So sitting in quiet, he heard them right through,
Then said, "For this riot, to-morrow will do,"
And very composedly sat down to drinking.

He was next day at dinner, lords, ladies, and all,
When Jarl Rollo, the sinner, stalk'd into the hall,
And seating him coolly, *sans* fashion or form,
Roar'd hoarsely out, "Truly your climate is warm,

So I'll taste of your liquor before I begin !"
And he snatched up a beaker, and drank to the King.—
" Who the devil art thou ?" quoth King Charles, rather bluntly.

" Thou shalt find me the devil,—in manners at least,—
An' ye be not more civil to welcome a guest !
They call me Jarl Rollo, the King of the Sea,
And a thousand men follow my raven so free !
We have paid ye a visit on hearing your fame,
To ask how is it with you and your dame !"
Now King Charles was a churl, for he thank'd not Jarl Rollo.

" Beyond the dark water," quoth Rollo the Bold,
" They boast your fair daughter and treasures of gold ;
Having plenty of leisure, we came here to see—
For my men is thy treasure ! thy daughter for me !—
Ye are time-worn and listless, with foes cannot wage,
And my power resistless shall shield thy old age."—
" Grammercy !" quoth the King, " Don't you wish 'twas a bar-
    gain ?"

" What ho !" the Jarl thundered, " my merry men all !"
And some four or five hundred burst into the hall ;
Some with young infants pitching from spear unto spear,
The half-dead things screeching, oh ! fearful to hear !
And all sat down laughing, wild, reckless, and rude ;
Some the merry wine quaffing, some gorging the food,
And others the delicate women caressing.

Then, out roar'd the Sea-king, " My warriors behold !
Yield the treasures I'm seeking, thy daughter, thy gold !
At my name thou hast shook not, nay, bearded my might !
Now, mark me, I brook not such insult and slight !
When I cross the dark water no child's play is mine.
Thy gold and thy daughter, or this fate is thine !"—
And he struck out the brains of a page that stood near him.

As the ghastly mass, shivering, dropt dead and inert,
A grey-goose shaft, quivering, struck Rollo's mail shirt,
And a voice was heard shrieking, " Unhand me, ye knaves !"
And a boy to the Sea-king was dragged by his slaves.

Then the Jarl roar'd out, chuckling, "By Woden! ho! ho!
Why the babe and the suckling will next come as foe!
Did ye think, boy, a Northman's coat thin as a heron's?"—

"A curse on its thickness!" the bold boy replied,
"And a curse on the weakness and youth ye deride!
Had my arm back'd my spirit, foul fiend that thou art,
The fate that ye merit had flown on my dart.—
Thou to wed my loved sister, Gisella the fair!
Thou!—Ev'n God would assist her ere such marriage were!
Take our treasures, and go—but our bright one—oh, never!"

Quoth the Jarl, "Mighty pretty, my Dauphin of France!
Now you've finish'd your ditty, let's see how ye dance.
Fling a rope round yon rafter, and hang him thereto:
He'll be taller, men, after, an odd inch or two."—
'Mid the Northmen's fierce laughter, their pallid foe's moan,
A rope round the rafter is hastily thrown,
And the noose round the neck of the bold boy placed read;

Like the moaning blood-chilling of sleeping despair
Rose the wild wail, heart-thrilling, of Gisella the fair,
And rushing forth madly, she clasp'd the Jarl's knee,—
"Oh! take all—all gladly—take treasure—take me—
Only spare my loved brother, our darling, our joy!
By thine own fond dear mother, oh, spare my bright boy!"—
"Ha! ha!" roared the Jarl, "have you come to your senses?"

Then the boy cried, "No, never, dark demon of pride,
My life to deliver shall *she* be thy bride!"
His words were unheeded, for Charles (call'd the fool)
Had already conceded—child, treasure, and rule—
One claim ere the bridal's permission promised,
"That the Jarl left his idols, and gat him baptized!"
Then the Northmen all laugh'd, and their leader roar'd fiercely—

"I've been christen'd already some ten times before;
But, to pleasure the lady, I'll wash me once more—
Nay, her station to alter more quick than is wont,
Be her spouse at the altar, her son at the font."
So they went and were wedded, the fair to the stern;
And a sight none had dreaded they found on return:
The Northmen had hung the bold boy in their absence!

Then the fair girl, heart-riven, look'd up in despair,
And the vengeance of Heaven forgot not her prayer!
Though the Jarl got the dukedom of Normandy wide,
Great Heaven rebuked him by means of his bride.
Though he'd lands, castles, treasure, serfs many a one,
He lack'd heart-peace and pleasure, for heir had he none;
And for many a year did Duke Rollo live childless;

Till a wizard right evil, by magic's black art,
Gave the Duke, through the devil, the wish of his heart.
Loud and long the Duke's mirth rose when a glad son there came,
Though then died in the birth-throes Gisella his dame.
But that son, born of evil, God's vengeance fulfill'd —
He was Robert the Devil, and Rollo he kill'd,
And his son was the Norman that conquer'd broad England!

THE ABBOT'S OAK.

A LEGEND OF MONEY-HUTCH LANE.

BY R. DALTON BARHAM.

" In the parish of Redgrave, skirting the Park, is a manor bye-road, which has from time immemorial borne the name of Money-Hutch Lane. Tradition says that it derived its appellation from a treasure buried in its immediate neighbourhood, at the time of the suppression of the monasteries, one of which, a small offshoot from the great parent stem of St. Edmundsbury, stood in its vicinity. It is added, that though deposited under the guardianship of spell and sigil, it may yet be recovered by any one who bides the happy minute."—*Collect. from Hist. of Suffolk.*

THE Abbot sat by his glimmering lamp,
  His brow was wrinkled with care,
And his anxious look was fix'd on his book,
  With a sad and a mournful air;
    And ever anon,
    As the night wore on,
He would slowly sink back in his oaken chair,
While his visage betray'd from the aspect it bore,
That his studies perplex'd him more and more.

On that Abbot's brow the furrows were deep,
    His hair was scant and white,
And his glassy eyes had known no sleep
    For many a live-long night.
His lips so thin had let nothing in,
Save brown bread and water untemper'd by gin,
    During his sojourn there;
His hopes of succeeding at all with his reading
Seem'd to rest on his firmly abstaining from feeding,
    And sticking like wax to his chair.
One would think, from the pains which he took with his diet, he
Meant to establish a Temperance Society.
His fasting, in short, equall'd that of those mighties,
St. Ronald, Dun Scotus, and Simon Stylites—
      No wonder his look
      On that black-letter book,
    Had a sad and a mournful air.

But oh! what pleasure now gleams from his eyes,
    As he gazes around his cell!
The Abbot springs up in delight and surprise,
    "I have it! I have it! I have it!" he cries,
    "I have found out the mystic spell!"—
'Twas a wonderful thing for so aged a man
To hop, skip, and jump, and to run as he ran,
    But something had tickled him sore.
      He just stay'd to sing
      Out for some one to bring
    His best suit of robes, and his crosier and ring;
While his mitre, which hung by a peg on the door,
In his hurry he popp'd on the hind side before,
And then—though 'twas barely dawn of day,
He summon'd a council without delay,
With a hint that he'd something important to say,
And commenced his address in the following way :—

"Unaccustom'd, my brethren, as I am to speaking,
    To keep you long waiting is not my intention;
I'll merely observe, that the charm I've been seeking
    I've found out at length in a book I won't mention.

Yes, my brethren, I have found
　Where to hide our riches vast,
Buried deep in holy ground,
　I've found the spell that binds them fast.
　　The proud, the profane,
　　Will search all in vain,
If they hunt for them over and over again.
　　One day in the year
　　Was banished, I fear,
By some trifling *faux pas* in our Patron's career;
　That's the time, and that's the hour,
　When fails our Saint's protecting power;
　Gallant hearts and steady hands,
　Then, and then only, may burst the bands,
Our treasures may win, if their patience but lets them;
As for Harry the Eighth, I'm"—he cough'd—"if he gets them.

　" And now my brethren, all to bed,
　We'll consider our early matins as said;
　And if, by good luck, into any one's head
　A better device or more feasible plan
　To bother that corpulent, horrid old man,
And that rascally renegade Cromwell, than this come;
　　The morning will show it,
　　Then let me know it.
I'm sleepy just now—so good-night—*Pax vobiscum!*"

It's pretty well known in what way the Eighth Harry,
When wearied of Catherine, he wanted to marry
Miss Boleyn,—he'd other points also to carry,—
　Applied to the Pope for his aid;
　　Which not being granted
　　As soon as he wanted,
　The hot-headed monarch right solemnly said,
　For bulls and anathemas feeling no dread,
　　That the Pope might go
　　To Jericho,—
And instead of saluting his Holiness' toes,
He'd pull, without scruple, his Holiness' nose;—
That way he brought the affair to a close.
　　Things being thus,
　　Without any fuss,

He kicks out the monks from their pleasant locations ;
  To their broad lands he sends
   His most intimate friends,
And bestows their domains on his needy relations ;
   And sad to relate,
  As we are bound to confess it is,
   Pockets their plate
   For his private necessities ;
And whenever his Majesty finds a fresh dun arise,
Gives him a cheque on the abbeys and nunneries.
So you'll not be surprised that the very next morning,
As the Abbot his person was gravely adorning,
   A note by express
   Put all notions of dress
Instanter to flight by its terrible warning.
   I say by express,
   Though you'll probably guess
That no gentleman deck'd in gold, scarlet, and blue,
Walked round in those days, as at present they do,
Charging eight-pence for billets which shouldn't cost two—
(The reason, they say, for folks writing so few).
But a change, we are told, will be made in a trice,
And epistles of all sorts be brought to one price,
Despite the predictions of Mr. Spring Rice.
   We shall not for any
   Pay more than a penny,
No matter how great the dimensions or distance.
  An excellent plan for the public ; for then 'tis his
Own fault if any one spurns such assistance
  Nor writes every day to his fellow apprentices !
   All laud to Hill
   For this levelling bill,
Which will make, by the aid of the Whigs, its abettors,
The General Post a Republic of Letters.

As it's everywhere voted remarkably rude
Into other folks' secrets to peep and intrude,
My Muse, for the present, shall so play the prude,
   As not to let out
   What this note was about,
Or what it was stagger'd an Abbot so stout.

The result's all we care to make public in this story,
And to that we've a right, as mere matter of history.

On the night of that ill-omen'd day
A band of Monks pursued their way
From the postern-gate of that abbey grey,
    To the churchyard damp and drear.
      They bore three "hutches,"—
        In Suffolk such is
The word they use, as lately I've read
In Johnson, for boxes in which folks make bread.
The aged men totter'd with toil and with pain,
As to carry their burthen they strove might and main.
The Abbot march'd first in that slow-going train,
    The Sexton brought up the rear.
      Near a newly-made vault
      They came to a halt,
With no unequivocal symptoms of pleasure,
    Then each ponderous box,
    With its three patent locks,
They buried, and filled up the hole at their leisure.
They planted above, in a magical figure,
Five acorns as big as five walnuts, or bigger.
    Then the torches' fitful glare
    Fell on the Abbot's silvery hair,
(I allude to his beard—his head was bare,)
As he read from a book, what perhaps was a prayer;
But whether 'twas Sanscrit, Chinese, or Hindoo,
I believe not a soul of his auditors knew,
And it matters but little to me or to you;
      But you'll find in swarms,
      Similar forms,
      If you read Sandivogis',
      A learn'd old Fogie's
Dissertation "De Goblinis, Ghostis, et Bogis."
      "'Tis done—'tis done,"
      Cried the Abbot; "now run—
We need some refection. And, hark! it strikes me!
Our treasure here placed beyond all human reach is,
And safe as if stored in St. Benedict's breeches.

18

King Harry may come ; but he'll ne'er, in good sooth, pick
Up enough plate for a decent sized toothpick."

      *   *   *   *   *

'Tis said the course of true love never
Yet ran smooth ; in fact, if ever
    It does so run,
    It's very soon done ;
    Like ladies, they say,
    ·Who have their own way,
It dwindles as snow on a very warm day ;
And, although unromantic may seem the admission,
Dies from the want of well-timed opposition.

    But so mournful a fate
    Seems not to await
The lovers whose griefs I'm about to relate.
    A noble pair,
    One wondrous fair,
  One manly, tall, and debonair,
Are whispering their vows in the evening air.
    Vain, vain,
    Hapless twain !
The Lady of Bottesdale ne'er may be
Mate to a squire of low degree !
Ralph of Redgrave is stout and true,
Ralph of Redgrave is six feet two,
As he stands in his stocking without his shoe ;
But, like Tully, his family's rather new,—
    And, what is far worse,
    Ralph's private purse
By no means is heavy, but quite the reverse,—
Two failings which make an indifferent catch
For a lady of title in want of a match.
    That lady's papa is stingy and close ;
As for his features—one look is a dose
    He is ugly and old,
    Unfeeling and cold,
With a *penchant* for nothing but bank-notes or gold.
His estates, too, are mortgaged or sold ; for the fact is, his
Youth had been spent in most dissolute practices,

Gaming, and drinking,
Cock-fighting, and winking
At ladies, without ever dreaming or thinking
His means were all gone, and his credit fast sinking;
While he'd now to "come down" with a pretty smart fine
For sundry exploits in the Jacobite line!—
A mode by which Tories in those days were pepper'd,
As you find if you read Mr. Ainsworth's "Jack Shepperd :'
All these things induced him to aid the advances
(Not being the person to throw away chances)
Of a wealthy old lord to his fair daughter Frances,
Which he thought no bad spec to recruit his finances.

Slowly and sadly the lovers were walking,
On their hardships, and some other odd matters talking ;
 The lady had said
 That rather than wed
An old noodle just ready to take to his bed,
 She'd perish outright,
 Were it only to spite
Her father for taking such things in his head.
 Ralph then swore he
 Would die before he
Allowed any man, baron, viscount, or earl,
To walk off to church with his own darling girl.
But, meanwhile, as dying was rather a bore, he
Would first tell the lady a singular story.

 He said,—"At Preston's bloody fray,
 As night closed o'er the well-fought day,
 An aged man sore wounded lay,
 And just as two troopers were ready to twist,
The old gentleman's neck, with one blow of his fist,
He, Ralph, strongly hinted they'd better desist.
 Then the old man smiled a remarkable smile,
 And clasping that same stout fist the while,
Acknowledged his kindness, and swore, too, that *dem it*, he
Would serve him in turn at his direst extremity.
That, last night, which must still more remarkable seem,
That remarkable man had appeared in a dream,

And had bid him, without any nonsense or joke,
Wrap himself up snug and warm in his cloak,
And meet him at twelve by the " Abbot's old oak."

Meanwhile the clouds were collecting on high,
Darker and darker grew the sky,
And a rain-drop moistened that lady's eye
    As big as a half-crown piece.
The lady she sighed, perchance for a coach,
Threw on her lover one glance of reproach,
    And one on her satin pelisse.
At this moment, when what to do neither could tell, a
Page appeared, bearing a brown silk umbrella.
    I don't mean a page
    Of this civilized age,
In a very tight jacket, with very short tails,
Studded all over with brass-headed nails;
But an orthodox page, who, on bended knee,
Said, "Miss, be so good as to come and make tea."

    Ralph instantly rose;
    One kiss ere he goes—
The page most discreetly is blowing his nose,—
And, before you can thrice on John Robinson call,
Ralph has cleared with a bound that garden wall.
    With no less speed
    He has mounted his steed,—
    A noble beast of bone and breed,
    Of sinewy limb,
    Compact, yet slim,
" Warranted free from vice and from whim."
Meanwhile the rain was beginning to soak
Through a very bad shift for a MacIntosh cloak,
    Which—a regular *do*,—
    When only half new,
Ralph had bought some time back from a parrot-nosed Jew,
Trusting his word, with no further thought or proof,
For it's being a patent-wove, London-made waterproof,—
A fact, by the way, which most forcibly shows men
How sharp they must look when they deal with old clothesmen.

Little reck'd Ralph of the wind and the rain,
On his inmost heart was preying that pain
Which man may know once, but can ne'er know again:
    That bitterest throe
    Of deepest woe,
To feel he was loved, and was loved in vain.

Now fiercer grew the tempest's force,
And the whirlwind eddied round rider and horse
As onward they urged their headlong course.
    O'er bank, brook, and briar,
    O'er streamlet and brake,
    By the red lightning's fire
    Their wild way they take.
A country so awkward to go such a pace on,
Might have posed Captain Beecher, Dan Seffert, or Mason.

    At once a flash, livid and clear,
Shows a moss-grown ruin mouldering near;
The horseman stays his steed's career,
    And slowly breasts the steep.
As slowly climbs that ancient mound,
His courser spurns the holy ground,
Where the dead of other days around
    Lie clasped in stony sleep.
And mark against the lurid sky
An oak uprears its form on high,
    And flings its branches free;
A thousand storms have o'er it broke,
But well hath it stood the tempest stroke,—
It is, it is the Abbot's oak,
    It is the trysting-tree.
An hour hath passed, an hour hath flown,
Ralph stands by the tree, but he stands alone.
Till, surmising his dream is a regular hoax,
He "confounds," with much energy, "Abbots and oaks,
And old gentlemen dying from Highlanders' strokes,"
Then enters a shed, which, though rather a cool house,
    Might serve at less need
    To hold him and his steed,—
As it formerly served the old monks for a tool house.

Another hour was past and gone,
Another day was stealing on,
When Ralph, who was shaking
With cold, thought of taking
A nap, and was just between sleeping and waking,
Was roused by his horse, who stood trembling and shaking.
He opens his eyes,
To raise himself tries,
But a weight seems to press on his arms, chest, and thighs;
Like a lifeless log he helplessly lies—
Then conceive his amazement, alarm, and surprise,
When on every side,
In its ancient pride,
He sees an old monastery slowly arise;
Chapel and hall,
Buttress and wall,
Ivied spire, and turret tall,
Grow on his vision one and all.
Airy and thin,
At first they begin,
To fall into outline, and slowly fill in;
At length in their proper proportions they fix,
And assume an appearance exactly " like bricks."

From the postern-gate of that abbey grey,
A band of monks pursue their way,
Till they came to the Abbot's oak.
Ralph sees an eye he before has known—
'Tis the eye of their leader—fixed on his own!
It is, it is,
The identical phiz,
Of his friend, or one precisely like his!
These words from his thin lips broke :—
"This the time and this the hour,
Fails the saints' protecting power,
Gallant heart and steady hand,
Now may burst the charmed band—
Now—" Here the knell
Of an abbey bell
On the ear of the wondering listener fell;

As if the sound
His limbs unbound,
His strength, so strangely lost, is found.

Howling, fled the wild nightmare,
As Ralph leaped forth from his secret lair,
And gained at a bound the open air ;—
He gazed around, but nothing was there!
Nothing save the roofless aisle,
Nothing save the mouldering pile,
Which look'd, in the deepening shade, half hid,
As old and as ugly as ever it did.
The storm had passed by,
And the moon on high
Beamed steadily forth from the deep blue sky.
One single ray through the branches broke,
It fell at the foot of the "Abbot's old oak."

Still in Ralph's ear the words were ringing,
The words he had heard the old gentleman singing,
"This the time, and this the hour."
He felt that the tide at last was come, now or
Never to lead him to fortune and power.
Of his trusty blade
He very soon made
An apology—poor one I grant—for a spade.
And proceeded to work, though new at the trade,
With hearty good will, where the roots seemed decayed.
With labour and toil
He turned up the soil,
While he thought—
As he ought—
On that adage which taught
"Perseverance, and patience, and plenty of oil!"
Till, wearied grown,
Muscle and bone,
His sword broke short on a broad flag stone.

     *   *   *   *   *

In Redgrave church the bells are ringing;
To Redgrave church a youth is bringing
His bride, preceded by little boys singing,—
A custom considered the regular thing in
Times past, but gone out in these latter days,
When a pair may get married in fifty queer ways.

In Redgrave church blush bridesmaids seven,
One had turned faint, or they would have blushed even;
In Redgrave church a bride is given
In face of man, in face of Heaven.
In her sunshine of youth, in her beauty's pride,
The Lady of Bottesdale stands that bride;
And Ralph of Redgrave stands by her side;
　　　　But no longer drest
　　　　In homely vest,
Coat, waistcoat, and breeches were all of the best;
　　His look so noble, his air so free,
　　Proclaim him a squire of high degree;
　　The lace on his garments is richly gilt,
　　His elegant sword has a golden hilt,
　　His " tile " in the very last fashion is built,
　　　　His Ramillie wig
　　　　Is burly and big,
And a ring with a sparkling diamond his hand is on,
Exactly as Richardson paints Sir Charles Grandison.

　　　　Nobody knows
　　　　Or can ever suppose,
How Ralph of Redgrave got such fine clothes;
For little Ned Snip the tailor's boy, said,—
And a 'cuter blade was not in the trade,—
That his master's bill had been long ago paid.
Ah! little, I ween, deem those simple folks,
Who on Ralph's appearance are cracking their jokes,
How much may be gained by a person who pokes,
At the right hour, under the right sort of oaks.

SALLY IN OUR ALLEY.

BY G. K. GILLESPIE.

I.

OF all the girls that are so
  smart,
There's none like pretty Sally,
She is the darling of my heart,
And she lives in Our Alley.
There's not a lady in the land,
  That's half so sweet as Sally,
She is the darling of my heart,
And she lives in Our Alley.

II.

Her father, he makes cabbage-
  nets,
And through the streets does
  cry 'em,
Her mother, she sells laces long,
To such as please to buy 'em,
But sure, such folks could ne'er
  beget
So sweet a girl as Sally;
She is the darling of my heart,
And she lives in Our Alley.

III.

When she is by, I leave my
  work,
I love her so sincerely :
My master comes like any Turk,
And bangs me most severely.

IN SARAM.

BY G. K. GILLESPIE, M.A.

I.

ANTE alias splendet specie pulcher-
  rima Sara,
Formosas superans effigie egregiâ.
Urget amore mihi pectus mentemque
  puella, et
Angustâ in Nostrâ vivit honesta
  Viâ.
Virgineo in cœtu nullas dulcedine
  Saræ,
Nobilibus natas, invenias similes.
Implet amore mihi mentem pectusque
  puella, et
Angustâ in Nostrâ vivit honesta
  Viâ.

II.

Institor huic pater est, portans qui
  caulibus apta
Retia per vicos clamitat assiduè
Digna viro est uxor, merces cui fim-
  bria longa est
Vendita, siqua velit fœmina compta
  emere.
At tales talem quam dulcis numina
  Sara
(Nobilis est certè !) non generâsso
  sinunt.
Est mihi deliciæ cordi mentiquo
  puella, et
Angustâ in Nostrâ vivit honesta
  Viâ.

III.

Adveniente illà fabricam inceptosque
  labores
Desero continuò, victus amore meo:
Tunc irâ fervens improvisusque magister,
Ut Saracenus, adit, me baculo
  feriens.

But let him bang his bellyful,
  I'll bear it all for Sally;
She is the darling of my heart,
  And she lives in Our Alley.

At quamvis feriat donec satiabitur
  iste,
Omnia pro Sarâ perfero, sic peramo.
Firmat amore mihi pectus mentemque
  puella, et
  Augustâ in Nostrâ vivit honesta
    Viâ.

IV.

Of all the days that's in the
  week,
I dearly love but one day,
And that's the day that comes
  between
A Saturday and Monday.
For then I'm dress'd in all my
  best,
  To walk abroad with Sally;
She is the darling of my heart,
  And she lives in Our Alley.

IV.

Hebdomadæ ex omni spatio serieque
  dierum
Solem unum expecto, suavis et est
  mihi lux.
Isque dies Lunæ imperium ac Sa-
  turnia regna
Disjungit, veniens lumine propitio.
Tunc etenim spatior Sarâ comitatus
  amicè,
Vestituque nitens, splendidiùs so-
  lito.
Fert mihi lenimen curæ dulcissima
  Sara, et
  Augustâ in Nostrâ vivit honesta
    Viâ.

V.

My master carries me to church,
  And often am I blamed,
Because I leave him in the lurch
  As soon as Text is named.
I leave the church in sermon-
  time,
  And slink away to Sally;
She is the darling of my heart,
  And she lives in Our Alley.

V.

Ad templum Domini me ducit sæpe
  magister,
Sæpe at nequitiam corripit illo
  meam:
Scilicet aufugio furtim falloque ma-
  gistrum,
Sacro argumento vix bene pro-
  posito.
Dum monet Orator populum horta-
  turque disertus,
Ad Saram effugio, dulceque collo-
  quium.
Implet amore mihi mentem pectusque
  puella, et
  Augustâ in Nostrâ vivit honesta
    Viâ.

VI.

When Christmas comes about
    again,
Oh! then I shall have
    money,—
I'll hoard it up, and—box and
    all—
I'll give it to my honey.
And would it were ten thou-
    sand pounds,
    I'd give it all to Sally ;
She is the darling of my heart,
    And she lives in Our Alley.

VI.

Quum volvente anno Christi Natali-
    tia orta
Sint, nummûm mihi erunt in loculo
    cumuli.
Omnes servabo, atque ipsâ cum
    pyxide Saræ,
Tempora quum veniant, melligenæ
    tribuam.
Atque utinam innumeras mihi opes
    fortuna dedisset !
Sara suo totas exciperet gremio.
Est mihi deliciæ cordi montique
    puella, et
Angustâ in Nostrâ vivit honesta
    Viâ.

VII.

My master, and the neighbours
    all
Make game of me and Sally,
And, but for her, I'd better be
A slave, and row a galley.
But when my seven long years
    are out,
    Oh! then, I'll marry Sally,
Oh! then we'll wed, and then
    we'll bed,
    But not in Our Alley.

VII.

Irrident flammam vicini atque ipse
    magister
Quæ me illamque urit, ludifi-
    cantque facem.
Sed, sine amore tuo, præstaret, SALLI,
    revinctum
Servi me vitam remigio trahere.
Quum tamen elabens lentè confecerit
    annus
Septimus orbiculum, Sara mihi
    uxor erit.
Tum vero thalamum celebrabimus
    atque hymenæos,
    At procul Angustâ ibimus usquo
    Viâ.

HORACE TO LYDE.

BY C. H. LANGHORNE.

Oh come, Lydè, come to my own Sabine hill,
And we'll list to the fall of the dancing rill;
The privet and wind-flower our couch shall be:
Oh haste, Lydè, haste from the city to me!

Lucullus's gardens are rich and rare,
Every shrub of the East grows there;
Balsam and nard, and cassia sweet,
And Syrian palm in his gardens meet.

The psittacus whistles among the trees,
And the monkey swings to the westland breeze,
And the mighty elephant wantons at will,
And the river-horse frisks and drinks his fill.

But, though rich and rare his gardens be,
Mine, though poor, is more meet for thee;
'Tis a turfy bank on Lucretili's slope,
Where the latest violets their eyelids ope.

Digentia's ripple is sweet to hear,
And Philomel charms the tranced ear,
And Phyllis is waiting to crown our board
With apples and nuts from the autumn hoard.

Such is our fare—we ask not for more;
The mighty haunch of Laurenian boar,
Or surmullet large as large can be,
Let them go to Apicius, but not to *thee*.

Phyllis shall cool the Falernian wine
In the running stream, while our brows we twine
With the glossy bay-leaf, and the chaste orange flower,
And I'll sing to my love in my chestnut bower.

Lydè, love, Lydè; I long for thee,
Faunus has hastened over the sea;
Mænalus knows his foot again!
I am left alone in my wild domain.

Come, and I'll touch my Latian lyre,
With somewhat of old Anacreon's fire;
Thy beautiful eyes my theme shall be,
How can I fail when I sing of *thee?*

I'll show thee where Sylvan sports by day,
And the Naiads glide on their watery way,
And Patula tends the corn with a smile,
And poppy-crowned Ceres looks on the while.

Come, Lydè, leave the haunts of men,
Thou must never quit thy Flaccus agon;
My hyacinth blossoms a spell shall be,
They will charm my Lydè to live with me.

Care was not made for charms like thine;
It has dulled the glance of thy sparkling eyne;
It has dimmed thy roses in haggard Rome;
Come and look bright in my Sabine home.

A DELECTABLE BALLAD OF THE JUDGE AND THE MASTER.

BY TOM TAYLOR.

THE stout Master of Trinitie
  A vow to God did make,
No Judge, no Sheriff, through his back door
  Their way from court should take.

And syne he hath closed his big, big book,
  And syne laid down his pen,
And dour and grimly was his look,
  As he called his serving men:—

"Come hither, come hither, my porter, Watts!
  Come hither, Moonshine, to me!
If he be Judge in the Justice Hall,
  I'll be Judge in Trinitie.

"And Sheriff Green is a lordly man
   In his coat of the velvet fine ;
But he'll rue the day that he took his way
   Through back-gate of mine !

"Now bolt and bar, my flunkies true,
   Good need is ours, I ween ;
By the trumpet so clear, the Judge is near,
   And eke bold Sheriff Green."

Oh, a proud, proud man was the Master to see,
   With his serving men behind,
As he strode down the stair with his nose in the air,
   Like a pig that scents the wind.

And they have barr'd the bigger gate,
   And they have barr'd the small,
And soon they espy the Sheriff's coach,
   And the Sheriff so comely and tall.

And the Sheriff straight has knock'd at the gate,
   And tirled at the pin ;
"Now open, open, thou proud porter,
   And let my Lord Judge in !"

"Nay, Sheriff Green," quoth the proud porter,
   " For this thing may not be ;
The Judge is Lord in the Justice Hall,
   But the Master in Trinitie."

Then the Master smiled on Porter Watts,
   And gave him a silver joe ;
And, as he came there with his nose in the air,
   So back to the lodge did go.

Then outspoke the grave Lord Justice,—" Ho !
   Sheriff Green, what aileth thee ?
Did the trumpets blow, that the folk may know,
   And the gate be opened free."

But a troubled man was the Sheriff Green,
   And he sweated as he did stand ;
And in silken stock each knee did knock,
   And the white wand shook in his hand.

Then black grew the brow of the Judge, I trow,
    And his voice was stern to hear,
As he almost swore at Sheriff Green,
    Who wrung his hands in fear.

" Now, out and alas, my Lord High Judge,
    That I this day should see !
When I did knock from behind the lock,
    The porter thus answered me :
' That thou wert Lord in the Justice Hall,
    But the Master in Trinitie.'

" And the Master hath bid them bar the gate
    'Gainst Kaisar or 'gainst King."
" Now, by my wig !" quoth the Judge in wrath,
    " Such answer *is not the thing.*

" Break down the gate and tell the knave
    That would stop my way so free,
That the wood of his skull is as thick to the full,
    As the wood of the gate may be !"

That voice so clear when the porter did hear,
    He trembled exceedingly ;
Then soon and straight he flung open the gate,
    And the Judge and his train rode by.

TOM TAYLOR is one of the most scholarly and accomplished writers
on all sorts of subjects of the present day. The story told, in this admirable old English ballad of his, is strictly true in every particular,
Lord Denman, one of the judges of Assize for the Norfolk Circuit, and
the celebrated Doctor Whewell, the Master of Trinity College, Cambridge, being the chief characters in the little drama, which was very
interesting whilst it lasted. The Master's Lodge at Trinity has been,
since Henry the Eighth's time, the home of the judges of the Cambridge
Assizes. Lord Denman, on this celebrated occasion, thought that he
had as good a right to return from court to his lodgings through the
back or front gate of Trinity, as he might think proper, and took it into
his head to choose the former. Doctor Whewell, the greatest man in the
world within the precincts of his own domain, and certainly anything

but the smallest beyond them, issued his orders that the judges were to enter by the front gate; and, in order that his mandate should not be misunderstood, he went himself and saw that the porter secured the back gate. Lord Denman, however, made his way in by the mere force of will, as Gloucester did through the Tower gates against the Bishop of Winchester, in Shakespeare's Henry the Sixth. Porters Watts and Moonshine were living entities, and Green was High Sheriff of Cambridgeshire at the time.

Mr. Taylor, the author of the ballad, was then in his undergraduate career. He was elected a Fellow of Trinity shortly after he took his B.A. degree with high honour, having been bracketed first with Mr. Goodwin, head of the first class of the Classical Tripos. He was afterwards called to the bar in the Inner Temple, and went the Northern Circuit for a few years, where he gave promise of future eminence in the legal profession, although his literary tastes led him to devote no small portion of his time to one or other of the leading publications of the day. He was one of the chief contributors to 'Punch' when Jerrold and Thackeray wrote their best things for it; and has written, taking quantity and quality together, for the stage more successfully than any living dramatic author. He is Secretary of the Board of Health, a branch of the public service attached to the Home Office, and is at present in the prime of his intellect and manhood, after having already realized a handsome fortune by his rare and versatile genius and marvellous industry.

THE COBBLER OF TOLEDO.

A LEGEND OF CASTILE.

You've all of you heard, or you've all of you read,
Of a little old cobbler whose dwelling is said
To have been nothing more than a stall or a shed,
Where he couldn't stand up without bumping his head.
But which still, as the choicest authorities say,
Both served him for kitchen and *salle à manger*.
This same little cobbler—so fickle is Fame—
Has never yet figured in rhyme with *a name;*
And even the place of his birth or location,
His life, death and actions, his language and nation,
Are all alike left to our imagination.

Yet he lived and he died;
He'd a language beside,
And a mother of whom he was haply the pride.

I've traced them all out with much trouble and pain,
And I've taken a journey expressly to Spain
To search all the archives—I hope not in vain,—
As I found that this maker of shoes for " the million,"
Was born at Toledo—a thorough Castilian.
Toledo's a city renowned through all ages,
In clerical tomes and historical pages,
For bishops and warriors, princes and sages,
And sword-blades, which even in these modern days
(When we're giving up fighting and choleric ways)
Are confess'd to be matchless in " temper"—a rarity
Scarcely more known to our peace-men than charity.

In one of the streets of this city of steel—
This Sheffield and Birmingham store of Castile—
Stood a gloomy old mansion, with windows so few,
And so closely barred up, how the light could get through
Was a puzzle to all who beheld them the more,
As the street was so narrow and dismal before,
That no ray of the sunlight had ever been known
To wriggle its way down and burnish one stone.

Like a little excrescence below this great hall
Projected a queer little, black-looking, stall,
Whence the sound of a hammer assail'd you, together
With odours of beeswax and blacking and leather.
    And if you look'd *in*,
    In the midst of the din,
    And the gloom and the smell—
    And the dirt, too, as well—

You might see a small body, a very big head,
Two eyes very bright, and one nose very red,
Two hands very large and as grimy as soot,
And not the least sign of a leg or a foot.

Don't fancy, I beg,
That there *wasn't* a leg—
But merely their owner, a cobbler at work,
Tuck'd them quite out of sight as he sat *à la* Turk.
And *this* is "the cobbler who lived in the stall
Which served him for kitchen and parlour and all:"
And this is the cobbler—Pedrillo by name—
Whose wonderful story my verses proclaim.

One day, as Pedrillo sat mending the sole
Of a shoe that its owner had worn to a hole,
And stitching, and waxing, and pegging, and thumping,
And filing, and smoothing, and 'clicking,' and 'clumping,'
He somehow got thinking on all sorts of things
And all sorts of persons, from cobblers to kings.
Pedrillo was not a philosopher, nor
Had he ever much practised at thinking before;
Or, at least, I much doubt till that moment if ever he
Had made the remotest approach to a reverie.

Yet, how charming a reverie *is*
When the mind and the heart are at rest,
When we shake off the clay of the world
And we dream of some land of the blest!

How pleasant to loll at one's ease—
Arms a-kimbo and eyes on the ceiling—
And shut out, in an opium trance,
(If we can) ev'ry earthly-born feeling!

But we're apt to do just the reverse—
Begin thinking of every evil—
Our pains, and our debts, and our sins,
Our long balance sheet with the devil.

"Ah, Life thou'rt at best but a dream!"
Is a saying each dreamer well knows—
And oh, what a deuce of a nightmare
Doth trouble some mortals' repose!

How we fret, and we fume, and we snore,
    How we kick off the clothes, how we quake—
How we fight with the phantoms we raise :
    And how stupid we look when we wake !

Yes—we've taken a great deal of trouble
    To suffer a great deal of pain ;
And when we awake to our folly,
    We turn round and act it again.

It's needless to point out our madness,
    We see it and feel it *within*—
But the spendthrift goes deepest in debt when
    The least he's encumber'd with " tin."

        I don't mean to say
        'Twas at all in this way
The thoughts of Pedrillo attempted to stray.
        He thought of his life
        Of struggle and strife
'Gainst the pangs of necessity, sharp as his knife.
        He thought how much fate
        Had bless'd all the great
Who roll'd by his stall in their coaches of state.
        He thought of his soul—
        What a dark little hole
It was shut in, in *this* world—as blind as a mole.
        He wished he was rich—
        How quickly he'd pitch
This shoe to the dev'—— here he made a false stitch.
        He thought he could spend
        Heaps of gold without end
And wear more new boots than he e'er got to mend.
        He thought how he'd dine
        And what oceans of wine
He'd swallow of Spain, and of France, and the Rhine.

Till the very idea of extensive potation
Produced on his brain an uncommon sensation,
And made him feel dreamy and vicious ;—at least
He fancied he'd like to try thrashing a priest!

And this terrible notion so tickled his brain
That he burst into laughter again and again,
As he thought of his reverence dancing with pain.

When a wicked idea gets into the head
There's no guessing the lengths into which it may spread:
It expands ev'ry moment and gets more defined,
Till it seems to fill up ev'ry nook of the mind,
And leaves not a square inch of virtue behind.

And so with Pedrillo : each moment there fled
Some good little thought that remained in his heaa,
And its place was supplied by a bad one instead ;
Till at length, quite o'erwhelmed in the vortex of evil,
He cried, in the midst of his fanciful revel—
"I should like to have one little peep at the devil!"

Rat-tat-tat-tat—a whole shower of knocks
Come pattering down on his dark little box,
And he starts from his day-dream and sees with amaze
A very tall man with a sinister gaze,
Who stands at his window, and lifting his foot
Shoves it in as he utters—"*there*—make me a boot."

Pedrillo feels sick—he's half ready to faint,
His horror no language of mine could e'er paint
As he grasps—not a foot—but a hoof hard and thick,
Just such as tradition assigns to Old Nick!
While the owner cries, "Now then, you booby, be quick—
Take the measure at once, sir—what makes you so slow ?
Hang the fellow, my dinner's all spoiling, I know—
I've got a roast heretic waiting below."

Half dead with the fright which he's trying to smother,
Pedrillo contrives in some manner or other,
To measure the hoof with his tape ; while the "gent"
Casts on him a glance of such evil intent
That cold perspiration commences to ooze
From the top of his head to the soles of his shoes.
"Now make that boot well, or you'll be in a mess,
And bring it home quickly, sir—*there's my address :*"

And he throws down a card with a sulphurous smell,
And one word of four letters—I'd rather not tell
What it was, but the reader will guess pretty well.

'Tis now the merry month of May
And all Toledo's streets are gay.
The bells peal forth a merry chime
In honour of the joyful time:
From steeple tow'r and mansion-top
In graceful folds bright banners drop,
Shallop, and barge, and tiny boat,
Across the glittering Tagus float,
Bearing their smiling freights along
To mingle in the gladsome throng
That revel in each street. The song,
The joyous laugh, the pleasant jest,
The strains of music—all attest,
Mid sighs of mirth and sounds of glee,
The noisy reign of revelry.

Let's follow in the motley train,
And listen to the blithesome strain
Yon maiden sings: how rich and clear
Each cadence strikes the listener's ear!

I.

Ye nobles and gentles come near,
  And list to the glee-maiden's lay;
Fair ladies, approach ye, and hear
  The words from my lips as they stray:
'Tis love is the theme of my song,
  Love's praises my verses proclaim,
And to you all his honours belong—
  For without you he is but a name.

II.

Say, is there a jewel on earth
  So brilliant, so priceless as this?
Does one hour of a lifetime give birth
  To a joy like the lover's pure bliss?

It glows like a furnace in youth ;
In manhood more constant its flame;
In age its companion is Truth—
In each—'tis Love only—the same !

III.

'Tis a gleam from some Angel-built sphere,
The dowry our maker hath given,
To prove, while we're sojourning here,
That we still have a portion of Heaven.
It knows not the leav'n of despond ;
It fears not the clouds that impend,
But sees the bright vista beyond,
And vanquishes Fate in the end.

IV.

Let Wealth be your mistress alone—
Let Glory allure you awhile—
Yet Love shall still claim you his own,
You shall turn from all else for his smile.
You shall taste all the pleasures that fall
From the bounty of Heaven above,
And confess you would barter them all
For one moment of exquisite Love !

Now look to the right and you see a great crowd,
With a man in the centre who's bawling aloud
Some speech, or some verses, or songs, which appear
To please the rude folks who're collected to hear.
The language, you'll notice, is not over choice,
Nor sung in a very melodious voice ;
And therefore, good reader, I strongly advise
That we move t'other way.   Up yon narrow street lies
The Cathedral :—I fancy we'd better go there,
Because we're in Spain, and of course you're aware,
Whenever a " rumpus " takes place in that land,
For fun or for fighting, the Church bears a hand,
To help in the " scrimmage :" and mightily grand
Are the shows she gets up, though 'twould puzzle to say
Where the deuce she can raise all the money to pay

For such costly affairs : but the utmost that *I* know
About it, is simply—she *does* get the "rhino."

And now I remember—I very much doubt
If I've told what these holiday scenes are about.
It's simply his Catholic Highness of Spain,
Who had buried one wife, has just married again ;
And so all his people go mad for a day,
And rejoice at the deed in an orthodox way.

We stand within the sacred pile—
The long, broad nave, the narrow aisle,
E'en to the very altar's stone,
Scarcely one spot untrodden own.
Yet solemn silence reigns around,
Save when the silver bells' light sound
Proclaims the Host :—then bows each knee
Before the symbol'd Majesty
Of Christ Incarnate : each one there
Mutters his penitence and pray'r ;
While pealing forth, the organ's note
Seems through the vaulted roof to float,
Rearing aloft its solemn tone
To bear its praise to God's high throne.

The hymns are sung, the mass is said ;
The crowd of worshippers has fled.
Deserted e'en by monk and priest
    The lofty temple's aisles are bare :
The gorgeous altar in the east—
    No suppliant form is kneeling there !

The motley crowd that whilome trod,
With silent step, the house of God,
Now dance the gay-deck'd streets along,
Or shouting join the ribald song.

And such is man ! thus vain his mind
And fickle, as the veering wind :
Now Pleasure, and now Heav'n his text—
This hour a Saint—a Satyr next !

In a dark little street is a " hullah-ba-loo,"
And shouting, and yelling, a precious "to-do ;"
    What hustling and rushing
    And running and crushing,
    And pulling and tearing,
    And laughing and swearing!
What masses of people all crowding to see
The fun or the fight, or whate'er it may be!
While each asks the other as fast as they run,
" Holloa—what's the row there ? *do* tell us the fun :
What the deuce are they doing ? do *you* know, or *you ?*
Are they baiting a badger, or shaving a Jew ?"

In that dark little street is the dark little stall,
Where our poor little cobbler's at work with his awl—
At work when the rest of the city's at play—
At work on this glorious festival day!
The crowd are astounded—they can't make it out—
So they yell to the cobbler, and holloa and shout,
And they bid him come forth and partake of the revel,
And pitch all his leather and tools to the devil.
" That's just *it !*" cried Pedrillo, as soon as he heard
The multitude utter that last naughty word.
" Just *it*, my old beeswax ? just *what ?* my old Turk ?"
" Why—it's just for his worship, I mean, I'm at work."
" His worship—what worship ? hang me if I know
What you mean." " Why—his worship that lives *down below.*"
And here poor Pedrillo turned awfully white,
And even his nose grew pale with affright.
" He's mad," cried the mob—" pull him out of his hole."
" Oh mercy ! not yet—I've not finished the sole !"

In spite of his cries poor Pedrillo is seized,
And dragg'd from his hole, and most ruthlessly squeezed,
And carried in triumph, still grasping a shoe
Half finished—not fit for a Christian or Jew ;
But a queer looking thing, made I scarcely know how,
And exactly the shape of the hoof of a cow!
    Away they all run
    In the height of their fun,

And bear off their prize
Amid laughter and cries,
And huzzahs for the cobbler, who, first of his trade,
A shoe for his evil-named Majesty made.

In the midst of their running they suddenly stop,
And cease from hurrahing; and quietly drop
The load that they carry: then hasten away—
And, before the poor cobbler could manage to say
One word to his captors, they'd left him alone,
With his comical shoe, sitting squat on a stone.

But, absorbed in one notion, he falls to his work
(Still seated, of course, as before—*à la* Turk)
And marks not the place where he's left in the lurch—
Alas! 'tis the porch of Saint Anthony's church!

With stately step and solemn mien
A black-rob'd priest is shortly seen
Emerging from the door that lies
Behind Pedrillo: and his eyes
Rest on the cobbler in surprise!

The latter stitches as before,
Unconscious of his visitor,
And heeding not the open'd door.
The priest stands still in dumb amaze
At the strange sight that meets his gaze—
The cobbler with his absent air,
And the queer shoe he's making there.

At length his holy indignation,
At such an act of profanation,
Burst forth in words—"Holloa! you hound,
How dare you work on holy ground!"

Pedrillo slowly raised his head,
Not heeding what the priest had said,
But slightly startled by the sound:
And then he turn'd himself half round,

And saw, with supernatural fear,
A black-rob'd priest standing near.
In fact, he thought the figure must be
His most Satanic Majesty!

And so he cried—"What *shall* I do?
I've not quite done your worship's shoe;
I'm hard at work, sir—this is it—
Perhaps you'll try how it will fit
Your worship's hoof—that is—I mean—
Your worship's foot—I'd never seen
One like it till your worship came—
So, if I've fail'd, you mustn't blame!"

Thus saying, he held out the cloven-hoof'd boot,
And gravely laid hold of his reverence's foot.

Then—oh for the pen of old Homer to trace
The passion that darken'd the holy man's face!
His eyes were half-red and his cheeks were half-black,
And he rush'd at the cobbler, and caught him a whack
With his toe on the nethermost point of his back,
That sent him a summerset, tumbling and sprawling,
Into the street, and with agony bawling.
      And before he could rise,
      Or had finished his cries,
Before the whole truth could have enter'd his mind,
Before he could rub where he smarted behind—
He was seiz'd on the spot, and with smart expedition,
Clapp'd into the jail of the fell Inquisition!

———

Fair Spain, sweet Spain, the brightest gem
In all Europa's diadem!
Land of the sun, the flow'r, the vine—
Land of a race once half-divine:
Land of fair scenes, and fairer ladies,
Whose forms, from Pyrenees to Cadiz,
May match with all the world can boast,
From Ind to Russia's ice-bound coast!
Land of romance—the rich, deep, store
Of poet's lay and monkish lore!

Birth-place of men whose ev'ry name,
Writ in the muster-roll of Fame,
To ev'ry age, 'neath ev'ry zone,
Attest their glory and thine own!

How art thou favor'd, glorious land!
What gifts thou hast at Nature's hand—
Climate and soil, and hills and vales,
And flowing streams—all that avails
To charm the eye or glad the heart,
Or sense of gratitude impart
To God above, whose hand benign
Hath bless'd thee thus—all, all are thine!

And yet, what art thou?—lost, debased—
Thine annals past in glory traced—
Thy present but a wretched blank,
Or viler stain! Where shalt thou rank
Among the nations of the earth? Ay, thou,
Once crown'd with honour—sunken now
Below the meanest state enslaved
Where once thy flag victorious waved!

And why is this? what spell hath wrought
  A change so fatal to thy fame?
What sad reverse, with ruin fraught,
  Hath swept away thine ancient fame?

Alas! within thy bosom cherish'd,
  The deadly canker-worm hath grown,
And day by day thy weal hath perish'd
  'Neath his corroding sting alone.

Yes! History's impartial page,
  Thy glory and thy fall that tells,
Shall point to ev'ry future age—
  "The land is cursed where Priestcraft dwells."

In a dark, dismal dungeon, where never a ray
Of sunlight has ever been tempted to stray;
Where the walls are all damp and all mildew'd, and where
An uncommonly scanty supply of fresh air

Is deem'd quite enough to supply the vitality
Of any imprison'd remains of mortality;
Where a heap of foul straw is to serve as a bed,
While the rats, by the dozen, run over your head,
And tickle your visage with tail and with claw,
Or vary the pleasure by taking a gnaw
At your toes, when they're hungry; where lizards and toads
Crawl out from the chinks of the pavement by loads—
In this highly-delectable tenement, all
That remains of Pedrillo lies chain'd to the wall.

Poor fellow! a visage so hollow and wan,
Scarce ever belonged to the form of a man.
His eyeballs so glazed, and his eyelids so blue,
And his skin of a greenish and yellowish hue;
His hands were so bony, so long and so thin,
So grizzled the beard that hung down from his chin;
So wasted his limbs, and his round little nose
So completely deprived of its *couleur de rose*—
That no eye could have ever detected, at all,
The poor little cobbler who lived in the stall,
Except that one hand, to its "cunning" yet true,
Still grasp'd the remains of an odd-looking shoe.

Pedrillo 'd been tried for the wicked pretence
Of mistaking a priest for Old Nick—an offence
Pronounced, with veracity, quite "diabolical"
By the holy Inquisitors—meek Apostolical
Lambs, who've been famed, in all countries and ages,
As patterns of Christians and virtuous sages.
The verdict was "Guilty," of course—'t wouldn't "pay"
To let a man off when they'd bagg'd him—to say
That they'd made a mistake: and besides, just of late
They'd been scarce of offenders in Church or in State,
And wanted a Jew or a heretic sadly—
And so poor Pedrillo was pounced upon gladly.

A little discussion between them took place,
Regarding the punishment due to his case.
Some voted for roasting—some hinted at flaying—
Which others declared to be trifling and playing.

The President wouldn't agree to the roasting,
And seized the occasion for modestly boasting
How mild and how gentle *his* sentiments were.
The fact is, his house stood just facing the square
Where the stake was erected when sinners were burnt,
And from many a past sad example he'd learnt
That the smell of a roast was so highly unpleasant—
He'd the strongest objection to try one at present.

And so, in the end, they decided on " mercy"—
Or, rather, what *I* should call just *vice versâ*—
That is—" out of care for his poor sinful soul,"
They left him to die, like a rat, in a hole.

   And thus our poor Pedrillo lay,
   Wasting his wretched life away :
   Dying by inches—dying slowly—
   Condemn'd by wretches self-styled "holy."

   Oh, God ! and can thy lightnings spare
      The impious creatures who profane
   The sacred livery they wear,
      And take Thy holy name in vain,
   To sanctify a deed of blood,
   And name that deed " Religious, good !"

   How vain the question ! look, weak man,
   Beyond thy frail life's little span—
   See Retribution's work begun—
   God's name avenged—and Justice done !

In a dark little street is a dark little stall,
And a plump little cobbler at work with his awl.
Who is it ? Pedrillo ? by Jove it's the same !
How on earth did he get there ?   What influence came
To set him at liberty ? see him at work,
Sitting just as before on his board *à la* Turk !
And he's stitching with vigour, he's making a boot—
Not a cloven hoof'd thing, but one fit for a foot.
And how happy he looks ! and how plump and how red !
How punchy his body, how shiny his head !

And he sticks to his trade like an honest Castilian—
Making highlows and mending the soles of the million.

Now touching his freedom:—it chanced one fine day
That some two dozen Jews were all sentenced to pay
A very large sum for some very bad deed,
Regarding some matter of conscience and creed;
And finding the prison was rather too small
(In addition to those it contain'd) for them all,
A "weeding" took place—and 'mongst others, Pedrillo
To a Hebrew in trouble relinquish'd his pillow.

And such—without varnish, invention, or mystery—
Is the true, undeniable, record and history
Of the "little old cobbler who liv'd in a stall
Which served him for kitchen and parlour and all."

MORAL.

There's a saying so stale that it's grown to an epigram—
Of course you all know it well—"*Ne sutor crepidam
Ultra:*" And some sleepy folks may opine
That such is the moral of *this* tale of mine.
They're mistaken: such "morals" belong to the past—
They won't do for these days—we're a great deal too fast
For such slow-coach old maxims. What! "stick to our last?"
Nail the doctor to physic, the lawyer to law,
The parson to preaching!—a pretty fine saw
For this age of progression!—when ev'ry man's head
Is so full of the things he has heard, seen, and read—
It's not easy to say where our knowledge *can* stop
When our brain is as full as a pawnbroker's shop.

No, no—I've got something much better—much truer—
Much more to the purpose—and certainly newer
To tell you. It's this:—if you ever give way
To an evil-born thought—if you let your mind stray
In a naughty direction, don't think me uncivil
If I say that *you* 're making a boot for the devil.
And that very same boot—when your virtue's clean gone—
You'll see him some day when he 's "trying it on."

THE LORD PROTECTOR'S GHOST.

A BALLAD.

BY CHARLES KENT.

₊ Very shortly after the Restoration the dead body of Cromwell was removed from its place of burial in Westminster Abbey, and having been drawn upon a hurdle to Tyburn, was there dragged out of its coffin and suspended, with fiendish exultation, upon the gallows by the hands of the public executioner.

SAUNTERING o'er the moorland lonely—
  Darkness dappling into day—
Lo! one courtly gallant only,
  Humming a blithe roundelay.

Ringlets trailing on his shoulders;
  Tufted lip and tufted chin;
Eyes that seem to seek beholders—
  Love for handsome looks to win.

Less than love were niggard payment,
  Music as each footfall stirs,
Rustling in that broidered raiment,
  Jingling in those burnished spurs.

'Tis a thing of silken splendour,
  Perfumed lace and velvet gear,
Flourished with the gauds that render
  Gay the roystering cavalier.

'Tis a pampered lord of revels
  Loitering from a banquet home,
Fearing neither God nor devils
  Where his wayward pathway roam.

Drinking deep from flagons brimming,
  Wine has flushed his cheek and brain;
Yet with heated senses swimming,
  Calm he lounges o'er the plain.

Whim-inspired, his sleek roan scorning,
  And his gaily liveried groom,
Quaffs he here afoot the morning,
  Brushing through the flowery broom—

Brushing through the dewy brambles
　　Leisurely as o'er a lawn,
Not yon dismal scene of rambles
　　Darkling at the glint of dawn.

Sudden sounds of doleful anguish,
　　Ghastly gleams of lurid light—
Gleams that fitful rise and languish—
　　Glimmer through the gloom of night.

Startled, pale, aghast, affrighted,
　　Lo ! the gallant plain doth see,
By the ghostlike radiance lighted,
　　Grim and gaunt—the Tyburn tree.

And beneath the gibbet standing—
　　Horror in its lifeless eyes—
On each lineament the branding
　　Token of a form that dies—

Rotting, mouldered, blue, abhorréd,
　　Yet with aspect calm and grand,
He who though uncrowned his forehead
　　Reigned—the Ruler of the land.

Hark ! the Awful Phantom uttering
　　Woeful words and dire to hear,
Words that breathed through black lips muttering,
　　Chill the reveller's bones with fear.

"Minion!" cries the dreadful Spectre,
　　" I am he who once did wield
Mighty England's glorious sceptre ;
　　Led her armies to the field ;

"Scattered all her ills and terrors,
　　As the winnow drives the chaff ;
And for all her tyrant's errors
　　Gave her right with scorn to laugh.

" Traitorous knaves with plots designing
　　Trembled at my sheathless sword,
Knowing that its splendrous shining
　　Was the glory of the Lord !

" Nations awed before my power,
   Monarchs shrinking from my blow,
At my coming, cursed the hour
   Britain first became their foe.

" Arbiter of peace and battle,
   In my grasp the bolts of war
Routed warrior-hosts like cattle,
   Hurled the victor from his car.

" Holland, with her navies scattered,
   Saw our banners sweep the main,
Saw them flout where low lay shattered
   In the dust the pride of Spain.

" Scotland's ancient brand fell broken
   When it crossed my iron rod ;
Erin knew her doom was spoken
   When my foot was on her sod.

" Distance, impotent to sever
   Britons from my sheltering fame,
Found them guarded, wheresoever,
   By the terror of my name.

" We were scatheless, free, defiant—
   Bent to none but God the knee,
On His holy aid reliant,
   Perilous though the path might be.

" Now ! with tarnished standards lowered,
   Draggling at the heels of France :
Fallen—not with fate untoward,
   Cloven helm and splintered lance :

" Shameless—stripped of pride and splendour,
   Like a craven knight who yields—
England to chicane doth render
   Glory won on foughten fields.

" Harlots throng the Cæsars' palace ;
   Bastards drain the realm of gold ;
Panders drug the royal chalice ;
   Rank and place are bought and sold.

20

" Puniest state of meanest power
    Britain's stingless wrath contemns,
Now when by old Julius' Tower
    Dutch ships ride upon the Thames.

" Yet with dastard shields scarce dinted,
    Plumes uncropped though blurred and torn,
Ye, whose recreant brows were printed
    With a villain brand of scorn—

" Palterers with kingly vigour,
    Lords in form, at heart but slaves,
Human ghouls, with coward rigour,
    Dragging dead men from their graves :

" Ye who, while this shape was breathing,
    Trembled from my glance away,
When my soul had left its sheathing
    Basely spurned the crumbling clay—

" One whose guards were freemen serried,
    One before whom millions bowed—
Spurned me powerless, lifeless, buried,
    Haled me from my mouldering shroud :

" On a murderous hurdle drew me—
    Lord of earth from sea to sea !—
Through my corpse in mockery slew me,
    Hung me on the felon's tree.

" Viler vengeance never mortal
    Dreamt of out of Hell's black womb,
Bursting ev'n Death's sacred portal,
    Rifling ev'n the awful tomb.

" Hence, the princely race ye cherish—
    Tawdry trifle of a day—
Quickly from the throne shall perish,
    Swiftly from the world decay !"

Dismal sounds, the soul appalling,
    Ring the gallant's brain around,
Horrid gleams about him falling,
    Swooned upon the dewy ground.

Grimly looms the gallows o'er him:
Not a living thing doth stir,
Where no longer frowns before him
Ghost of kingly Oliver.

MR. BARNEY MAGUIRE'S ACCOUNT OF THE CORONA-
TION.

Air—" The Groves of Blarney."

OCH! the Coronation! what celebration
  For emulation can with it compare?
When to Westminster the Royal Spinster
  And the Duke of Leinster, all in order did repair!
'Twas there you'd see the New Polishemen
  Making a skrimmage at half after four,
And the Lords and Ladies, and the Miss O'Gradys
  All standing round before the Abbey door.

Their pillows scorning, that self-same morning
  Themselves adorning all by the candle-light,
With roses and lilies, and daffy-down-dillies,
  And gould and jewels, and rich di'monds bright.
And then approaches five hundred coaches,
  With General Dullbeak:—Och! 'twas mighty fine
To see how asy bould Corporal Casey,
  With his sword drawn, prancing made them kape the line.

Then the Guns' alarums, and the King of Arums,
  All in his Garters and his Clarénce shoes,
Opening the massy doors to the bould Ambassydors,
  The Prince of Potboys, and great haythen Jews;
'Twould have made you crazy to see Esterhazy
  All jools from his jasey to his di'mond boots,
With Alderman Harmer, and that swate charmer,
  The famale heiress, Miss Anja-ly Coutts.

And Wellington, walking with his swoord drawn, talking
  To Hill and Hardinge, haroes of great fame:
And Sir De Lacey, and the Duke Dalmasey,
  (They call'd him Sowlt afore he changed his name,)

20—2

Themselves presading Lord Melbourne, lading
  The Queen, the darling, to her royal chair,
And that fine ould fellow, the Duke of Pell-Mello,
  The Queen of Portingal's Chargy-de-fair.

Then the Noble Prussians, likewise the Russians,
  In fine laced jackets, with their golden cuffs,
And the Bavarians, and the proud Hungarians,
  And Everythingarians, all in furs and muffs.
Then Misthur Spaker, with Misthur Pays, the Quaker,
  All in the Gallery you might persave ;
But Lord Brougham was missing, and gone a-fishing,
  Ounly crass Lord Essex would not give him lave.

There was Baron Alten himself exalting,
  And Prince Von Schwartzenberg, and many more,
Och ! I'd be bother'd and entirely smother'd
  To tell the half of 'em was to the fore ;
With the swate Peeresses, in their crowns and dresses,
  And Aldermanesses, and the Boord of Works ;
But Mehemet Ali said, quite gintaly,
  " I'd be proud to see the likes among the Turks !"

Then the Queen, Heaven bless her ! och ! they did dress her
  In her purple garments and her goulden Crown ;
Like Venus or Hebe, or the Queen of Sheby,
  With eight young ladies houlding up her gown.
Sure 'twas grand to see her, also for to he-ar
  The big drums bating, and the trumpets blow,
And Sir George Smart ! Oh ! he play'd a Consarto,
  With his four-and-twenty fiddlers all in a row !

Then the Lord Archbishop held a golden dish up,
  For to resave her bounty and great wealth,
Saying, " Plase your Glory, great Queen Vic-tory !
  Ye'll give the Clargy lave to dhrink your health !"
Then his Riverence retrating, discoorsed the mating ;
  " Boys ! Here's your Queen ! deny it if you can !
And if any bould traitour, or infarior craythur,
  Sneezes at that, I'd like to see the man !"

Then the Nobles kneeling to the Pow'rs appealing,
  " Heaven send your Majesty a glorious reign !"
And Sir Claudius Hunter he did confront her,
  All in his scarlet gown and goulden chain ;
The great Lord May'r, too, sat in his chair, too
  But mighty sarious, looking fit to cry,
For the Earl of Surrey, all in his hurry,
  Throwing the thirteens, hit him in his eye.

Then there was preaching, and good store of speeching,
  With Dukes and Marquises on bended knee :
And they did splash her with real Macasshur,
  And the Queen said, " Ah ! then thank ye all for me !"
Then the trumpets braying, and the organ playing,
  And sweet trombones, with their silver tones ;
But Lord Rolle was rolling ;—'twas mighty consoling
  To think his Lordship did not break his bones !

Then the crames and custard, and the beef and mustard,
  All on the tombstones, like a poultherer's shop :
With lobsters and white-bait, and other swate-meats,
  And wine and nagus, and Imperial Pop !
There was cakes and apples in all the Chapels,
  With fine polonies, and rich mellow pears,—
Och ! the Count Von Strogonoff, sure he got prog enough,
  The sly ould Divil, undernathe the stairs.

Then the cannons thunder'd, and the people wonder'd,
  Crying, " God save Victoria, our Royal Queen !"—
Och ! if myself should live to be a hundred,
  Sure it's the proudest day that I'll have seen !
And now I've ended what I pretended,
  This narration splendid in swate poe-thry,
Ye dear bewitcher, just hand the pitcher,
  Faith, it's myself that's getting mighty dhry.

ELEGIAC TRIBUTE TO THE MEMORY OF THOMAS HAYNES BAYLEY, ESQ.

BY MRS. C. BARON WILSON.

FAREWELL to thee, sweet melodist! thy minstrel lay is o'er,
  Thy lyric harp shall tune its string to music's voice no more ;
But like the rose-leaves, when they fall, though scatter'd on the
    ground,
The sweetness of the poet's song still breathes a fragrance round :
And thus thy minstrel memory is still embalm'd by death,
And holds a spell o'er feeling hearts, that fleets not with the
    breath.

Oft in the gay and crowded scene, where Pleasure's votaries meet,
Thy songs from woman's syren voice shall flow in accents sweet :
Oft shall the listening lover steal, from music's tuneful strings,
A hope that she who breathes the strain may feel the words she
    sings:
And though beneath the willow's shade thy broken lute is hung,
In memory still is treasured deep the strains that lute has sung.

I well remember when thy lute first woke its dulcet lay
In years long past, when life for me was one bright summer day ;
Thy songs are twined with memories I never can forget,
That 'mid the wither'd waste of life my heart keeps verdant yet :
And when I think the hand is cold, those tuneful chords that
    pressed,
Mine eye a pensive tear will dim, a sigh escape my breast.

Alas! each hour but shows me more the poet's fatal doom,
Writ in misfortune's clouded page! though radiance may illume
The chequer'd path he treads awhile, sorrow and cankering care,
Coiled like the worm within the bud, are ever hidden there !
And such a fate, alas! was thine, oh ! sweetly gifted bard,
And such will be to thousands more, the child of song's reward !

A flame too delicate for earth, his spirit feels the chill
Of worldly woes, with keener sense, and a more sickening thrill ;
He cannot wrestle with the throng, or struggle 'mid the crowd
Like other minds, but sinks o'erpowered, his strength too quickly
    bow'd :

And many a wasted frame can shew, and broken spirits tell,
How sad a doom is his who owns the poet's gifted spell!

Farewell! and may the verdant turf lie lightly on thy breast,
And flow'rets blossom from the sod where thy cold ashes rest;
May pity's tear bedew the spot, and lovers' accents breathe
A fond regret for him who sleeps, that flowery turf beneath:
And many a kindred spirit come, in spring's returning bloom,
To hang a wreath of tribute-flowers upon the poet's tomb!

AS I LAYE A-THYNKYNGE.

THE LAST LINES OF THOMAS INGOLDSBY.

As I laye a-thynkynge, a-thynkynge, a-thynkynge,
    Merrie sang the Birde as she sat upon the sprayc;
      There came a noble Knyghte,
      With his hauberke shynynge brighte,
      And his gallaut heart was lyghte,
        Free and gaye;
As I laye a-thynkynge, he rode upon his waye.

As I laye a-thynkynge, a-thynkynge, a-thynkynge,
Sadly sang the Birde as she sat upon the tree!
      There seem'd a crimson plain,
      Where a gallaut Knyghte lay slayne,
      And a steed with broken rein
        Ran free,
As I laye a-thynkynge, most pitiful to see!

As I laye a-thynkynge, a-thynkynge, a-thinkynge,
Merrie sang the Birde as she sat upon the boughe;
      A lovely Mayde came bye,
      And a gentle youth was nyghe,
      And he breathed many a sighe
        And a vowe;
As I laye a-thynkynge, her hearte was gladsome now.

As I lay a-thynkynge, a-thynkynge, a-thynkynge,
Sadly sang the Birde as she sat upon the thorne;
    No more a youth was there,
    But a maiden rent her haire,
    And cried in sad despaire,
        'That I was born!'
As I laye a-thinkynge, she perished forlorne.

As I lay a-thynkynge, a-thynkynge, a-thynkynge,
Sweetly sang the Birde as she sat upon the briar;
    There came a lovely Childe,
    And his face was meek and mild,
    Yet joyously he smiled
        On his sire;
As I laye a-thynkynge, a Cherub mote admire.

But I laye a-thynkynge, a-thynkynge, a-thynkynge,
And sadly sang the Birde as it perch'd upon a bier:
    That joyous smile was gone,
    And the face was white and wan,
    As the downe upon the Swan
        Doth appear,
As I lay a-thynkynge—oh! bitter flow'd the tear!

As I laye a-thynkynge, the golden sun was sinking,
O merrie sang that Birde as it glitter'd on her breast
    With a thousand gorgeous dyes,
    While soaring to the skies,
    'Mid the stars she seem'd to rise,
        As to her nest;
As I lay a-thynkynge, her meaning was exprest:—
        'Follow, follow me away,
        It boots not to delay,'—
        'Twas so she seem'd to saye
        'HERE IS REST!'

THE END,

DILLING AND SONS, PRINTERS, GUILDFORD, SURREY.